Rough Diamond
Rough Justice

By

Avien Gray

In memory of my best friend
– a great friend –
and others too.
RIP

To Janet
A Wonderful Lady
Without her this book would not have been written
Thank You

Facebook profile: Avien Gray

Twitter – X profile: @aviengrayauthor

Author's Note

During the late eighties and early nineties few people had cell phones – and none of the existing phones had cameras. There were no portable laptops or iPhones and the Internet was in its infancy, so there was neither Wi-Fi nor social media. Give or take half an hour, pubs opened only from 10.30am to 2pm and then from 5pm to 11pm. To book a room in a hotel, you had to make a phone call and to book a holiday you went to a local travel agent to pick up a brochure. To watch a movie, you'd go to a cinema or your local high-street video rental store.

People in the UK were allowed to own handguns.

Prime Minister Margaret Thatcher resigned in 1990.

SLR cameras were loaded with mostly 35mm Ilford black and white or Kodak colour film and camera lenses were focused manually.

Prologue

Once upon a time, two young men started off their careers as professional photographers. They'd grown up together and were the best of friends. One eventually fulfilled a long-held aspiration: he became a Metropolitan police officer. Several years later, he joined the Royal Protection Team. Meanwhile, his best friend became a member of MI5.

Part One

The enemy of my enemy is my friend

1

Surrey, England – 1992

It is a fact of life: one day you are going to die.
So you will have just the one question: When?

Only the sound of distant rifle fire echoed across the English countryside.

Cain was alone on the range. He preferred it that way and besides, for the time being, he had company enough. He removed his Beretta .9mm semi-automatic pistol from his shoulder holster. He checked the time on his Breitling – a quarter past three – he turned to face the next target. 'Ready when you are.'

Some thirty feet downrange, several life-sized photographs of the world's most infamous dictators were staring straight back at him. And in recognition of such men – narcissists who believe the world revolves around them – their images had been placed standing in the line of fire with their backs against a wall. Cain racked the Beretta's slide, sending the first round into the chamber, and taking aim, he looked straight into the haunted eyes of a dead man staring straight back at him. But they did not belong to any of the world's most infamous.

You again, he thought.

And with characteristic ease, he tightened his finger on the trigger.

Bye.

Rapid-fire sent more than just a few rounds into the dead man's head, and his heart didn't fare much better. The Beretta's slide finally locked back, Cain blinked, and the eyes were gone. Bright rays from the afternoon sun then broke through gaps in the clouds. The shafts of light transformed the distant photographs into silhouettes and cast their perforated shadows onto the ground. Cain looked down at his own, outstretched shadow lying on the hardened earth beside him.

Another dead body lying in the darkness.

But his outstretched didn't stay for long. The clouds soon closed in, the silhouettes morphed into photographs again, and the mere shadows of their former selves simply melted away.

Cain reloaded and holstered his Beretta, dropped his Peltor ear guards down to his shoulders and gave his Serengeti shades a nudge. And raising his arms to give his aching body a stretch – with a bit of a groan – he glanced up at the all too familiar delights of an English summer.

'At least it isn't raining,' said a familiar voice.

Cain turned to see ice-cold cans of tonic on an esky. Jerry stood close by, six feet tall, fit and agile, with his gun bag by his side.

'Agent Edwards,' Jerry said.

'Detective Sergeant Davis.'

'Afternoon.'

'Typical police officer,' said Cain, 'sneaking up behind a defenceless law-abiding citizen and scaring the hell out of me.'

Jerry smiled; he'd heard it all before. 'Sod off.'

The two young men continued along their well-trodden path of jests and gibes until they came face to face. And for the first time in not such a long time, they embraced like lifelong, best friends do.

'Glad you're all in one piece,' said Jerry. 'How are you feeling?'

'Just a few aches and pains. They'll be gone in a day or three.'

As they drew back from each other, Jerry surveyed the cuts and bruises on Cain's face.

'Now I can see why you've been hiding out for the past few days. You must be this week's most battered member of MI5's investigative surveillance team.'

'I think I'll transfer to your Royal Protection Team to have an easier life,' Cain bantered.

Jerry smiled. 'Sod off.'

'Might do.'

Jerry knew Cain would soon enough get around to telling him about most of what had happened, as he would, had their roles been reversed. It was something their mutual high levels of government security clearance allowed them to do.

Therefore, Jerry had no reason to ask, no reason to delve, just make light of things, go with the flow, and all in good time, much of the *who, what, where, when, why,* and *how* would be revealed. Jerry was also well aware of Cain's fighting prowess. As teenagers they had always trained together and been awarded their *Ryukyu Kobujutsu* karate black belts on the same day. They were also both members of the six-foot club and, being lightweights, they had reach and agility beyond most others.

'Mmm,' said Jerry, with a curious frown. 'Even those Serengeti shades of yours do not hide a simple reality. There are some things you just cannot knock into shape.'

Cain grinned and removed his shades.

'Nice one,' said Jerry. 'Your black eye is almost the same colour as our black belts.'

'At least it's just the one black eye.'

'Hang on a sec, where's your Canon sure-shot camera? I'll take a picture.'

'On your bike.'

Jerry picked up the cans and handed one to Cain. 'You shouldn't have upset her,' he quipped with a feigned look of seriousness.

Cain placed his finger on the tab. 'Pop off.'

'Cheers,' Jerry said, raising his can.

'Chugalug. For my first taste of sin.'

After a few more light-hearted comments, Cain reached down to the esky, flipped up the handle and gestured towards one of the pub-style garden benches. 'Let's go take a seat.'

'Why not,' Jerry said, maintaining his usual composure and stepping back to pick up his gun bag.

'By the way, did I tell you I had a stakeout in West London last weekend?'

Jerry straightened himself up. 'Was it by any chance one of our usual *filet mignon* kinds of steak?'

'Not quite,' said Cain with a sense of detachment. 'This one was a rare cut,' he sighed, 'of a slightly more, let's say, bloody kind.'

2

The Previous Weekend.
In The Early Hours Of Saturday Morning – 1:00am

From his vantage point, cloaked in the darkness of a vacant fourth-floor office window, Cain looked out over a tranquil garden square; one of the most famous in London. To avoid the unwanted attention of any prying eyes he remained concealed within the curtained, layered folds of a draped blackout. Out of sight, out of mind.

He fidgeted again on the upturned beer crate he was sitting on. He finished eating the last of a Marks & Sparks egg mayonnaise sandwich, quenched his thirst with a swig of Lucozade and placed the empty bottle down on the dusty floor beside him. It would come in handy later, something to pee in.

Only hours earlier, an MI5 director had informed Cain of an unexpected, spur-of-the-moment mission. The honcho of an organisation involved in the illegal trafficking of cash, drugs, guns, and girls from Africa into Europe and the UK would be receiving a visit from a kingpin.

Cain's director had said, "The MTSA (Modern Slavery & Trafficking Agency) do not know his identity, whereabouts or the time he is due to arrive. They need pictures of him. They want to trail him, but not arrest him. Therefore, since you started off life as a photographer and take better pictures – especially under difficult circumstances – than the rest of us, I've loaned you to them. At the end of the stakeout, give the films to Agent Omara, who will be with you, and go your separate ways."

'Understood.'

The near-skeleton of a building Cain and Agent Omara would be hiding in was undergoing restoration. It was a work in progress that left the floors, stacked with building materials, tools and an exposed pipe or two, an obstacle course of all things incomplete, waiting for the morrow. However, at six o'clock on a Friday afternoon, the workmen gave their time-clock a last punch. It left the residents of the garden square with a quiet weekend ahead, and the deserted building – with just a few lights on in the hallways to assist the night-guard making his rounds – deathly silent. It was the perfect location for the Agency's forty-eight-hour stake-out.

Also, hours earlier, in a race against time, the Agency's facilitators had retrieved a damaged door from a street skip around the corner next to the stakeout site and hung it in the open doorway of the fourth floor office, where Cain and Agent Omara would be hiding. It would provide a necessary degree of security, while an unexpected jagged gap at its base, would allow a small shaft of hallway light to provide just a scattering of detail across the office floor.

When the entrance of an apartment building on the other side of the tranquil square began to open, Cain leant forward. Two bodyguards emerged. He framed them in the crosshairs of his Nikkor 600mm telephoto lens and pressed the shutter release; only the whisper of the Nikon's motor drive disturbed the silence. He watched through the lens, waiting for the bodyguards to make their next move, but they just stood motionless in the light of the open doorway, giving the impression they were waiting for someone or possibly something to arrive or leave. Cain gave the deserted square another quick scan, but there was no sign of life. However, up in the apartment buildings opposite, an occasional light being switched on or off, mostly behind curtained windows, made him aware: insomniacs were on the prowl.

In the depths of the darkened office, the faint sound of the Nikon's motor drive alerted Agent Omara: Cain was taking photographs – someone was on the move. He quickly dropped his pen and notepad into his briefcase and placed it under the upturned beer crate he had been sitting on. As he turned off his torch he saw what appeared to be a ghost-like shadow, flicker across the shaft of hallway light from under the door. Remaining motionless, waiting for his line of sight to fully adjust to the darkness and distance across the room, his eyes were soon transfixed by an array of dust particles, dancing like fireflies on the edge of the small shaft of hallway light from under the door.

The only other person who could have legitimately been in the building at such a time was the night-guard, but he had been moved to another location for the weekend, miles away.

Agent Omara's alarm bells began to chime. He undid the top button of the night-guard's uniform he was wearing and got to his feet.

Seconds later, Cain felt the firm grip of Agent Omara's hand on his shoulder, a simple sign for silence. He glanced up to acknowledge the warning and turned his focus of attention back to the lens.

One of the bodyguards – Cain had nicknamed Watch-Man – was checking his wrist for a second time. He looked up and turned to his partner to exchange a few words before he strolled down the short flight of steps to the pavement below. Headlights then entered the garden square, sending a swathe of light skimming across the railings, the hedgerows, and empty park benches. And shape-shifting shadows curved their way around the parked cars, the lampposts and Watch-Man, standing by the kerb. Watch-Man raised a hand as the glowing red brake lights of a black cab brought it slowly to a stop. He stepped forward, but he didn't open the door. Instead, he placed his forearm on the edge of the roof and leant over the passenger window.

Agent Omara knelt down beside Cain and looked out to see what was going on. 'Tell me,' he whispered.

'The *For Hire* sign and interior light are both off. No one's getting out. I can't quite see from this angle if he's talking to the driver or a passenger.'

'Deliberately hiding?' Agent Omara murmured.

'Could be.'

Agent Omara turned himself around, carefully moved one of the layered folds of the draped blackout and looked through the spy-hole at the small shaft of hallway light from under the door.

At the same time, Watch-Man stepped away from the cab, glanced down at his wrist again, pulled a Zippo lighter from his pocket, flipped the lid, and lit the cigarette already between his lips.

Realising the implications, Cain called out quietly, 'Harry, Watch-Man is smoking a cigarette.'

Agent Omara turned back to Cain. 'If either of the bodyguards are smoking,' he said, 'they cannot be on duty. They cannot be waiting for their honcho or anyone else to leave.'

'Or anyone else to arrive.'

'Or are they? We may have a problem. Bear with me.'

Cain stayed silent and Agent Omara turned back to look again, through the spy-hole.

Down in the square, Watch-Man somewhat theatrically gave his partner a wave before he drifted up the steps at a leisurely pace – exhaling smoke-rings into the early morning air – leaving the cab waiting by the kerb behind him.

Cain was beginning to get the distinct impression he was watching a staged performance when the penny dropped. He again called out quietly, 'Harry. Urgent.'

'Talk to me.'

Cain summarised Watch-Man's antics: 'It's not Watch-Man, it's Watch Him. We're being set up.'

'A distraction? I think you may be right.'

Agent Omara undid the last of the buttons on the night-guard's jacket he was wearing, reached inside, and withdrew his Browning .9mm semi-automatic pistol.

Cain immediately sensed a change in the temperature of the room. A plethora of murderous scenarios instantly raged through his subconscious. A feeling of anger and frustration came to the fore and clenching his empty hand – members of MI5 were not allowed to carry guns – a subliminal, almost imperceptible inkling of fear touched his psyche.

A second later, Agent Omara took a breath and raised his Browning .9mm pistol. The ghost-like shadow was back. 'Sorry,' he whispered, 'there are gunmen at the door. Stay down.'

When death and danger are upon you, the slow-motion movie in the mind distorts time.

What might seem like an eternity is, in fact, only a second – or seven.

Agent Omara disappeared around the draped blackout, distancing himself from Cain and away from the pathway of light about to invade the room. He hunkered down behind one of the pillars – it was all the protection he had. Well, almost.

Cain immediately reached for the only semblance of a weapon he had: a switchblade in the watch pocket of his jeans. He laid himself down on the floor and eased aside the edge of the draped blackout just enough to see.

Tick-tock… Time had moved on. Seven seconds…
and then it began.

A shotgun blast blew the door open and two gun-wielding silhouettes burst in. Amid a deafening exchange of gunfire and blinding muzzle flashes, the leading gunman's shotgun blasted buckshot into the draped blackout. Cain felt the layered folds shiver against him. Buckshot ricocheted off the walls around him and then everything happened at once.

The leading gunman took a bullet to his chest and fell to his knees, leaving the trailing gunman a step behind, firing a revolver. And perhaps more by luck than judgement, a bullet found its mark. Agent Omara stumbled and fell back against a wall.

As the trailing gunman slowly stepped to one side, aiming his revolver into the darkness, trying to track his target, the wounded gunman, kneeling and coughing up blood, slammed the shotgun's barrel against his legs. The tremor immediately caused his aim to fleetingly falter. He looked down.

'Help me,' the kneeling gunman begged. But anger rather than compassion overwhelmed his comrade. He stepped behind a pillar for cover, pointed his revolver down at the head of his kneeling cohort, pulled the trigger – and Agent Omara fired again.

Cain's loyalty immediately came to the fore. Keeping a grip on what he knew would not be enough – the switchblade – he crawled his way out from under the folds of the draped blackout, across the obstacle course of all things incomplete, towards his target.

The trailing gunman fired a last shot and immediately opened the revolver's cylinder to reload. Seeing the empty shell casings falling to the floor, Cain got to his feet, went for it and the revolver's cylinder closed. The trailing gunman thumbed back the revolver's hammer, glanced around the pillar, and as he turned into the darkness to shoot again, Cain came up on his blind side, grabbed hold of the revolver's barrel, and pressed the button on his switchblade. In a raucous millisecond, the blade flicked out, the revolver fired, Cain stabbed the trailing gunman in the chest, and Agent Omara fell silently to the floor.

Cain felt a vice-like grip around his wrist. Up close, he realised he was up against a giant of a man: a muscle-bound hulk, some ten kilos heavier, but an inch or two shorter. Cain pulled back, the blade came out and the giant choked a spray of blood and saliva over him. He instinctively kicked low, but a taekwondo-style jockstrap did its job, the giant didn't even flinch. Cain twisted and turned, but he couldn't break free as the giant pushed and shoved, refusing to let go.

When Cain was slammed against a wall, he came to terms with a fateful reality: if he were to survive, if he were to break free, he would have to drain the lifeblood out of the giant. He karate-kicked the heel of his Timberland boot against the giant's knee and pushed with all his might. As the giant went sideways, they tripped the dark fandango, turned cartwheels 'cross the floor and, weaving the blade between them and the revolver around them, the bullets continued to fly.

Seconds later, the revolver's hammer finally fell on a spent chamber. *Click!*

At that moment of realisation and hesitation, Cain and the giant stared into each other's eyes. They both felt and they both smelt each other's heaving breath – and the giant choked directly into Cain's face. Cain tried to turn his head away, but not far or fast enough. He felt the splattering of the giant's blood, sweat, and saliva across his mouth and, gasping for breath, he tasted it. He instantly gagged, his stomach convulsed, and his Marks & Sparks sandwich rose to the occasion. He vomited straight into the giant's face. The giant roared, spitting out blood and bile, let go of the empty revolver, and elbowed Cain's head aside.

Remaining manacled in the grip of the giant, Cain took punches to his stomach and face before he grabbed his chance. Leaving himself open, he swiped the butt of the revolver into the side of the giant's head with all his might. The giant reeled back. Cain stepped round, turned out and, finally twisting free of the vice-like grip around his wrist, he pirouetted Tai Chi-style and slashed the blade across the side of the giant's throat.

In the blink of an eye, the giant retched, raised a hand to his bleeding jugular, and grabbing hold of Cain's wrist again, he collapsed, dragging Cain down with him. When he hit the floor, his head struck a stacked row of steel joists and Cain crashed into the base of a workbench.

In the quiet of the aftermath, Agent Omara regained consciousness. He was glad to be alive, and thankful no one was pointing a gun at him again. Feeling pain, he checked the bullet wound to the top of his leg. He breathed a sigh of relief: his artery was undamaged. He undid his tie to use it as a tourniquet.

Several yards distant, Cain gradually turned himself onto his side to free his wrist, but he came face to face with the dying giant lying next to him. Their eyes met.

In the far reaches of Cain's mind, a door slowly opened. He didn't ask it to, it just did, and stepping through, into a darkened place he did not know, he felt himself crossing a threshold into a world he had yet to encounter.

Where am I?

A shiver ran down his spine.

As Cain turned, the door slowly closed – and to the sound of a last wheezing, dying breath, so did the giant's eyes.

Agent Omara checked his Browning .9mm pistol – just in case. He placed the only clean thing he had, a handkerchief, against the flesh wound to the side of his head and silently wincing from the pain he cast a wary eye across the office floor. Bathed in the hallway light now spilling through the open door, the leading gunman – whom Agent Omara had shot in the chest – was lying with blood pouring from the fatal bullet wound to his head, with his shotgun still in one hand. A few yards away, a blood-covered Cain and the second gunman were lying deathly still, deathly quiet.

Dear God, no.

'Cain,' Agent Omara called softly, 'talk to me!'

The words resounded through Cain's subconscious, breaking the spell. He looked up to see Agent Omara sitting with his back against a wall.

'Harry, you were shot. Thank God you're alive. You OK?'

'Just about, thanks to you, and the Kevlar helped. You're lying in a pool of blood. You hurt?'

'I'm fine. Not my blood.'

'What about the man next to you?'

'Both the gunmen are dead,' said Cain, sighing. 'Ready for the encore?'

Agent Omara showed a momentary look of admiration. 'You'd better get up then.'

'Will do.'

'Sorry I didn't help you back there,' said Agent Omara, 'but I was out of it for a minute.'

'Harry, we're both alive, you're all in one piece . . . well, just about. Nothing else matters.'

Cain got himself up onto one elbow, coughed to clear his throat, and after spitting on the floor to get rid of the taste of vomit, he wiped his mouth on his sleeve.

Agent Omara noticed the blood-covered switchblade in Cain's hand and realised how the second gunman had been killed: Cain wasn't supposed to be armed.

Cain got to his feet and, giving himself the once-over, he noticed blood dripping from his hands and clothes, splashing down into the dead-pool beneath him. He looked to Agent Omara. 'I'd better not help you, Harry.'

'I'll manage,' Agent Omara replied sympathetically, while checking the time on his wrist. 'The clock's ticking, so let's get started,' he added, holding out his hand. 'Give me the switchblade. Quickly, now.'

Cain stepped forward and handed it over before drying his hands on his clothes as best he could. Agent Omara wiped the switchblade's handle clean with the gloves he had been wearing, placed his own blood all over it, and tossed the lot into the air. Cain followed the trajectory as the gloves peeled off, leaving a trail to where the switchblade landed next to the pool of blood, next to the dead giant.

Agent Omara said, 'The neighbours must have heard the

gunfire. They will already have dialled 999. If the emergency services arrive before my people, let's not implicate you in the deaths.'

'Understood Harry. Thank you.'

'Get my briefcase, it's under the armchair,' Agent Omara said, pointing to the beer crate.

'Sheer luxury,' Cain commented, lifting it up.

Agent Omara took the briefcase and managed a smile. 'Take the film out of the camera but leave the rest where it is. No time to pack.'

'OK.'

Cain easily negotiated the obstacle course on the floor, now illuminated by the hallway light. He swept aside the buckshot-ridden folds of the draped blackout, grabbed his jacket and backpack hanging on the tripod and slung them over his shoulder. He pressed the rewind button on the back of the camera and flipped the lever. As the film re-wound he moved the tripod to one side, changed the angle of the camera, and altered the point of focus on the 600mm telephoto lens to infinity. Nobody would now have a clue as to who or what had been photographed. He looked out across the garden square but there was no sign of life: Watch-Man, his partner, and the black cab were gone.

The sound of the motor-rewind coming to a stop gained Cain's attention. He opened the back of the camera, removed the 35mm cassette, and returned to Agent Omara, who was talking on a cell phone. Cain stayed silent.

Agent Omara ended the call.

Cain said, 'Just to let you know, the bodyguards and the black cab are gone.'

'We were set up,' Agent Omara concluded.

As instructed, Cain placed the 35mm cassette into Agent Omara's now open briefcase, closed the lid, and spun the dials.

'Time for you to go,' said Agent Omara. 'The streets are dark, mostly deserted, you should be able to get to the car without being see–' Agent Omara grimaced from the pain.

'You sure you're OK, Harry?' Cain asked.

'Yeah, I'll survive.' Agent Omara gave Cain a quick look. 'You're covered in blood. Thank Christ it's not your own.

When you get to the car, don't try to drive anywhere. Just hide on the back seat. The Litter Man will be with you within twenty minutes, driving one of the Agency's covered transporters.'

'Got it Harry. No problem.'

Agent Omara knew Cain was not carrying any form of ID.

'If the police catch up with you before you get to the car, just collapse and feign unconsciousness. When they see the state you are in, they will think you're injured, so just play along, let them take you to a hospital. Keep your eyes closed and your mouth shut. Don't say a word to anyone, don't tell them anything, not even your name.'

'Understood.'

'My colleagues will soon pick up on where the police have taken you. They will come to collect you.'

'Got it Harry.'

'Just one last thing, we know the bodyguards will stay with their honcho, but we don't know who else might be out there–'

'A getaway driver,' Cain interrupted, 'or whoever Watch-Man was talking to in the cab.'

'Possibly.'

'Don't worry,' said Cain, tapping his Kevlar-jacketed chest with his clenched fist. 'I'll keep an eye out for anyone hanging around.'

'Make sure you do. You will have noticed the bodyguards, and the gunmen were all black men. Just remember we blend into the darkness better than you whiteys.'

Cain grinned. 'Thank you for reminding me Harry – I'll take extra care.'

'Make sure you do. Now go. And don't leave a trail of bloody fingerprints behind you.'

Cain quickly made his way down the four flights of stairs to the lobby, where the sight of a man covered in blood entering the building brought him to a standstill. He stared at his mirror image reflected in the glass panels of the swing doors. The terrible state he was in was a reminder of why he had not helped Agent Omara: HIV and AIDS. Cain suddenly saw his reflection move, but he hadn't. He realised the swing doors were slightly ajar; the locks were broken. The false move jolted him into action. As he watched his doppelgänger put his jacket on, stick his bush hat on his head, and sling his backpack over his shoulder, he noted the bottom halves of the swing doors were wood panelled. He would crawl along the floor and use them as cover to look out around the garden square, to make sure Agent Omara was safe. His doppelgänger stepped forward and dropped to the floor.

Meanwhile, hidden under a broken streetlamp and an overhang of trees in the square, a third gunman was waiting impatiently behind the wheel of the getaway car, counting the seconds since hearing the last gunshot. It had been too long: there was no sign of his two accomplices. Leaving the getaway car was forbidden, but he had to: one of the accomplices was his brother. With his Colt .45 in hand, he climbed out of the car and checked the street. Glancing up at the darkened, fourth-floor office window again, he saw a glimmer of light: not a good sign. He cautiously started climbing up the side of the steps to the building's entrance. On reaching the top of the steps, he pinned himself against the wall by the side of the swing doors.

Kneeling on one knee, Cain knew if he pushed the swing doors open a millimetre or two allowing him to take a peek, his line of sight would be too restricted. So instead he raised his hand to adjust the brim of his bush hat, to lessen the reflections in the glass panels and take a glimpse over the mid rails, to see if any gunmen were loitering on the sidewalk below or coming up the steps.

As the gunman peered around the jamb of the swing-doors, movement down at waist level caught his eye: a bloodied white man's hand, in front of a bush hat. An open cuff of a bloodstained sleeve. A six-inch scar along the side of the white man's wrist.

The gunman raised his Colt .45 but anxiety about his brother had caused him to make a mistake. Realising he was too close he tried to step back, but too late.

Catching sight of the Colt's muzzle, Cain instinctively pushed the swing doors against it, leapt to his feet, rammed his elbow through the glass and, turning sideways-on, he broadsided the swing-doors against the gunman's arm. As the glass shattered, the Colt .45 fired and the gunman, caught off balance, tripped and plunged back down the steps, leaving Cain diving for cover. The gunman, momentarily lying on the pavement, taking in a snail's eye view of the entrance to the building, could see there was no sign of movement. He assumed the one shot he had fired had hit the white man. As he scrambled to his feet thinking about what could have happened to his brother, and what the hell to do next, the distant sound of approaching police sirens left him with no choice. Leaving uncertainty behind him, he ran over to the getaway car to make his escape.

From behind broken glass Cain heard the roar of an engine, the screech of tyres, and the sound of approaching sirens, immediately followed by the lightning strikes of flashing blue lights criss-crossing the walls around him.

Harry will now be safe. Time to go.

Cain ran along the hallway and crashed through the emergency exit at the rear of the building. Finding himself in a courtyard, he climbed onto some dustbins, jumped over the wall, and dropped down into a deserted alleyway. He hurried to a car parked in a side street and hunkered down in the back, catching his breath. As the events of the past few minutes reeled through his mind in slow motion, he came to terms with a simple reality, he had just killed a man. He waited, expecting guilt or perhaps conscience to overwhelm him. But instead, a subliminal sense of achievement flooded through him. The image of the dying gunman, however – an image he would never forget – lingered in his subconscious.

A stream of light slowly passed through the car's interior, followed by the sound of an engine coming to a stop. Cain should have been keeping an eye on the street, but he had been totally immersed in his thoughts and lost track of time.

The back door of the car opened; Cain looked up to find himself, staring down the barrel of a Browning .9mm semi-automatic pistol – and at arm's length the blurred image of the Litter Man's face behind dark glasses under a baseball cap.

'Password?' the Litter Man said.

'Zorro,' Cain replied. 'Bit of a mess, I'm afraid. But I'm not injured.'

'Let's get moving,' said the Litter Man, lowering his weapon.

Hiding in the shadows, crouched down behind metal railings on the basement steps of one of the Georgian houses lining the street, a black man named Zokwana, made a note of the car's licence plate number. And as the six-foot tall, slim, agile white man took a quick look around the street before getting into the driver's seat, he caught only a glimpse of a very bloodied face, hidden under the bush hat.

I followed you. Whoever you are, he thought, *one day we will meet again.*

3

There Was This Chap Carrying A Rose & Scroll
Over One Shoulder

Cain finished telling Jerry about the stakeout.

'What a night,' said Jerry. 'Thank goodness the media were unable to identify you or the agent you were with, whoever he was.'

'I'm glad the agent survived.'

'You saved his life.'

'We saved each other.'

'And for you,' said Jerry with a look of understanding, 'a first kill. Incredible.'

Cain gave his arms a stretch and with a bit of a sigh replied, 'Now you know, let's go have a shoot.'

'Why not.'

Some time later, Cain and Jerry fired double-taps to their targets' heads to finish the session. They reloaded and holstered their pistols and slipped their Peltors down to their shoulders.

'Those last shots will decide the winner, I think,' Jerry said as he flicked the target-retrieval switches and glanced downrange.

'Fingers crossed,' Cain replied.

Jerry raised a hand, flipped his middle finger over the index, and in the manner of a casual salute he touched the side of his head. 'Touch wood.' He folded his arms as he inspected their targets – pictures of Mugabe and Gaddafi. 'Bugger,' he said, realising he'd lost the session by a whisker. 'Must've been the breeze,' he quipped.

'Must've,' Cain said with a grin as he very theatrically shielded his Serengeti shades with the palm of his hand and looked up at the lifeless Union Jack on top of the flagpole.

Jerry ignored the 'act' and started unclipping the targets.

The sound of a latch on the well-weathered Edwardian wooden gate, clicking open interrupted them.

18

Cain lowered his hand. 'Ah, must've been the breeze,' he suggested.

'Sod off.'

They both turned to see a member of the sporting gentry walking towards them. In his mid-forties, the chap wearing the customary Tattersall check shirt, plain tie, a Beaver of Bolton tweed waistcoat, breeks and Oxford brogues, carrying a Purdey shotgun – a Rose & Scroll – over one shoulder looked very grand. He raised his hand to tip his cap.

It was not unusual for a member of the rifle, shotgun and aristocratic double-barrel named fraternity, to be strolling through the hundreds of hectares of the shooting clubs' quintessentially English countryside. However, it was unusual for such a very grandly dressed chap – compared to Cain and Jerry's very casual summer attire – to enter the handgun range. The chap's hair, just like Jerry's was very neatly trimmed, whereas Cain always kept his a little longer.

Cain gave the chap a discreet once-over.

One of the photos in the Shooting Times & Country Magazine has come to life.

Cain imagined retriever gun dogs coming to heel, but the Edwardian gate closed with a click without them – and time moved on.

'Good afternoon,' the chap said.

'Good afternoon Mac,' Jerry replied.

Jerry's casual welcome suggested he already knew Mac. It left Cain with the distinct impression the encounter was more than just coincidence.

Mac-the-chap, Cain thought resorting to his tendency for using nicknames.

Jerry made the introductions and with firm handshakes all round Jerry said, 'Glad you could make it, Mac. Good to see you.'

'You must be Mac,' said Cain. 'What did you make?'

Mac smiled. 'Jerry has told me about your sense of humour,' he responded with the calm of an aristocratic Oxford education.

'Oh. Really?'

'Yes. Really.' Mac surveyed the cuts and bruises to Cain's face. 'Interesting,' he said, with an air of curiosity. 'Did someone not like your last joke?'

'At least I managed to dodge the bullets.'

The subtlety of Cain's remark was not lost on Mac, whose affable manner gave nothing away. 'Always the best option,' he replied.

'Always.'

'Shall we?' said Jerry, gesturing towards the bench they were using. 'Best place for you to lean the Purdey, Mac.'

'Good idea.'

Taking Jerry's lead, the three men ambled over to the bench, talking about all things guns and bullets, passing the time of day. As Mac rested his Rose & Scroll on the lid of the esky, subtly closing the 'bar', he eyed the unclipped targets Jerry was holding. 'May I?' he enquired.

'Please do,' said Jerry, laying them on the bench.

As Mac examined the bullet-ridden mugshots of the world's most infamous dictators he quite unexpectedly discovered the untouched charms of a Page 3 Girl.

Cain said, 'Always good to be able to trade a nipple for a nose.'

Jerry smiled. 'Cain only keeps her photo because he likes looking at *them*.'

'I suspected as much,' Mac said, maintaining the banter.

After chatting amiably for a few minutes, Mac gave Jerry a relaxed 'bye for now' Spock eyebrow and took a seat. Jerry picked up his jacket and put it on. 'If you will excuse me gents,' he said, adjusting his collar and holster, 'I have a couple of calls I need to make.'

'We'll be here,' Cain said.

As the gate latch clicked shut behind Jerry, Mac started the conversation.

'Jerry tells me you two shared a flat together in Windsor, before he joined the Met. You considered joining with him but decided not to. Please tell me why?'

'Jerry wouldn't change his name to Hutch. Plus, we needed a Windsor 351 V-8, not a Windsor flat, so the idea fell through.'

'*Starsky and Hutch*,' said Mac. 'A memorable TV series.'

'One of the engines used in Starsky's Gran Torino was a Windsor 351 V8. Not many people know that. Perhaps we should have gone for *Morse* instead, Jerry likes Jags. Or better still, *The Sweeney* – more our style.'

Mac smiled. 'What was the real reason?'

'The police in the UK do not carry guns. It's something Jerry was able to come to terms with when he joined the force, before he became a member of the Royal Protection Team, who are permanently armed.'

'Thankfully they are.'

'I believe when you are working on the front line, so to speak, when push comes to shove, you have to sink to the level of those you are up against, or you lose or die. Hence, you have to be carrying a gun.'

'Is that why you decided to join the investigative surveillance side of MI5 instead?'

'Yes. It keeps me in the background. When the laws change, let me know and maybe I'll think again.'

'Perhaps I will.'

Cain removed his Beretta from his shoulder holster, dropped the mag, slipped the slide, and placed the disassembled parts on a cloth to give them a clean.

For the next few minutes, Mac deliberated on the role of the police force, the will of the people, and the law of the land; Cain could not help but notice how Mac said, 'with their hands tied behind their backs', more than once.

Mac concluded, 'Compromise is always a dangerous road to go down.'

'Yes it is.'

Mac went on to describe the various branches of law enforcement, the diversity in colour and creed of the people who joined up, and the different backgrounds from which they came.

Cain said, 'A motley crew of the disciplined kind.'

'It takes all kinds to fight all sorts.'

'It does.'

'I met with Jerry two months ago. My people have been keeping an eye on you ever since. I wanted to know what you get up to when you're not working.'

Cain dropped a spot of Hoppe's oil on the Beretta's frame, thinking about his past few weeks' social activities. 'Guess I'll have to start checking my rear-view mirrors more often.'

'There's no need. The tracking device on your vehicle has already been removed.'

Mac saw a flicker of scepticism, perhaps concern, on Cain's face. He guessed what Cain was thinking. 'Variety is the spice of life,' he said, 'but let's not tell the husbands or fiancés of the various young ladies you met up with.'

'Let's not,' Cain agreed.

'I think now would be a good time to clarify a couple of points.'

'OK.'

'When I first spoke to Jerry on the phone, I arranged to meet him forty-eight hours later, allowing him time to make the obvious, covert enquiries about me.'

'What did he find out?'

'I am just an ordinary, nine-to-six, five-days-a-week security clearance officer.'

Cain grinned. 'Of course you are.'

'When I met with Jerry I told him you were being considered for a promotional move from your MI5 investigative surveillance team. And because he is your best friend you were both the subject of a routine personal security check. When I discovered you were both coming here to the range today, I decided it would be a good opportunity to watch you shoot, meet up with you both, and have a chat.'

Cain realised Mac was maintaining a more formal rather than amiable manner, just like an army colonel would when in conversation with one of his junior officers, preserving the line between them.

Cain asked, 'How come Jerry never told me about your meeting?'

'When I asked him not to he gave me his word he would not tell you. His word – like your own – is beyond question.'

'It is.'

'You never make promises.'

'We never do. It is a word we prefer not to use.'

Mac reached over to Jerry's gun bag and magically removed a folder from under it. 'But you do, on occasions, tell a little white lie,' Mac said, raising his Spock eyebrow.

'Don't we all? It's only if those little white lies graduate into big lies, provoking a knock on the door, do the problems begin.'

'Would that be a knock on the door by the police,' said Mac, 'or a husband?'

'Touché.'

Mac smiled, opened the folder, and continued with his narrative. 'Apart from your obvious skills with ladies and handguns, you have a driver's licence, a motorbike licence, and a pilot's licence.'

'I do. I fly light aircraft.'

'And like Jerry, you're a karate black belt.'

'We also practice Tai Chi – and we're pretty good at backgammon too.'

'A throw of the dice can only result in a win or lose situation.'

'We only throw dice when we're playing games.'

Cain closed his eyes. He reassembled his Beretta, placed the full magazine back into place, and racked the slide, sending the first round into the chamber. He returned the gun to his shoulder holster and opened his eyes.

Mac said, 'To coin a phrase, I see you prefer not to be blindsided.'

'Don't we all.'

'Your file here,' said Mac, 'tells me you were born in November. Being a Scorpio must explain why you have – as Jerry mentioned – a no-nonsense, straightforward more a free-spirited attitude to life.'

'Sounds about right.'

'I can also see, when your MI5 investigative surveillance team was in a confrontational situation on two separate occasions you stepped forward into the front line.'

Cain simply grinned with a bit of a shrug.

'During the first encounter,' said Mac, 'you karate-kicked a man to the ground and during the second encounter, you twisted and broke a man's arm before you fractured another's ribs with several punches.'

'Being a black belt certainly helped.'

'You have no regrets? No qualms?'

'None. Especially since the first man was a convicted arms

dealer carrying a pistol, and the other two were known terrorists, both carrying combat knives. If I'd been armed I would probably have just shot them.'

Mac smiled in apparent agreement. 'In respect of your time with MI5, what I know about you from your file here, and what I have learnt about you during these past two months from my people keeping an eye on you, I formed an idea. However, in light of what happened last weekend, that idea has now become a reality.'

Mac's last comment should have taken Cain by surprise, but it didn't. Mac noted the lack of reaction.

'So,' said Mac, 'I believe you have a natural ability. And to use your own words from a few minutes ago it is now time for you to 'think again'. And yes, as I am sure you have already guessed, I know it was you at the stakeout who knifed the gunman to death.'

Cain looked up at Mac, and once again, looked straight into the haunted eyes of a dead man staring straight back at him.

Mac said, 'You will never forget the face of the first man you kill.'

Cain blinked and the eyes were gone. But Mac's use of the word 'first' remained etched in his subconscious.

Mac asked, 'Where did you get the switchblade?'

'A Spanish friend gave it to me as a present. They are easy to open and close with one hand, especially when opening a Marks & Sparks sandwich.'

'A handy friend to have.'

'The blade or the friend?'

'The friend.'

'She is.'

'A *she*?'

Cain nodded. 'Her name is Sofia.'

'Interesting,' said Mac. 'How many switchblades do you have?'

'Several. I know they're illegal, but MI5 Agents don't carry guns so I carry it only to use as a last resort.'

Mac smiled. 'Rest assured, you are not the only one. Talking of protecting people, Agent Omara was very relieved to learn the single shot he heard after you left him did not injure you. He sends his regards. He is well on the road to recovery. On a personal level, I would like to thank you for saving him.'

'We saved each other,' Cain said.

'You understand why you are not allowed to know where he is or visit him?'

'Yes. Please tell him I owe him a beer.'

'Consider it done.' Mac turned a page of the file. 'I understand you have an exceptional memory.'

'I have. But it's not quite a photographic memory. Sorry, what is your name?'

Mac showed a look of amusement. 'For the moment, let's just say I run a specialist Government organisation. Tell me about the gunman you came up against when you were trying to leave the building you and Agent Omara were holed up in.'

Cain retold what had happened.

Mac said, 'You didn't see his face.'

'No. I was too busy looking at the barrel of the Colt .45. I just saw his hands before he fell back down the steps, they were black.'

'He didn't see your face.'

'No, my old bush hat did its job.'

'Do you think, when the gunman looked down at your hand adjusting your bush hat, he could have seen the scar on the side of your wrist?'

Cain pondered for a second. 'Not sure.'

'Just so you know, Jerry told me how you got the scar. He also told me you never button the cuffs of your shirt.'

'I just prefer them left open.'

'You have quite a tan.'

'I like lying in the sun, reading a book, written by one of my favourite authors.'

'Anyone in particular?'

'Wilbur Smith, Tom Sharpe, Dean Koontz, Jeffrey Archer.'

'Good choices! I've looked at your wrist many times this afternoon, but I noticed your scar only occasionally because I know it's there.'

Cain rested an elbow on the bench, arm wrestling-style, exposing the scar. 'It makes me a cut above the rest?'

'The scar runs along the little finger side of your wrist there, and the tail-end of it curves to the inside. If you hand somebody something, or vice versa, it is almost completely on the other person's blind side. It's hardly noticeable.'

Cain twisted his arm around to take a look. 'It happened when I was twelve years old. When I joined MI5, it was deleted from my medical records to prevent anyone using it to trace my identity.'

'You've watched the news?'

'The nine o'clock news said a Kevlar jacket saved the life of an undercover police officer, or perhaps a DEA Agent on secondment from a foreign agency.'

'It will have explained to the gunman why there was no return fire,' said Mac, 'and why he was not pursued. Also, the media will never be told which country the supposed DEA agent is from. It will keep the gunman guessing.'

'I have to know: did the gunmen find out we were on the fourth floor because of something I did or didn't do? Did I make a mistake?'

'I appreciate you wanting to know. The simple answer is no. Neither you nor Agent Omara did anything wrong or made any mistakes. As you are aware, the stakeout was part of an early investigation into an organisation involved in the illegal trafficking of cash, drugs, guns, and girls across Africa, into Europe and the UK. The Agency had been informed an unknown kingpin was going to be meeting with the honcho of the organisation in his apartment. Unfortunately, the honcho was tipped off that a rival gang was watching him, so he decided to send a message. You were attacked. I'm afraid there is nothing more I can tell you.'

'Understood.'

'The police found the getaway car on the following day, parked in a side street off the Stockwell Road, near Brixton. One of the neighbours living in the square made a note of the registration number before it drove off and called 999.' Mac closed the folder. 'How are you feeling?'

'Just a few aches and pains. Nothing to worry about.'

'Nightmares?'

'No.'

'The doctor gave you the all-clear physically. How about

26

your mind?'

'I see the dead gunman's face occasionally – and those dead man's eyes, staring straight back at me.'

Mac gave Cain a knowing smile. 'It is a common phenomenon among a select few people like you and me. We'll have a chat about it later. You'll be pleased to know the results of the blood tests carried out on the dead gunmen have all come back negative. No infections, diseases, HIV or AIDS. You are all clear.'

'That's a relief.'

Mac checked the time on his wrist. 'It's getting late.'

Cain was momentarily silent, thinking about what Mac had said earlier:

"You will never forget the face of the first man you kill."

Those words had remained etched in Cain's mind. He looked Mac in the eye. 'The specialist government organisation you run is an assassination squad.'

'We're known as the Trailing Arrest Team, but in reality, we are the Bureau. We find, track, and eliminate our country's enemies. Now you know, where do *we* go from here?'

Cain grinned. 'You tell me.'

'Welcome aboard,' Mac said, holding out his hand.

Mac then explained to Cain what would be happening in the coming days and weeks.

'Understood,' Cain said.

'Jerry's waiting for your call. Tell him to come and join us.'

Cain pressed the speed dial on his mobile.

'Hello,' Jerry said.

'Hi. Did you know Mac is a recruitment officer for the Hare Krishnas? I've ordered you a tambourine.'

Jerry laughed and Mac smiled.

'Come and join us.'

'On my way.'

When Jerry arrived, the three men sat talking for some time about the security of various organisations, their mutual high levels of government security clearance, and the Royal Protection Team. Mac eventually rounded off their conversation. 'We all know, even with our best friends, we can only tell each other so much about what we do, what we see, where we go, who we meet, and why.'

'Of course,' said Jerry. 'We live by the rules.'

'Always,' Cain agreed.

'Congratulations,' said Mac. 'I can confirm you have passed the security check. It is now time for me to go.' All three men got to their feet; Mac lifted his Rose & Scroll off the lid of the esky and placed it over his shoulder. 'The bar is now open. You can celebrate Cain's promotional transfer from MI5's investigative surveillance team to the Trailing Arrest Team.'

And with handshakes all round, pleasantries and courtesies were exchanged. A minute later, the sound of the old gate latch clicking shut confirmed Mac had left.

Jerry opened the lid of the esky. 'Beer?'

'Good idea.'

Cain raised his can. 'Chugalug.'

'Cheers. Congratulations.'

As Cain took a swig of his beer, Jerry saw the scar on Cain's wrist and remembered what had happened when they were twelve years old.

Cain had been in the lead as they ran at full speed across their school's gymnasium to get outside for a session of sport. At the exit, Cain's hand had inexplicably missed the handle on the door and smashed through one of the small panes of glass. Despite the door being on a hydraulic overhead closer, it had been ajar at the time allowing Cain's momentum to do the rest. He tripped on the step and, falling to the ground, his wrist had caught on a piece of the now broken glass on the lower edge of the smashed pane.

Jerry had been surprised to see Cain sit up, look at the six-inch gash on his wrist, and shrug. Getting to his feet, he'd simply said, 'Let's go see a teacher.'

In hospital, Cain's wrist received twenty-one stitches.

Cain finished his beer, crushed the empty can in his hand, and tossed it into the air. Jerry looked over the end of the bench at the waste bin down on the grass beside them. *Clunk.*

Cain looked downrange at the life-sized photographs of the world's most infamous dictators staring straight back at them and casually remarked, 'Where is Stormin' Norman when you need him?'

The waste bin antics of the U.S. Army General Stormin' Norman Schwarzkopf when he was conducting his daily press briefings during the Iraqi Gulf War had gained him world fame. He had pulled toy soldiers, symbolising the enemy troops, off the battlefield map on the wall and, to exemplify their mounting losses, he had theatrically dropped them into a bin on the floor. The ensuing loud *clunk* had prompted laughter from the assembled media, and merriment from his millions of supporters around the world watching him on live TV.

To assist the war effort, the American Defence Intelligence Agency (DIA) had created a 'Most Wanted' pack of picture playing cards – handed out to the allied troops – to help identify Saddam Hussein's henchmen in the post-war manhunt.

It had proved to be an inspiration for Cain. He had created the life-size photographs of the world's most infamous dictators and placed them where he believed they truly belonged: on the range, in the line of fire, with their backs against a wall.

'Can the can,' Jerry said.

'I'll drink to that one,' Cain grinned, gesturing with an empty hand.

Jerry calmly shifted himself into typical police officer mode to analyse as only a best friend could, how Cain felt after having committed potentially a once-in-a-lifetime action: a first kill. 'You still feel no sense of remorse or regret?'

'The only regret I have is not having had my Beretta with me. If I had, I'm sure I would have been able to prevent the agent being shot.'

'You think about it a lot?'

'Being in the apartment alone these past few days I've only thought about how I might have been able to skip the dark fandango.'

Jerry got the gist of Cain's variation to the lyrics of a great song and smiled. 'Turned cartwheels cross the floor.'

'The room was humming harder.'

'Until you hit the floor.'

'And the ceiling flew away.'

'But it wasn't *harder* for you, was it?' Jerry suggested.

'No it wasn't. Killing the gunman to save the agent and my own life came naturally. When I was waiting in the back of the car for the Litter Man I simply felt a sense of achievement.'

'Who would have believed a young man who started off life as a professional photographer would work for MI5 and end up knifing a man to death?'

'Who would have believed a young man who started off life as a professional photographer would become a Metropolitan police officer and then a member of the Royal Protection Team. One day, you might have to kill someone to protect the Royal Family.'

'No problem, we're two peas in a pod.'

Jerry's last succinct comment was followed by a moment's silence, leaving them both with their own conscience and thoughts on what the future may bring.

All men are ordinary men; the extraordinary men are those who know it.

Gilbert K. Chesterton

4

Setting Precedents – For Good & For Bad Reasons

The third gunman, the driver of the getaway car, was sitting in a greasy spoon-style café in Brixton, south London. On the table, among the half-empty coffee cups, bottles, and glasses, an untouched bowl of jollof rice and chicken slowly cooled to room temperature. He looked down at the old newspaper in front of him and began to read again the story:

'The two men, believed to be African nationals, were killed by an undercover police officer on secondment from another country. The deaths are being treated as a drug-dealing related incident . . .'

Isolated in his own world of anger and frustration, the gunman reflected again on the identity of the man who had killed his brother who remained a mystery. He folded the newspaper along its now well-creased lines and placed it on the table.

Sitting opposite, Zokwana watched the gunman and waited for an appropriate moment to resume their conversation. He huddled his elbows forward on the table, ready to show compassion, ready to say or do whatever was necessary to get his own way. 'Reliable sources have told me the police officer you want has been sent back to whichever country he came from. But I will track him down.'

The gunman looked up.

'This is not Africa,' said Zokwana. 'We have no suspects. We have no one to question. No one to use our unique black-room methods of torturous persuasion on.'

The gunman sighed, looked down at the table again and Zokwana continued.

'I have to thank you for allowing me to hunt for this undercover police officer. If you had started making enquiries, you would have put yourself in the spotlight and drawn unwanted attention to those around you. It would not have been long before you found yourself on the wrong side of your own people, as well as the law. I care about you. It is not a situation I want you to put yourself in. I cannot begin to imagine how difficult this must be for you.'

The gunman stared up from the table. 'I have to find the police officer who kill–'

'Yes, you do,' Zokwana interrupted, 'but remember, the British do not even know you are in their country. You are not here legally.'

The gunman was silent.

'We have worked for our honcho for several years now. You and your dear brother – God rest his soul – have always been there to deal with our enemies. On that night I was in the taxi, talking to the bodyguard as a distraction, allowing your brother and the other gunman to get into place without being detected. However, we now know the men in that fourth-floor office building were police, not our competitors, not our kind of people. We've never come into direct contact with law enforcement before. It is not something we want to start doing now.'

What Zokwana did not mention was how, on the night of the shoot-out, after the taxi had dropped him off at their rendezvous point, he had heard the last single shot being fired. How he had seen and followed the white man running out of the alleyway into a side street and into a car. Nor had he told their honcho, divulging such information would not fit into his personal plans.

Zokwana said, 'I will soon be returning to South Africa. When our people take control, we will be presented with many opportunities that can only be exploited our way, the African way. A temporary change of scenery would be good for you too. It will allow time for things to calm down here, for people's tongues to loosen, names to be divulged, and locations revealed. It will be exactly what we have been waiting for. You will then be able to–' Zokwana left the rest of his sentence to the vengeful imagination of the gunman.

The gunman sighed again.

Zokwana got himself up, moved to the end of the table and sat next to the gunman. 'In my country,' he said, placing a comforting hand on the gunman's arm, 'I will need a man I can trust by my side.'

A man I can tell what to do.

'But, I have to find the bastard who murdered my brother,' the gunman replied.

'I agree,' said Zokwana softly, 'but if you are with me when I find out where the murderer is located, I will arrange a new passport for you. It will provide you with a new identity. It will allow you to legitimately travel to wherever the murdering son of a bitch is located. It will allow you to carry out whatever you have decided to–' Zokwana again indulged in his mind game: leaving the rest of his sentence to the vengeful imagination of the gunman.

There was a long silence. The gunman knew there was logic to what Zokwana was saying. He gave his bruised shoulders and elbow – the result of falling down the steps – a stretch and started rubbing the cuff of his shirt. In his mind's eye he could see the one and only thing he knew he would never forget: the six-inch scar along the side of the white man's wrist.

Guessing what the gunman was thinking about, Zokwana said, 'For the time being, not telling anyone about the scar will work in our favour. It will not draw any undue attention to us. Trust me, it will be our way of finally identifying the murderer.'

Zokwana glanced up at the clock on the wall and decided he had wasted enough time on this particular issue. He played his ace card. 'Lastly, if you wish, I can arrange for your brother to be flown to a church on the outskirts of Johannesburg. The bishop there is a good friend of mine.'

The gunman stopped rubbing the cuff of his shirt. Zokwana showed the most affable look of understanding. 'If you will allow me to be with you we could attend your brother's final farewell together, on African soil.'

After a moment's contemplation, the gunman spoke. 'I agree. Thank you, sir. It will be a privilege to be with you in South Africa.'

***

News of Cain being involved in a car accident soon spread throughout his world.

His reported injuries enabled him to take time away, without raising the suspicions of his fellow MI5 Agents, ladies in his life, or other people he knew. It would be three months – convalescing can be a lonely time – before he was seen again. But in reality it was a stratagem, the beginning of his intensive training with the SAS and members of the Bureau on how to eliminate people.

His graduation was unique: he was given the details of a known terrorist who lived in Cricklewood, London. Ten days later, he was watching the somewhat inebriated terrorist leave the Crown pub late at night to walk home alone. In a quiet street, Cain pulled a silenced Beretta from his shoulder holster and shot the terrorist dead. The back doors of a van parked nearby opened immediately and the Litter Man helped Cain lift the dead body into the back.

Soon after, having poured litres of water onto the pavement to clear away the blood, the Bureau's Litter Man drove off. Cain removed his wig, false moustache, and spectacles. It started to rain. The terrorist's body was never found.

Cain was now a member of a Bureau no one had ever heard of and never would, because to all intents and purposes, it didn't exist. A Bureau with one strategic priority:

> When the transgressions of a target of primary interest ascended to a hearing.
> When there was only the one judge – Mac – in session and no jury:
> Cain would carry out the sentence with characteristic ease.

A week later, on a Friday evening, Cain arrived back in London. Jerry was at home already, stocking up the fridge and decanting a bottle of their favourite Saint-Émilion red wine.

'Great to see you,' said Jerry, and they embraced like best friends do.

'My first whole weekend off in months – we can go have a steak tomorrow.'

'Perfect.'

As they chatted, Cain talked about his work on the Trailing Arrest Team, though he didn't divulge everything. They ordered a pizza home delivery.

Jerry smiled. 'So we both now carry guns every day.'

'Guess we do. My Beretta 92 in a shoulder holster.'

'And my Glock 19 in a waist holster.'

In the late of night, lazing in the lounge, Cain placed a single ice cube in each of their highball tumblers. The cubes would keep the two fingers of J&B for Cain and Jameson for Jerry *cool for the gang*. It was a ritual they had started in a garden shed, when they were too young for anyone to know or even suspect. When they reached adulthood it became a tradition they indulged on the balcony of their Windsor flat overlooking the Thames and Windsor Great Park.

Early on Saturday evening, after a lazy day, they went to one of their favourite restaurants, located on the South London, Thornton Heath Pond roundabout to have a steak.

On Sunday morning, they cooked themselves a full English breakfast and, as always, read every word of *The Sunday Times* before eventually heading out to a restaurant for a traditional Sunday lunch: roast lamb with roast potatoes, vegetables, and mint sauce.

Later that evening – with their iced J&B and Jameson – watching episodes of one of their favourite TV series, *The Sweeney*, Jerry couldn't resist the temptation. Looking at the Beretta 92 resting in Cain's shoulder holster he said, 'Shall we call you Regan, Danger Man, The Prisoner, or Callan?'

'Touché.'

5

Several Years Later: August 4th, 1996

In the grounds of a very famous English manor house, Cain was standing at the edge of the forest floor, wearing a police officer's uniform. He felt for the monocular tethered around his neck and looked out across the green expanse of the polo pitch. Some two hundred yards distant a line of tethered ponies, a 1960's convertible Aston Martin, a Bentley, and a Range Rover or three provided the perfect backdrop for the Prince and his friends.

As for the young Princes, they were playing with their young chums: polo without the ponies. And not far away, under the shade of a canopy, the Princess – always there for her boys – in the company of various titled ladies, kept watch on her hobby-horse jockeys.

On such a very private day, out of the public eye and out of sight of Fleet Street's finest, the Royal couple appeared to be relaxed – providing they kept their distance – and comfortable, each with their own kind of people.

The only reason the Princess was attending the very private, unofficial, last polo game of the year was because her boys had asked her to. It would be a grand finale for them in every sense of the word.

Cain spotted DS Jerry Davis in the background.

See you tonight.

Cain took one last look at the aristocrat he would be keeping a very close eye on, let go of the monocular, and checked the time on his wrist. The first chukka would begin in thirty minutes at three o'clock, gaining everyone's immediate attention. It would allow him – unnoticed – to enter the parking area and attach a tracking device under the aristocrat's newly purchased Jaguar XJ saloon.

The sound of a snapping branch then gained his full attention. Expecting it to be the police officer he had been walking with who had gone off on a recce into the forest, he waited for the officer to reappear. But instead he heard a jumble of words – in some form of Arabic he did not understand. However, the last word was unmistakable, '*Inshallah* (God willing).'

Another man's voice declared, '*Allahu Akbar* (God is great).'

Cain could not believe what he was hearing. He stayed silent, carefully unbuttoned the jacket of the uniform he was wearing, reached for his Beretta in his shoulder holster, and cautiously moved forward through the undergrowth. He brushed against greenery, ferns, and shrubs, following the telltale signs of human activity: a snapped branch, a trail of trampled grass, a broken stem or two.

'Dear God, no,' Cain said quietly, as he came across the police officer he had been walking with, lying motionless amid the foliage under an old oak tree. As he approached he could see the officer's throat had been cut wide open. Realising Jihadists had infiltrated the grounds, he was left with just one thought:

Snipers or bombers or both? Are there just two?

Cain scoured his close proximity just to be sure, checked his back again – just in case and raised his monocular to scour the area. On penetrating the distant layered folds and filtered sunny glades of the forest, a movement, no more than a butterfly alighting honeysuckle, caught his attention. He saw a gloved hand holding a rifle, under the outline of a sniper's scope, before in the blink of an eye, it was gone. He immediately let go of the monocular, dropped to the ground and, breaking protocol, he reached for his mobile and dialled direct. Jerry was very surprised to see Cain's number on his Royal Protection Team's cell phone. It had never happened before because Cain was not supposed to know the number. He sensed a problem. He answered. 'What's happening?'

'Code Red,' Cain said quietly. 'We have two Jihadists on the polo pitch's southern line. One is carrying a sniper's rifle, moving towards the centre of the southern line. I don't know where the second one is. They have already killed a uniformed police officer. I don't know if there are more than two. You need to move now.'

Despite having a number of obvious questions for Cain,

Jerry's professionalism immediately came to the fore. While ushering his Principal to safety, he made his coded announcement on his Royal Protection Team's police radio.

'You are wanted on the phone sir. Yes, they are waiting on the southern line, sir.'

Jerry and his team then placed themselves as human shields around the Royal family, and calmly swept them off to safety, behind an unawares aristocratic 'wall' of – fame – guests.

Meanwhile, Cain spoke on his police radio.

'Understood,' a voice replied. 'Stay where you are.'

Cain didn't take much notice when the calls of an agitated woodlark taking flight, broke the natural silence of the forest. He glanced up, looked around, but the sky was clear.

Gunfire from the centre of the southern line instantly shattered the calm of the afternoon, causing the aristocrats to ask what was happening. Cain realised armed police officers had taken down one of the Jihadists. He looked up again.

Where the hell is it. Should have been here by now.

He heard a bluster of words in Arabic coming from close behind him, then silence.

When death and danger are upon you, the slow-motion movie in the mind distorts time.
What might seem like an eternity will, in the event, only be a second – or ten.

Staying crouched down, Cain silently and very slowly turned, contorting his body. Stretching his arms, he coaxed the Beretta's trigger – the sights a blur – and scoured the undergrowth. All he needed was just the slightest of movement, any telltale sign.

From absolutely nowhere and with deafening force, a tornado suddenly struck the forest floor. Cain instantly broke left, keeping his back to the winds. The Jihadist immediately turned away and, shielding his eyes from the profusion of flying foliage, he did not see the gun-pointing figure rising up and open fire. Two bullets entered the Jihadist's head, and the dead man standing fell to the ground. The tornado immediately spiralled away, the profusion of flying foliage began to settle – and a false sense of calm pervaded the underlying charge on the forest floor.

Cain wanted to check the body just to be sure, but the word body morphed into bait, then into bomb, so he left it alone. Crouching down by a tree he spoke on his police radio. 'I have killed a Jihadist at my location.'

'Stay where you are.'

'Understood.'

'Chopper finally got here to help you.'

'Perfect timing.'

'Technical problem delayed it. No guns, but great pilot.'

'I heard the Jihadist talking before I shot him. Did the chopper's infra-red see anyone with him?'

'I'll double check. Wait one.'

'Will do.' Cain kept low, keeping an eye on everything around him.

The voice came back on the radio. 'Chopper pilot says infra-red shows no one else. All clear.'

As Cain continued to look around, his mobile rang. He answered.

'We're on the move now,' said Jerry, as he closed the rear passenger's door of his Principal's Range Rover. 'Thank you for everything. Gotta go.'

The line went dead. Cain changed the frequency on his police radio and listened.

'Purple 5:2 shadow is clear. The Principal is secure. The . . .'

Hearing the calm transmissions, Cain breathed a sigh of relief. There was just one thing on his mind. He made his way carefully over to the dead Jihadist, got down on his knees and started rummaging through the foliage around the body. He soon found the Jihadist's cell phone. He checked the times on the incoming and outgoing call lists then spoke on his police radio. Having agreed joint tactics, Cain said, 'On my way.'

After a short run – staying out of sight, out of mind – Cain arrived at the back door of the manor house to be met by a member of staff holding a waiter's uniform on a clothes hanger. Cain quickly changed and, minutes later, he was walking among the remaining aristocrats and invited guests, gathered under the canopy. They were all talking about what had happened, speculating about why it had happened, having drinks, and waiting for the delayed first chukka to – hopefully – begin.

Cain looked down at the dead Jihadist's cell phone lying on the tray of drinks he was carrying and pressed the button. He was calling the last number the Jihadist had been talking to, seconds before being shot. One of the invited guests immediately reached for the cell phone in his pocket and answered the call. 'Where are you?'

'Look behind you,' Cain said quietly.

The invited guest turned and Cain, standing to his side, not behind him, slowly ambled towards him. As Cain reached for his Beretta, concealed under his waiter's shirt, gunfire rang out. Cain felt the bullets strike him and, to the sounds of screams and panic around him, he fell to his knees.

Having shot Cain the gunman turned to find his next target, but he took two bullets to his chest and fell sideways onto one of the drinks tables, causing several astonished, seated aristocrats to tip their chairs and fall backwards onto the grass. Cain watched an armed, plain-clothes officer put a gun to the head of the guest still holding the cell phone in his hand.

Got the bastard.

Cain looked down at the wound to the side of his stomach and his bleeding right hand. He groaned and collapsed onto the grass.

*When you are right, too soon you will
be judged to be wrong.*

A Mr. Anonymous

6

Several Days Later

Cain was in a room in a private hospital when he regained consciousness.

He heard one of his favourite songs and opened his eyes. He saw a blurred image of Jerry and heard a voice call out, 'He's awake, get the doctor.' He felt someone grip his left hand.

Hours later, Cain had a semblance of awareness – and on the following afternoon, he was fully conscious, listening to Jerry telling him what had happened, getting things into perspective.

The guest who had answered the cell phone was a multi-millionaire Arabic grandee who had several friends in both the British Government and in the City of London. Unbeknown to anyone, he was also a leading Jihadist. He had cajoled a member of parliament into taking him to the polo match as a guest. Once there, he was going to do whatever he could to help his followers assassinate members of the Royal Family. He would then return to his own little fiefdom to be honoured. He'd also had his illegally armed bodyguard with him, posing as his PA.

'The bodyguard was the one who shot you,' said Jerry. 'Unfortunately, as he drew his gun, a man and woman stepped in the way of the armed police officer watching your back. That split second allowed you to be shot. We can only assume the bodyguard saw you drawing your Beretta from under the tray of drinks you were carrying. The first bullet hit the side of your stomach and as you turned, the other two went through the tipping tray of drinks to hit your Beretta and fracture your hand and fingers.'

Cain looked down at his arm in a sling, his hand and fingers in a splint. His look of vexation, acrimony, and regret said it all.

Jerry said, 'The police officer is mortified.'

Cain looked up. 'We all did the best we could in extreme circumstances. Please tell the officer I would be honoured to have him watch my back any time.'

'Will do. Just so you know, it was the chopper that brought you here. The pilot was–'

The surgeon entered the room to examine his patient. 'Afternoon. How are you feeling?'

'Not too bad. Thank you for looking after me.'

Cain was informed the bullet wound to the side of his stomach had caused no major long-term damage. The surgeon said, 'I doubt if many people will even notice the scar. But if they do, and you need a reason, just tell them you fell onto something short and sharp.'

'Good idea, will do.'

'Your Beretta and the tray you were holding probably saved your life. However, your right hand is a problem. Your index and middle finger bones have been fractured. And your metacarpal bones in your palm have been peppered with fragments of tin and glass. Because you have more than one fracture on two fingers it is going to take at least four to five months to get back to normal.' The surgeon saw the look of disappointment on his patient's face. 'Rest assured; your hand will get back to normal. I give you my word.'

On the following morning, a man who looked every inch a Whitehall civil servant, wearing a three-piece suit and carrying a briefcase, walked into the room. 'You are Agent Smith?'

The man had used the pseudonym registered on the hospital's patients listing.

'Who's asking?'

'I am Mr. Trenchard.'

'Where are you from?'

'Your superiors.' Trenchard opened his briefcase. 'I have a statement for you to sign.'

Cain leafed through the pages. At best, the statement, couched in ambiguous terms, represented a total distortion of the facts. Whereas, at the very worst, it could have been construed to be an admission of an unauthorised killing: guilt. He considered signing it *Mickey Mouse,* just to annoy Trenchard, but he didn't. 'Thank you for the opportunity,' he said quietly, looking down at his arm in a sling, and hand and fingers in a splint. 'How am I supposed to sign it?'

'I do have your best interests in mind. I'm sure you'll find a way.'

'Thank you,' said Cain, surreptitiously pressing the alarm button, 'but I'll give it a miss today.'

'You should reconsider,' Trenchard retorted.

Voices were then heard in the hallway and armed officers entered the room. Cain said, 'This man is here under false pretences. Please remove him.'

Trenchard looked shocked. 'You can't just–'

'I'll hang on to this,' Cain interrupted, holding the statement out of Trenchard's reach.

Ignoring the comment, Trenchard leant over Cain, trying to grab the statement – and losing his balance, he accidentally placed a hand on Cain's wounded stomach instead of the bed. Cain reacted angrily, elbowing Trenchard in the throat. As the armed officers grabbed hold of the choking Trenchard to escort him out of the room, he attempted to retrieve his briefcase.

'Please sir,' said one of the officers, 'come with us.'

'Bye, Trash-card, sorry, I mean Trenchard,' Cain sneered as he picked up his mobile, lying on the bed beside him.

Mac answered, listened, and made a call on another line.

Within minutes, Trenchard was arrested. One of the officers re-entered the room, picked up Trenchard's briefcase and politely asked Cain to place the statement back inside it.

'Go ahead,' said Mac's voice, instructing Cain.

'Will do.'

***

In early September, a rather slow-moving Cain, his arm still in a sling and hand and fingers in a splint, arrived in Mac's office. Shaking hands – injured-man-style – they avoided the friendly embrace. Cain sat down and they talked about his recovery until coffee arrived and they got down to business.

Mac said, 'The Jihadist gunmen were from Iraq – al Qaeda. The assassination attempt was in retaliation for Operation Desert Storm. Al Qaeda wanted to do what the IRA did in 1979 – when they murdered Lord Mountbatten – take out a member of the Royal Family.'

'Why are we not surprised?'

'The member of parliament who was supposedly cajoled into taking the leading Jihadist as a guest to the polo match was actually paid to do so. He's been taking backhanders for years. He is now being meticulously investigated. We wait to see what is uncovered.'

'He will get his just deserts.'

Mac nodded. 'The death of the Jihadist gunman you shot in the forest has been attributed to the dead officer who had been walking with you. He will be remembered as a true hero.'

'God bless him.'

'Because you were dressed as a waiter and did not fire a gun, you've been described as a servant to the Royal Family who was accidentally shot. Buckingham Palace has refused to name you. Your identity will forever, especially since you were wearing a false beard, remain anonymous.'

Cain showed a look of relief. 'We know the Princess only attended the last polo match of the year because her boys asked her to, it was almost a grand finale of a different kind.'

'Almost. But thanks to you and those around you, it wasn't. The aristocrat you were about to start following – the one who is connected to the laundering of money for crime lords – is none the wiser. He will soon lead us to those he is dealing with. But for you the case is closed.'

'As is everything,' Cain responded with a look of regret.

'Temporarily not permanently,' said Mac 'The leading Jihadist's lawyer released a statement, claiming his client had found the burner phone on the grass by the side of the polo pitch. And would have, but for all the commotion caused by the unexpected departure of the Royal Family, handed it in to the police.'

'Pack of lies.'

'He was released on bail and twenty-four hours later he disappeared. The media are saying he fled the country.'

Seeing the look on Mac's face, Cain asked, 'Where is he?'

'We interrogated him.'

'I bet that hurt.'

'It did.'

'Never to be seen again?'

'A dead loss,' said Mac. 'Tell me, did you ever watch the TV series, *Yes Prime Minister*?'

'Margaret Thatcher's favourite. I've seen every episode.'

'You are aware the political shenanigans performed by the senior Whitehall officials and the Prime Minister depicted in the series are true to life.'

'Sadly, yes.'

'Consider your encounter with Trenchard in the hospital to be one of those episodes. Trenchard was just doing what he was told to. The statement he wanted you to sign was indeed to quote your own words: "At best, the statement, couched in ambiguous terms, represented a total distortion of the facts. Whereas, at the very worst, it could have been construed to be an admission of an unauthorised killing: guilt." Those in Whitehall were just doing whatever they had to, to achieve their own personal agendas.'

Cain showed a look of contempt. 'To get their next pay-offs.'

'At the very least.'

'And, as always, we are waiting for the next episode.'

'Very true.'

Looking down at his damaged hand and fingers, Cain frowned. 'I reached a score helping to save members of the Royal Family.'

'Twenty notches on the bedpost.' Mac arched a knowing eyebrow. 'Regarding your hand, the doctors have informed me you will need several months to get yourself back to being one hundred per cent. You are also owed many weeks' leave. It has been a busy year for you, so I have decided, after the doctors have given you the all-clear, it would be better for you to spend the winter in warmer climes, exercising on a beach, getting yourself back in shape.'

'Seriously?'

'You are still a young man, months away will do you no harm, especially since you will continue to receive your salary. Her Majesty has also arranged a Royal bonus to help you along your way.'

Mac waited for a response, but Cain stayed silent, looking

down again at his hand and fingers with a look of regret, perhaps frustration.

Weeks later, Cain put on a brave face to meander with Jerry along their well-trodden path of jests and gibes. For the first time ever, they would be going their separate ways. They were at Jerry's new home, his lifelong dream: an 80ft barge, the *Disponible,* moored on the Thames near Tower Bridge. The boat's name, being French for *available,* alluded wryly to both men's bachelor status.

Jerry smiled. 'I'll let all our female friends know I am now truly alone and available.'

'And truly capable,' Cain quipped. 'By the way, I almost forgot to tell you. Since you're a member of the Palace Pups, and we both saved the lives of members of The Firm, I put half the money Her Majesty gave me into your account this morning, halfsies.'

The Royal Protection Team were a very close-knit, independent team, respected for its unquestionable loyalty to the Royal Family. A loyalty only equalled by the Royal Family's love and respect for their faithful, two and four-legged pets. This had led to Cain nicknaming Jerry and the Team the Palace Pups.

'Thank you,' said Jerry. 'I'll use the money to pay for the flights when I visit you. Never forget the Royal Family's love and respect for their faithful two and four-legged pets. If ever you need anything, HRH will be more than willing to help you.'

'Nice to know.'

Jerry removed a Nikon F camera with a 35-70mm zoom lens from the bag he was carrying and handed it to Cain. 'Present for you. Thought you might like to take a picture or two while you're away. You'll be a photographer again.'

Cain grinned appreciatively, 'Great idea! Thank you for putting a shutter release screw-on button on it.'

'In the old days we always had them on our cameras. It will help your fingers.'

'Memories.'

'See you in a few months' time.'

And they gently embraced like best friends do.

From his window seat on a 747 jet leaving Heathrow, Cain looked down at the grounds of Windsor Castle. A lady wearing a headscarf and long tweed coat, accompanied by a gentleman in a bowler hat and navy jacket, were riding their respective chestnut and grey mounts along a track by the Thames, across from Datchet village.

'Morning your Majesty,' Cain said quietly.

Passing over Windsor Great Park, the 747 banked left, nosing south. Cain caught sight of the hundreds of acres at Bisley shooting ground, where it had all begun.

C'est la vie. Who knows what the future may bring?

Part Two

Australia

Life, Love, and Death

7

Nothing Lasts Forever

When the wheels touched down in Sydney, Australia, Cain felt, as the crow flies, he'd got as far away from it all as he could.

For the first few weeks he stayed in a hotel near Sydney Harbour, from where he could explore the city at an easy-going pace, visit the various tourist attractions, and catch a coach or three for a number of sightseeing trips to various outlying districts.

It did not take him long to realise, he was now in a country where nothing was demanded nor expected of him. And having left the umbrella weather behind him, he soon came to appreciate the benefits of the warmer climes, the constant blue skies, and the wonderfully relaxed Ozzie way of life.

He eventually relocated to a hotel on the coastline to fulfil a lifelong dream; spending Christmas and New Year on Bondi Beach, overlooking the Tasman Sea, to watch the sunrise, top up his tan, and read his favourite authors' latest novels.

But of course, on New Year's Eve, Cain had missed being with Jerry on the 80ft deck of the *Disponible,* listening to Big Ben bringing in the New Year, popping a cork or two and watching the fireworks. However, Jerry had missed it too. He was up in Norfolk on the Sandringham estate protecting The Firm – leaving the deck of the *Disponible* deserted under sky-filled pyrotechnics.

'Happy New Year,' they said to each other on the phone.

'See you soon.'

One afternoon on Bondi Beach Cain was finishing a takeaway chicken salad. He removed an ice-cold can of Victoria Bitter from his cooler bag and placed it into his newfound discovery, a stubby holder to keep it cool. 'Chugalug,' he said quietly to no one, and took a sip watching the girls go by.

For my next taste of sin. When I get my hand and fingers back to being a hundred per cent.

49

Out of the corner of his eye, he saw it coming he deflected the shot with his arm and gave the kids a wave. 'Happy New Year,' he called out. 'Bend it like Beckham.'

The kids all laughed. 'Happy New Year mate,' one shouted back – and the culprit kicker chased after the ball.

The brief encounter reminded Cain of one of his life's rules: 'I grew up with children. I know what they're like. No thanks.'

It had guaranteed him and Jerry their bachelor status. He laid down, removed his Serengeti shades and closed his eyes. He still had months of leave left to go.

Go where?

One morning, on the terrace of a café, Cain was reading a newspaper article about Australia's most famous movie stars. He remembered, weeks earlier, he'd stood on the top of Sydney Harbour Bridge, where Paul Hogan had worked as a rigger. He looked at the change on the small plate the waitress had placed on the table, picked up a 20-cent coin and flipped it into the air. It landed on the table; the platypus on the upside made his decision for him. Inspired by the memory of the *Crocodile Dundee* movies, he decided he would head for the Blue Mountains, follow a storyline or two out of the movies, and follow in the footsteps of the Aboriginal people: he would go walkabout. It would be a 4000km-plus journey across the southern breadth of Australia to Perth on the western coast – the most isolated capital city in the world.

Taking his time and managing to take a picture or two using his thumb, Cain encountered all manner of life – wild and otherwise – along the various bus ways, tourist routes, and the off the beaten tracks he chose to explore.

In an Outback café a hundred miles from anywhere, he unexpectedly spotted a baby kangaroo – a joey – in the pocket of an apron, hanging on a kitchen door.

'That's how we always take care of them mate, when they're orphaned,' said the short-order chef in his apron and toque.

Cain took a photo, took a seat, and the chef poured him a coffee.

In a village on the edge of a eucalyptus tree forest, Cain was in a local store looking at picture postcards of Australia's most venomous when he caught sight of one of the UK's most deadly.

Looking at himself in the mirror, he had his backpack and camera slung over one shoulder, but something was missing: his gun. He looked down at his hand and fingers in the splint, unsure of when he would feel the weight of his loaded shoulder holster again. His reflection then gave him a momentary look of regret – he turned and walked away.

April 1997

On the eve of a full moon, Cain reached the last leg of his journey: the 1200km expanse of the Nullarbor Desert. It was definitely not a place to go walkabout, so he hitched a ride on the Pacific Indian locomotive to take him along the world's longest, 478km dead-straight track to the halfway point, Kalgoorlie, the gold mining centre of Australia.

He stepped out onto the platform and into the 35°C heat of the day. He took a breath and gave his Serengeti shades a nudge. It was definitely going to be a day to be indoors with the air-conditioning, rather than out and about.

In a gold merchant's showroom, a gold flake in a heart-shaped pendant necklace caught his eye.

'Lucky lady,' the merchant remarked, as he gift-wrapped the necklace.

'She will love it,' Cain said. It would be a present for Sofia, his wonderful Spanish friend, who always provided him with the switchblades.

'Anything for you sir?'

Cain had never been one to wear any personal items that could be left behind, lost or torn off, especially when on an assignment. 'Very tempting,' he said, 'but old habits die hard. I only ever wear a watch.'

As Cain bid his farewells a beautiful, slim, blonde young lady he had seen in another showroom came out of a private office. As they both headed for the exit to the showroom Cain said pleasantly, 'Morning, we seem to be crossing each other's paths today.'

On hearing Cain's accent, the beautiful young lady asked, 'You are English?'

'Yes, from London.'

And having noticed the Nikon camera slung over Cain's shoulder, she enquired, 'You're a photographer?'

'I will be, once I've learnt how to put the film in the camera.'

Looking up to get the measure of the Englishman – he was some six-inches taller – she replied, 'Somehow, I think you already know how to put the film in the camera.'

'Might do.'

As they went out into the heat of the day the beautiful young lady smiled in amusement. 'You're on holiday?'

'Sort of,' said Cain, holding up his hand with his fingers in the splint. 'A car door slammed onto my hand, forcing me to take a few months off.'

Cain went on to introduce himself, expecting the beautiful young lady to do the same but she didn't Hence his professionalism told him not to ask – just go with the flow. 'I still manage to take a picture now and then using my thumb.'

'I have often thought I would like to learn about photography, but I don't have a proper camera.'

'Having one would certainly help.'

'It would. 'So what do you think I should buy?'

'Lunch.'

And with smiles all round, walking to a restaurant the beautiful young lady introduced herself: her name was Riley.

Over steaks and salad they talked about cameras, travel, Australia, and gold. They were quickly relaxed and content in each other's company, to the point where Riley was soon slicing up Cain's steak for him.

'So a million dollars in gold weighs fifty kilos. Not a matchbox option,' Cain said.

'Yet the 68-carat pear-shaped diamond Richard Burton bought for Elizabeth Taylor in 1969, only weighed just thirteen grams.'

Cain did a quick mental calculation. 'Thirteen grams is just one seventy-seventh of a kilo – but it's also worth a million dollars. An interesting comparison.'

Riley smiled. 'All that glitters is not gold.'

Cain grinned. 'Diamonds are forever.'

Over an ice cream dessert, Riley mentioned – without going into detail – she was in Kalgoorlie for only a few hours to collect some gold jewellery for clients.

Cain grinned, 'Now I know why you only had water with your lunch. You rode here on your bicycle.'

Riley laughed. 'I actually flew myself here in my Cessna 172 light aircraft.'

'How wonderful. The same aircraft I learnt to fly in.'

Riley looked surprised. 'You really have a pilot's licence?'

'Might do.' Cain lifted up his backpack, delved inside and handed his GA pilot's licence and passport to Riley. 'Please, take a look,' he said.

'Now I know why you have a Breitling Navitimer watch on your wrist.'

'It was a present from my best friend when I got my licence.'

'He didn't get one too?'

'No. He's into boats.'

Riley viewed Cain's passport and pilot's licence for a few long seconds – and looking up she made an invitation. 'Would you like to fly back to Perth with me?'

'I would consider it an honour.'

'And just to be safe,' said Riley. 'You will have to show your pilot's licence and passport when we check in.'

'Of course,' said Cain. 'Hang on to them.'

Riley smiled brightly as she placed them in her briefcase, and they continued chatting affably as they waited for the bill.

An hour later, Cain and Riley took off in *Jumbo,* her Cessna 172. During a delightful ninety-minute flight to the west coast and along the coastline to enjoy the views, Riley occasionally allowed Cain to have his hand on the yoke... before she landed them in Perth.

After having refuelled and parked *Jumbo* in a hangar, the contented couple walked out to Riley's 4x4. She drove to a small motel conveniently located on the edge of the city centre. Riley told Cain she was going to be busy the next day – Friday – and the weekend ahead, so Cain gave her the number of his Australian mobile.

Riley smiled. 'I'll definitely give you a call on Monday.'

'Any time.'

'We can probably meet up on Tuesday.'

'I'll spend the long weekend having a wander around. Look forward to seeing you.'

And they kissed Spanish-style, cheek to cheek.

8

Finding A Gem

Cain walked along the Avenues Of Honour in Kings Park – overlooking the Swan River and city beyond – to the War Memorial. After he had taken his time to pay his respects to those who had made the ultimate sacrifice, he sat on a park bench for a moment's reflection. He touched the side of his stomach, where he had been shot.

It's good to be alive.

On the Saturday afternoon, Cain was exploring the shops and streets when he heard the unmistakable sound of Harley Davidsons coming his way. As he stood by the kerb, watching the Hell's Angels pass he couldn't help but notice embossed on the backs of their leather jackets the greatest name of all time. A name he knew he would never forget: Coffin Cheaters.

Next day, he visited the tourist centre, picked up a map, explored the local Sunday markets, wandered the nearby streets and visited a bar or two where he read the local papers to get a degree of perspective on what was going on in the most isolated city in the world.

On Monday, Cain relaxed on a near-deserted beach to top up his tan and have a read. He dropped a can into his stubby holder and thought about the beautiful Riley. As the sun slipped towards the horizon, only an albatross, high on the wing, saw the long shadows gently performing the karate *Katas,* followed by a Tai Chi *form* or two before wading into the soothing depths of the perfectly warm Indian Ocean.

Tuesday

Cain and Riley were on the veranda of a Bohemian-style restaurant, relaxing in comfortable peacock chairs enjoying a glass of wine, browsing the menu, passing the time of day.

Over a lazy lunch of raw fish salads, roasted lamb and steak, they whiled away the hours talking about life, countries, and cameras. In a nearby park, Riley got to take her first-ever photographs – of ducks and black swans in a lake – with a proper camera.

'I definitely like the sound of the motor drive,' said Riley, looking through the viewfinder and pressing the shutter release again. 'I could get used to this.'

'Perhaps you will.'

They sat on a park bench where Riley was guided through the process of unloading and reloading the camera. 'So,' said Riley, 'you really do know how to put the film in the camera.'

Cain grinned, remembering his comment on the first afternoon they had met in Kalgoorlie.

'Touché.'

During the next seven days, Cain and Riley met up almost every day for lunch or dinner in different parts of the city, before exploring the sights hand in hand. It was a time when they both came to the realisation they were relaxed, content and wonderfully happy being together.

On the afternoon they celebrated their anniversary – knowing each other for two weeks – on the veranda of a restaurant, Riley said, 'You have never asked me what I do for a living.'

'From the moment we first met I realised you prefer to divulge information about yourself in your own time.'

'That's just the way I am. Bit like you.'

'Touché.'

And with smiles all round, Riley said, 'Let me tell you a story.'

'OK.'

'My fascination for diamonds, started at an early age when my mother, a wonderful Ingrid Bergman lookalike – caught me in her bedroom, sitting at the dressing table going through her jewellery box. I'd put a ring on my thumb. I loved the sparkles.

'My father is a highly successful businessman – he says it runs in the family. He always explains with a tone of amusement how we come from a long line of entrepreneurial ancestors in London, England. Or at least they were until they were arrested in the1850's by the Peelers Police Force. Brought before the Court, sentenced by the Beak and put on a Convicts Ship, bound for Perth.'

Cain grinned, 'Sail away, sail away, sail away.'

Riley laughed… 'When I decided to start my own business, I opened an up-market jewellery showroom, on the ground floor of a building owned by my father, bless him. It soon became very successful, allowing me to leave my staff to run what was in reality the showcase for a much bigger enterprise.

'The wave of wealth sweeping across Asia provided our city with tourists of a slightly different kind. Regular weekend visitors, who came to Perth in their private jets to stay on the top floor of the Burswood Hotel, free of charge for a reason: they gambled at the top tables of the invitation only *High Roller's International Room* in the casino next door.'

As Riley took a sip of her wine… Cain showed a look of admiration. 'Fascinating.'

'Those *High Rollers*,' said Riley, 'also proved to be regular visitors to a top table of a slightly different kind. A top table on the top floor of the three-storey building owned by my father. It was where I established my own, Investors Diamond Showroom, catering for the world's – mostly from around Asia – elite 1% billionaires. And to ensure total professionalism, I tempted two independent Master Diamond Cutters from New York – by paying them more than just a salary – to work with me, rather than just for me. To cater for my clients every need. So now you know.'

'Incredible,' said Cain. 'You are absolutely wonderful.'

***

When Jerry landed in Perth for his holiday, he was not surprised to see a very suntanned Cain, waiting in the arrivals lounge.

'Agent Edwards,' Jerry said.

'Detective Sergeant Davis.'

'You're looking well.'

'Getting there,' said Cain holding up his hand with his fingers in the splint.

And they embraced like lifelong, best friends do.

From the back of a taxi – Cain's hand prevented him from hiring a vehicle – they talked about all the things they might want to do for the next two weeks.

'Now I'm here,' said Jerry, 'you'll have something to do when you are not seeing Riley.'

'True, and when I do it will be the three of us together.'

'From what you have told me I really am looking forward to meeting her.'

'Probably tomorrow night.'

In the small motel, Jerry unpacked his suitcase in his room next to Cain's and took a shower to freshen up.

Over a leisurely breakfast they talked about how life had been treating them since Cain had left the UK. And whilst taking a stroll around Perth's city centre, Jerry mentioned a few things he would like to do, and places he would like to visit.

By the end of the following evening Jerry and Riley truly liked each other. It was the beginning of a great holiday.

When all three of them were together, Jerry was able to enjoy all the luxuries of a personal tour-guide, without the crowd, which suited them all. And on a couple of occasions, watching the *Spirit of Ecstasy* leading the way, Jerry was able to sit in a Rolls Royce – without members of the Royal Family around him – having a relaxing time.

Jerry collected an assortment of stubby holders, decorated with various designs, a boomerang or two and a few souvenir magnets for the old fridge door.

The whole holiday left Jerry wishing Riley had a sister.

At the airport. 'Stay in touch,' said Jerry. 'Let me know what you decide to do.'

'Will do,' Cain responded. 'Take care.'

And they embraced like best friends do.

***

Several days later, while chatting on the phone, Riley suggested they spend the afternoon sunbathing. 'Great idea,' Cain responded, realising he would see Riley for the first time without any clothes on – well, almost.

On Scarborough Beach, Cain and Riley stripped off and gave

each other the most obvious once over. 'You're beautiful,' Cain murmured, surveying her slim, trim, tanned body and perfect breasts.

'Thank you,' said Riley, eyeing Cain's tanned frame. 'I can see being a karate black belt keeps you in shape. You have a small scar on the side of your stomach.'

'I tripped and fell onto something short and sharp when I was having a morning run through a woodland. I had to have a couple of stitches.'

Seeing the effect she was having on him – under his loose fitting beach shorts – Riley stepped forward and they wrapped their arms around each other. 'There's something I have to tell you,' she said quietly.

On hearing the seriousness of Riley's tone and seeing the expression on her face, Cain showed a look of understanding. 'OK.'

Riley nervously looked up at Cain and stood on her tippy-toes. 'I know you really like me but I'm in love with you.' She took a breath. 'I have to tell you why I have never slept with you.' Hesitantly, she spoke five simple words.

Cain stared down into Riley's tearful eyes and grinned. 'Perfect,' he said.

'Oh really?' Riley replied, dropping down onto her heels. 'Wh–'

'I grew up with children. I know what they're like. No thanks.'

'So you will stay with me?'

Cain then made the ultimate choice of his life. 'Forever,' he said, as he dropped to his knees. 'Will you marry me?'

Riley immediately burst into tears. 'Yes,' she said.

Cain got to his feet, they hugged and kissed, leaving those five simple words – *I can never have children* – to never be spoken again.

Later that afternoon, Riley's 4x4 came to a stop outside Cain's motel. 'I'll collect you in two hours at six o'clock.'

'OK. Where are we going?'

'Not telling you.'

At 6:20pm, Cain watched the Spirit of Ecstasy lead them through the gates of Riley's mansion-like home. Aside from the

Rolls-Royce Silver Shadow they were riding in, there was a Mercedes-Benz and a 4x4 in the driveway: Riley had clearly been born with the proverbial silver spoon in her mouth.

'A magnificent property,' Cain said.

'I live here with my parents.'

'Will I be meeting them?'

'Not on this occasion – they're down in Mandurah visiting friends.'

Out on the patio, the contented couple finished their steaks and salad and Cain topped up their glasses of red wine.

'Thank you for once again cutting up my steak,' Cain said.

'Thank you for cooking them on the barbecue.'

'Wonderful meal.'

Whilst again talking casually about Riley's clients, the elite 1% she commented, 'The million dollar diamond Richard Burton bought for Elizabeth Taylor was one of many. My favourite was the Krupp diamond he purchased the year before, in 1968.'

'You certainly have an endless knowledge about diamonds.'

'To quote you from when we first met – might do.'

'Smarty pants,' Cain responded with the biggest of grins, 'you never cease to amaze me.'

Riley then waggled her head from side to side. Cain saw the sparkles in her ears.

Riley sang, 'Twinkle, twinkle little star.'

Cain crooned, 'How I wonder what you are.'

'Up above the world so high.'

'Like a diamond in the sky.'

'Twinkle, twinkle little star.'

'How I wonder what you are.'

And they both burst out laughing.

'A wonderful lullaby,' Cain eventually said.

They wandered up onto a first-floor balcony overlooking the ocean to watch the last of the sunset morphing into twilight. Cain leant against the balustrade while the remnants of the afternoon breeze – the *Fremantle Doctor* – kept them close. Riley nestled against Cain as he wrapped his arms around her. The effect she was having on him was, again, easy for her to feel.

Riley waggled her head again, from side to side to show off

her earrings. 'They're pink diamonds from the Argyle diamond mine here in Western Australia, up in the Kimberley district. They are beyond rare.'

'Like you,' Cain whispered.

Riley turned in Cain's arms so they were face to face. 'Now tell me. Which do you prefer? Kalgoorlie and kilos or me and carats?'

'Kilos or carats . . . mmm,' Cain said, feigning indecision.

Riley closed an eye, hunched up her shoulders, screwed up her face, and stuck her tongue out.

'You are indeed stunningly beautiful,' said Cain. 'When did you escape from Notre Dame?'

They both laughed and Riley, with a certain rhythm, wriggled and writhed herself back into shape.

'You are perfect,' Cain said, and they kissed...

Lying in bed, Riley was totally at ease in Cain's arms. 'You can teach me all about taking photographs,' she said, 'and I'll teach you all about diamonds.'

They kissed to seal the deal. 'Ladies first,' Cain whispered, anticipating pillow talk of a very different kind.

'We'll start with the 4Cs.'

'Come again?' Cain quipped.

'I will,' Riley giggled. 'The 4Cs stand for colour, clarity, cut, and carat weight,' she managed to say before she arched her back and breathed in deeply, as Cain eased her legs apart. 'I'll tell you in the morning,' she sighed.

As the sun rose, Cain woke to the unmistakable calls of kookaburras in the trees and a beautiful young lady – sound asleep – contentedly wrapped around him. It was confirmation of their love and fascination for each other.

A week later, Cain went to see an orthopaedic surgeon Riley had recommended to have his hand examined. The prognosis confirmed the obvious: his fingers would need several more months to get back to being one hundred per cent.

In a stationery shop, Cain faxed a copy of the medical report to London – and back in his motel room he used his burner phone to make a call.

'Morning,' Mac said.

Mac completely understood the physical compromise Cain had to live with – and greatly appreciated his honesty regarding his relationship with Riley.

'I now live in a different world,' Cain said.

'For the time being, let's just leave you on sick leave. That way you will continue to receive your salary during the months ahead, but on one condition.'

'Of course.'

'Give me your word you will let me know when your hand is back to being one hundred per cent.'

Cain understood Mac was hoping – in the months ahead – his relationship with Riley would come to an end, he would return to the UK, and return to the Bureau. He realised there was no point in speculating with Mac about what the future may or may not bring.

'I give you my word.'

Mac signed off: 'My door is always open to you.'

Cain then phoned Jerry to update him on what had happened with Riley.

'You're engaged,' said Jerry. 'Congratulations.'

'Thank you. You will have to be my best man at the wedding. So we will arrange everything around when you can have the last two weeks of your annual leave.'

'I'll let you know.'

'Try to make it towards the end of the year, when it is summer here so you can avoid a couple of weeks of the winter in the UK.'

'You don't mind waiting.'

'Not at all. Riley is insisting you have to be here.'

After clarifying a couple of points, accompanied by good-humoured comments they brought their conversation to an end.

'Will get back to you as soon as I can,' Jerry said.

'Look after yourself.'

After Cain had met with Riley's parents on several occasions, he moved into their mansion.

On their first night of living together, Riley found a small gift on her pillow. She unwrapped it and placed the gold flake in a heart-shaped pendant necklace around her neck.

The following days, weeks, and months became an astonishing learning curve – in every sense of the word – for Cain. It was a time when his almost photographic memory served him well; a time when he discovered there were few regulations in the diamond industry, variety was the spice of life – and a million dollars in diamonds would easily, unlike gold, always fit into a matchbox. It was something that appealed to his more a free spirit attitude to life.

And beyond all expectations, his mentor became his everything: totally in love with each other, they did just about everything together.

9

November 1997

Gianni Versace had been murdered outside
his home in Miami, Florida.
The world was still mourning the tragic death of
a Princess in a car crash in Paris.

Many people said it was a year
they would always remember.
Whilst for Cain and Jerry, it was a year they would never
forget.

Early on a quiet Tuesday morning, Cain and Riley were relaxing on the patio reading the papers and drinking coffee. It had been another long weekend of meetings with several of her elite 1% clients. Riley's cell phone rang. 'Hello.'

Cain was already well aware Riley and her parents were going to fly down to the Margaret River wine region to stay with old family friends for a few days. It was something they were now able to do more often because Cain would stay in Perth to look after things. He always believed it best, Riley should have time with the two daughters, her lifelong friends, without him. But when the family came to stay with Riley's parents, they would all go out to dinner together and Cain would often act as a chauffeur for Riley and the two daughters.

Cain could clearly hear what Riley and her two friends were talking about on the phone, so when she plonked herself on his lap he played along.

'I think I need to fly down to the vineyards to pick up some wine and keep up my flying hours.'

'What a good idea. Why don't you take your parents with you, have lunch with your girlfriends, and if you decide to sample the wine, you could have dinner with them and stay a while.'

'Oh,' said Riley with a flutter of her eyelids, 'why didn't I think of that?'

'As one pilot to another, I think *Jumbo* would appreciate having the dust blown off him,' Cain said, wrapping his arms around Riley.

The laughter on the other end of Riley's phone was clearly audible. 'Tell her what you want, what you really, really want,' the background audience sang.

'We'll be taking off at 11:30am, see you soon. 'Bye!' Riley hung up, totally at ease with Cain fondling her gently. 'Nice to know both your hands are now feeling normal.'

'I love to keep abreast of things,' Cain murmured as, accompanied by an exchange of seductive comments, he piggy-backed Riley up to their bedroom.

Riley and her parents landed safely at the Margaret River airfield – and before driving off with their family friends, she phoned Cain to let him know all was OK.

'Love you,' Riley said.

'Love you too.'

In the background, Riley's two girlfriends both joyfully shouted, 'Phone you on Friday.'

'Byyyyyyeeeeee.'

'Have fun.'

That evening, Cain took Bill and Greg, Riley's two master diamond cutters, out for a steak at one of their favorite restaurants. From day one all three men had got on well together. Lunch or dinner was something they always did at least once a week with Riley.

On the following morning, Cain started his day by cooking himself an English breakfast before doing paperwork, making phone calls, and having a coffee.

And on Thursday, Cain was out and about doing everything on his To-do list.

Friday Afternoon

At the Margaret River airfield, having loaded up *Jumbo*, the two families bid their farewells and, as always, the hosts drove off

to park in a lay-by near the end of the airfield to give Riley and
her parents a wave as they flew above them.

Riley phoned Cain. 'Boo! It's me.'

'What a surprise. All OK?'

'We'll tell you all about where we went for brekkies, lunch,
and dinner when we get back.'

'I thought you might.'

'We'll be taking off in twenty minutes.'

'In *Jumbo*,' said Cain. 'Or are you doing a Harry Potter on a
broomstick?'

'I'll fly *Jumbo*. It will be easier to bring the wine.'

'The corkscrew is ready and waiting.'

Several more amusing, sensual one-liners were exchanged
before they rounded off their conversation.

'I'll be waiting for you at the airfield,' Cain said.

Riley giggled. 'Love you.'

'Love you too.'

'Byyyyyyeeeeee.'

An hour later, Cain finished the paperwork and phone calls –
for Riley – and put the kettle on to make himself a coffee. He
thought about the tragic death of Princess Diana: he understood,
better than most, what a difficult past couple of months it had
been for the British Royal Family, Jerry, the Royal Protection
Team, the British nation, and the people around the world. In an
effort to lift Jerry's spirits, he decided to give him a wake-up
call about his upcoming trip.

'Morning,' said Cain. 'Paradise calling.'

'Sod off.'

They both laughed – like best friends do.

'The sunbed is waiting by the pool. The barbecue is waiting
for a steak. Your dry cider is in the fridge. And to round off the
evening, the freezer is full of ice for our J&B and Jameson.'

'Great, just what I need to unwind.'

'We'll be at the airport to meet you.'

'And I'll be at your wedding to see you off.'

'You always have been and always will be the Best Man.'

'Gotta get myself ready, talk to you later.'

'Take care.'

Cain was getting ready to leave for the airfield when the doorbell rang. On opening the front door he was surprised to see two police officers. 'Afternoon gentlemen, to what do I owe the pleasure?' Cain said cheerfully. Then he saw the looks on their faces.

A minute later Cain was sitting on a sofa with his head in his hands, tears running down his face. *Jumbo* had crashed, Riley and her parents had been killed.

Some fifteen minutes later, the police officers left Cain. He sat alone with the numbing pain only such a loss can bring, flooding through every fibre of his being. An hour later, he started doing what he knew he had to. He phoned the family down in Margaret River, the diamond cutters Bill and Greg, the manageress of the ground-floor jewellery showroom, and the wedding organisers to tell them the tragic news.

Afterwards, devastated and exhausted, his mind reeling, he poured himself a very large J&B and went upstairs. Since first meeting Riley, he had become the son her parents never had. And after Riley told Cain her secret – something he was ecstatic about – he had been destined to become the son-in-law they always wanted.

Cain stepped out onto their bedroom balcony. The scent of Riley's favourite incense, *Nag Champa*, lingered in the air. He walked back into their bedroom, where the emptiness was overpowering, the silence deafening. He got their photo albums out of her wardrobe. He sat on their bed turning page after page, staring down at the photographs of the two of them together: on beaches, in parks, in the Outback, in restaurants, and at barbecues with Riley's parents, business associates, and friends.

A picture of them riding bicycles on the car-less Rottnest Island reminded him of the gibe he had made on the first day they had met about riding a bicycle to Kalgoorlie. Turning a page, he saw the picture of the two of them standing by *Jumbo*. He hugged Riley's pillows: he could feel her, smell her, taste her, and from somewhere real or imagined, he didn't know, he heard *Ringo Starr* singing:

Every time I see your face
It reminds me of the places we used to go

The tears streamed down his face.

During the rest of the afternoon and evening, Cain fielded the inevitable calls offering their condolences and support for the days ahead. In the silence of the early hours of the morning, he was on their bed. He slowly picked up the phone and pressed the speed-dial button.

'Hello,' said Jerry. 'Good timing, I've just set foot, back on the *Disponible.*'

'Are you alone?'

'Yes.'

'There's no easy way to tell you this. *Jumbo* crashed a few hours ago. Riley and her parents are dead.'

'Dear God, no.' There was a pause and Cain heard his friend take a deep breath. 'I'll fly out as soon as I can.'

'No, don't do that Jerry. I've had a long think about you coming back to Perth. I can't cope with you being here for all the wrong reasons. After Diana's death you've been through enough for one year. You don't want to have to go through it all again. Let's just remember Perth like it was when we were all here together.'

Jerry sighed. 'The best holiday we ever had.'

'It was. Let's meet up when . . . well, whenever, I–'

Jerry filled the silence. 'Do you have anyone with you?'

'Not at the moment. Bill and Greg, the two diamond cutters we had dinner with when you were here, will be with me in the morning. Please excuse me, I've had enough for now, let's talk again later.'

As Cain put the phone down – the two men at opposite ends of the world, wiped the tears from their eyes.

10

Grief

Despite Cain's natural fortitude and resilience, it soon became clear to those around him, his taking on of the mantle of responsibility, of doing what had to be done was more than just taking its toll.

A bleary-eyed Cain was in the study, contemplating what the authorities had just confirmed: Riley had not made a distress call over the radio or signalled an SOS by transponder; the aircraft's squawk-code had remained the same to the end.

The ATSB (Australian Transport Safety Bureau) had been unable to find any structural or mechanical reason for *Jumbo* to have crashed. And the coroner's report had concluded there was nothing to suggest Riley may have been incapacitated in some way by a sudden medical condition. Cain gazed out of the window, but his sleepless, bloodshot eyes were staring into oblivion.

On the day of Riley's and her parents' cremations, the service overflowed with people, condolences, tributes and a plethora of tears.

The sound of *Sarah Brightman* and *Andrea Bocelli* singing *Time To Say Goodbye* floated over the assembled mourners as everyone whispered their personal farewells.

In the quiet of the evening, Cain sat alone on a darkened patio, looking at an empty chair. The words of a *Simon and Garfunkel* song drifted through his head:

Hello darkness my old friend . . .

The song's lyrics had a vastly different meaning for a man like him.

The following day, Mac phoned Cain again to express his condolences before they had a long chat. Cain was well aware — because of what he was — if the cause of death of anyone closely associated with him could not be established, it had to be flagged as suspicious and handed over to the Bureau for further investigation.

Cain said, 'I'll be driving down to the crash site tomorrow.'

'Let me know if you find anything the authorities have overlooked.'

'Of course.'

'My door is always open to you.'

'Thank you.'

Three days later, Cain was talking with Jerry, who was waiting in Buckingham Palace for his day to begin. They talked about how things were progressing.

'I drove down to the crash site.'

'How was it?'

'*Jumbo* nose-dived into the ground; Riley and her parents would have been killed instantly. I then drove on down to Margaret River to stay overnight with Riley's parents' friends and their daughters. On the following morning they took me to the airfield. They went through everything they all did before *Jumbo* took off. I spoke to the airfield staff. Nothing–'

'Sorry,' Jerry interrupted, 'Principal is on the move, have to go.' He hung up.

Cain understood the pressures Jerry faced as a Royal Protection Officer at the best of times, let alone the worst. He totally understood why Jerry had – not for the first time and not for the last time – abruptly ended a call.

'Nothing suspicious happened,' Cain said quietly to no one listening.

***

Sitting in the front passenger seat of the Royal limousine, heading out of London towards Windsor, Jerry could not help but think about why *Jumbo* had crashed.

'Jerry, what is the latest?' HRH enquired.

Jerry looked over his shoulder, appreciating HRH's concern and choosing his words carefully, leaving out the word *crash* for another day:

'Unfortunately sir, we still do not know why the plane went

70

down.'

***

Without Riley, the elite 1% top-floor business wasn't a business anymore.

Everyone associated with Riley on a day-to-day basis had always looked forward to seeing her. On the rare occasions she had not been with Cain, associates had always enquired, 'Where is Riley today? What's Riley up to mate? Send her our best wishes. Send her our love.'

Cain had got used to being told he was the luckiest man alive, followed by good-humoured threats of death and destruction if he ever upset her. But not anymore: periods of awkward silence now lingered around a void of what could never be said again.

Cain met with lawyers – now the executors for Riley's and her parents' wills. He sat quietly in their office, listening to the details. Everything her parents owned would be sold, accumulating several million Australian dollars. They had no living relatives to leave their money to, therefore friends, a number of business associates, and Cain would all be the beneficiaries, receiving a percentage of whatever the total amount would be.

Riley had done something similar: leaving the diamonds she had in stock to friends, a number of associates, Bill, Greg, and Cain.

Riley's lawyer said, 'Riley and I were well aware you never asked to be legally a part of her business or a signatory for her bank accounts.'

Cain had been staring out of the window. He looked to the lawyer. 'I trusted her implicitly. There was no need. We'd agreed we would get around to sorting it out with you after we were married.'

'She adored you for your trust,' said the lawyer, handing Cain a cheque.

Seeing the seven-figure sum, Cain was lost for words.

I'd give it all up to have her back.

As Cain wiped tears from his eyes, the other lawyer very politely placed a box of tissues by his side and confirmed, 'In due course, we will inform you of exactly how much Riley's parents left you.'

Bill and Greg were leaving for Hong Kong and pastures new. Cain gave them a lift to the airport. After unloading the suitcases, an air of sadness hung over them all.

Cain said, 'Thank you for all your help these past few weeks.'

'Thank you for putting so many members of the elite 1% clients directly in contact with us,' said Bill.

'You deserve it.'

'If you hadn't, we would not have been invited to Hong Kong by one of them. Are you sure you do not want to join us?' Greg added.

'Not for now,' Cain demurred – he had to stay away from anyone who reminded him of his time with Riley. 'I'll come visit you sometime.'

'We look forward to seeing you,' Bill said.

'Take care,' Cain concluded, and with an air of sorrow, regret, they embraced as great friends do.

Watching Bill and Greg walking away, Cain came to terms with the inevitable: he also had to move on. But where would he go?

On the following morning in the deserted mansion, a fatigued Cain received a call from another of his and Riley's business associates and friends: the chairman of West Australia's Diamond Merchants' Association.

'Bill and Greg informed me you will also be leaving Australia.'

'I have to,' Cain responded.

'I understand, but where will you go?'

'I'm not sure.'

'Please, let's meet up before you make any decisions. Are you free for lunch?'

A car came for Cain at one o'clock and, out of respect, he was taken to a newly opened restaurant on the outskirts of the city that held no memories for him.

Staying in Perth for Christmas was not an option for Cain, and neither was going back to London: Jerry was up in Norfolk on the Sandringham estate, protecting The Firm.

Grief is a fickle thing. It hits you in ways and at times you are least prepared for. Leaving sadness and/or depression to be brought on by the realisation you are now alone. Possibly causing you to isolate yourself whilst reflecting on things you did with your loved one or focusing on memories from the past. It can last a long time.

In a travel agent's, Cain decided he would catch a flight to a country he had never been to, where no one would know him. He would stay in a luxury hotel, where his room would have its own private balcony so as to avoid coming into contact with those celebrating the Christmas holiday. He would also, by being in a country where the sun was shining, not have to contend with the unpredictability of a thing called weather – and on New Year's Eve he would fly on to his new destination, to arrive on New Year's Day. It would be from where – regardless of how long it was going to take he would embark on a journey down a long road called grief, to a place only he could find. A place called acceptance.

But unless the reason for *Jumbo* crashing could be established, his journey would always be hampered by a nagging doubt, an echo from his previous life in the UK: had his past life with the Bureau finally caught up with him?

Sitting on the Qantas 747 as it taxied out to the runway, Cain unfolded the tissues to touch the pink diamonds, the gold flake in a heart-shaped pendant, and their engagement rings lying on his favourite photographs of the two of them together.

As the plane took off he looked down at Scarborough Beach in the distance. He could see Riley standing on her tiptoes, looking up at him, with their arms wrapped around each other: *forever*, he had pledged.

He closed his eyes to watch the magic movie in his mind as they revisited all the places, the islands, parks, the Outback,

beaches and restaurants they had been to together.
But only diamonds are forever.
A tear ran down his cheek.

> *For all sad words of tongue and pen,*
> *the saddest are these:*
> *'It might have been.'*

John Greenleaf Whittier

Part Three

Land of The Free and Home of The Brave

Life Moves On

Life's A Circle

11

The Beginning

On the morning of January 1st, 1998, Cain landed in Miami, Florida.

Happy New Year: if only.

From the back of a taxi driving along the coastline, Cain was watching the world go by. He momentarily remembered his meeting in Perth with the Chairman of the Diamond Merchants' Association. It left him with an overwhelming sense of gratitude.

I would never have had this opportunity without your help. Thank you.

From a small motel in Fort Lauderdale, he ventured out into his new environment. He wandered the streets to get his bearings, browsed the shops to see what was on offer – and early in the evening he went to one of the restaurants on the beachfront to have a quiet bite to eat.

And from dusk to dawn, trying to contend with the reality of life and death, he heard – real or imagined – *Noel Harrison* singing *The Windmills Of Your Mind*:

Like a door that keeps revolving in a half-forgotten dream
Or the ripples from a pebble someone tosses in a stream

Lovers walk along the shore and leave their footprints in
the sand
Is the sound of distant drumming just the fingers of your
hand

Like a circle in a spiral, like a wheel within a wheel
Never ending or beginning on an ever-spinning reel
As the images unwind like the circles that you find
In the windmills of your mind.

On the following morning, a bleary-eyed Cain set about doing everything he could to keep himself occupied and keep his mind focused on the future. He went to a bank, opened an account and deposited the lawyer's cheque, the 'gift' from Riley. He wandered more streets again to see what was on offer, stopped into a real estate agent's to see what was for sale, and chose a restaurant overlooking the main waterway for a quiet lunch. During the afternoon he checked out the locations of several apartment buildings.

In the evening he went for a run before drinking too much in his motel room – and with tears in his eyes he curled himself up on the bed and fell asleep.

Saturday – January 3rd

The sight of Jerry walking through the arrivals lounge at Miami International Airport raised Cain's spirits to an all-time high. And for the first time in a long time they embraced like best friends do.

'Great to see you,' Jerry whispered.

'It's been too long.'

Cain picked up Jerry's carry-on. 'I've hired a 4x4. We'll take the scenic route up the coast back to Fort Lauderdale. Better than being on the freeway.'

'Perfect,' Jerry agreed, grabbing his suitcase. 'Nice to see your hand is back to normal.'

And taking a first step, they meandered along their well-trodden path of jests and gibes.

After Jerry had unpacked, they wandered out of the motel to one of the beachfront restaurants to have lunch, enjoy the view, and talk about what they would be doing in Florida.

Jerry knew Cain would soon enough get around to talking about what had happened in Australia. So, he had no reason to ask, no reason to delve, just make light of things – go with the flow – and all in good time all would be revealed.

'I've been promoted, I'm now Detective Inspector Jerry Davis – and on Monday February 2nd I will start my new role as the personal bodyguard to a member of the Royal Family.'

'Congratulations! Who is it?'

'Don't be Naïve.'

Cain grinned; Jerry had used an anagram of a nickname – known within certain circles – for a particular member of the Royal Family. And shaking hands, Cain quipped, 'You truly are a senior Palace Pup now.'

'Sod off.'

'Tonight we will celebrate.'

That evening they enjoyed a New York strip and bottle of red wine in a great steak house.

On Sunday – the real estate agent's open-house day – Cain and Jerry were standing on the balcony of a sixties tenth-floor penthouse overlooking the beach.

Back in the UK, Cain and Jerry had developed a lucrative sideline in buying and selling or renting out residential properties. It had been nothing more than an enjoyable, money making hobby. They both had a keen eye for a good deal. It allowed them to increase their savings for their bucket list. Apart from declaring what they were doing to their bosses in writing (a requirement of their professions), they never told anyone.

Looking down from the balcony, they watched the security guard checking in a car at the barrier before directing the driver to the visitors' parking area. It was one of the most secure buildings Cain had been told about. As they admired the magnificent views along the coastline.

Cain realised overlooking the beach was now a way of life he was not prepared to live without. And being on the east coast of a country he would now see the sunrise not the sunset. It would give him a new perspective on life. A new dawn. A new start.

From the shorter side of the L-shaped corner balcony the panoramic view across the hundreds of miles of navigable canals and waterways was truly breathtaking for a boat lover like Jerry. He admired the yachts, sailboats and cruisers, moored at the end of the detached properties front gardens, lined with palm trees. Truly a sight to behold.

'The Venice of America, the yachting capital of the world,'

sighed Jerry. 'A dream come true.'

'You'll have the same view from your bedroom,' said Cain, gesturing with a hand. 'Let's go have a look.'

Jerry stood at his bedroom window. The expression of appreciation on his face said it all.

The apartment was wonderfully furnished with king-sized lounger suites, beds, en-suite bathrooms and, of course, the classic American-style walk-in wardrobes. Later, they wandered around the underground car park, the gardens, the barbecue area, and the swimming pool. It all left Cain with just the one thought in mind:

This is perfect.

On the following day, Cain's bank transferred the funds to his appointed lawyer to pay for the apartment, to get the obligatory paperwork started, and Cain was handed the keys.

Twenty-four hours later, Cain and Jerry were sitting at the kidney-shaped kitchen island having a chat. Cain handed Jerry a set of keys and the alarm codes written backwards on a sticky-note.

'I'll keep them with the ones we have for our London properties,' said Jerry. 'A new addition to our collection.'

'Of course.'

Cain placed his US bank statement in front of Jerry, who stared at it, astonished. 'Now you know how much Riley left me; how much we can now add to our savings for when we retire.'

'Incredible.'

In the light of the early evening, they went to a seafood restaurant overlooking the main waterway and enjoyed oysters, prawns, and the catch of the day, watching the boats passing by. Strolling back to the apartment at a leisurely pace, they paused on a drawbridge to enjoy the view.

'Reserved for the *Disponible*,' said Cain, pointing at an empty mooring in front of another million-dollar property.

Jerry smiled. 'Perfect for when we retire.'

'Fingers crossed.'

Jerry raised a hand, flipped his middle finger over the index, and in the manner of a casual salute he touched the side of his head. 'Touch wood.'

Now Cain's hand was back to normal, he did the same – and with smiles all round, they continued on their way.

Back in the apartment, for the first time since Australia, Cain placed a single ice cube in two highball tumblers and poured a finger or three of J&B for himself and Jameson for Jerry. Settling into easy chairs out on the balcony, they raised their glasses. 'Cheers.'

As Cain eventually started talking about Australia, Jerry calmly shifted himself into police officer mode to subtly analyse Cain's time in Perth with Riley, both before and after her death, to make sure nothing had been overlooked. By the early hours of the morning, a deep sense of sadness had engulfed the balcony.

'When I waved to Riley and her parents in *Jumbo* it was the last time I ever saw them,' Cain said quietly.

Jerry stayed silent.

Cain looked out at the horizon and into the darkness beyond. 'On the following Friday afternoon, I spoke to her for the last time on the phone and then she was gone,' he sighed. 'Forever. *Jumbo,* like everything else the family owned, was always one hundred per cent. The hangar in Perth where they kept it was under 24-hour CCTV surveillance. The tapes were reviewed, but none of the ground crew or other pilots ever touched *Jumbo* or did anything that could be construed as suspicious. If *Jumbo* was sabotaged in some way it could only have happened at the Margaret River airfield. When I drove down to see the crash site, I went on to Margaret River to stay overnight with Riley's parents' friends and their daughters. On the following morning they all took me to the airfield. They went through everything they'd done before *Jumbo* took off. I left them in tears to go and speak to the airfield staff. But they said they had not seen anything or anyone suspicious.'

Cain momentarily paused to top up their glasses.

Jerry quietly asked, 'Nothing suspicious ever happened in Perth?'

'No, nothing,' Cain murmured. 'None of the family, our friends or the bodyguards protecting our elite 1% clients ever had any reason to bring something or someone to our attention.'

Cain glanced at Jerry. 'You saw what our life was like when you came to visit us.'

'I did. It was paradise – the best holiday we ever had together.'

A somewhat drained Cain conveyed the last of his thoughts: 'Surely if it had been an accident, if *Jumbo* had failed in some way, the ATSB would have found something.'

'Or the doctors,' Jerry said quietly – not wanting to use the word autopsy, because of all it implied. 'Would have found something.'

'If . . . if only I had–' Cain sighed, but he trailed off.

If had been the key word to much of what Cain had spoken of during the course of the evening. It was now crystal clear to Jerry what was troubling Cain: he blamed himself for Riley's and her parents' deaths. He believed if he had been with them, he would have saved them all. He was mired in guilt and regret.

'There are too many *ifs* in the world,' Jerry quietly commented. 'You have to stop blaming yourself.'

Cain slowly placed his empty glass on the table and raised the palms of his hands to his eyes, holding back the tears – without success.

Jerry got to his feet, leant over, and placed a hand on Cain's shoulder. 'I'll go make some coffee,' he whispered.

Nothing had been overlooked.

***

Meanwhile, back in London, Mac was sitting at his desk, having a morning coffee.

Knowing Jerry was in Florida, he checked the clocks on the wall. The time was 3pm in Perth. He picked up the phone and dialled the number. He would just check if there was any further news from Australia before they finished for the day.

On the day of Riley's and her parents' funeral, Mac had opened an investigation into the murder of a KGB defector in London. Behind closed doors, it was believed the death had been a Kremlin-sanctioned contract killing carried out by an *Agent* of a poisonous kind – with a very Cossack flavour.

The contract killing prompted Mac to consider if Riley's autopsy could have missed something. But it was all too late. Riley – along with her parents – had already been cremated.

Mac eventually ended his call to Perth and closed Riley's file on his desk. The case would remain flagged as suspicious. Long-term, he believed, if Riley's death had not been just an accident, there would eventually be a trail to pick up on and he would find it.

The words *Open Verdict* did not sit well with him, and neither did the thought that Cain's past had, in some way, finally caught up with him.

12

Cain was at the kitchen island pouring coffees when Jerry, having watched the sun rise, walked in from the balcony. 'It's going to be another beautiful day.'

'It is. Brunch at Denny's,' Cain suggested.

'Good idea.'

'If you want to try those horrible grits, you're more than welcome.'

'Not such a good idea.'

After brunch, it took Cain just twenty minutes of multiple-choice questions and fifteen minutes on the road to obtain his key ID for everything – his US, driver's licence. They then drove to a garage showroom where Cain purchased a gun-metal grey Jeep Grand Cherokee, ready for collection at the end of the week.

A combination of business and pleasure took them to Sawgrass Mills, the second largest shopping mall in Florida. First off, they purchased a couple of pairs of 34x36 inch jeans – unavailable in the UK – a couple of souvenir T-shirts, and a few more magnets for the old fridge door. And in a tech shop they purchased their first ever laptops, a step into the world of new technology, along with a printer for Cain.

That evening the two young men were back in the apartment, looking at their laptop screens, registering their Hotmail addresses – a new world of communication.

'Talking of whatever next,' said Jerry, 'when are you going to introduce yourself to your new diamond business associates?'

'At the end of the month. Call me old-fashioned, but–'

'Old-fashioned,' Jerry interrupted with a smile.

Cain managed a grin. 'I didn't want anything interfering with our time together.'

'Perfect,' Jerry said, and opening the recently released Microsoft Word, he started putting together a *To Do* list for

Cain to keep him busy, keep him on track.

On the following day, Jerry was well aware, getting Cain to start shooting again would be a major step on his long journey down a road called grief to a place called acceptance.

Cain walked out of his bedroom into the kitchen to see his shoulder holster – the one he used to wear in the UK – lying on the kitchen island.

Jerry said, 'Thought you might like to have it to get your fingers on the trigger.'

Cain sighed. 'My mind has been on other things.'

'How long since you fired a gun?'

'Not since the polo ground shoot-out.'

'Eighteen months ago. Since we are in the US of A, the world of guns, shall we give it a try?'

Cain picked up his shoulder holster for a moment's contemplation. 'OK,' he said.

'Winner buys the wine.'

'You'll be buying the steaks then.'

'Sod off.'

On an indoor shooting range above a gun shop, Cain racked the slide of a Beretta .9mm semi-automatic pistol, sending the first round into the chamber and taking aim, he tightened his finger on the trigger. The rapid-fire sent several rounds into the target's head – and its heart didn't fare much better. The Beretta's slide finally locked back, Cain blinked – and Jerry opened fire.

At the end of the session, they dropped their Peltor-style ear guards down to their shoulders tidied up and threw the empty cans of Coca-Cola – Stormin Norman-style – into the bin. *Clunk.*

'Like old times,' said Jerry, as they examined their last targets.

'Looks as if I'll be buying the steaks.'

Down in the gun shop, encouraged by Jerry, Cain purchased his two favourite weapons: a Beretta .9mm, semi-automatic pistol and a Colt Python .357 magnum revolver. He also purchased two of the recently released, new generation polymer pistols, a Glock 27 – the perfect size for a concealed ankle holster

– and Walther P99, to give them a try.

Cain would return in a week or so – after the authorities had put him in the system – to collect the guns, along with two extra mags for each of the three semi-automatics, plus an ankle holster, and ammunition.

Out in the car park, Cain pressed the button and opened the door of his new Jeep Grand Cherokee only to find he wasn't on the driver's side. 'How many times am I going to do this? I keep forgetting it's different here,' he said with a tone of frustration, shaking his head.

'You are not doing it every time,' said Jerry, putting a comforting hand on Cain's shoulder. And trying to be supportive he added, 'Just a momentary lapse of concentration. We know what you're going through. Let's try not to dwell on it.'

'At least I've stopped putting my left hand down when I want to undo my seat belt.'

One afternoon, Cain and Jerry were ambling back from Miami South Beach along Ocean Drive when they came to a stop on the sidewalk by the main gates of the Casa Casuarina, a magnificent mansion: home to the late Gianni Versace. They were standing on the very spot where the famous fashion designer had been murdered.

For Jerry it brought back memories of the death of a Princess, when the car she was in had crashed on the Pont de l'Alma tunnel in Paris, some four months earlier.

During those times, and because Jerry had been in the UK and Cain in Australia, they had only been able to talk cautiously on the phone. Jerry had been able to disclose only a few lesser-known facts. Now, they were face to face.

As they slung their cameras over their shoulders and continued on their way, the subject of security, personal safety, and the Royal Protection Team came to the fore.

Cain and Jerry glanced at each other. Jerry smiled. 'Let me tell you a story.'

'OK.'

'*Il était une fois à Paris* (Once upon a time in Paris).'

The roaming pair rounded off Jerry's visit with a five-day leisurely drive down the length of the Florida Keys. They stopped off at Key Largo, where they had their photographs taken beside *The African Queen:* a thirty-five-foot steamboat used in the 1951 movie of the same name, starring Humphrey 'Bogie' Bogart and Katherine Hepburn.

Jerry posed Bogie-style, holding a bottle of whisky. 'I'll have this photo sepia-toned and put it on a wall in the *Disponible,*' Jerry said.

'I'll drink to that one,' said Cain. 'Bogie would love it.'

On the following day, having made numerous stops along the way to enjoy sessions of *Ryukyu Kobujutsu* karate on deserted beaches, and having driven over the expanse of the magnificent Seven Mile Bridge, Cain and Jerry arrived at their final destination, the southern-most tip of America: Key West.

They soon found themselves in Ernest Hemingway's favourite bar, Sloppy Joe's, where they tried a pint or two of Spearfish Amber and Sloppy Joe's Island Ale. Afterwards, they took a leisurely stroll along Whitehead Street.

Standing on the first-floor veranda of Ernest Hemingway's exquisite home, they leant side by side against one of the pillars, overlooking Hemingway's writing room: a simple, separate single-storey building surrounded by beautiful gardens. Inside, Cain and Jerry could see the great author's chair in front of his typewriter on the table, waiting for the next chapter to begin. But in reality, Hemmingway had committed suicide in 1961.

'We will have to write that book when we retire,' Cain said. They looked at each other with knowing smiles.

'All those secrets,' said Jerry. 'Perhaps we will.'

And time moved on.

When Cain and Jerry entered the departure terminal at Miami International Airport, they continued along their well-trodden path of jests and gibes, laughing together and shaking hands for the last time for perhaps a long time they embraced like best friends do.

Cain was now alone again taking a slow drive, along the coast, back to Fort Lauderdale. Time to get started.

The Next Chapter

Ready To Roll

At the crack of dawn, Cain began his first day of being alone again. He went for a run, gave his Jeep a once-over at the car wash, had a shower back at his apartment, and went shopping.

On the following day, he started getting himself organised. While having a coffee on the kitchen island, he opened his post. The documents for his newly registered company, GemGia, had arrived. He somewhat reluctantly opened the envelope stamped with an Australian postmark. He read the letter from Riley's parents' lawyers. He couldn't believe what he was reading: a cheque for AU$950,000. A tear ran down his cheek.

After depositing the cheque in the bank, he went to a restaurant on the beach to have a coffee and have a think. He would visit England to see Jerry, but he would never live there again. Nor would he return to Western Australia: he would, for the rest of his life, always be wherever the sun was shining – on a beach.

Back in the apartment, looking at his laptop screen, he moved the mouse and ticked off another box on his *To Do* list and sent his first proper email to Jerry. The Internet would now allow them – with the press of a button – to leave the longest of messages for each other 24/7.

He finished his two-fingered symphony with a single, coded line:

Give me a call when you are home alone so we can have a long chat. I need to cheque *something with you.*

Cain now had a place to live, wheels, a bank account, a landline, and a lawyer. He was now where he needed to be: in a position of accountability, credibility, and respectability. He remembered his meeting with the chairman of the Diamond Merchants' Association in Perth.

Thank you again.

He dialled the number.

Early next morning, he took a fifteen-minute drive, heading north along the beach road, and came to a stop. Ahead of him, a one-mile strip of prestigious, twenty storey-high, beachfront apartment buildings – home to many in the retired Jewish community – was basking in the heat of the morning sun.

Named the Galt Mile, the prestigious apartment buildings were the home to many of the diamond industries' most esteemed – and now retired – old masters from New York, who had offered to take Cain under their wing.

Cain soon found common ground with his retired seniors, who found the younger man – someone new, someone different – an unforeseen but very welcome inspiration. They'd liked the way, after watching an old James Cagney gangster movie together on TV one afternoon, how Cain had nicknamed them the Galt Mile Gang.

In time, their yet-to-retire counterparts in New York were introduced to Cain and they became the Manhattan Mob. And before too long he was a regular and welcome guest of theirs too. He purchased diamonds through them, they cut his *rough* – and in time he was given a greater insight into the many secrets of a very protective profession.

Cain then contacted his old friends Bill and Greg, who had moved from Perth to Hong Kong. After reminiscing about the good old times in Perth, they soon moved on to chatting about how looking after their elite 1% clientele was going.

Rounding off their conversation on a positive note, Cain said, 'I owe you a steak.'

'We'll have it in our favourite restaurant here in Hong Kong.'

'Hopefully one day soon.'

'Stay in touch.'

'Will do.'

As time moved on, Cain eventually managed to tempt the old masters into occasionally reviving their professional skills. He purchased a top-floor apartment on the Galt Mile and turned the master bedroom into a masters' diamond-cutting room. The rest of the apartment was converted into a Galt Mile Gang hangout.

Everything the chairman of the Diamond Merchants' Association in Perth had done for Cain had turned out well. By nature, Cain had always been a bit of a loner and after Perth, he was spending more time than ever by himself. 'No woman would put up with me,' he often replied if tackled about his personal life, before politely moving the subject of conversation on to other things or moving himself on to other places.

He decided to get a USA motorbike licence. It would be a welcome commitment: a two-day course over a whole weekend to keep him occupied, to keep his mind off other things.

In Florida, the 'Home of The Brave', the law allowed people to ride without wearing a crash helmet. Cain soon discovered the thrill, both mentally and physically, of cruising the coastline on a hired Harley Davidson Road King with the wind in his hair. It appealed to his more free-spirited attitude to life and now, after what had happened in Perth, his same attitude to death. He remembered the name of the biker gang he had seen: Coffin Cheaters.

Late one morning, after shooting on a range, Cain visited the local police station. He submitted his application forms and his IDs to the officer on reception. He had his mugshots and fingerprints taken. He booked his ability test for the following day.

Weeks later when his permit arrived in the post, he looked at himself in the mirror. 'Seen better,' he said quietly, and staring at his Beretta in his shoulder holster, he felt a slight niggle in his subconscious.

Need to carry it, like to carry it, or prefer to – just in case?
The conundrum left him with one last thought.
But will the day ever come again when I have to?
On the following day he went back to carrying a handgun day and night.

One evening, Cain was having a quiet drink with the most senior of all the old masters; the one with whom he had spent the most time: Joseph.

'You have a type of sadness that stops you sharing your life with another,' Joseph said.

Cain had learnt whatever Joseph, a true old-style gentleman, had to say, his perception and sense of understanding always made his words truly worth listening to. When Joseph leant forward, topping up their glasses, Cain saw once again the number tattooed on his arm. The number provoked Cain to contemplate if the *Old Master's* words were based on observation. Or were they perhaps, a reflection of an untold past personal experience? But Cain did not ask. Instead, he found himself gazing into the eyes of the beautiful Riley, her pink diamonds in her ears, the gold flake in a heart-shaped pendant around her neck, the engagement ring on her finger, while the scent of *Nag Champa* filled his mind. Cain breathed out long and slow, reaching forward for his glass.

Joseph seemed to read Cain's mind. 'Always try to remember the good times, rather than the bad one,' he condoled.

14

Two Years Later – July 2000 – Threshold

In the early hours of the morning, Cain folded Riley's pink diamonds, the gold flake in a heart-shaped pendant and their engagement rings, along with his favourite photographs of the two of them together into some tissue paper and placed them in a small envelope. He realised his life with Riley had been one of contentment, serenity, and tranquillity; a dream come true, a once-in-a-lifetime experience that would no longer give cause to depress him. It would instead be a reason to inspire him.

He wandered out onto the balcony to watch the morning sun rising over the horizon. He had reached the end of the road called *grief.* He had found acceptance. His days would now begin with a new perspective on life: a new start, a new dawn.

Several weeks later, Cain was wandering along Las Olas Boulevard when he noticed an empty police patrol car with the driver's door open on the other side of the road. A couple of steps further on, he could see a uniformed police officer struggling with a man on the ground. A couple of cars passed by, but nobody pulled over to assist.

Cain immediately imagined it could be Jerry and ran across the road. Getting closer, he could see the officer was trying to disarm the perp, who had a revolver in his hand. The revolver fired; the bullet pinged a lamp-post. Cain placed his thumb between the revolver's hammer and the next round in the cylinder, preventing the perp from firing it again.

'The next bullet will go through your head,' Cain said.

The perp looked up and straight down the barrel of Cain's Glock 27. Cain kept the barrel pointing, allowing the exhausted police officer to take possession of the revolver and handcuff the perp's wrists around the lamp-post.

As the police officer walked back to his patrol car and radioed for help, the perp sat looking up at the bullet in the lamp-post.

Nobody noticed the man who had intervened, walking away. It had been the first time Cain had held a gun in anger since saving members of The Firm.

But the incident on Las Olas Boulevard had been short and *sweet*, and that was the problem: he had not been left with a bad taste in his mouth. He remembered what Mac had occasionally said: "It is a common phenomenon among a select few."

The words, along with the incident, scratched away at Cain's subconscious. He soon came to realise there was something missing in his life, but he wasn't quite sure what it was. He walked past his favourite steak house and along the waterways, deep in thought, back to his apartment.

He poured himself a J&B and wandered out onto the balcony. He looked out to the horizon into the darkness of the night – and from somewhere, he heard Simon and Garfunkel sing: *Hello darkness my old friend . . .*

The song's lyrics had a vastly different meaning for a man like Cain.

He looked down at everything below him – and his mind finally synced. Despite his wealth, something had been missing from his quiet life: challenges, fortitude, pressure, risk:

The Edge.

In early August, Cain was sitting in a deli on East Oakland Park Blvd, sharing a Reubens and a bagel or two with the Galt Mile Gang.

He had just returned from a visit to the Manhattan Mob in the Big Apple where, apart from dealing in diamonds, he would take on the role of courier to deliver an occasional present, along with a message or two, between Mob and Gang.

As they talked, a Fox News presenter interrupted their conversation. Everyone looked up at the screen on the wall: the anniversaries of the death of a Princess and the murder of Gianni Versace were being remembered again. It made Cain think back to Jerry's latest visit, when they had been walking a familiar path along Miami South Beach.

'We will have to write that book when we retire.' Cain had suggested.

'All those secrets . . . perhaps we will.'

'Cain, are you OK?'

The sound of Joseph's voice jogged Cain's line of thought back to the present, he looked up. The Fox News tributes to Gianni and Diana were over – and the latest news was back on the screen. Time to pay the bill.

Outside in the car park the Gang all shook hands, bid their farewells, and went their separate ways. But Joseph was still standing by the front of Cain's Jeep, gesturing with a closed fist and raised thumb – hitch-hiker-style.

Cain grinned. 'Would you like a lift?'

'Thank you.'

Out on the road Joseph said, 'You seem to have been distracted these past few days.'

'Just a bit restless,' said Cain. 'It'll pass.'

'Has it anything to do with the police officer on Las Olas Boulevard?'

Cain had not told anyone about the Las Olas incident, but Joseph always seemed to know what was going on. Cain glanced at his smiling passenger. 'MOSSAD keeping a check on me again?'

'How did you guess?'

Cain was never quite sure if Joseph was serious or not.

Joseph said, 'Florida has been good for you, Cain. And you have been good for us. Having watched the news this morning, I use the following words with a degree of reluctance. Perhaps you have outlived us, so to speak.'

'Outliving people is a habit I seem to have developed.'

'Tomorrow never dies,' said Joseph, gesturing to a roadside billboard advertising a weekend of Bond movies at one of the local drive-in theatres.

'Die another day then,' said Cain. 'A good title for the next Bond movie. I'll suggest it to Cubby Broccoli, if I ever meet him.'

'Unfortunately, you will not be able to. He died a few years ago.'

'Oh, really?'

'Fraid so.'

'I rest my case,' Cain said with a tone of predictability.

'Perhaps,' Joseph suggested, 'you need a change of environment?'

'Somewhere with a beach and a climate, not weather,' Cain stipulated.

'What if I could trade you a degree or two of milder weather, for wine, women, and song, plus a carat or three?'

Cain grinned, waiting for Joseph to continue.

'Let me tell you a story about an old friend of mine, a man named Moshe. He is a renowned master diamond merchant.'

'OK.'

A few minutes later, Cain had parked his Jeep outside Joseph's apartment building. His curiosity had been aroused. 'Intriguing.'

'Moshe now lives in Johannesburg. He has an office in the famous Jewel City.'

'I've heard so much about it; I've often thought about paying it a visit.'

'As I mentioned earlier, what if I could trade you a degree or two of milder weather, for wine, women, and song, plus a carat or three?'

'I think you might be able to,' Cain responded appreciatively.

Part Four

Cape Town, South Africa.

Hello Darkness My Old Friend

There is no such thing as coincidence . . .
or is there?

15

On the slopes of Table Mountain, the streets are uphill all the way. Life can be a bit like that sometimes, especially in a country with a population of only forty-five million, plus an annual murder rate of twenty thousand plus – and that's just the people.

"Go have a look," Joseph had said. "Take a pragmatic approach."

Cain followed the words of wisdom. He settled himself into a small hotel in the centre of Cape Town, conveniently located within walking distance of everywhere and everything to keep life easy. He hired a car and explored the wine lands, their village-sized towns, and the beaches around the Cape of Good Hope. It was a time when his natural desire to stay away from the crowd, along with his professional ability to blend into the background came to the fore, allowing him to observe a vastly different way of life, especially at night.

One afternoon, Cain climbed Platteklip Gorge to reach the famous flat top of Table Mountain and found a place to sit. The view of City Bowl below, defined by Signal Hill, Lion's Head, and Devil's Peak, was a steep contrast to the vast flatness of Florida. And the distant panorama, from the Twelve Apostles mountain range across the Atlantic Ocean towards Robben Island, was truly breathtaking. It was a reminder of why he loved to overlook a beach. He stayed for some time, bathed in the coolness of the afternoon breeze – a sou'easter called the 'Cape Doctor' – breathing in the air, long and slow, thinking about the future.

If all went to plan, he would be flying from Cape Town up to Jo'burg on a regular basis. His past flying, from Fort Lauderdale up to New York, had always provided him with a welcome break and a change of scenery: it would be the same in South

Africa. He peered down the one thousand-metre north face of Table Mountain to the wild lands below.

I've already found The Edge.

And with a bit of a grin, a bit a shrug, he decided he would make the call to the man named Moshe, the old master's friend in Johannesburg, and book a flight.

***

Rumours about Moshe's private life rivalled the renown of his thirty-year plus career in the diamond industry.

Some years earlier, he had been shot and his family killed when Jihadists had launched an attack in Israel. His pain and suffering had been immense, unimaginable. After attending his family's funeral, he respected the requisite thirty days of *Shloshim* before leaving the country.

It did not take long for the media to report: the terrorist responsible for planning the attack had been killed – along with several of his operatives – when the building they were meeting in was blown up. Several days later, an accomplice was shot dead in his car. And last of all – in every sense of the word – another operative and his family were killed when hand grenades were thrown through a window into their home.

The subsequent rumblings in the Knesset prompted a number of questions, but MOSSAD denied any involvement, leaving the media to suggest, the deaths were the result of Jihadist infighting.

"Welcome to New York," Joseph – the old master – had said.

"Good to see you again my old friend," Moshe had replied, and they had embraced like such men always do.

It had been the start of a long journey for Moshe, down a long road called grief, to a place only he could find. A place called acceptance.

A year or so later, early one winter's morning, Moshe was amid the usual hustle and bustle of Midtown Manhattan, trudging his way through the aftermath of another 'snowmageddon', when an image of Frosty the Snowman in a shop window convinced him the day had come.

I've had enough.

He walked into the warmth of his morning café, ordered his usual coffee with bagels, removed his burner cell phone from his briefcase and dialled the number. It was time to take his last bite of the Big Apple and seek out warmer climes.

For the rest of the week, he had considered his options. He thought of moving to London, but looking up at the clouds he had no desire for more of the same: a thing called weather.

On the Friday evening, he'd taken a flight down to Florida to stay with Joseph his old friend, Cain's acquaintance, for the Christmas and New Year's holiday. They talked about many things, along with where Moshe should go and why.

On a hot, sunny January morning in 1997, Moshe landed at Johannesburg International Airport, South Africa, where he could trade a degree or two of milder weather for something new – a variation of his menu, plus a carat or three.

Since leaving Israel, Moshe had never installed a landline phone in his home or office, nor had he ever used a computer or laptop. His burner cell phones were his only method of communication with the outside world. He only gave his numbers to a select few people and answered calls from even fewer of them. Simply put, if you wanted to meet with Moshe – assuming you managed to contact him in the first place – you made an appointment, you arrived at his office in Jewel City, you waited. And then you waited some more.

***

Late one afternoon, Cain eventually stepped into Moshe's office, and they met for the very first time. Cain removed a large envelope from his backpack and placed it, as instructed, on Moshe's desk.

'What's this?' Moshe enquired.

'Letters and photographs from our friend Joseph in Florida and–'

'The Galt Mile Gang,' Moshe interrupted.

Cain grinned. 'Yes. They all asked me to convey to you their very best regards.'

'Thank you.'

As Moshe opened the envelope, Cain laid out his rough on the master's bench.

Moshe gave the rough no more than a cursory glance. He looked at the clock on the wall and said, 'There's not enough time now. Come back tomorrow at 9am.'

Cain sensed Moshe wanted to look at the contents of the large envelope more than the rough. 'OK, I'll see you in the morning,' said Cain affably. 'Have a good evening.'

'Shalom.'

At the start of their first day together, Moshe thanked Cain for his initial act of trust: leaving his rough on the bench. As the hours passed, Moshe soon came to appreciate why Cain had been recommended in the letters and featured in so many of the photographs delivered in the large envelope on the night before. By late afternoon, Cain's amicable character, along with his humour and respectful nature, had more than aroused Moshe's curiosity.

'See you again tomorrow at 9am,' Moshe said.

'I'll bring coffee and doughnuts.'

The Masterclass.

At the end of their second day together, Moshe knew the old master in Florida – his great friend Joseph – had been right: Cain was an opportunity for him to 'turn a page' in his life and start afresh.

The following days soon turned into weeks during which, encouraged by Cain, Moshe installed a fax machine in his office – the first step on the ladder to reopening his world of communication.

Moshe expressed his appreciation to Cain. 'Thank you for convincing me.'

'Any time.'

'Fax off,' Moshe suggested.

Cain laughed – and for the first time in a long time, a smile appeared on Moshe's face.

But of course one of the main reasons people sent a fax was so they could talk about whatever had been sent. Hence, Moshe soon agreed to the installation of an office telephone landline. The weeks turned into months – and time moved on…

Moshe could easily have been mistaken for the Hollywood actor F. Murray Abraham. However, his personality was such that nobody ever dared to suggest it. Although he rarely smiled or laughed, he did possess a dry sense of humour, a great sense of irony, and an old-fashioned belief in what friendship and loyalty ought to be. He never mentioned his family, talked about his past or private life, or enquired into other people's. However, on the day he spotted a pilot's magazine in Cain's backpack, his powers of gentle coaxing came to the fore, he persuaded Cain to take him flying.

They took off in a Cessna 172 – a *Jumbo* – the perfect high-winged aircraft for sightseeing and having a good time. They flew around Jo'burg to enjoy the view and glided over the bushveld to see the wildlife. On several occasions, Moshe placed his hands on the yoke to get a feel of what it was like to control a plane. Flying low, along the Limpopo River, they spotted crocodiles.

Moshe's favourite WWII air force movies then came to mind: *The Battle of Britain* and *633 Squadron*. He thought too of the Hollywood actor James Stewart, who had been a heroic, WWII bomber pilot.

'Don't forget,' said Cain, 'if at any time I say I have control, you just let go of the yoke.'

Moshe glanced to his left and nodded to Cain. 'Understood.'

Following Cain's instructions, Moshe went on to do Spitfire climbs, followed by Stuka dives and a 360-degree roll. He had achieved a life-long ambition.

In a restaurant that evening, the two men were talking about all things flying. Cain realised, by piloting an aircraft for the first time since leaving Australia, he had lifted a monumental weight off his shoulders. As the evening progressed, the two men's unquestionable trust in each other allowed Cain to tell Moshe about the death of Riley and her parents.

'I understand what you went through,' Moshe said, before he quite unexpectedly told Cain about the death of his family.

Minutes later, Cain showed an expression of the greatest respect. 'You have been through far more than I ever will.'

'We have both been through more than enough,' Moshe

commiserated. 'I left Israel because I had to get away, like you had to get away from Australia. I believe whoever carried out the subsequent reprisal killings across the border, on those Jihadists and their accomplices who murdered my family, and sadly, others too, was completely justified.'

'An eye for an eye: if only the whole world felt the same.'

Moshe smiled – a rarity – without comment.

Cain momentarily contemplated what Moshe had *not* said:

Perhaps we have had very similar, but very different lives. Perhaps.

'I miss my family terribly,' Moshe sighed, bringing the subject to a close.

With confidences having been shared, Cain refreshed their glasses and placed the bottle back on the table. They silently looked down at their drinks for a long few seconds. Cain was once again considering why *Jumbo* had crashed, why Riley was no longer with him and, after what Moshe had said, if he would ever have a reason to carry out reprisal killings.

'Always try to remember the good times, rather than the bad time,' Moshe said quietly.

Cain showed a heartfelt look of appreciation. 'Joseph said those same words to me.'

Moshe raised his glass. 'Our friend also said them to me. To our fondest memories.'

'To our fondest memories,' Cain whispered.

Thereafter, Cain and Moshe had no further discussions about the sad times. From that day, when travelling on the streets and across the deserts to the diamond mines of South Africa, the ease with which Moshe always handled firearms and dealt with danger told Cain what he did not need to ask. And Cain's habit of carrying a Glock 27 in an ankle holster and switchblade in the watch pocket of his jeans told Moshe what he already suspected.

16

One Year Later – Rough Ride

The time was 11:55pm on a dark, deserted, poorly lit street on the outskirts of Cape Town.

In the darkness of the sidewalk, a few rats scavenged amongst the tipped-over bins of the week and the 'garbage' of the day. One rat got too close, a foot kicked out and it scurried away.

The traffic lights – 'robots' – turned to red as a sedan approached the lingering stem of a Y-shaped intersection. The sedan's driver, a young Xhosa intelligence agent, cautiously slowed the vehicle to a crawl.

The young Xhosa agent, in his twenties, and the Afrikaner commander, in his forties, instinctively double-checked their mirrors and the street around them. They wanted to make sure they were not being approached by gun-packing, rapist-carjackers who were always on the prowl, between dusk and dawn.

The agent stopped the sedan some five yards short of the 'robots', just in case, and slipped the gearshift into first, just to be ready.

The commander glanced over at the clock on the dash and up at the red 'robots'. 'It's been a long day, let's put the blues on.'

'Good idea sir.'

As the commander reached up to place the strobe on the roof, the agent spotted the outline of a four-door BMW saloon entering the lower stem of the Y-shaped intersection. 'I know it's a Saturday party night,' said the agent, 'but try turning your lights on.'

The agent's words gained the commander's immediate attention. He eyed the speeding BMW heading their way.

'No lights on,' said the commander. 'And in the middle of the road, breaking the speed limit, it should be taking the right hand fork at the 'robots'.'

The commander placed a hand on the 12-gauge, pump-action shotgun lying by his side.

'Must be partygoers on their way from one *shebeen* to another *shebang* sir,' the agent surmised as he flicked the switch on the dash, turning on the flashing blue light. 'That should slow them down sir.'

The oncoming BMW swept through the junction – instead of turning right – and its headlights burst into life.

'Attack,' the commander instinctively called out, racking the shotgun's slide sending the first shell into the chamber.

> When death and danger are upon you, the slow-motion movie in the mind distorts time.
> What may seem like an eternity will, in the event, only be a minute . . . or fifteen.

Seeing the BMW crossing the central white line between them, the Xhosa agent backhanded the sedan's indicator lever and flicked the switches on the dash, sending blinding full-beam headlights and spotlights into the attackers' eyes. Bullets then shattered the sedan's windscreen.

As the BMW skidded to a halt, blocking the sedan's path, momentum threw the doors open. Booted feet kept them that way – and a trigger-happy gunman fired again. The killers found their feet, decamped their vehicle, and with arms outstretched, barrels pointing, they opened fire.

'Back up, back up,' the commander ordered.

A blood-covered hand, already reaching for the gearshift, got it into reverse.

Against the barrage of enemy fire, the commander's salvo of Hunter-4 buckshot – used to bring down 'game' – blasted a hole through his already shattered windscreen, raking the attacking gunmen – and amongst those who had dared to venture, the dead and dying fell.

From the tipped-over bins of the week, the 'garbage' of the day stepped out. High on a crystal-meth, called *Tik,* and seemingly oblivious to everything going on around him, Tik the shooter aimed both his pistols at the reversing sedan heading his way and opened fire. As intended, the gunmen's combined barrage, from front and back, finally completed its task, mortally wounding the driver.

'Comman–' the agent called out, but before he could utter another word, his arms slumped from the wheel.

The commander grabbed control of the sedan and, catching sight of the BMW now heading towards them, realised there was no way out.

Put our backs to the wall; fight it out.

The sedan mounted the kerb. A tyre exploded, it crashed into a lamppost, and juddered to a halt as the engine stalled. The commander felt the grip of his young agent's bloodied hand on his arm. He turned; their eyes met.

'*Hamba, hamba mhlekazi* (Go, go sir),' mouthed the young agent in his native Xhosa tongue and, using the last of his strength, he turned his back on Tik The Shooter standing in the street, putting his body in the line of fire to protect his boss. More rounds entered the young Xhosa agent's head and back, killing him instantly. The commander pushed the passenger door open and a bullet hit his shoulder, flipping him out onto the sidewalk. As he gritted his teeth against the pain and crawled for cover, the flashing sedan's blue light disintegrated, the windscreen collapsed, and the relentless barrage of gunfire suddenly trailed off into silence.

Meanwhile, Cain had been driving back into Cape Town when he rounded a bend. In the distance, he could see a flashing blue light on the roof of a crunched-up car against a lamppost amid a range of unrelenting muzzle flashes from the middle of the street. And a BMW, with its headlights shattered, coming to a stop. He slowed his Jeep Grand Cherokee to a crawl and scanned the street around him.

It's probably another gang against the police shoot-out.

Cain switched off the Jeep's headlights, checked his mirrors and reaching for the Glock 27 in his ankle holster – just in case – he watched the distant, flashing blue light disintegrate into the darkness and the muzzle flashes fade into the depths of the night.

Cain buzzed down his window to have a listen.

Can't hear a thing.

The emergency response units were not yet on their way.

Cain could make out the shapes of the gunmen, standing still.

Why aren't they leaving?

The gunmen standing in the road stared in disbelief through the sedan's windscreen. 'Shit!' one of them shouted. 'It's not him; it's not the white motherfucker.'

Another gunman stood up on the side sill of the BMW and gazed at the dead agent behind the wheel. 'Can't be,' he bellowed. 'It's the fuckin black bastard. The white motherfucker ain't drivin.'

All eyes instantly turned to where *the white motherfucker* was taking cover – down on the sidewalk – against the side of the sedan, by the knocked over bins. The commander painfully reached for the cell phone in his jacket pocket and pressed the button.

'Good morning, sir. How can–'

'Alpha Red,' interrupted the commander, giving his location.

'Already on our way sir, stay with–'

The line went dead. The commander crawled to the back of the car to be by the pole to have a better chance of protection, especially if he needed to stand when shooting.

'Can't see the white motherfucker,' a voice shouted.

'Is he dead?' another voice yelled out.

Shotgun blasts, followed by the sound of a screaming man falling to the ground, instantly gave the gunmen their answer. The commander, standing behind the pole, immediately ducked down and the unrelenting barrage of gunfire resumed.

Cain, now viewing the scene through his monocular, immediately recognised the shotgun; it was a military-style version of a pump-action 12-gauge issued to law enforcement officers. But the white man firing it covered in blood, however, was not wearing a uniform. Cain got the distinct impression he was looking at a plain-clothes officer, who with fair hair had to be an Afrikaner.

Cain could never turn his back on a law enforcement officer in trouble. He slipped the monocular into his jacket pocket and turned his focus of attention to Tik the Shooter in the middle of the road, firing at the Afrikaner.

Time was of the essence.

And the red 'robots' silently turned to green.

Cain slammed his foot to the floor. The Jeep accelerated hard, leaning out wide across the centre line and bearing down on its targets. Knowing what was about to happen, Cain elbowed the driver's door open and wedged it ajar.

Tik The Shooter fired another few rounds before the sound of a vehicle's horn made him glance over his shoulder, but too slow, too late. The Jeep Grand Cherokee's bull bars slammed into his back and carried him forth as a one-time mascot, on the front bars of Chrysler's toughest.

The other gunmen behind the BMW were momentarily transfixed by the surreal image of Tik the Shooter flailing, his eyes wide, mouth agape, and legs grotesquely splayed, hurtling towards them. In the blink of an eye, the Jeep's headlamps burst into life. Cain immediately saw the wave of light wash across the heels of a running man fleeing into the darkness – and *tap! tap!* – two bullets cracked the Jeep's windscreen, missing Cain by a whisker. The Jeep crashed into the BMW, glass shattered, metal fragmented, and bodies were crushed and thrown aside. As the two vehicles separated, the BMW rammed itself against a utility pole, the Jeep tripped sideways onto the kerb and Tik the Shooter's remains were laid to rest. Cain dived out of the Jeep and rolled onto the sidewalk, from where he surveyed the carnage around him, realising for the first time since 1996 he had killed a man – or was it two? He waited, expecting guilt or perhaps conscience to linger in his mind; instead he was overcome by a sublime sense of achievement.

In the silence of the aftermath, illegally connected power lines fell from the utility pole to snake and flash their way across the sidewalk. And leaking petrol, tainted red, bled its way along the gutter.

Tick-tock... Time had moved on. Fifteen minutes... and quiet prevailed.

Cain had just the one thought in mind:

The running man, did he keep on going or has he doubled back?

Cain made eye contact with the fair-haired, blood spattered Afrikaner, who – looking more like Mortensen than McKellen – acknowledged his saviour with a wave. Cain pointed into the darkness and gave a tactical hand signal to confirm a man was on the loose. The commander acknowledged the warning and, grimacing in pain trying to stem the flow of blood from the bullet wound to his shoulder, he looked down at his dead agent, slumped behind the wheel.

'You shouldn't have. God Bless,' he whispered, respectfully acknowledging the sacrifice the young agent had made.

As the commander scanned his surroundings, he saw an arm and the legs of one of the dead gunmen lying in the road slowly moving. The commander painfully removed his pistol from his shoulder holster and made his way around the bonnet of the sedan, towards the gunman.

As the gunman eased himself onto his side he saw the armed white man coming towards him. He glanced over at his own pistol lying in the road, but it was out of reach.

How the hell can the white motherfucker still be alive?

'Please don't shoot me,' the gunman called out desperately, 'I'll tell you everything you want to know.'

The gunman's words echoed along the all-quiet intersection and into the darkness beyond. Gunfire rang out and the gunman pleaded no more.

Cain tried to see where the shots had come from, without success. He realised the man who had disappeared into the darkness had doubled back.

The commander, being blindsided by the wreckage of the BMW, was unable to return fire. Nor was he – with the bullet wound to his shoulder – able to give pursuit. Instead, he cautiously made his way across to the Jeep, eased himself down next to its driver, and tended his wound.

'You OK?' said Cain, keeping an eye on the darkness. 'Can I help–'

'I will be fine,' the Commander interrupted, and giving his saviour, a quick once-over, he expressed his appreciation. 'Thank you for intervening.'

'Pleasure.'

In the distance, the sirens of the emergency response units were getting louder with every second. Cain realised he had no time to waste. He sensed seniority in the manner of the wounded Afrikaner and dispensed with the pleasantries. 'My name is Cain. I'd really prefer to be left out of this situation. My Jeep here, it was stolen an hour ago. I'll report the theft to the police in the morning. I have to go now.'

'I am Commander van Rensburg,' said the Afrikaner. 'As you can hear, the cavalry are on their way. Although their sounds will have frightened off whoever it was hiding in the darkness back there, be careful. Now go. We will meet again.'

As Cain reached higher ground, he turned to see the BMW engulfed in flames. He raised the monocular to his eye: the swathe of light illuminated the commander being ushered into the back of a 4x4, escorted by two other vehicles... They then all sped off.

When Cain reached the apex of the hill he took a last look down at the flames, at the flashing blue and red lights, and all the activity now going on around them.

On the following day, the TV news and daily tabloids reported:

Rival gang members were shot dead at the scene of a road traffic accident in the early hours of Sunday morning. It is understood two stolen vehicles, a BMW saloon and Jeep, were involved in a collision, before they were engulfed in flames.

Police are looking for the driver of the Jeep, a black male in his early thirties who – an eyewitness has confirmed – fled the scene.

WTA – Welcome To Africa.

17

Rough Calculations – A Week Later

High on Devil's Peak – the mountain, not the drug – Commander van Rensberg drove onto the spacious forecourt of an imposing three-storey, modern detached, private residence.

The buzz of a motion sensor told Cain a vehicle was on his property. He stepped out onto the first-floor balcony – enclosed by solar-tinted glass – from where he could observe without being seen. He was not too surprised when he saw the commander getting out of a vehicle. He had not expected such a man to phone first to make an appointment. Watching his visitor, who in the warm light of the day looked even more like Mortensen than Mckellen, he noticed a solitary car, parked a short distance along the drive.

Unusual.

Awareness made Cain pick up his binoculars for a closer look, but the early afternoon sunlight reflecting off the car windscreen and lowered sun visors prevented him from seeing if there were any people waiting inside. Cain lowered the binoculars and looking down at the commander again, he placed a reassuring hand on the Walther P99 tucked in his waist.

The commander readjusted his arm in a sling – and glancing up, he gave the property a quick once over: The sundeck on the top floor was a perfect aerie for a bird's-eye view of the surrounding area, City Bowl below, the coastline, and beyond. Whereas the first-floor balcony left him with just the one thought in mind:

Is it smash-proof or bullet-proof, solar-tinted glass? Is Cain behind it, watching me?

Below the balcony, the pair of double-sized garage doors provided access to what had become a standard feature in a modern-day, mountainside residence. The whole of the ground floor would be a parking-lot. The colour of the garage doors did not escape the Commander's notice.

Royal Blue. How very English. Just like Cain.

The Commander looked at the perimeter wall on either side of the property topped with the usual mix of electric fencing, razor wire – and to cap it all, the glint of sunlight reflecting off pieces of jagged, broken glass, completed the list of deterrents.

Looks more like a fortress.

The Commander opened the back door of his vehicle, lifted a brown paper bag off the back seat and closed the door with a shove of his foot. As he headed for the front gate in the perimeter wall a buzzer sounded, locks clicked, and the gate opened. After he had stepped through, a quick look back confirmed the gate was already closing behind him.

At the top of a short flight of steps, the commander saw a veranda running along the length of the side of the property, overlooking a simple garden laid to lawn.

The top half of a stable-style front door on the side of the property then opened.

'Commander, what a pleasant surprise,' said Cain with a welcoming grin. 'Good to see you.'

'Afternoon,' said the commander – and seeing the design of the front door, memories of a TV series came to mind, arousing an inspirational remark. 'Is Mr. Ed in?'

'Hang on, I'll find out.' Cain glanced over his shoulder and opened the lower half of the door. 'Mr. Ed will be with you in a sec,' he joked, and the commander laughed.

Handing Cain the paper bag, bottles clinking together provided a very suitable sound for such an occasion. 'Thought we should have a drink,' the commander suggested.

'What a good idea. How's your shoulder?'

'Fortunately, the bullet missed the bone, so not too serious.' Shaking hands, injured-man-style, the commander maintained his grip for a moment longer. 'You helped save my life, please call me Marius.'

'Any time. Will do, Marius.' Cain stepped aside, and Marius entered a world of open-plan living: L-shaped loungers covered with cushions, around a freestanding fireplace, along with an array of indoor plants – exhibiting a tranquil life – gave him a very welcoming first impression. Sensing Marius' natural curiosity – and wanting his own satisfied. 'Please, take a look,' Cain said with an inviting gesture.

Cain and Marius stood on the first-floor balcony, overlooking the spacious forecourt, the drive, and a small quadrangle of a park. It mimicked all the characteristics of a bigger than normal window box, preventing Marius from seeing down into the splendour of Cape Town's natural amphitheatre, City Bowl, some three hundred metres below.

But on the upside, Marius had no such obstacle in his way: it was a near-perfect panorama, stretching from Table Mountain on his left, across the gap to Lions Head, and along the ridge to Signal Hill and the ocean beyond. It was truly breathtaking.

'Lekka view,' Marius said, using the unique, Afrikaans adjective *lekka*, meaning – regardless of whatever the subject of conversation may be – the best, fantastic, the greatest.

'It's the reason I chose this spot to have the house built.'

'Good choice.'

Marius was also scanning the small quadrangle of a park – the window box – its copse of trees and stands of umbrella pines, looking for anything or anyone out of place or hanging around for no apparent reason. But apart from a plastic bag or two – the 'Plast-a-teak' flora of South Africa – caught on the park's perimeter fence, there was no trace of movement or any sign of life.

'By the way,' said Cain, 'the car on the drive there. Friends of yours?'

Marius appreciated the advantage of being behind tinted, bullet-proof glass: this was a place from where one could watch, but not be seen. He noticed Cain's binoculars hanging on a hook. 'Can you see who's in the car?' he asked.

'Fraid not. The sun is reflecting off the windscreen and the sun visors are down.'

'The two men inside are my most trusted,' said Marius. 'Things have been somewhat hectic recently.'

Having just met Marius, Cain knew better than to delve any further.

Two black men were sitting in the parked car.

The driver – with an eye on the rear-view mirrors – kept the engine ticking over.

While the passenger – with a finger on the trigger – kept an eye on the drive ahead.

The sound of the bottles in the bag clinking together again, conveniently moved the subject of conversation on to other things.

'Time to pop a cork,' Marius suggested with a smile.

'Or two.'

Chatting amiably as they strolled back through the world of open-plan living, Marius noticed something was missing.

I'll check out the rest of the floor to confirm it.

A pair of reclining leather reading chairs sat on either side of a coffee table, which accommodated a bottle of J&B and Jameson next to some highball tumblers along with magazines and paperbacks: very relaxing.

Near the base of the floating-style staircase – leading up to the top floor – Marius was taken by surprise at the sight of a stripper's X-Pole. 'Something different,' he said, and with a feigned look of expectancy, he gestured with his 'good' hand, up towards the opening in the ceiling. 'I can imagine,' he speculated.'

'Unless you borrow a couple of the girls from the Czarina's pole dancing strip club,' Cain suggested, 'you'll have to.'

'Ah, the Russians: always a handful.'

'In every sense of the word.'

Cain placed the bag on the counter of the kitchen island and, taking out the bottles, he looked at the labels and grinned. 'Saint-Émilion – one of my favourites. Thank you.'

'Pleasure.'

Not wanting to inhibit Marius' natural curiosity, Cain again said, 'Please feel free to have a wander.'

Keeping the small talk going, Marius ambled off to the all-glass sliding doors at the rear of the kitchen. Out on the patio, two rocking chairs with a coffee table between them under a lemon tree looked very inviting, as did a pub-style garden bench, set near one of that most revered of Afrikaans altars – a braai. Marius ambled back to a pair of five-foot tall viper bowstring plants standing sentry by the entrance to the dining room.

Inside, a Georgian mahogany cabinet occupied one wall and an old, wooden eight-seater railway sleeper dining table in front of another set of glass sliding doors looked out onto the veranda and the simple garden laid to lawn.

A cork popped.

Walking back to the kitchen island, Marius said, 'I really like the framed collections of vintage cigarette cards you have hanging on the walls. The images of civilian and military aircraft, soldiers in uniform, tropical birds, butterflies, and Hollywood stars are all very impressive.'

'Thank you, I'm a touch old-fashioned.'

And having checked out the rest of the floor to confirm it, Marius could clearly see there were no photographs on the cabinets, the tables or walls, not even an obligatory Polaroid picture stuck on either of the American-style fridge doors. In essence, there was nothing to suggest Cain even had a past. Marius considered it to be somewhat unusual, especially for a man who was known to enjoy taking photographs.

Cain and Marius raised their glasses.

'Thank you again for intervening,' said Marius. 'I owe you one. Cheers.'

'Glad I could help. Thank you for bringing the wine. Cheers.'

Marius placed his glass back down on the counter, slipped his arm out of the sling, and removed his jacket, revealing his .9mm pistol in a shoulder holster.

'A Beretta,' Cain commented. 'My favourite when I'm out and about.'

Marius hung his jacket on the back of one of the swivel stools, sat on another next to it, and glanced at Cain's Walther P99 tucked in his waist. 'Nice one.'

'I prefer it when indoors – just in case.'

'I understand.'

On the open page of the *Cape Times* newspaper lying on the counter, an update on the Afghan conflict prompted a few comments on the wars of the day and those from the past. Marius reminisced for a few minutes about the South African Special Forces, the Hunter Groups, and the border skirmishes on the Caprivi Strip. Cain got the impression he was listening to a voice of experience, but he didn't say it. Marius went on to make a few light-hearted comments about history, about life in general, and about the British living in South Africa.

Appreciating the humour, Cain said, 'Bearing in mind the Boer Wars came to an end in 1902, nearly a hundred years ago, do you think there is any chance the Afrikaans people may one day soon stop blaming the British for everything that has happened to them ever since? Will they ever let bygones be bygones?'

'I doubt it. But give them time.'

'No rush,' Cain said, and with smiles all round, he topped up their glasses.

'What were you doing before you came to South Africa?' Marius enquired.

Cain innocently mentioned his time in the UK, taking photographs, and his buying and selling residential property, nothing more. The subject of conversation moved on to the inevitable: the night they first met.

Marius asked, 'You saw the newspaper reports?'

'Yes. They said the Jeep's black driver, fled the scene.' Cain looked at his hand. 'I didn't think I was so tanned.'

'It was the least I could do to help divert any attention away from you.'

'Appreciated. Thank you.'

Cain realised to enquire about the lack of detail in the various newspaper reports would best be left for another day, as would asking Marius why he had hitched a ride in the 4x4 convoy before the emergency response units had arrived. But Cain understood it would appear a little odd if he allowed the newspaper's oversights – deliberate or otherwise – to pass without comment. 'I noticed the story made no mention of law enforcement being involved in the shooting,' said Cain. 'All for a good reason, I'm sure.'

'There are some things best left on a need-to-know basis.'

'Or a don't-need-to-know basis. To save you asking,' said Cain, adhering to the protocol of his past life in London, 'I have not told anyone about the night we first met. Next week sometime, I'll mention to a couple of people my Jeep has been stolen.'

Marius was quick off the mark. 'By mentioning it next week, those people will assume your Jeep has just been stolen and not associate it with what really happened two weeks earlier. Your discretion is appreciated. Have you replaced your Jeep?'

'I'll order a new one in a week or two,' said Cain, picking up the bottle and topping up their glasses. 'But it's going to take more than just a few weeks to get here. So I bought myself a two-year old Mercedes saloon to use meantime.'

'Good choice.'

'Something different.'

Cain and Marius were both well aware of the crime rate in South Africa: fifty murders a day; forty-plus shootings a day; one hundred sex crimes.

Marius said, 'I'm glad you saw the gunman on the loose. Thank you for warning me.'

Expecting his comment to take Cain by surprise, Marius watched for a reaction but there wasn't one. However, Cain instantly remembered he had used a military tactical hand signal to warn Marius: a mistake. He gave Marius the same tactical hand signal again. 'Good job I watch all those war and spy movies.'

The subtlety of Cain's response was not lost on Marius, who smiled. 'Although your Jeep was a write-off, forensics told me the driver's door had already been wedged open before impact. Good thinking.'

'I have a GA pilot's licence; I fly light aircraft. We are taught to lock-open the doors before a forced landing to prevent anyone from getting jammed in on impact.'

'By using a policeman's truncheon?'

Cain grinned. 'It was a present from my best friend; he's a police officer in London. Any chance of getting it back?'

'When the investigation is over, I'll get it for you.'

'Thank you, much appreciated.'

'Where is your friend stationed?'

Cain gave a brief resume of Jerry's career.

'Royal Protection, the elite,' Marius said.

'I'll introduce you next time he comes to Cape Town.'

'I look forward to meeting him. You have probably already

guessed; the attack was an assassination attempt on my life. But unfortunately it was the young man driving who was killed instead of me. I know his family well; I attended his funeral yesterday.'

Cain had not seen any mention of the funeral in the *Cape Times* or on the TV news. And Marius not referring to the deceased individual by name or rank had not escaped his attention.

'Please accept my condolences.'

Marius is more than just a police officer.

'Thank you, it should have been me who was killed. I always drive when I am in a motor vehicle. But I wasn't driving because . . . well, it doesn't matter now.'

Marius was quiet for a moment. Cain understood how he would always be asking himself: What if I had been driving? If I had done this? If I had done that? Would my driver still be alive?

To help deflect Marius' feelings of sadness, Cain calmly suggested, 'If I had turned up seconds earlier who knows what might or might not have happened? There are too many ifs in the world. Don't blame yourself.'

Marius sighed again and raised his glass. 'To a brave young man.'

'To absent friends,' Cain responded, raising his glass.

And my beloved Riley.

As Marius placed his glass on the counter, he subtly checked the time on his watch. 'The police enquiries are, of course, ongoing. Although there's not a great deal I can tell you, there are a couple of things I would like to mention.'

'Please do.'

'The identity of the running man who carried out the *coup de grâce* on one of his own and made his escape remains a mystery.'

'Talking of mystery, do you know who ordered the hit?'

'I'm afraid I cannot go into detail,' said Marius with an air of caution. 'However, I can tell you, the criminal records and tattoos on the dead gunmen prove they were or had been members of the notorious 33s gang – a starting point for the police investigation.'

'Is the number by any chance an indication of their IQ?'

Marius appreciated the humour. 'I think it would be fair to say yes for quite a few of them.'

'I've heard various stories about the 33s.'

'Haven't we all.'

'Not the sort of people you want to get on the wrong side of.'

'Very true – which brings me to my next point. 'Your Jeep was registered to an off-the-shelf company. I assume it is a precautionary measure.'

'Purely for reasons of safety.'

'Of course. All being well, no one will be knocking on your door any time soon. But if they do . . . ' Marius fleetingly glanced at the Walther P99 on Cain's waist.

Cain got the inference. 'I'll let you know.'

'I'll bring the body bags.'

Cain grinned. 'Where are the 33s based?'

'Ironically, they operate out of the Pollsmoor Maximum Security Prison, located in the Cape Town suburb of Tokai.'

'Seriously?'

'Yes.'

'Do they rent a suite or are they just visitors?'

Marius smiled and checked the time on his watch again. 'We will have to save the rest of our conversation about the 33s for another day.'

'Time to go?'

'Unfortunately, yes.'

Cain helped Marius on with his jacket. 'It's been good meeting you again.'

'Let's have lunch one day,' Marius said.

'Good idea.'

'I'll give you a call next week.'

'OK.'

With his jacket on, Marius turned so he was eye to eye with Cain – and time stood still.

Cain had not missed the similarities between Marius and Mac, back in London. He wondered if Marius was also supposedly just another ordinary, nine-to-six, five-days-a-week, pen-pushing security clearance officer?

Marius' people had done their homework. He knew more about Cain than he cared to divulge. But there was one thing he had to mention. 'I have to tell you,' he said, 'you killed two gunmen that night. The one you gave a *lift* to and one standing by the BMW.'

'Pity it wasn't three,' Cain quipped.

'I know we can never tell each other everything,' Marius said.

Cain grinned. 'You mean about the pole?'

'Of course,' Marius smiled.

Once they were down the internal stairs and through the security door into the garage, Cain pressed the remote. One of the garage doors opened up and over… and in the warm light of the afternoon sun, Marius ended their farewells in his native Afrikaans language:

'*Gaan goed* (Go well).'

Cain and Marius had established an understanding and an unspoken trust between them had been formed. It was the founding of an allegiance for whatever the future may bring.

TIA – This Is Africa.

18

Old Friends – Business

On the following morning, Moshe was absorbed in his world of diamonds.

Sitting at his merchant's bench with his elbows resting on a velvet placemat, he was analysing the finished cut diamond – clasped in tweezers – bathed in a circle of florescent light, through his vintage, 10x magnifying loupe.

He was eventually nudged back into the real world by his Telkom landline playing its tune. Glancing down at the caller ID, he jabbed the button. 'One moment – I think the correct expression is go fax yourself.'

Hearing Moshe's gibe echo down the line, Cain grinned. In his mind's eye he could see Moshe sitting on the grand old leather chair, deep in analysis, surrounded by instruments, and devices.

Cain had already decided, when it came to telling Moshe about how he had helped to save Commander Marius van Rensburg's life, and their meeting a week later at the 'fortress', he would stick to the protocol of days gone by. He would wait – like he and Jerry always had when discussing more serious things – until they were face-to-face.

'Morning,' Moshe eventually said on the phone. 'I have just finished the oval-shaped 2-carat from the consignment you picked up in Lesotho last month.'

'How's it looking?'

'As we expected,' Moshe said with an air of professional reserve.

'A journey always worth the effort. They are incredibly honest, trustworthy people.'

'Indeed.'

As they went on to discuss their itinerary for the weeks ahead, Cain picked up the page Moshe had faxed him an hour earlier to pencil in suitable dates for several meetings and journeys to the diamond mines. Moshe then – in his inimitable way – moved the subject of conversation on to other things.

'I bumped into Zhang, the young Chinese salesman yesterday. He told me the miserly merchant he is working for here in Jewel City has again delayed paying him and Hadley, his office manager, their commissions, arguing over the amount. To cut a long story short, he's had enough. He's going back to China to live with his parents in Guangzhou. He's–'

'What a coincidence,' Cain interrupted.

'Why do you say that?'

'I had an email from Bill and Greg in Hong Kong this morning. They want to open an upmarket investment diamond showroom in Guangzhou. They said it would cater for the country's top people who like to flaunt themselves in front of friends and associates. Apparently, in China, it's often more about the ceremony than the actual purchase.'

'Sounds impressive.'

'If they go ahead it will enhance the business they have been doing with Kay and Susie Su – the two Chinese ladies – these past three years. However, it will of course remain separate from Bill and Greg's and our own dealings with the elite 1%.'

'Indeed. You said *if* they go ahead,' Moshe queried. 'What's stopping them?'

'They cannot find a top-class, trustworthy Chinese salesman, who is fluent in English, to be part of such an enterprise.'

'Zhang has a reputation for being a great salesman rather than a businessman. He has been in to see me on various occasions to seek advice. His English is 95%, his writing too, and of course, he is fluent in Cantonese and Mandarin. Hadley is a well-respected manager. They have become very good friends. Apparently, Hadley and his wife, although they are still living under the same roof, are no longer sleeping under the same ceiling. His wife has filed for divorce.'

'Is she also an American?'

'No, she's from Prague.'

'So they will definitely be going their separate ways.'

'Indeed. And having an American passport, she can now go wherever she wants to.'

'You said Hadley and Zhang have become very good friends.

Perhaps, they could be what Bill and Greg are looking for?'

On the following day, after meeting with Hadley and Zhang, Moshe faxed their CVs to Cain, who looked them over before emailing them to Bill and Greg in Hong Kong. Once they had expressed an interest, Cain paid for Hadley and Zhang to fly to Hong Kong to be interviewed. Within two weeks, they were hired. Cain nicknamed them H&Z.

Bill and Greg persuaded one of their elite 1% clients – one of the many they had first met in Australia – to make a capital investment of US$450,000. As a sign of good faith, Cain invested a much smaller amount on behalf of himself and Moshe.

Cain and Moshe became non-executive directors of the investment diamond showroom for one main reason: being based in South Africa would truly enhance the reputation of the new business and authenticate their supply of genuine South African diamonds. No other company in China had those credentials. Cain used his London-based company, GemGia, to sponsor Hadley for a Chinese work visa that had to be renewed on an annual basis. And last of all, Cain transferred US$5,000 into Hadley's personal bank account to pay off his debts and allow him – for the benefit of Bill and Greg – a financially clear-headed fresh start.

Bill and Greg would, for the first few months, alternate their time between Hong Kong and Guangzhou to be with H&Z, Kay, and Susie Su. It would be something new, something different, allowing them – as they could now well afford – to venture out on a more regular basis.

Kay was an authority on Chinese company formation, accountancy, and tax regulations. She was the perfect person to register the company, look after the accounts and, on a part-time basis, oversee the day-to-day running of the showroom and tend to the requirements of her own very wealthy clientele.

Susie Su, a director in a financial consultancy business, would continue to introduce her privileged and influential Chinese clients into the world of the investment diamond showroom. Both ladies had an impeccable reputation for honesty and integrity, for which they were well respected.

Having Hadley's white face in the showroom – on a day to day basis – would always arouse a great deal of interest. It would be a reminder to the Chinese how H&Z had both lived and worked in the diamond industry in South Africa. A fact of life no other company in China could make claim to.

'I'll buy you the steaks,' Cain said, rounding off another of his and Moshe's conference calls with Bill, Greg, Kay, and Susie Su.

'We'll have them in one of our favourite restaurants here in Hong Kong,' Bill said.

'Look forward to seeing you in a few weeks' time,' Greg added.

Moshe would not be going to Guangzhou: his first step on the ladder to reopening his world of communication did not, for the time being at least, extend that far east. And besides, his and Cain's commitments for the weeks ahead were more than enough to keep him in Jewel City.

19

Two Years Later: 2003 – Week One – Rough Town

It was a Monday afternoon. Cain left the dojo; he looked up at Table Mountain and the blue skies above – spring was in the air.

In his lightweight backpack – slung over his shoulder – he had his keys, his wallet, his mobile – and his coiled Black Belt on top of his karate gi, with his Glock 27 pistol at its centre.

Cain walked up Kloof Street, a one-mile mix of upmarket bars, boutiques and al 'fresco dining at the *high-end* of town – in every sense of the word.

Three blocks away, in a side street, two black men were sitting in a Land Rover, waiting for a call. The passenger checked his Colt .45 and slipped it back into his shoulder holster.

'What's the white man's name?'

The driver placed a S&W .38 revolver into his waist – and keeping watch on the passing traffic, he answered, 'Cain.'

Cain walked off Kloof Street into a quiet avenue of trees, where parked cars dotted the kerbs – and the usual scattering of street-litter paved the way. A teenager standing on the street corner, watching the world go by took a last drag of his cigarette and, without looking, he flicked the butt into the air and raised his cell phone to his ear. '*Jahela* (Hurry),' he said in his Zulu tongue. 'The white man is here.'

Cain was some twenty metres into the avenue, when two black men emerged from the shadows ahead. One of them leaned against a lamppost, while the other stood impassively on the sidewalk with a hand inside his jacket, blocking the way.

Lamppost-leaning folded his arms and gazing down past the approaching white man, he nonchalantly moved his head from side to side watching nothing in particular – but watching, always watching; neither black man moved.

Cain instinctively slowed his stride and turned to check the area behind him. A Land Rover swerved into the avenue, veered across the centre line towards him and entering an empty parking space, the front wheels mounted the kerb and came to a stop. Cain glanced over his shoulder, Lamppost-leaning and the sidewalk blocker were now only feet away. They both opened their casual jackets, giving Cain a quick glimpse of their .38 revolvers tucked in their waists. Cain heeded their warning by keeping his hands where they could be seen as he slowly turned to put his back against the sidewalk's hedgerow.

The Land Rover's doors opened, and the two black men stepped out with handguns pointing. Cain stared down the barrel of a Colt .45 and straight into the haunted eyes of a dead man, staring straight back at him. He immediately blinked and looked again but the ghostly eyes were still there.

You again. It's been a while.

In his mind the pages of history turned back to the stake-out – in 1992 – overlooking the tranquil garden square in London.

I wonder what Agent Omara is up to these days? Wish you were here.

A sigh of resignation, perhaps contempt was Cain's only hint of a slightest emotion.

Who would have guessed, the first man I killed had an identical Twin Brother.

He stood waiting… waiting to die.

'Shit Happens,' a voice said.

Nobody moved.

The Land Rover's driver lowered his revolver, stepped around the front of the vehicle and walked to within spitting distance of his target, but he kept his saliva to himself. He savoured the white man's predicament: and a short vertical scar creased with his smile, under the left of a pair of very wild eyes.

Cain realised, with an inward sigh of relief, since no attempt was being made to physically harm or steal from him, the 'troop' were on an errand of some sort, rather than a killing spree – well; not just yet.

'Good evening, Mr. Cain,' said the driver. 'My name is Windows. Thank you for taking the time to stop and talk to me.'

Windows was a product of Township poverty, a poor education, and gangland influence. He had a memory like an elephant, was extremely dangerous, and had a reputation to go with it, as his police record would prove. In true Township tradition, when he was given the name of a stranger he would automatically prefix it with the title Mr. or Miss.

Cain said, 'Thank you for giving me the opportunity. TIA.'

The nickname Windows was given in the diamond industry to windowers: people training to become diamond cutters. Cain had no idea, however, if this Windows – carrying a .38 revolver – was one of them. On the other hand of course, when Windows was born, his father could have been a cat burglar who decided to name his son after his preferred choice of entry.

Good job he wasn't a sex maniac, Cain thought.

Windows slipped his .38 revolver into his waist and gestured towards the living twin. 'Now, before I forget, let me introduce you to Lastly.'

'Evening,' Cain said.

The twin brother did not respond.

'Lastly is a quiet one,' Windows said.

'Seems to be.'

'He is aiming the Colt .45 at your head for a reason.' Windows waited for a response.

Cain gave Windows a nod of acceptance and, intent on keeping the whole 'troop' relaxed, his professional ability to appease came to the fore. 'I understand you have to be cautious. Thank you for being so considerate to a foreigner in your country.'

Windows stepped forward and, shaking hands with Cain, South African black man-style – double grip, two position hold, three-time crunch – he made an offer Cain could not refuse. 'Now we are friends Mr. Cain please, allow me to give you a lift to your car.'

A minute later Cain was in the Land Rover *riding shotgun* – without the barrels – and Windows started the engine.

'You are a Land Rover fan?' Cain asked, taking the lead.

'Oh yes, I am a big England fan,' said Windows. 'The Arsenal, the Rolling Stones, I will see them all when I go to England,' he bragged.

Cain gave Windows a side-glance to check for any possible hint of a lie as he asked, 'You have been to England?'

'No, not yet, but Lastly has. He will show me around. We will start a business in London together.'

'Good luck,' said Cain encouragingly. 'Just the two of you?'

'Sadly, yes. Unfortunately, Lastly's twin brother was killed in London many years ago. Our business will be a tribute to him.'

'How tragic,' Cain said, with an appropriate tone of regret.

'Yes, it was a very sa–'

The Land Rover's back door opened, interrupting the thread of Cain's easy-going cross-examination. Cain looked over his shoulder to see Lastly climbing in at exactly the wrong time.

Windows put the wheels into motion and as he changed gear he changed the topic of conversation. 'You see, Mr. Cain, you are the man who knows much about cutting and selling rough diamonds, and I am the man who knows much about finding and supplying rough diamonds: the perfect formula for us to start a venture together. Simple, yes? You agree?'

Arriving at a private parking lot, Cain pressed his remote. The gate opened and Windows drove in. Cain pointed to his Mercedes. 'Of all the people in South Africa, why are you asking me?'

'Because you are not an Afrikaner – you are a white foreign bastard. It is what we prefer.' Windows glanced at Cain, waiting for a response to his slight, but none came. 'You see, Mr. Cain, being white you can go where we are still not welcome. And we, the black citizens of Africa, can go where you are not wanted and will never be invited. But both ends make a one, yes? We will join forces.'

'Anything is possible. We could of course just go our separate ways. I'll take the sidewalk down to the beach, and you can take the tarmac to your friends.'

'Ah, Mr. Cain, you are a joker,' said Windows, bringing the Land Rover to a stop and switching off the engine. He then turned in his seat to face Cain and held out his hand. In the centre of his palm was a small, odd-shaped ice cube. It showed no signs of melting. Windows smiled. 'Please take it.'

Cain took the rough diamond and rolled it between his

fingers and thumb. One of its sides had been polished, allowing a trained eye, looking through a merchant's 10x magnifying loupe, to see inside and carry out the mapping of its internal features.

'I appreciate you are a man who deals in diamonds,' said Cain, 'but one who carries a .38 revolver.' Cain looked from the rough to Windows. 'Is it real?'

'Yes, it is Mr. Cain, and so is the diamond. I have many talents. Try taking a deep breath before you speak again.'

Cain breathed in deeply before he slowly exhaled. The fog of his breath engulfed the rough in his hand and cleared instantly, indicating it was a genuine diamond and not a silicon carbide fake, namely *moissanite*, used by conmen.

'It is a flawless 3-carat,' Windows proudly announced as he placed a spliff between his lips. Lastly leant forward, struck a match, and held up the flame. Windows relaxed back into his seat, slowly exhaled, and watched the smoke drift out into the early evening air. 'Please, keep the rough. The first of many.'

'Thank you.'

Cain unzipped his backpack, placed the rough inside and discreetly left it open – just in case.

'Now Mr. Cain, before we leave–'

'Missing you already,' Cain politely interrupted.

Windows showed just a hint of a smile, 'I will phone you tomorrow to arrange a time to take you to the person who requested the meeting.'

'Who is he?'

Windows glanced down at Cain's backpack. 'I am sure the 3-carat rough will grant you the patience to wait to find out.'

'I'm afraid it will not. If you prefer not to tell me, sadly, I will have to return it to you.'

Windows' ever-wide eyes flicked a look to Lastly in the rear-view mirror. Lastly leant forward and pointed his Colt .45 at Cain.

Cain reacted instinctively: his hands enveloped the Colt, his foot hit the dash and, leveraging Lastly's left arm forward, shoving Windows aside, he whacked Lastly's face into the back of the head restraint – and falling back, Lastly's nose left a trail of blood.

As Cain immediately racked the Colt's slide to ensure there was a round in the chamber he felt a strange coarseness against his fingers... and Lastly, finding himself looking down the barrel of his own Colt .45, decided to literally take a back seat on proceedings.

Windows, having grabbed for his .38 revolver in his waist, had only succeeded in dropping burning ash into his lap. 'Ow, shit!' he exclaimed as brushing it away he found himself looking down the barrel of a Glock 27. 'Ah, Mr. Cain,' he said, raising his slightly burnt palms, 'please let us remain calm.'

'I think we should.'

'You are wishing to know who is pulling the strings?'

'Good guess.'

'But first, let us remember Mr. Cain, we are friends now, so you have no reason to be pulling the trigger.'

'Tell me!'

'Minister Zokwana would like to meet you to discuss a number of business proposals.'

'It's a simple request. Why not just invite me without the 'troop' and all the guns on the avenue?'

'TIA.'

'Does the minister know?'

'He would not object.'

'What are the minister's business proposals?'

'I don't know, you will have to ask him yourself.'

'I will.'

Cain realised anything else he wanted to know would only come from a face-to-face meeting with the minister.

Time to go.

Cain opened the passenger door, backed out of the Land Rover and, standing in the doorway, out of arm's reach, he looked at the side of the slide on the Colt .45 to see what had caused the strange coarseness against his fingers. 'A strike-pad from a box of matches,' said Cain. 'Must be a real frightener when someone asks you for a light?'

Windows and Lastly remained silent just staring back.

As Cain used the hem of his shirt to wipe-away any trace of his fingerprints on the Colt, he realised Minister Zokwana would get Windows to repeat verbatim what had been said. But

Windows would not want to tell the minister about the punch-up. Cain decided he would give them a script to help them out.

'Please thank the minister for the diamond.' Windows nodded without comment and Cain continued in his most affable manner. 'I would appreciate a call from the minister tomorrow to confirm a time and place for our meeting. I will make my way to wherever it is going to be. Now gentlemen, we have had a slight misunderstanding here this evening. I believe we were all partly to blame. May I suggest we allow ourselves to forgive and forget.' Cain eyed Windows. 'After all, as you mentioned, we are friends now.'

Windows nodded again, without comment.

In a final effort to calm the situation, Cain held out an olive branch. He placed Lastly's Colt .45 on the passenger seat and backed away. 'Let's let bygones be bygones. It will allow us, when–'

'When we next meet,' Windows interrupted.

Cain immediately got the gist of Windows' sardonic tone. He held up his hand, pressed the remote and, gesturing towards the parking lot gate, he said, 'Gentlemen, thank you for your time. You have thirty seconds.'

Neither Windows nor Lastly uttered a word, but the looks on their faces said it all.

Cain closed the Land Rover's passenger door, the engine started and drove off.

Minutes later, driving back to the 'fortress', Cain contemplated his unforgiveable tactical error in the Land Rover. He should have allowed Lastly to shove the Colt .45 in his face and Windows to threaten him. But he hadn't.

All because Lastly was left-handed, giving me an advantage.

Windows, and especially Lastly, whose reputation as the muscle of the pairing had been seriously compromised, would now want to meet up with Cain again for just one reason: payback for the punch-up in the Land Rover, a bury-the-hatchet of a very different kind. His actions had given them both a much better idea of what he was capable of; what they were up against.

An unforgiveable mistake. Never again.

Cain had to ask himself: If Lastly had seen the scar, would

he have recognised it? Or if it resembled something he had been told about, who could have told him?

Finally, if Lastly were to discover the white man's true identity . . . well, there were no limits to what people like Lastly would do just for fun, let alone revenge. Cain did not want to be spread-eagled on a slab, while Lastly played out his very own personal, very slow, revengeful version of a *Dexter* fantasy.

Cain came to terms with a simple reality: he was only ever going to be left with just the one option.

KIA – Killing In Africa.

High on Devil's Peak, Cain checked his rear-view mirror one last time, he did not see the Land Rover or any other vehicle following him – just the haunted eyes of a dead man staring straight back at him.

Or are they the eyes of a living man?

Scanning the drive ahead, Cain said, 'Evening, Egg. What's happening?'

But the ostrich egg-shell lamp, glowing through the bullet-proof tinted glass on the first-floor balcony, had already told Cain what he wanted to know. The internal motion sensors had not been triggered. No one had broken-in.

He drove onto the forecourt, did a U-turn and pressed the remote. One of the two double-sized garage doors, he had nicknamed Ladysmith began to open, and Kimberley, stayed closed. He reversed the Mercedes into the garage, opened the driver's door, and stood with a hand on the Glock 27 in his backpack, waiting for Ladysmith to close – just to be safe. He walked over to the alarm panel by the security door and tapped in the code. The incessant beeping ceased, and silence prevailed. He turned to look at his gunmetal grey Jeep Grand Cherokee on the other side of the garage. The vehicle looked pretty standard, but the cross-rail roof rack, bull bars, blind-spot mirrors, smash-proof glass, and second antenna, all waiting to ride on puncture-proof tyres, told quite a different story: he was living in Africa, not the Land of The Free.

When Cain's new Jeep had eventually arrived, months after helping to save Commander Marius van Rensburg's life, he'd come to appreciate how his Mercedes saloon was less conspicuous in a line of traffic and less noticeable to a wandering eye, especially when parked somewhere around Cape Town for an overnight stay. Hence he had decided to keep it.

He turned to pass through the internal security door. At the top of the internal stairs he adjusted the dimmers, flicked the toggle and pressed the button. The sound of Pachelbel's *Forest Garden* music, drifted across his world of open-plan living. He checked the time on the distorted Gaudi clock, lingering like a ghost mask from the movie *Scream*, over the edge of a shelf on the wall. It's sliver-style hands both pointing downwards, towards a couple of its warped Roman numerals made it look comical.

The clock was a surprise gift Cain had recently received from Sofia in Spain. After their subsequent phone call, he had couriered two more ostrich eggshell lamps, hand carved in different ways, to Sofia. She now had eight around her home and office. She absolutely adored them.

He wandered into the kitchen; it was too late to phone anyone. He opened the fridge doors.

Inside it was all booze and fun, but not tonight. He took out a can of beer, pulled the tab – pop – and took a swig.

On the kitchen island, he removed the rough from the side pocket in his backpack and rolled it between his fingers and thumb. Minister Nathi Zokwana was the head of the Government's Task Team for Minerals and Energy – in other words, rough diamonds.

Since leaving London, Cain had always maintained – wherever he may be – his natural desire to stay away from the crowd, along with his professional ability to blend into the background of mainstream, everyday activity. A trait that ensured, in South Africa, only a select few people, who lived up in Jo'burg and Lesotho, knew he traded in diamonds. Whereas, down in Cape Town, his reputation for being a bit of a loner who traded in residential real estate to make a living – and had an interest in photography – provided a perfect nondescript way of life to keep him under the radar.

However, Windows had said: "You are the man who knows

much about cutting and selling rough diamonds." So how did the minister know?

On the avenue of trees, Cain had been caught in a trap by Windows and the 'troop'. He should have seen it coming. How? He wasn't quite sure. But he should have. And grabbing Lastly's gun in the Land Rover had been an unforgiveable, tactical error. They were two incredibly rare, if ever, inexcusable mistakes within minutes of each other.

Cain stood up, clenched his hand around the rough in his palm, raised his fist and slammed it down, crushing the now empty can with a single strike.

Never, never again.

Up on the top floor, Cain sat at his Edwardian roll-top desk, made a note of the Land Rover's licence plate number on a sticky note and stuck it on his laptop.

Inside one of the desk's secret compartments, he pressed a button and, with a push of his heel against the floor, his old Chesterfield captain's chair slowly swivelled him around. Across the room, the lens of an ancient Gandolfi field camera – sitting on its equally aged wooden tripod – was focused on a framed copy of a Monet painting on the opposite wall. As the water lilies started floating to one side, taking the wall with them, opening the secret door, Cain got to his feet.

In the diamond room, Cain switched on a fluorescent lamp, revealing the professional merchants instruments and devices on a bench. He glanced down at the Remington 12-gauge pump-action shotgun leaning in a corner: it would always provide the final solution. He pulled up a chair, put a drop of cleaning liquid on a cloth, wiped the rough, placed it on the bench, and put on a pair of white cotton gloves.

'So you want to become a girl's best friend? Don't we all,' he said, glancing up at the Sara Moon pictures of Jacqueline, Jennifer, Christine, and Moshgan hanging on the wall. The pictures were the only female company he maintained on a permanent basis.

He pressed the retractable tip of the diamond tester against the rough: the sound of a buzzer and a line of illuminated LED lights confirmed it was genuine. Next, he placed the rough on the seat of the electronic scales and closed the sliding glass panel; a carat weight of 3 (600 milligrams) showed on the screen. On the glass stage of the colorimeter, the rough gave a reading of E – the top grades being D to F. As he held the rough up to the light in a pair of lockable merchants tweezers, he brought his 10x magnifying loupe up to his eye. Looking in through the one polished side, he could see no inclusions or imperfections, confirming it was of the highest quality. Windows had been right. He folded the *rough* into one of the uniquely designed, diamond merchant's 8x4cm envelopes, called a *brifka* and wrote the number 3 in the bottom, right-hand corner.

The 4Cs: colour, clarity, cut, and carat-weight, then came to mind.

But – and there is always a but – in the diamond industry, there was a rarely mentioned fifth *C*: it stood for confidence. Or more specifically, the confidence you have in the person you are dealing with. But that fifth C, in this particular scenario, being the very corrupt Minister Zokwana, left Cain with just the one thought in mind:

With how many strings attached?

OIA – Only In Africa.

Tuesday – Rough Options.

Cain had long suspected Marius was the South African equivalent of Mac in the UK, but he had never probed, and Marius had never divulged the activities of The Institute.

Marius, aged forty-five, was now the same age Mac had been in 1992 when he had first met Cain with Jerry at the gun range. Time and tide, however, wait for no man. Although Cain was still some ten years younger than Marius, it was no longer the Colonel talking to his Lieutenant: the dynamic had changed.

Cain powered up his laptop, took a sip of his coffee and picked up the phone. Marius answered. '*Goeie more* (Good morning),' he said, speaking in Afrikaans – like the Afrikaans people often do – when starting or ending a conversation.

'Morning Marius.'

'To what do I owe the pleasure?'

'Are you sitting comfortably?'

'Just having a Rooibos tea. I'm listening.'

Cain went through the details of the previous evening's events – and rounded off his narrative by mentioning the date Lastly's twin brother had been killed in London, inferring Windows had told him.

'Quite an evening,' said Marius. 'Especially when you are given a 3-carat rough diamond. I'll make a few enquiries. I'll see what I can dig up.'

'Are you by any chance free for lunch?'

'Surprisingly, yes.'

'Vasco's?'

'Good idea – how about three-thirty, after the lunchtime rush?'

'See you there.'

At 3.25pm, Cain stepped into the world of the Orange Free State. The Afrikaners sitting at tables and standing at the bar turned to eye the lone Englishman before returning to their conversations in their own language.

The barman acknowledged Cain's order with a nod and picked up a glass. Two minutes of harp, surge and settle allowed the black velvet to achieve its crown before the barman placed a pint of Guinness on the bar. As Cain took a sip and wandered over to an empty table in a quiet corner the barman picked up a pen and started his tab.

Welcome to Vasco's.

A few minutes later, Marius entered. Relaxed and unassuming, the man who was more Mortensen than McKellen, wearing a jacket to conceal his shoulder holster and holding a local newspaper in one hand, acknowledged a couple of familiar faces with a smile and gave the barman a nod.

Marius greeted Cain. '*Namiddag* (Afternoon).'

'Good to see you.'

Marius slipped the newspaper he was holding across the table and took a seat. 'Have a read of what's inside when you are alone, back at the 'fortress'. Have you–'

A very attractive, slim young waitress with long, brown hair in a pigtail, wearing a T-shirt and mini skirt, arrived with Marius' Guinness.

'Thank you, Lara,' said Marius. 'You look wonderful.'

Lara smiled. 'Thank you – what would you like to eat?'

'Could we have two of your perfect peri-peri chicken with rice, please?'

'Perhaps,' Lara replied. When she finished writing the order on her notepad, she quite unexpectedly dipped her pencil into Marius' Guinness, gave him a fleeting glance, and walked away.

Seeing the heart-shaped outline inscribed in the froth of the Guinness, Cain said, 'Lara's new here. You seem to have made an impression.'

Marius glanced at Lara going through the door into the kitchen. 'I'll have to have a word.'

'Chugalug,' said Cain, raising his glass. 'For your first taste of sin.'

'I should be so lucky. Cheers.' Placing their drinks back on the table Marius asked, 'You've not heard from the minister or Windows today?'

'No, not even a postcard.'

Marius showed a look of amusement. 'Perhaps it's a deliberate delaying tactic, to keep you in suspense. Let's see what unravels in the next day or two.'

'By the way,' said Cain, 'any luck with the licence plate number of Windows' Land Rover?'

'It's registered to an address in Guguletu Township. We know it well – a no-go area for any white man, but we keep an eye on it.'

Cain grinned. 'I'll leave your people to it.'

'Thought you might.' Marius instinctively checked again for anyone watching. 'The minister,' he said, 'has recently been linked to some of Africa's most powerful crime kingpins. But this goes beyond the usual realms of bribery and corruption.'

'It's an ongoing investigation?'

'Yes. I have good reason to believe he is acting as a go-between, facilitating easy passage for the trafficking of cash, drugs, guns, and girls into and through South Africa to neighbouring countries.'

'Typical politician,' said Cain with an air of cynicism. 'Always on the take.'

'And being the head of the Government's Task Team for Minerals and Energy, he certainly knows where to lay his hands on a bit of rough in every sense of the word.'

Cain grinned. 'Good comment.'

Lara arrived with the plates of perfect peri-peri chicken and placed them on the table. 'Enjoy your meal. Would you like two more drinks?'

'Please,' Cain said – and Marius simply smiled.

Once Lara was out of earshot, Marius said 'Our turn to eat.'

Cain knew he was not referring to the peri-peri chicken.

The phrase *Our Turn To Eat* referred to the day-to-day activities of a vast number of African politicians who always had their noses well and truly in the trough and their fingers in the till. And when the next political *party* – in every sense of the word – took over, nothing ever changed. It reminded Cain of the famous 1991 novel Marius had lent him, *Fishing In Africa,* by Andrew Buckoke. When Cain had read it, if he had not known the names of some of the countries mentioned had been changed, or the various leaders referred to had already died, he would have thought it had been written on the day before and not twelve years earlier. Africa had got the western world hook, line, and sinker.

Cain grinned, 'Bon appétit.'

As they were eating, Marius said, 'Remember, whatever the minister asks you to do, he is not the top dog here. He is simply obeying orders, regardless of the cost to you or anyone else. So be careful.'

'We wait to hear.'

Wednesday – Rough Choice

Cain finished discussing all things business with Moshe on the phone.

Cain had already decided when it came to telling Moshe about his encounter with Windows and Lastly, he would stick to the protocol of days gone by: he would wait, like they always did when it came to discussing more serious things, until they were together in Jo'burg.

But before that happened, Cain would meet with Minister Zokwana to discuss, as Windows had mentioned, a number of business proposals. The face-to-face encounter would allow him to get a better idea of what the member of the *Our Turn To Eat* Club was really up to and, more importantly, see if and when he was being lied to.

'Talk to you later,' Cain said.

'Shalom.'

With a glass of iced water in hand Cain wandered out onto the sundeck and into the 22°C heat of the morning to have a think. He looked up at the flat-topped summit of Table Mountain, already covered with the stream of candyfloss-looking cloud – *the Tablecloth* – rolling into place. It would soon start slowly pouring down the vertical front of the mountain for several hundred metres, until the leading wisps of candyfloss would appear to have come to a stop and just hang in the breeze. It never ceased to amaze him.

Cain's eyes wandered across the gap to Lion's Head and along the ridge to Signal Hill. The sound of the noon-day cannon suddenly echoed across City Bowl.

Cain checked the time on his Breitling: high noon.

In the late of the afternoon, Cain was sending a fax to Moshe to round off the day when his mobile rang. He checked the caller ID; *Peter* showed on the screen. He pressed the button. 'Beer,' Cain said.

'Hi Cain, good idea. If you're lazing on the sundeck, I'll be passing by in twenty minutes. You want me to pick you up?'

'Evening Peter – can I sit in the back?'

'Piss off,' Peter said disparagingly, hanging up.

Cain closed-down his laptop… and minutes later headed for the pole.

Out on the forecourt he waited for the Kimberley garage door to close before he crossed the drive, sat on the wall, and scanned the small quadrangle of park a few feet below. He noticed a motionless bergie, a tramp, sitting in the shadows of a distant, small copse of trees.

Is he alive?

It was unusual for a bergie to be so high up on the mountain slopes. They tended to stay lower down, where the flatter terrain made it easier for them to push their obligatory mobile homes: supermarket trolleys. As Cain checked the park again for any sign of a trolley, a flash of flame from a striking match and curl of cigarette smoke rising through the branches proved the bergie was alive.

A BMW crossed the drive and pulled up beside Cain. The window buzzed down and Peter, having all the traits of a retired English police officer, greeted Cain in his usual way.

'Evening all.'

'Hi Peter.'

'What are you looking at?'

'There's a bergie under one of the small copse of trees, but no supermarket trolley.'

'Suspicious. Pity he's not a corpse in the copse instead.'

Cain grinned. 'He's just lit a cigarette. Let's nickname him Smokey to give him an identity.'

'Good idea.'

Cain took a last look before walking around the BMW, opening the front passenger's door and taking a seat. As they moved off, Smokey the supposed bergie – watching, always watching – made a note of the time.

Peter, a retired Special Branch officer, had been assigned to Margaret Thatcher at Number Ten when she became prime minister. He had stayed with her to the end.

When he had completed his LS and GC, he was still a young man. He moved to Cape Town, where he had initially run the security for Margaret Thatcher's son, Mark, who lived in the Cape's most affluent area, the Constantia Wine region.

However, word soon got around, convincing many of the region's wealthy people to ask Peter to take on the mantle of watching over the security of their own properties, along with their personas, stroking a pet doglet or two – and an occasional ego or three.

When Jerry had taken his annual leave to visit Cain in Cape Town for the very first time, an evening visit to Carlton's to meet Peter and have a perfect steak, had been top of the to-do list. Jerry and Peter had soon discovered they had quite a lot in common as they traded stories about legends of the police force and those they'd known. The jokes and insults about politicians raised an eyebrow or two, while comments about Margaret Thatcher and The Firm always prompted looks of admiration. And so meeting in Carlton's became an annual event.

'How was your day?' said Cain, knowing Peter always had his finger on the pulse. 'Anything exciting been happening?'

'There was a shooting at two o'clock this morning. I haven't stopped all day; I need a beer. I bloody well hate having to get up in the early hours.'

'What, not *up* in the biblical sense?'

Peter glanced at Cain. 'Piss off,' he said, and with smiles all round he continued. 'The shooting happened at a country residence being renovated, out in the Constantia Wine Region. The thieving bastards wanted to steal a load of Italian marble, delivered on the previous day. They did the usual trick of building up a bit of speed before turning off the engine, turning off their lights, turning off the road, and freewheeling up to the property. But the guard saw them from his lookout on the top floor, and quietly called for back-up. Anyways, to cut a long story short, during the exchange of gunfire the guard shot dead one of the bastards before they all scarpered.'

'Just the one dead?'

'The police checked the hospitals,' Peter replied bringing the BMW to a stop.

The two men ambled through a casual lounge where a couple were sitting in a bay window eating pizzas and salad. At another table, a group were playing 'loser buys the drinks' backgammon. And two ladies relaxing on a sofa enjoyed an Orgasm and an Old Etonian while waiting for the restaurant to open. Having climbed the four steps up to the area of the old oak bar, Cain and Peter settled themselves on stools at a table in a quiet corner.

'So,' said Cain, 'did the police find any dead or wounded at the hospitals?'

'Quite a few, but none of them were connected to our shoot-out.'

Cain grinned. 'Situation normal then. The guard did well.'

'Yes, he did. He's a bright lad. I sometimes think he's too good for guard duty he-'

Their conversation was interrupted by Sharlise and Tarah – two very gorgeous waitresses – each carrying a pint of Stella and a Jägermeister shooter. And after Hugs and kisses all round – Spanish-style – their conversation was interrupted. 'Evening gents,' a voice said.

'Well, well, well,' said Peter, 'As I live and breathe if it isn't Jason Carlton.'

The men all shook hands, as was the Carlton's tradition.

'You're late again,' said Peter with a wry smile – and giving Tarah a wink, he suggested, 'Go get the visitors' book for Jason to sign.'

Tarah's eyes widened in acknowledgement, but she didn't go anywhere: it was all part of a humorous routine.

'Tell me Jason,' said Peter, 'Any chance of your brother making an appearance? Or is he still sulking from the thrashing at backgammon I gave him last night?'

Cain enquired, 'You're the reigning champion?'

'I am,' said Peter with a wry smile. 'By the way, Jason, would you like a drink? Or aren't you staying?'

'Don't mind if I do,' said Jason. 'An Amstel, if you would be so kind.'

'Where's our favourite barman, Leo?' Peter asked.

Jason turned to see there was no one behind the bar. Sharlise appeared by Jason's side with a huge smile on her face. Jason looked questioningly at her. . .

'I don't know where Leo is,' said Sharlise, handing Jason his Amstel. 'I give up.'

Sensing skulduggery. 'Tell me,' Jason said.

'What?'

'Sharlise . . .'

'Oh, there he is!' Sharlise said, pointing at the bar.

In unison, everyone turned to stare at Leo, now standing behind the bar, wiping his eyes with tissues.

Cain said, 'He becomes so very emotional when he sees us.'

And everyone – except Leo – burst out laughing.

'Evening Leo!' Peter called out, 'Good of you to come back.

Better late than never. Don't worry about us, we're just paying customers.'

'Bog off,' Leo said, looking at the crowd, revealing very red eyes.

'Jesus Christ,' said Peter. 'I've told you about that bending over game and the ring of fire.' More laughter followed.

'How?' Jason said, staring at Sharlise.

'Oh, all right then, if you insist,' Sharlise beamed. 'When Leo went to get his pizza from the kitchen this evening, he wouldn't let any of us near it. But when he got back behind the bar I undid an extra button on my blouse and pressed myself against the far end. My boobs did the rest.' The men all looked at Sharlise's breasts. She breathed in with the biggest of smiles – and continued with the story. 'While I was having my pressing engagement and Leo was getting my drinks order together, Tarah sneaked out of the kitchen and round the bar and up the steps. She used one of the long teaspoons Cain got for us to quickly slip the sauce, *el hot es-peciale*, onto Leo's pizza.'

'That must have taken some planning,' Cain said.

'Not really – we practised when Leo was in the kitchen, keeping guard on his pizza.'

Everyone again erupted into laughter, and even Leo managed a smile. It was just another one of the many games they all frequently played.

Jason finished his beer and, with the girls in tow, feigning reluctance, they went off to check on the evening's preparations for the restaurant, leaving Cain and Peter to their own devices.

Cain said, 'It's been a truly memorable day for you, Peter.'

'It has. By the way, a chap I know is selling his property down in Constantia, he wants a bigger one. He hasn't given it to a real-estate agent yet, so I asked him to hang on for all the obvious reasons. Would you like to take a look? I can meet you in the morning. I'll buy you coffee and carrot cake at Melissa's, our favourite breakfast restaurant.'

'Coffee and carrot cake – something you know I can never refuse,' said Cain. 'OK.'

'Meet you at the usual spot in the car park,' Peter said, as they both threw their dice to see who would go first for their session of backgammon.

Sometime later, when Carlton's relaxed 'sundowners' gave way to the evening's gathering of diners and drinkers, Cain's natural desire to stay away from the crowd came to the fore. He checked the time on his wrist.

'Time to go?' Peter suggested.

'Good idea.'

And with their tips – in every sense of the word – in place, Cain and Peter enjoyed their farewell hugs and kisses with Sharlise and Tarah and shook hands with Jason.

A few minutes later, Cain gave Peter's BMW a wave.

See you on the morrow.

Cain looked down into the small quadrangle of a park. Under the small copse of trees, just a flicker of light from the end of a cigarette glowing in the darkness told him what he needed to know. He turned away, crossed the drive, pressed the remote, took a last look around, and Kimberley opened.

Meanwhile, down in the park, Smokey – watching, always watching – made a note of the time.

Thursday

Cain stepped out onto the first-floor balcony, from where he could see but not be seen. He scanned the small quadrangle of a park. *Smokey* was still there, and Marigold, the maid, was crossing the drive.

Down in the garage, Ladysmith opened. 'Morning, Marigold,' Cain said, initiating their usual bout of greetings and chit-chat, like they always did. Minutes later, Cain checked the time on his wrist. 'I have to go,' he said.

'Have a good day.'

Cain drove the Mercedes out into the 24°C heat of the day and came to a stop watching – Marigold had already pressed the button – Ladysmith close. He gave his Serengeti shades a nudge, checked the drive again, and switched on the air-conditioning. A minute later he turned onto Duval Drive, a twisty dual carriageway that snaked its way around the base of the mountain.

Duval Drive just happened to have a nickname too – the

Mercedes Bends. It had to be done: Cain pressed the button and stepped on the gas. The gears dropped down, *Tina Turner* stepped up and, to the tune of *River Deep, Mountain High,* six cylinders of Stuttgart's finest powered the Mercedes from the sun-baked city suburbs of the north to the affluent, luxuriant, Constantia wine region in the south. Home to the rich, the famous, the Smiths, the Gettys, the movers and shakers – plus an occasional rock star or two.

In a quiet corner of the village shopping centre's car park, under the shade of trees, Cain pulled up alongside Peter's BMW. He opened his door. 'Morning,' he called out.

Peter buzzed down his window and theatrically took a sniff of the air. 'Morning. I can smell your brakes. You scorched the Bends again.'

'Just a touch.'

'I have to make a stop on the way,' said Peter. 'I need to have a quick word with the guard who shot the robber.'

'OK.'

Cain eased his six-foot tall frame onto the front passenger seat of Peter's BMW, but he couldn't get in, there wasn't enough legroom: the seat was too far forward.

It wasn't like this *when I got out last night.*

Guessing a female had been the last person to hitch a ride – perhaps of a slightly different kind – Cain slid the seat back. 'Did you decide to do it in the bed or the car last night?' he speculated.

'Piss off,' said Peter with a smile. 'Before I forget, was Smokey still in the park when I dropped you off last night?'

'Unfortunately, yes. I saw the glow from the end of a cigarette – and this morning a puff of smoke in the air.'

Several miles further on, a ragged police tape hanging from the main gate of a country residence marked the location. The guard who had done the shooting, walked down the drive, from where the body for evidence, forensics and photos had all been taken – and a workman was hosing down what remained.

Peter opened the car door. 'Morning, Cebo! How's my star guard today?'

Appreciating the compliment, Cebo grinned, 'Morning boss, I'm good. Everything OK, yes?' he asked with an air of expectancy.

'Yes, all OK,' said Peter. 'I spoke to the police again this morning. They confirmed what I said to you yesterday, it's a clean kill, so no worries. But you will have to wait until the inquiry is completed before you are officially informed.' Peter removed an envelope from his jacket pocket and covertly handed it to Cebo. 'There's US$200 for you – don't spend it all at once! Well done.'

Seeing Peter's gesture, Cain unzipped his backpack and discreetly removed US$200 from the US$1000 he always kept hidden at the base of a pocket liner.

'By the way,' said Peter, 'let me introduce you to a friend of mine, Cain.'

'Morning sir.'

'Morning Cebo, good to meet you,' said Cain and, shaking hands South African black man-style – double grip, two position hold, three-time crunch – he discreetly handed Cebo the US$200. 'Please take this, just in case you do spend it all at once.'

Totally surprised, Cebo said, 'Thank you sir.' He quickly glanced over his shoulder to make sure none of the workmen were watching and slipped the notes into his pocket. 'If there is ever anything I can do for you sir, please let me know.' Cebo said, expressing his gratitude.

'I'll keep it in mind. You take care now.'

Cebo turned to Peter, and they walked away to have a quiet few words.

Driving the BMW, Peter gave Cain an appreciative glance. 'Thank you for giving Cebo the US$200. You didn't have to.'

'Any time – giving him a bonus for putting his life on the line, protecting property, getting shot at, and killing one of those thieving, murdering bastards is a pleasure.'

'I wish everyone had your attitude towards the guards.'

'Just one thing,' said Cain. 'Why hasn't Cebo been suspended, pending the inquiry?'

'I must admit, it is normal procedure, but the police told me he is allowed to stay on the job.'

'Unusual.'

'Yes, it is. I don't understand the whys and wherefores, but there you go. Perhaps he knows someone in high places.'

'Perhaps he does.'

A few miles down the road, Peter turned the BMW into the driveway of the house the owner was hoping Cain would buy. Hoping he would not have to pay the estate agents 5% plus VAT fee. Hoping he would negotiate a deal with Cain so they were both financially better off... An hour later, the owner accepted Cain's offer.

Back in the BMW, Cain said, 'Thank you Peter, I think I need to buy you brunch.'

Starting the engine, Peter smiled. 'Coffee and carrot cake.'

'What a good idea.'

Friday – Rough Assessment

Cain sat in the diamond room completing his roundup of the week's events. On the map in front of him, his finger followed his line of thought to the residence of Minister Nathi Zokwana.

He read again through the documents Marius had given him between the folds of the newspaper in Vasco's, bringing him up to date on the minister's activities and involvement in the trafficking of cash, drugs, guns, and girls. It was again a reminder of how he had killed Lastly's twin brother all those years ago in London. He checked his mobile, but there were no missed calls or messages.

Although he believed payback for the punch-up in the Land Rover was now Windows' and Lastly's priority, he could not understand why Minister Zokwana had not contacted him or, at the very least, instructed Windows to pass on a message of some sort.

Early that evening, after the rush-hour traffic and to avoid the TGIF – Thank God It's Friday – crowds in the bars and restaurants, Cain drove down to his favourite takeaway fish and chip shop in City Bowl. Once back at the 'fortress', he switched on the TV and sat with a beer watching *Attenborough In Africa*, enjoying his cod and chips with a sprinkling of Heinz Tomato Ketchup.

Cain stepped out onto the first-floor balcony. He picked up his binoculars and scanned the small copse of trees in the park. Smokey, was still there, looking up at the 'fortress', lighting another cigarette.

Are you watching everyone or are you watching just me? Time will tell . . . tick, tock.

He checked the time on his watch. He went for a leisurely drive to pick up his mail, stop off at the dry cleaners, buy a local newspaper and have a late afternoon lunch in one of the al 'fresco restaurants on Kloof Street.

Back at the 'fortress', he was pleased to know he had not been followed.

Later that evening, Cain sat watching an episode of *Top Gear*. And after he'd made himself a cold meat salad for dinner he watched *CSI Miami*. The locations in the episode were places he had visited with both Jerry and members of the Galt Mile Gang, bringing back fond memories of days gone by.

Just after midnight his mobile rang, he checked the caller ID, and pressed the button.

'Hello,' said Tarah. 'I'm leaving Carlton's.'

'Make sure someone escorts you out to your SUV.'

'Of course.'

'See you in a sec.'

Cain wandered up onto the top-floor sundeck to take a look around. In his mind's eye he could see Tarah being escorted by either a male member of staff or customer to her SUV. It was a courteous, obligatory offer no female, leaving Carlton's alone, ever refused.

A flash of light, from down in the park, immediately confirmed to Cain, Smokey was still there, lighting another cigarette. The man's presence was a stark reminder of how the simple act of opening a garage door could be an unavoidable dice with death. Cain dropped himself down the pole to the first floor, wandered down the stairs through the security door into the garage – and with his Walther P99 tucked in his waist he pressed the button.

Kimberley opened and he walked out into the early morning air to check the drive.

An SUV turned onto the forecourt and came to a stop next to him. The driver's window buzzed down. 'Oh hello, fancy seeing you here,' Tarah mischievously remarked.

'I just happened to be passing.'

Tarah glanced up at the first-floor balcony. 'Egg is like a beacon.'

'Well, at least you won't get lost.'

Tarah playfully stuck her tongue out, slowly drove into the garage, and with Cain pressing the button again, Kimberley closed behind them.

Tarah stepped out of her SUV. She was wearing a tight T-shirt, mini-skirt, and trainers, looking more Cruz than Hayek. 'Boo,' she said. They hugged and kissed. 'Are you ready for this?' she sighed.

Up in the open-plan living room, a very radiant Tarah gave Cain a quick peck on the cheek then headed up the stairs with a glass of red in one hand and her overnight bag in the other. Cain kept an eye on Tarah's legs – all the way up to the top . . .

Cain settled himself on one of the sofas, knowing: after Tarah had showered and changed, his mobile would ring.

He had started seeing Tarah, who was ten years younger, many months earlier. She was one of several females who, for a number of different reasons, lived by a simple philosophy: I will see you Cain, if and when I want to, no questions asked, no strings attached. It was a perfect ideology for Cain. Especially since he now lived by an equally simple decree: I will never live with anyone again, never be married, and never have children.

His mobile rang: it was Tarah. 'Hello, mischief.'

'Ready?'

'See you in a sec.'

Cain pressed the button on the stereo and *Supertramp* sang: *The Logical Song:*

When I was young, it seemed that life was so wonderful.

One of Cain's casual shirts, floating above a pair of stripy thigh-length socks came sliding down the X-Pole – with a glowing Tarah inside them. She came to rest on six-inch heels. Her session on the pole – of gently gyrating, and provocatively pouting with phenomenal rhythm – mesmerised Cain. She eventually spun herself around the pole one last time and completed her performance with a flourish.

Cain stood up. 'Bravo,' he applauded. He then bowed in appreciation and Tarah curtsied.

'I'm all hot now,' she said seductively, walking towards him and wearing only the most mischievous of looks.

Enveloped in Cain's arms, Tarah felt his erection against her. She rubbed against him a little. 'I think I may have drunk the wine a little too quickly,' she whispered. 'I was nervous.'

'You were fantastic.'

'Thank you. I've had a really busy week; can we have a lazy day tomorrow on the sundeck.'

'I'll slowly cover you with Piz Buin.'

Looking into Tarah's eyes Cain just knew. He lifted her into his arms and carried her up the stairs. In bed, he laid down beside her, she snuggled up, he stroked her wild hair away from her face, and gently kissed her on the end of her nose.

'After a long day, the spirit is willing, but the body is weak,' he whispered.

But Tarah hadn't heard him.

> *There are times when all the world's asleep*
> *The questions run too deep*
> *For such a simple man...*

> *Supertramp*

20

Monday – Week Two Begins – Rough Idea

Cain sat at his Edwardian desk, turning the pages of his diary. He looked at the week ahead.

Wednesday! It could be a perfect opportu–

His phone rang, interrupting his train of thought. He checked the caller ID. 'Morning Moshe.' After their customary pleasantries they got down to business, looking at their commitments for the days and weeks ahead.

'I'll fax you a copy of our schedule,' Moshe said.

'Thank you. Talk to you later.'

'*Shalom.*'

Cain turned back the pages of his diary to look again at the week ahead.

I must drop into the martial arts shop.

He spent the next couple of days in the diamond room, talking to Moshe, tending to business, and after having lunch with his conveyancing solicitor, he ticked a box long overdue.

Wednesday

It was a day of union protests and marches in Cape Town's City Bowl. Many businesses and stores had closed, ordinary people were not walking the streets. Everyone wanted to avoid what would inevitably end in rioting.

Cain had had a chat with Jerry on the phone, playing catch-up.

'When I'm finished in Guangzhou, I was thinking I could come back via the UK so we could have some time together in London before we fly back down to Cape Town for your annual leave.'

'It's been a while, good idea,' said Jerry. 'I'll buy you your first pint of London Pride.'

'Make that two.'

'Gotta go. Time to get ready.'
'Talk to you later.'
'Bye.'

In the late of the afternoon, Cain racked the slide of a silenced, throwaway Beretta and slipped it into his shoulder holster. He still believed Windows and Lastly had one priority: payback for the punch up in the Land Rover. Therefore the unattended dojo would provide them with a perfect opportunity.

It left Cain with just the one thought in mind:

What if Lastly has now been informed of the white man's true identity?

Cain realised, that being the case, Windows and Lastly would want to keep him alive so Lastly could carry out a very slow, revengeful version of a *Dexter* fantasy. It left Cain with no choice. He would have to shoot first and if they were still alive, if they knew he had killed Lastly's twin brother, he would ask one simple question: Who told you?

Cain parked the Mercedes in a small, virtually empty car park next to the dojo. On a normal day it was always packed, so he never bothered to try. There was no security or CCTV. He looked around for any sign of Windows, Lastly or the 'troop', but there was nothing.

At the door of the deserted dojo, respecting protocol, Cain bowed and removed his trainers before entering. He crossed the room, placed his backpack on a bench, laid out his training weapons, and pulled on his newly purchased martial arts weight-lifting gloves. The scar on his wrist was now covered. He walked to the door at the rear of the dojo, checked for any signs of tampering and, finding nothing, he made sure it was securely locked.

Standing in the centre of the dojo, he faced the wall of mirrors. His reflection bowed, before he worked through the various stages of his half-hour warm-up.

Minutes later, Windows entered the dojo. He hadn't bothered to remove his shoes.

He's had no training, good to know, Cain thought.

'Mr. Cain, afternoon.'

'Fancy seeing you here,' said Cain, before he quite obviously looked at the door. 'I see you've lost Lastly.'

'He is away for a few days.'

'He will not be joining us?'

'Sadly no,' Windows sighed. 'But I am here now. So let us talk the business.'

Windows was very wide-eyed again and juggling his words: he was high on drugs.

'Minister Zokwana has not phoned me yet.'

Windows immediately used the universal gesture of dislike towards another: he folded his arms across his chest and glared at his enemy. 'So, what to do Mr. Cain?'

'How about asking the minister to phone me?'

Windows remained silent, weighing up his options. Cain turned his back and walked away to provoke a reaction from a man he knew would never go anywhere alone. Windows somewhat exaggeratedly cleared his throat and footsteps tapped the floor; Cain glanced over his shoulder. A gunman with a revolver in hand had entered the dojo, leaving just the one thought in Cain's mind:

If only the gunman had been Lastly. Tap-tap.

'That is far enough Mr. Cain,' said Windows. 'Do not reach down into your backpack. You will not need your Glock 27. Please come back, we are not finished yet.'

Cain took hold of what looked like a long broom handle leaning against the wall bars and turned to face his opponents. 'This is called a *Bō*,' he said, walking back towards the centre of the dojo. 'It is made of red oak. It is 180cm long and weighs 500g.'

On reaching the point of no return, the centre of the dojo, Cain stood to attention with the *Bō* at his side, facing his doppelgänger in the wall of mirrors, keeping an eye on Windows and the gunman.

Windows unfolded his arms and gestured to the gunman. 'Allow me to introduce you to Gospel.'

Cain stepped his left foot forward, rotating the Bō upwards – windmill-like – to above his head where it came to rest, pointing horizontally at his reflection in the wall of mirrors.

Windows glanced at Gospel with a look that said it all.

What's the white shit up to?
Gospel simply shrugged.
Haven't a fucking clue.
Cain stepped his right foot forward, rotating the *Bō* downwards until the tip appeared to strike his reflection on the top of his head. Cain then stepped his right foot back and, rotating the *Bō* once more, he returned to the set position, ready to strike again. Cain had just completed the first stage of a *Ryukyu Kobujutsu Bō kata*. Watching Cain repeat the act several times, Windows became increasingly bored.

'Block him,' Windows shouted looking at Gospel.

Keeping an eye on the *Bō*, Gospel strolled over and placed himself between Cain and the wall of mirrors. Cain immediately realised; Gospel was the sidewalk-blocking gunman who had been with Lamppost-leaning on the avenue of trees.

'You again,' said Cain. 'You seem to be developing a propensity for getting in my way.'

Without waiting for an answer, Cain stepped forward and repeated his first stage of the *kata*. Gospel aimed his .38 revolver and Windows placed both his hands behind his back.

Cain could see the gap between the tip of the *Bō* and the .38's muzzle was one metre. He took a short step back and, rotating the *Bō*, he pulled it back further than he previously had, completing the deception. Having watched the *Bō* more than the man, Gospel failed to notice the physical gap between the two of them had been reduced: he believed he still had the trajectory of the *Bō* etched in his mind.

In the wall of mirrors, Cain glanced at Windows, now holding a baseball bat in one hand, swinging it pendulum-like by his side – and savouring the white man's predicament, his short vertical scar creased with his smile, under the left of a pair of very wild eyes.

The stage was set. Payback.

When death and danger are upon you the slow-motion
movie in the mind distorts time.
What may seem like an eternity will, in the event, only
be life slowly coming to an end.

Cain relaxed the grip of his left hand on the *Bō* and tightened his right hand, waiting for Gospel to trigger the outcome.

Tick, tock.

As Gospel glanced to Windows for instruction, Cain swept forward, jabbing the *Bō en flèche*-style – straight as an arrow. The tip of the *Bō* instantly struck Gospel's trigger finger. Gospel howled, his aim faltered, the .38 revolver fired, and Windows cried out in pain. Cain wheeled the *Bō* sideways, striking Gospel's gun hand – and the .38 revolver tumbled to the floor. Cain instantly reverse-wheeled the *Bō*, slamming it into Gospel's knees, sending him crashing down. Catching sight of the baseball bat flying through the air, Cain whipped the *Bō* around and the deflected baseball bat whacked the back of Gospel's head, rendering him unconscious.

'Fuck you, white shit,' Windows raged, falling to his knees, grappling with his bloodied, soggy T-shirt, trying to stem the flow of blood from the bullet wound to his side.

Looks painful, Cain thought. *I know how much it hurts.*

As Windows got his hand on his revolver. . .

'Easy does it,' said Cain, pointing his silenced Beretta. 'Now toss it away, not towards me.'

Windows did what he was told and seeing Cain now getting closer, he let rip, '*Yooo* white shit, yooo some kinda marshal art mojo motherfucker or what?'

As Windows doubled over in pain, Cain stepped around him and removed the only cell phone he was carrying from his back pocket.

'Password?'

'Go fuck yourself.'

Cain returned the Beretta to his shoulder holster and poked the *Bō* into Windows' bullet wound. Windows' face contorted. 'Jesus fucking Christ,' he gasped.

'Tell me.'

'One, two, three, four.'

'Original,' said Cain, keying in the password. 'Thank you.'

Hearing a grunt from Gospel lying on the floor, Windows vented his anger. 'Look what yooo done yooo arsehole. Yooo Fuck–'

The *Bō* struck the side of Windows head, rendering him

unconscious and Cain walked away.

At the door to the dojo, Cain turned and bowed. 'Sayōnara.'

The *Bō* had kept any blood spatter away from Cain but, just to be sure, he went through a doorway, dropped his backpack to the floor and dropped himself down into the shallower end of the swimming pool, keeping the hand holding the Beretta above the water.

Dripping wet, Cain headed for the car park. Windows' Land Rover was parked inches from the driver's door of his Mercedes. He compared the two vehicles side by side, remembering what Windows had said when they first met: "I have many talents. Try taking a deep breath before you speak again."

Cain took a deep breath, counting from one to ten to stop himself from sticking his switchblade into each of the Land Rover's tyres. He leant the *Bō* against the back of the Land Rover, and with a downward kick, he snapped it in half, picked up the pieces, and dumped them in the boot of his Mercedes. He opened the passenger door, climbed across into the driver's seat and came face to face with the steel reality of the Land Rover beside him: it was definitely too close for comfort. It was a reminder of what his Jeep had done to another of Germany's finest – the BMW – on that fateful night when he had written it off while rescuing Commander Marius van Rensburg. It convinced him: the time had come to make contingency plans for on and off the road.

On his way back to the 'fortress' – using one of his burner cell phones – Cain rounded off the conversation. 'I will make payment within 24 hours. Thank you.'

The Cleaning Crew would now be on their way to the dojo. They would collect blood samples from the floor for analysis and erase all traces of the night's encounter. Cain knew, by time they arrived, Gospel would already have picked up Windows – dead or alive – and left.

Back at the 'fortress', Cain walked out onto the first-floor balcony from where he could see but not be seen and picked up his binoculars. He watched Smokey down in the small quadrangle of park, under the small copse of trees – watching, always watching – press a button on a cell phone.

Windows' cell phone began to ring. Cain pressed the button.

'Hello Windows,' a voice said… 'Windows, can you hear me?'

Cain could see Smokey's lips moving. He pressed the button, the line went dead, and turning off the phone, he came to terms with a simple reality: Smokey is watching me.

Some twenty minutes later, having showered and dried himself off, Cain stood at the kitchen island and poured himself a glass of his favourite red wine. As he gave himself a bit of a stretch, he spilt a few drops onto the counter. The drops gave his brain a nudge about HIV and AIDS… he stopped pouring.

South Africa was said to have more people with HIV and AIDS than any other country in the world. The government had refused offers to provide free or cheap anti-retroviral treatment because it was unsure of what the long-term side effects might have on people.

The South African Health Minister, Manto Tshabalala-Msimang, in yet another act of gross stupidity, had advocated a 'cure' diet of garlic, olive oil, and lemon.

And to compound it all, the Pope's subsequent first-ever visit to South Africa outraged everyone worldwide when he stated: 'AIDS was a tragedy that cannot be overcome by money alone, that cannot be overcome through the distribution of condoms, which even aggravates the problems.'

Cain sliced a lemon, but for a vastly different reason: a *Vera Lynn and supersonic* – a gin & tonic. He topped up his highball tumbler with ice, poured the tonic, and walked out onto the patio. He sat in solitary silence in a rocking chair under the lemon tree, holding a half-empty glass of *G&T* in one hand and a fully-loaded, silenced, throwaway Beretta in the other. He looked up towards the sky and started counting his chances.

Thursday

In the warmth of the rising sun, Cain was jogging on the mountain trails of Devil's Peak. Pushed to the limit, breathing heavily, and sweating profusely, he reached the remnants of the Kings Blockhouse Watchtower and slowed his pace to take a breather, appreciate the solitude, enjoy the view.

In the distance, a three-masted tall-ship – on some epic, global voyage – was entering Table Bay. Its arrival reminded Cain of the great novels written by Wilbur Smith. And with a bit of a grin he decided he would not wait to watch for two of the greatest lines to happen:

No monsoon in the bay today . . .
The anchor drops from the hawsehole. . .

He watched the rush-hour traffic down on the plains slowly grinding to a stop. He looked out to the horizon and beyond, and heard *Jimmy Cliff* singing:

It's gonna be another bright (bright) bright (bright)
sunshiny day
I can see clearly now the rain is gone
I can see all obstacles in my way...

Cain turned to face the rising sun.
I wish I could see all the obstacles in my way.
He stood to attention, closed his left hand over his right fist, breathed out long and slow, and bowed towards the source of the heat of the day. Only a goshawk, high on the wing, saw the long shadows performing the Tai Chi Quan-42 Short Form.
A respite for peace of mind.

Later that morning, Cain powered along the *Mercedes Bends,* [Duval Drive] and for the last time *Janis Joplin* sang:

Oh Lord, won't you buy me a Mercedes Benz?
My friends all drive Porsches, I must make amends . . .

Cain pulled in at Robbie Tripp Motors, a dealership whose reputation for honesty and integrity was beyond question. 'When you've sold it,' said Cain, talking to Dennis the salesman, 'give me a call and I'll let you know where to deposit the money.'

'Will do.'

As they shook hands, the taxi arrived. Cain left the showroom, knowing everything would be absolutely fine.

Back at the 'fortress' Cain called Marius to give him a run-down of the previous evening's events.

'I'm glad you are all in one piece,' Marius said.

'As we speak, I'm faxing you the list of calls and contacts from Windows' cell phone.'

'Thank you,' said Marius. 'I have it, I'll see what I can dig up.'

'If Windows is still alive, he will not be able to hide the fact he's been shot from Minister Zokwana.'

'Nor will he dare lie to the minister.'

'Instead, he will just bend the truth a bit. Or maybe skirt around the issue with a smidgen of his well-practised, artful evasiveness, putting the blame on everyone else but himself. Namely me.'

'It would certainly be interesting to be a fly on the wall when Windows tells his story.'

'Do you think Gospel will back him up?'

'Probably, I think err . . .' Marius paused.

I'll save my speculation until a body is found.

'What are you thinking?' Cain asked.

'I'll let you know when it happens. But one thing is for sure: the minister will want verification. I believe it is fair to say you will be receiving the call you have been waiting for sooner, rather than later.'

'I have to go up to Jo'burg on Monday.'

'Say hello to Moshe for me.'

'Will do.'

'How long will you be away?'

'The whole week – I don't want the minister to get the impression I am running away or trying to hide from him. If I've not heard from him by the end of tomorrow I'll go to his residence on Saturday. If he's there, I doubt I will be able to see him at such short notice. But at least I will be able to leave a message and my visit will be logged with the guards. Going to his residence will be better than going to his government building, for all the obvious reasons.'

'I'm sure the minister will appreciate your discretion. I doubt if even he would want you to be seen by all and sundry in his building. He will of course, have quite a few questions for you.'

'I'll have quite a few for him too.'

'Haven't we all.'

Cain rounded off their conversation by telling Marius why he had decided to sell his Mercedes.

'Safer in the Jeep,' said Marius. 'Have a good trip.'

Early that evening, Peter phoned Cain.

'Having spent most of the morning stuck in traffic,' said Peter, 'it took me ages to get into Constantia. Someone had dumped a dead body by Kirstenbosch Botanical Gardens, near some minister's residence.'

'Only one?'

'Apparently. Makes a change. I had a chat with one of the police officers. He hadn't seen the body, but he'd heard the victim had been shot in the stomach and left to bleed to death.'

'TIA,' Cain said.

Could it be Windows?

'The officer reckoned the killing had all the hallmarks of another gang-related killing.'

'He's probably right.'

'The rest of my day was subsequently delayed and dragged out. I've had enough. I'm staying in tonight having a beer.'

'Time to relax . . . By the way,' said Cain, 'I've gone back to driving my Jeep full time, I prefer the higher view, I sold the Mercedes.'

'Why not. Chat to you on the morrow,' Peter signed off.

'Have a good night.'

At the kitchen island Cain loaded a tray with 400g *filet mignon* steak, salad, and wine. His mobile rang, but there was no caller ID. He pressed the button. 'Hello.'

'Good evening, Cain. Minister Zokwana.'

'Good evening, Minister.'

'I would like to meet with you tomorrow.'

'Of course, Minister.'

Some time after the call, Cain was sitting in a rocking chair under the lemon tree out on the patio. Amidst the lingering aroma of the smouldering red oak from the cut-up karate *Bō* on the braai, he savoured the taste of seared steak in his mouth. He held a half-empty glass of red wine in one hand and a fully loaded Walther P99 in the other. He looked up towards the sky, closed his eyes, and started counting his options.

Friday – Diamonds Are Forever

Out on the Mercedes Bends, Cain drove his Jeep at a more leisurely pace.

When he arrived at Minister Nathi Zokwana's residence, he eyed the muzzle of a shotgun barrel coming through the Judas gate towards him. He buzzed down his window.

'Good afternoon, sir,' said the guard. 'How can I help you?'

'Afternoon,' said Cain, handing over his photo ID. 'I have an appointment with the Minister.'

'Thank you, sir.' The guard gave the Jeep's interior a cursory glance, compared the photo ID with the living image, handed it back, and politely confirmed, 'You are expected sir.'

The guard stepped back, gave the CCTV a wave, and the gates opened... Cain drove in at a snail's pace – like a true professional – taking in every detail of everything around him, getting his bearings, getting a degree of perspective. Checking the driveway ahead, he spotted the welcoming committee: two AK-47s resting in the arms of two *Suits*. One standing by the steps of the Georgian-style residence and the other waiting between a Mercedes M-class 4x4 and an S-class saloon. Cain parked in front of the visitors sign, exited his Jeep and walked towards the suit by the steps.

'Good afternoon sir,' said the suit, gesturing towards the main entrance.

'Afternoon. Thank you.'

Cain climbed the short flight of steps to be greeted by a butler waiting in the open doorway. Having been taken into an empty drawing room, Cain stood admiring a landscape painting, of a Victorian farmhouse estate – above the fireplace – viewed from a hillside. It could have been just about anywhere in South Africa; however, the numerous baobab trees on a green landscape placed the location in the Limpopo province, an area bordering Botswana, Zimbabwe, and Mozambique.

The door opened and Cain turned to see a Rhodesian ridgeback enter the room, closely followed by a well-dressed, portly, smiling Minister Zokwana. 'Good afternoon, Cain,' the minister announced in the friendliest of manners, as the dog obediently came to heel.

When Zokwana and Lastly had arrived in Johannesburg back in 1992, they had visited the Bishop and laid Lastly's twin brother to rest.

"Finally got you here," Lastly had lamented, looking down at the coffin in the grave.

"Rest in peace," Zokwana had added, with his usual look of faked compassion.

Lastly had turned to Zokwana to express his gratitude. "Thank you for making this possible sir."

"It was the least I could do," Zokwana had said, placing a comforting hand on the gunman's shoulder.

Finally closed the bloody lid on this one.

Without delay, Zokwana had soon ensconced himself on the peripheries of Government and set about entering the world of politics; a task made easier by a simple reality: a vast number of the politicians had their noses well and truly in the trough and their fingers in the till. In almost no time at all, Zokwana had jumped on the political bandwagon of bribery and corruption. It did not take long before he was walking the Government's corridors of vice and exploitation. A pathway on which, by fair means or (mainly) foul, he successfully gained himself a first step on the political ladder to power.

Additionally, the opportunities presented by the South African gangs were far too great to resist. Accompanied by Lastly – who never stopped thinking about the undercover police officer who had killed his twin brother – Zokwana negotiated with the notorious 33s gang lord.

'Minister Zokwana,' said Cain in the most affable of ways.

'Good afternoon.'

The minister shook hands, white man western-style, instead of black South African-style. 'Good to meet you.'

'Thank you for inviting me.'

Minister Zokwana rather theatrically pulled on a short chain, bringing his pocket-watch into the palm of his hand to check the time. 'Coffee? Or would you prefer English afternoon tea?'

'Coffee will be fine, thank you Minister.'

The minister turned to the butler waiting by the door. 'Coffee for two.'

Whilst exchanging pleasantries the Ridgeback stretched itself out on a Persian rug and the minister gestured towards one of the two Chesterfield sofas facing each other across a coffee table. 'Please take a seat.'

Some ten minutes later, the butler placed a tray on the coffee table, and as instructed, left the room, closing the door behind him.

Leaning forward, the minister poured the coffee and got down to business. 'Lastly and Windows informed me your Monday evening meeting went well.'

The minister's comment prompted Cain to remember how he had given them a script to help them out, suggested we allow ourselves to forgive and forget, mentioned after all we are friends now, and held out an olive branch by placing the Colt .45 on the passenger seat.

'Yes Minister,' said Cain, 'all went well.'

'Please accept my apologies for not phoning and meeting with you earlier. Unfortunately, a number of political situations required my immediate attention. I'm sure you will appreciate I cannot go into detail.'

Cain gave the minister a nod of understanding. 'Of course sir.'

'Now, before we go any further,' said the minister, glancing down at Cain's right hand, 'Please show me the scar on your wrist.'

The minister's comment, as expected, took Cain by surprise. He showed a look of bewilderment, perplexity, his professionalism had come to the fore. 'You know about it, I can't belie–'

'Take your time,' the minister politely interrupted. Cain pulled up the cuffs of his jacket and shirt, leant forward and held out his arm. 'I always wondered what it looked like,' the minister said, handing Cain his coffee.

'Now you know, Minister.'

'Are you prepared to tell me what happened in London on that night, back in 1992?'

Cain maintained his true professionalism; he showed a look of consternation. 'Unfortunately, there is always a difference between how circumstances make one look and what the reality is.'

The minister nodded appreciatively. 'That can often be the case.'

Cain would now bend the truth to protect himself, Agent Omara, and those around them.

'Everyone knew I was a photographer in London. However, nobody knew I was taking photos for the police on occasions, it was a well-kept secret. I was never told who I was photographing, or why. And when I finished, the police always took the films from me.

'When the shooting in the building overlooking the garden square began, I stayed hidden within the curtained, layered folds of a draped blackout, from where I had been taking photographs. I was terrified, I dived to the floor to avoid the bullets. A minute later, one of the gunman tore through the layered folds. I assumed he was seeking cover. He was then shot several times and–' Cain closed his eyes, took a deep breath. 'Sorry minister, the memory of the dying gunman falling on top of me, covering me with all his blood is too much to...'

'Please take your time,' the minister said sympathetically.

'The police officer pulled the dead gunman off me, and when I told him I had not been badly injured or shot he told me to leave. I simply did as I was told. I got up and hurried away... At the entrance to the building, I was scared. I crawled along the floor to take a look from behind the swing doors to see if there were any more gunmen outside. I saw a gun through the glass, but I had nowhere to hide, I wanted to live, not die. I threw myself against the door. The gun fired and I fell to the floor, I was terrified. When I heard the approaching police sirens, I thought there would be a shoot-out, so I ran away… If I had been a police officer, I would have had a gun in my hand, I would have stayed and fired back to save myself and help the other police officer.'

'How terrible for you.' Minister Zokwana took a moment to contemplate the implications of what Cain had confessed to. 'No gun,' the minister eventually said. 'Did you know where the police officer who was with you was from?'

'No idea. I had never met him before that night, and I never saw or met him again.'

'Was he a black man?'

'No, he was white.'

That's one in favour of Harry.

'You then made your escape?'

'Yes. I managed to kick open the back door of the building and jumped over the wall into an alleyway–'

'Where I saw you,' the minister interrupted.

Cain displayed a look of absolute surprise. 'You saw me? You were there sir?'

The minister nodded. 'I was the man in the taxi in the garden square. I was told to talk to the bodyguards. I was on the periphery of what was going on. Like you Cain, I was just there doing what I was told to.'

'I understand.'

'When the taxi dropped me off around the corner of the square,' said the minister, 'I hid in a pre-arranged doorway – listening to the gunfire – waiting for the gunmen in the getaway car to pick me up. Minutes later after hearing the single, isolated gunshot, I saw a white man wearing a bush hat and carrying a backpack slung over one shoulder, hurry out of an alleyway at the back of the building. He appeared to be covered in blood, so I followed him to where he got into the back of a car in a side street.'

'Incredible sir,' Cain said, showing a calculated look of amazement.

'I hid in the shadows, crouched down on the basement steps of one of the terraced houses. At the time, of course, I did not know the white man I had followed was the same one who had been shot at in the entrance to the building. It was not until I met up with the gunman, hours later, when he told me about the bush hat, the backpack and blood, I realised the man he had encountered in the doorway was the one I had followed. And now of course I know the white man was you Cain.'

'Unbelievable,' Cain replied shaking his head with a look of astonishment. 'I have to ask, how do—'

'Please allow me to continue.'

Cain showed a look of frustration, respect. 'Of course sir.'

The minister momentarily contemplated everything Cain had told him and asked, 'When you met with Windows and Lastly some ten days ago, did you not recognise him as the twin brother of one of the gunmen killed on the fourth floor of the building or realise he was the gunman who had taken the shot at you in the entrance?'

Cain looked horrified, shaking his head. 'The gunman was Lastly. Unbelievable. Thank God we didn't recognise each other. I can't even begin to comprehend what could have happened.'

'You did not see the faces of the gunmen on the night of the shootings.'

'No sir. The one who fell on top of me was in darkness and when he was dragged off me he was face down. I only saw the other dead man on the floor from a distance, when I left the room. And when I saw the gun in the doorway, as I said, I was on an adrenalin rush. I was terrified I couldn't take my eyes off it, I never saw the gunman's, sorry Lastly's, face. I cannot begin to explain how terrible I felt. It haunted me for months.'

'Now you know it was Lastly who fired the shot at you, will revenge be on the top of your list?'

'I seek no revenge. From what you have told me sir, and having met Lastly, he is out of my league. I can only hope your influence sir, in telling him what really happened will placate any anger he may have against me.'

The minister again, momentarily contemplated everything Cain had told him.

'Tell me, why were you not in the driver's seat of the car?'

'I was hiding. I was scared. The police officer who did the shooting was supposed to be right behind me, but he wasn't. Nobody ever told me where he went instead.'

'Why did the police officer, (Litter man) who was driving the transporter, point a gun at you.'

'I was a civilian, not a police officer. I was not supposed to be alone. He did not know me. I had to give him the password.'

The minister again momentarily contemplated everything Cain had told him.

'We have also now,' said the minister, 'finally met.'

'Minister, I have to congratulate you,' said Cain. He bowed his head respectfully. 'You have won the day sir.'

What a charade.

'Thank you,' said the minister, puffing himself up grandly. 'Winning the day is something I am used to.'

The minister went on to indulge in a narcissistic summary of his political career.

'Very impressive sir, 'Cain said with a look of admiration.

The minister smiled. 'Thank you. And to save you asking, I have not told Lastly it was you in the doorway, back in 1992.

'Thank you minister.'

A veiled threat: you mean you haven't told Lastly yet.

'That, for now, is all I am prepared to tell you.'

'As you wish, Minister.'

'Did you ever take photographs for the police again?'

'No sir. My nerves had been shattered. May I ask, how did you discover my identity?'

The minister smiled. 'Many months ago, I was coming out of a bank in City Bowl when I saw a white man walking along the street with a light backpack slung over one shoulder. The rhythm of his gait reminded me of the blood covered man I had followed all those years before on the streets of London. When the white man, wearing a short-sleeved shirt, wandered into St George's Mall and sat down at one of the al 'fresco restaurants, I got the person I was with to sit at the table next to him. I'm sure you can guess what happened next.'

'I ordered a beer or a coffee.'

'It was in the late of the morning. You ordered a coffee. And when you raised your hand to take a sip, the person watching you – on my behalf – saw the scar on your wrist.'

'Incredible.'

'So you went from taking photographs to trading in

diamonds. Quite a step.'

'I still take photographs sir. I spent several years in America before coming to South Africa. My life, especially when compared to yours, Minister,' said Cain, stroking the man's ego, 'is a rather long, somewhat boring story. But of course if you insist–'

Minister Zokwana held up his hands, bringing the subject of conversation to a close. He glanced up at the clock on the wall and turning to Cain he said, 'Enough of the past for now, let's look to our future.'

There were many questions Cain wanted to ask the minister. But he knew they would have to wait for another time. He had to just go with the flow to retain his assumed innocence.

'Of course sir,' Cain said. He removed the *brifka* containing the 3-carat rough diamond he had been given from his pocket and placed it next to his coffee on the table. 'Windows gave me this when we met.'

'I told him to.'

'It certainly convinced me I had to meet with you minister, to discuss – as Windows had informed me – a number of business proposals. I will be going up to Johannesburg next week, is there anything I can do for you while I'm there?'

The minister fidgeted on the sofa for a second, building up to a faked look of appreciation. 'Ah, yes, thank you for reminding me,' he said as he reached under the coffee table and handed Cain a small wooden jewellery box. 'Please open it.'

Inside, there were four rows of *brifkas*. Cain ran his finger along the rows to see the carat weight of the rough inside each one – 3.1, 4.2, 2.6, 2.4 – written, as always, in the bottom right-hand corner. However, there were no notations to indicate their colour and clarity.

The rough has only been weighed and not yet professionally graded.

The circled numbers written in the top right-hand corners, ran from 1 to 99. Cain glanced down at the 3-carat *brifka* he had placed on the coffee table and, exchanging looks with the minister, he asked, 'You wish me to make the number up to 100 sir?'

As Cain reached over for his coffee on the table, the

minister's hand pushed the sugar bowl towards him. 'Sweetener.' The minister smiled with a look of appreciation. The subjects of bribery and corruption were now firmly on the table.

Cain had no option – he had to accept the payoff. He picked up the 3-carat *brifka* – instead of the coffee – and without a word being spoken, he placed it back in his pocket. And the minister, in true African tradition, by pretending what had just happened never had, politely continued their conversation: 'Your reputation and that of your partner Moshe, goes before you. I trust you both implicitly. Please take the first ten *brifka*s with you up to Johannesburg. Arrange to have them cut and certified. Let's see what we have.'

'Thank you sir, I'll tell Moshe. We will not let you down.'

Cain closed the box, placed it on the table, and put the ten *brifkas* in his jacket pocket. To an outsider, the conversation would have appeared to be more than affable. However, Cain had recognised the veiled threat the minister had made:

"I trust you both implicitly," – was what the minister had said:

I will have you both killed if you cross me – was what the minister had meant.

'Who would have thought,' said the minister, 'all those years ago in 1992, in London, we would be sitting here face to face with each other in 2003, in South Africa.'

'Meeting you, Minister, has been an honour.'

The minister smiled appreciatively and got to his feet, bringing the meeting to an end. 'I'll call you at the end of next week to arrange a time and place to meet again.'

In the lobby, bidding their farewells, Cain said, 'A privilege to have met you sir, and be a part of your enterprise.'

'Good to have you on board.'

'Have a successful time in Johannesburg. My regards to Moshe.'

'Of course,' said Cain, realising the minister's last comment was another veiled threat. 'I look forward to meeting with you again sir, when I get back.'

The minister gestured towards the butler waiting by the door and they went their separate ways. Walking down the steps, Cain noticed the suit – standing several feet below, with an AK-47 resting in his arms, had something he should not have had, along with a somewhat amateur demeanour.

I'll mention it to Marius.

Driving back into Cape Town, Cain was thinking about all the questions a first meeting with the minister had not allowed him to ask.

Do you just want us to cut diamonds for you? I'll add it to the list.

Cain's mobile rang. Although the caller ID was blocked, he pressed the button. It was the Cleaning Crew. They had analysed Windows' and Gospel's blood from the dojo for any contagion.

'You're all clear. Have a good weekend,' said a familiar voice.

'You too.'

We live to die another day.

FIA – Fighting In Africa.

In the late of the afternoon, having spent some time examining the rough diamonds, Cain was relaxing on a sofa, having a beer, talking on the phone.

Marius said, 'The body found by Kirstenbosch Botanical Gardens, near the minister's residence, is Gospel.'

'Windows must have killed him.'

'As I mentioned to you yesterday, I'll let you know when it happens.'

'Touché.'

'Windows could not let it be known, one of his own 'troop' had shot him, let alone shot him and lived. He got rid of Gospel to stop the truth coming out and to preserve his reputation. But of course, the main reason would have been for revenge.'

'TIA.'

'The police are treating the death as just another gang-on-gang killing. Bearing in mind there are fifty murders a day in South Africa, the *Docket* the police have opened will not be a priority.'

Cain went on to outline the relative points of his meeting with the minister but, for the time being at least, he again excluded any mention of the link between himself, Lastly and Zokwana.

'So,' said Marius, 'the ten rough diamonds the minister has asked you to cut for him are of the highest quality, just like the 3-carat he has given you as an incentive.'

'Incentive, bribe, payoff,' said Cain, 'they all fit the minister's intentions.'

'Unfortunately, we are left wondering if the minister knows Windows was shot, who shot him and, if he is still alive, what is he doing now.'

'The minister was deliberately evasive. I'll have to wait until I get back from Johannesburg and we meet again before I can ask any more questions. By the way,' said Cain, 'when I left the minister's residence I recognised a tattoo on the neck of one of the armed *Suits* standing several feet below me on the steps. Could the minister really be employing members of the 33s?'

'Well spotted. Just to clarify, such a man would be a rogue freelancer. An ex-member of the 33s, brought down from the north. I have not been informed officially of their presence at the minister's residence. '

Marius' comment seemed a little unusual. Cain decided to delve a little further. 'So you have been informed unofficially?'

'Let's just say I am aware of a situation.'

'So would they be protecting or watching the minister?'

'If it develops into something more,' said Marius, 'I'll let you know.'

'OK. Have a good weekend.'

'Have a good trip.'

When Cain finished the home-delivered pepperoni pizza he took a seat in his leather recliner. He topped up his J&B over ice and shifted himself into Jerry's typical police officer mode to analyse what Minister Zokwana had said.

However, some time later, what Marius had not said left Cain contemplating who, if anyone, at the minister's residence could be informing Marius unofficially of what was going on.

Part Five

Johannesburg, South Africa

Out In The Beyond

Earth provides enough to satisfy every man's needs, but not every man's greed.

Mahatma Gandhi

21

Monday – Week Three

At Johannesburg's International Airport, Cain collected his suitcase, collected his Glock 27 from the security kiosk and headed for the exit, where an unmarked 4x4-shuttle was waiting for him.

As the 4x4 entered the grounds of the very private Sempre Aqui Hotel in the suburb of Primrose. Cain looked back to see the solid steel cantilever gate closing behind him. Located at the end of a quiet cul-de-sac, the Sempre Aqui's policy of absolute confidentially allowed their guests total anonymity and ensured very few outsiders even knew it was there.

As always, Célia – the owner of the Sempre Aqui – greeted Cain at reception to sign him in. Their conversation was interrupted when Cain's mobile received an SMS. He took a quick look. 'It's Neilson and Catarina in Maputo, confirming they will be arriving tomorrow at around 4pm.'

'Yes, they will,' Célia said, handing Cain the key to his room.

'Be good to see them again.'

Once in his room, Cain called Moshe. They would meet up in Jewel City on the following morning. In the evening, they would have dinner with Neilson and Catarina. And on Wednesday, they would make an early start to rendezvous with Kobus at his diamond mine in the depths of the distant desert lands.

'We'll play the rest of the week by ear,' Moshe said, rounding off their conversation.

'See you on the morrow.'

'Shalom.'

Cain placed his karate and tai chi kit into his backpack. It was only a fifteen-minute jog to the dojo where South Africa's greatest martial arts master would conduct his classes, starting at 7pm.

'Jewel City – it sure is the jewel in the crap,' said the taxi driver, glancing at Cain in his rear-view mirror, coming to the end of their twenty-minute drive.

'Sure is,' Cain agreed, looking out at the never-ending decay and degradation on the downtown streets around them. 'Such a shame.'

In the 1950's, the residents of the exclusive, northern suburb of Sandton enjoyed a very horsey lifestyle. A hay-day of a slightly different kind. A memorable decade when Sandton was dubbed Johannesburg's Mink & Manure Belt.

In the late 1990's, the post-apartheid abandonment of downtown Jo'burg, in favour of the trendy suburbs of the north – especially Sandton – was well and truly taking its toll. Simply put, more than just a bucket load of the 'proverbial' had been shovelled downtown.

In 2003, Jewel City – the diamond centre of South Africa – was at the heart of the now forsaken downtown *dung-heap*. The six-block mini-precinct of multi-storey office buildings, car parks and restaurants – centred around a crossroads – looked quite ordinary at first glance. However the perimeter walls, topped with razor wire, electric fencing and CCTV, told a different story. The 250-plus diamond merchants and traders premises inside were well protected. Totally inaccessible to the general public, with only one way in – and one way out.

'Keep the change,' Cain said, handing the taxi driver a number of Rand notes.

'Thank you, boss. Take care, them's all crooks in there.'

Cain grinned. 'Some of them.'

Cain walked towards the guards, armed with pump-action shotguns, waiting at the barrier. He removed his Serengeti shades, handed in his Glock 27 and passed through the airport-style security checks without incident. Next, he stepped into one of the hateful man-sized, steel turnstiles – people would occasionally get trapped inside them – and swiped his Merchant's ID card to gain release. He pressed the speed dial on his mobile. 'Morning Moshe, I've just passed through the pirate's gibbet,' he joked.

'I'll get the coffee ready.'

In the entrance hall of Moshe's building, more armed guards greeted Cain; there was another round of security checks and a second pirate's gibbet. On the top floor, he exited the elevator, stepped into the mantrap cubicle made of bulletproof glass, and swiped his ID one last time. In the hallway, he looked up at the CCTV. The buzzer sounded and the door opened.

As Moshe poured the coffee, Cain unbuttoned his shirt, retrieved the leather wallet strapped to his waist, opened it up, and placed ten *brifkas* on his desk.

'What have you got there?' Moshe said.

'On Friday, I met with Minister Zokwana at his residence in Cape Town.'

'Interesting.'

'It's a long story.'

Moshe placed his coffee on his own desk, sat down, and got himself comfortable in his grand old leather chair. 'Ready when you are.'

Cain detailed his encounters with Windows, Lastly, and Gospel, his meeting with Minister Zokwana, and his conversations with Marius. Once again, however, he excluded any mention of the link between himself, Lastly and Minister Zokwana. Cain then answered a session of questions.

Finally Moshe said, 'I think it is fair to say the minister knows more about us than he's letting on. I agree with you, his comments have an underlying threat for both of us.' Moshe got to his feet. 'More coffee?'

'Good idea,' said Cain, checking the time on his wrist. 'Elevenses,' he announced, removing the bag of doughnuts from his backpack. 'Courtesy of the Sempre Aqui.'

As they finished their brunch, Cain held out a clenched fist. 'Present for you,' he said, dropping a *brifka* into Moshe's hand.

'I'll take a guess,' said Moshe, noting the number three written in the bottom right-hand corner. 'It's the *sweetener* the minister gave you.'

Cain grinned. 'The same one Windows originally gave me when I was in his Land Rover. Five minutes with a nail file should get it into shape.'

'I was just thinking the same,' Moshe, said with a now more often smile.

Hearing the fax machine burst into life, Cain was again reminded of how Moshe had reopened his world of communication.

'Go take a look,' Moshe said as he turned in his chair to his merchant's bench. Leaning forward, he flicked a switch and delved into the *brifka*. Cain watched the grand master resting his elbows on the velvet placemat in front of him and holding his vintage 10x magnifying loupe up to his eye to examine the 3-carat rough diamond clasped in tweezers.

Knowing it was best not to interrupt Moshe, Cain wandered over to the fax machine to retrieve the newly arrived pages. He sat at his desk, reading through the final rough diamond stock list from Kobus before he powered up his laptop to check his emails.

Some time later, Moshe turned to Cain with tweezers in hand. 'I agree with you. This sweetener and the ten rough he has asked us to cut for him are, at first glance, all of the highest quality.'

They were both on the verge of entering a world they had little insight into: where did the minister get the diamonds? What were the minister's business proposals? And where were Windows and Lastly?

'It is pointless speculating,' Moshe sighed, turning back to his desk.

'Next time we meet I'll have to find out a great deal more.'

'Indeed,' said Moshe. 'Now, let's take a look at our agenda.'

Both men looked down at their diaries and began to discuss their commitments for the days and weeks ahead.

Tuesday Evening

On the terrace of the Sempre Aqui, Cain and Moshe were sitting at a table.

Cain checked the time on his Breitling: 6pm. Two jet-black faces appeared on the terrace and rushed towards them. Cain and Moshe immediately got to their feet. Neilson and his wife,

Catarina, from Mozambique had arrived.

'Hey boys. How yooo doo-in?' Neilson said.

And whilst exchanging a stream of welcoming comments, pleasantries and humour they all hugged and kissed in the – unavoidably – all-embracing, wonderful, African Way.

Cain and Moshe had first met Neilson and Catarina at the bar of the Sempre Aqui, where Célia had introduced them. They'd all ended up having a wonderfully entertaining dinner together, an evening that turned out to be a prelude to doing business. Neilson was a successful entrepreneur who had connections in various countries.

In the months that followed, Neilson and Catarina came to be among Cain and Moshe's most important clients so whenever they visited Jo'burg, they would always all meet up to have lunch or dinner and chat about a carat or two.

On a business trip to Cape Town, Neilson and Catarina had stayed at the Mount Nelson Hotel, from where Cain and Moshe had acted as tour guides around the 'Mother City' and in the cable car to the top of Table Mountain. On their last night, they enjoyed dinner at the Miller's Thumb, a renowned seafood restaurant in Tamboerscloof. In return, Cain and Moshe accepted an invitation to visit Neilson and Catarina in Maputo.

Neilson had played an active part in the long Mozambique civil war, from 1977 to 1992. Experience that occasionally inspired an entertaining story of adventure or daring-do. However, Cain and Moshe were never really sure which side – *FRELIMO* or *RENAMO* – Neilson had been on: perhaps it had been both.

With their hugs and kisses – but not the banter – coming to an end, the content professionals settled themselves around the table and ordered their drinks.

It would be an enjoyable evening, playing catch-up – and when discussing a time and place to have lunch or dinner, Neilson and Catarina would, as always, have a *carat* of a slightly different kind on their menu.

Early next morning, Moshe drove onto the freeway, aiming his Toyota 4Runner towards the desert. It would be a near five-hour drive to Kobus' diamond mine, across what to some was known as Afrikaans country, by others: diamond country, and by Cain, bandit country.

From the gun bag on the back seat Cain removed two Mossberg, pump-action shotguns and laid them with the muzzles resting in the footwells. The two men instinctively felt for the Berettas in their shoulder holsters and gave each other a nod.

'Let's hope it's only time we have to kill today,' Cain said.

'Indeed.'

'How much did Neilson give you last night before you left?'

'Sixpence.'

Cain grinned. 'Don't spend it all at once.'

'It was a banker's draft for US$75,000.'

'What a surprise.'

'From Mozambique to China,' said Moshe, moving the subject of conversation on to other things. 'All is going well.'

'It certainly is.'

'When I was talking to Greg he mentioned again how white faces in the investment diamond showroom always arouse a great deal of interest, reminding customers of their connection to the South African diamond business, thereby enhancing our reputation.'

'No other investment diamond showroom in China has those credentials.'

'And being in Guangzhou, a city of 12 million in a country of 1.3 billion. We're doing well.'

Two hours into the journey, as Moshe skirted the Toyota around the community of Sandorp, Cain dialled a number on a burner cell phone.

Kobus answered, 'Yes?'

'Leaving.'

'Charlie Echo.'

'Charlie Echo,' Cain repeated – confirming the password – and the line went dead.

Ten kilometres further on, the Toyota turned onto the desert trails. All Cain and Moshe had to do now was avoid at all costs any entanglement with the fifteen thousand-strong Umthi Township folk, who lived in the heart of bandit country. Cain scoured the horizon.

Halfway there.

On reaching the end of their journey, Moshe drove the Toyota off the track and through an unmarked, broken gate, between collapsed fencing. They were three kilometres in when they stopped to take a leak and take a look. At the base of a three-hundred-metre elliptical quarry, two Volvo crawler excavators were loading six-wheelers with the contents from the pipe.

Two kilometres further on, the Toyota circled the main compound of men and machinery and parked in a quieter spot, at the end of a line of 4x4s and half a dozen Portakabins.

As Cain and Moshe stepped out into the 30°C heat of the day, a guard approached them. Seeing faces he recognised, he smiled but kept his shotgun at the ready. 'Morning boss.'

'Bravo Delta,' Cain said – instead of Charlie Echo – giving the pre-arranged password of the day. It was one of many simple variables used to thwart those who might have been listening to any cell phone communications.

'Morning,' Moshe said.

The guard nodded and lifted the tailgate of the Toyota – just to make sure no hijackers were on board – and continued on his way.

Cain and Moshe removed the aluminium cases from the back and set off to meet their host. Outside one of the Portacabins Kobus, his two sons, and one of his managers were all sitting in the shade of a patio-style umbrella on old sofas and armchairs around a table, playing a game and having a non-alcoholic drink.

Kobus was a married Afrikaner who – with his two sons, in their twenties – owned the independent diamond mine. He was a man of the utmost integrity who had been introduced to Moshe by Joseph, the old master from Florida.

Kobus' youngest son, with the biggest of smiles on his face, won the game.

'Eish, not again,' his elder brother said to a chorus of jokes and gibes. The players collected up the cards, 'cash', dice, and board on the table and placed them back in the Monopoly box, bringing the session to an end.

'Morning,' Moshe called out, gaining everyone's attention.

Kobus turned to greet his friends in Afrikaans:

'*Môre goed om jou te sien* (Morning good to see you).'

And with everyone getting to their feet, the greetings began.

Kobus took Cain and Moshe into his office, where maps, charts, and graphics flanked the framed aerial photograph of Kobus' kingdom on the wall. A Remington 12-gauge pump-action shotgun, leaning against the side of Kobus' desk, was always at the ready. Behind it, his old Chesterfield captain's chair was leaning somewhat precariously to one side in everlasting tribute to the teenage antics of his sons.

On the merchant's bench in the middle of the diamond room, the instruments and devices catered for the critical analysis of what some might say came from the 'rough' end of town. Whereas, back in Jewel City, Moshe's diamond room satisfied the sophisticated expectations of clients who preferred to stay on a more 'polished' side of the street.

Cain and Moshe opened their aluminium cases while Kobus took his trays of rough from his wall safe, placed them on the bench, and went to the fridge to get three bottles of water.

All three men took their seats. Kobus opened a dossier, flicked a few switches, and Moshe selected one of the rough and raised his merchant's loupe to his eye. Kobus was moving with the times, using modern technology, whereas Moshe was still strolling on the periphery of a bygone era. The only chips he wanted were fried ones wrapped in a newspaper with cod. Cain momentarily wondered how long it would be before Moshe, now the owner of a fax and phone, got a laptop.

Moshe selected his final rough diamond. 'That's it,' he said. All three men gave their eyes a welcome rub, got to their feet, and shook hands. Kobus checked the time on the clock on the wall: the process had taken ninety minutes. He picked up a walkie-talkie and ordered three beers.

As Moshe counted out the cash, Kobus' eldest son, Hennie, entered the diamond room, handed out the cans and switched on the money-counting machine. When Kobus took a phone call, Cain along with Moshe stepped outside to give Kobus some privacy. They sat in the shade to finish their beers. When Kobus eventually exited the diamond room he looked in fine spirits, but the few quiet words shared with Hennie by the door told another story.

'Everything OK?' Moshe enquired.

Kobus hesitated, unable to disguise a momentary look of concern. Moshe motioned to Kobus and Hennie to join him and spill the beans.

The phone call had been from a new client who had visited the mine a week earlier and left a cash deposit on the rough he wanted to purchase, now secured in a locked and signed diamond case. However, the new client was now demanding an immediate delivery to Jo'burg.

Under normal circumstances, Kobus would have taken any change of plan in his stride, but this was a new client, making an unprecedented demand. It was a circumstance he had never been confronted with before, especially at the present time, when he was temporarily short-staffed.

Moshe knew Kobus was thinking of something he would never ask for, because of all the inherent dangers it involved. Moshe glanced at Cain, who gave him a nod, and they made their offer. 'Why not travel back with us?'

Cain grinned, crushing his can. 'Cost you a beer.'

Moshe placed a comforting hand on Kobus' shoulder. 'Someone has to keep an eye on you.'

Relief showed on Kobus' face. 'Thank you, gentlemen,' he sighed and, turning to Hennie, he said, 'We'll go. Moshe and Cain will ride shotgun.'

Over by the Toyota, Cain handed Moshe his Kevlar vest and put on his own. 'This is an unusual situation.'

'Indeed,' Moshe agreed.

Cain reached into the back of the Toyota and pulled out an Uzi sub-machine gun. He racked the slide, sending the first round into the chamber. 'Lock and load.'

Some forty-minutes later Moshe looked in his rear-view mirrors. 'We have company.'

Cain turned to take a look out of the rear window, but the speeding Toyota's trail of swirling dust and flying sand stretched far and wide, obscuring the view.

'Just the one vehicle?' Cain queried.

Moshe stared at the mirror again. 'I can see only one vehicle; it's on the fringes of our dust trail, trying to stay out of sight.'

Cain checked the time on the cheap watch on his wrist. 'We just happen to be bang in the middle of bandit country.'

Moshe glanced down at the speedometer. 'At this speed, anyone else would be happy to stay back in the clear air, behind us.'

The inference was not lost on Cain. He picked up the walkie-talkie. 'Two calling one.'

'One receiving,' Kobus responded.

'We see you half a mile ahead. We have a vehicle closing in on us, we will check it out.'

Kobus immediately heeded the inference. 'We're looking for blockers ahead. We'll drop our speed by twenty.'

'Your speed down by twenty. Catch you when we can.'

Cain checked the Uzi before reaching over and delving into the bag on the back seat. He pulled out what looked like a pair of very large pince-nez spectacle frames, welded to the top of a large column of steel acting as a 'nose'.

Cain handed the 'nose' to Moshe, who dropped it into the slot of his reinforced driver's door, leaving the pince-nez specs peering out through the base of the window. Cain slipped the muzzles of both the Mossberg's barrels into the pince-nez.

Both men put their earplugs in before Cain held the wheel, allowing Moshe to cover both barrels with a black cloth and the *pince-nez* with the cuff of his shirt. Moshe then checked his mirrors again. 'It's a Pajero.'

'Wankers.'

'Why do you say that?'

'Pajero is Spanish for wanker.'

'The wankers have switched their headlights on to full beam,' said Moshe. 'They're coming.'

'We'll all come together, but not in the biblical sense.'

Moshe steered left, giving the Pajero room to come along

side.

Cain turned in his seat, with the Uzi at the ready, watching the Pajero gaining ground. 'Let's see if they take the bait.'

Moshe nodded in agreement, knowing his life now depended on Cain's instinctive reactions.

As the speeding Pajero came alongside; both vehicles started tunnelling into the wake of the swirling dust and dirt – from Kobus' Land Cruiser ahead – into a *Desert Storm.* All visions would now be impaired.

'The Pajero's windows are still up,' said Cain. 'Shotguns.'

In the blink of an eye, Cain laid the Uzi in his lap and placed his hands around both the Mossberg's stocks with his fingers coaxing the triggers. The Pajero's front passenger window buzzed down slowly, and Moshe glanced to his right to take a look. A black man, wearing a bush-style hat and huge sunglasses, gave Moshe the biggest of smiles, showing his teeth, and saluted him with the friendliest of waves. In response, Moshe buzzed down his window, a sign of good faith, before raising a hand as a casual salute – and Cain opened fire.

> When death and danger are upon you, the slow-motion
> movie in the mind distorts time.
> What may seem like an eternity will, in the event, only
> be a second . . . or nineteen.

The Mossberg's salvo of Hunter-4 buckshot – used to bring down 'game' – wiped away the big smile on the face of the Pajero's front-seat gunman: his sunglasses disintegrated, his skull fragmented, and his bush-style hat was blown away. The tinted glass of the Pajero's back-door then shattered, the back-seat gunman dived for cover, and a walkie-talkie fell to the floor.

'Jesus fuckin' Christ,' the blood-splattered Pajero driver screamed, glancing down at his passenger's shattered head – spewing brain, blood, and bone – cradled against him. As he tried to heave the body away, his hand inadvertently wrenched the steering wheel. The Pajero instantly swerved too sharply, tripped off the track, the tyres dug in, and it somersaulted into the air.

'You fuckin' idiot!' the backseat gunman shouted as he hit

the roof, causing him to pull the trigger of his AK-47. Spiralling rounds went into the air, several hit the Toyota, but Moshe didn't even flinch – and then he did.

Tick-Tock… Twenty seconds. Time had moved on…
and the Toyota came to a stop.

Looking at the Pajero on its roof with wheels spinning in the air, Moshe said, 'We should check it out, but we need to stay close to Kobus.'

'We do,' said Cain, handing Moshe the Uzi. 'Do it.'

Moshe took aim and bullets punctured the Pajero's tyres while others penetrated the interior.

Kobus' voice came back on the walkie-talkie, 'One calling two.'

'Two receiving.'

'We have blockers on the horizon.'

'We're done here,' said Cain. 'We're on our way.'

'Catch us when you can.'

Hearing what had been said, Moshe immediately handed the Uzi back to Cain and floored the Toyota's accelerator. Cain looked over his shoulder out of the rear window, but the speeding Toyota's trail of swirling dust and flying sand again stretched far and wide, obscuring his view. 'Do you think anyone was still alive?'

'I saw a leg move in the back.'

'A long walk.'

As Cain pulled the Mossberg's muzzles out of the pince-nez, he saw blood on the barrels. 'Moshe, you've been hit,' he exclaimed. 'You–'

'Just a flesh wound to the top of my arm,' Moshe interrupted. 'I'm OK. Tie the black cloth we used to cover the shotguns barrels around it to stem the bleeding.'

Cain leant around Moshe to do the necessary. 'The bullet's gone in and out,' he said. 'Nothing serious – you'll probably have to delay any desires to become a member of the Pajero Club for a few days.'

'Would that be a stroke of good luck or bad luck?'

Cain grinned – it was a moment's respite from the tension.

'Touché.'

Closing in on Kobus' Land Cruiser ahead, Moshe switched off the air-con, checked his mirrors again, and the first specks of sand tapped the windscreen.

Miles ahead, one of the blockers was bawling into his walkie-talkie, trying to reach his associates in the Pajero but getting no response. 'Jesus shit,' he bawled.

'Can you see it?' another asked.

The track, stretching to the horizon and beyond, kept the Toyota hidden in the wake of the swirling dust and dirt from Kobus' Land Cruiser. The blocker lowered his binoculars. 'I can't see if it's our Pajero behind the Land Cruiser or the white shits in the Toyota. Our people were supposed to flash their lights to let us know they were in position.'

Fear enveloped the blockers. 'Why's the fuckin' gunfire stopped?'

Cain spoke again with Kobus on the walkie-talkie. 'We're now behind you. We can see your rear fog lights.'

'Understood.'

Kobus turned to Hennie, who was driving. 'We are now in your hands son.'

The two 4x4s scythed their way across the desert floor, bearing down on the blockers. Kobus pressed the button. 'Thirty seconds to go.'

'Thirty seconds, ready,' Cain confirmed.

'We are going two o'clock right.'

'You are going two o'clock right, understood. We will maintain twelve o'clock straight and stop.' Cain turned to Moshe. 'On the mark twelve o'clock straight, handbrake turn, my side on. You sure your arm is OK?'

Moshe instinctively flexed his fingers and thumb. 'All OK.'

Kobus released the safety on his Uzi and turned to speak to his two lieutenants in the back. 'Ready, men?' he said with a nod.

'Ready, boss.'

Cain buzzed down his window. The traversing winds had their expected effect. He was left battling the swirling dust and dirt. He leveraged himself with a foot against the 'dash', with the Uzi jammed against his chest – and waited.

Out of desperation, the blockers opened fire on the approaching Land Cruiser. Kobus pressed the button. 'One calling, we are close. On the count: 3,2,1, NOW!'

The Land Cruiser instantly veered to the right, enabling Kobus and his crew to rake the roadblock with automatic fire. The Toyota blasted out of the dust trail, handbrake-turned side on and, through an erupting wave of dust and sand, Cain let rip with the Uzi. The blockers, realising they were outflanked and outgunned, tried to make a run for it. But they ran out of luck instead.

Kobus, with one of his lieutenants by his side, stepped out from between the blockers' vehicles. 'All dead,' Kobus shouted.

'All dead,' Cain called out.

The rumbling of the returning Land Cruiser and the blasting of its horn immediately gained everyone's attention. It skidded to a stop and the driver's door opened, 'Boss, boss, help,' the other lieutenant shouted as loudly as he could.

'Dear God, no!' Kobus shouted, rushing towards his blood-covered son Hennie, who was staggering forward out of the driver's door. And with his arms outstretched, he fell into his father's arms. 'Keep him up, keep his wounds away from the sand,' Kobus cried.

'Got it boss, we're here!'

Within minutes, the Land Cruiser's tailgate was up and the back seats were down. Cain stared at Kobus and his lieutenants as they tended to Hennie's wounds, stemming the flow of blood, saving his life. Hennie had taken a hit to his chest, and shrapnel to a leg. Although the dark colour of his blood did not bode well, he remained conscious – a positive sign.

Clasping Hennie's hand, Kobus pleaded, 'Stay with me son. You're going to be OK. We're getting you to the doctor.'

Cain saw Hennie's hand squeeze his father's hand. Seconds later, Kobus was ready to go.

He looked to one of his lieutenants. 'You drive.'

His other lieutenant raised a hand. 'I know what to do Boss. No problem.'

Kobus had been so totally consumed with concern for his son, it was only when he looked out at Cain did he realise they were one man short. 'No, not Moshe!' he gasped.

'Moshe is OK,' said Cain reassuringly, 'it's just a flesh wound to his arm. I'll take care of him. Now go Kobus, Hennie is the priority.'

Before Kobus could do or say anything more, Cain closed the Land Cruiser's tailgate and ran to the side to get away from the impending swirling dust and sand.

'Go!' Kobus cried, and the lieutenant at the wheel immediately floored the accelerator.

Minutes later, Moshe was sitting in the sand in the shade of his Toyota waiting for Cain to finish tending his wound. As Cain finished putting a sling round his arm Moshe said, 'We will have to go back to the Pajero. We must gather all the evidence we can to help Kobus find out who is responsible.'

'You mentioned you saw a leg move in the Pajero.'

'Just the one.'

'Let's go take a walk on the wild side.'

'I think,' said Moshe, 'I would prefer you to drive us there.'

Cain grinned, helping Moshe get to his feet.

Having back-tracked along their desert path, Cain and Moshe stood by the Pajero: it had been tipped back over onto its bullet ridden flat tyres. The driver had been left hanging out over the side of his open door; an almost headless passenger was lying across the front seats, and flies in their droves were already feasting on the leftovers. Moshe looked up at the Cape griffon vultures circling above the wreck. Their eight-foot wingspans silhouetted against the afternoon sun. 'They didn't waste any time getting here.'

'We're not far from their breeding ground,' said Cain, 'in the Magaliesberg Mountains.'

Moshe pointed with his good arm at a dust trail being left by a vehicle in the distance. 'We are too late.'

'Even when we shoot first and ask questions later, some bastard still gets away.'

'Let's do it,' Moshe said, handing Cain a pair of medical gloves from the first aid kit.

'I'll do the heavy lifting.'

'Thank you.'

The blood-saturated sand beneath the driver's door told Cain and Moshe all they needed to know: the driver hanging out over the side with a bullet to the head had been finished off by his own people. On the passenger's side, Cain dragged the headless body out onto the desert floor, checked the pockets and, finding nothing, he started searching the interior. Under the passenger seat he found a walkie-talkie. He could see it had taken a few hits and knocks and after trying a button or two, he could see it no longer worked. Placing it on the roof, he opened the back door. The butt of a semi-automatic pistol wedged between the driver's seat and centre console caught his eye. He pulled the blood-soaked pistol out of its jam; he felt coarseness against his fingertips and stared down at a strike pad from a box of matches, stuck on the side of the slide of the Colt .45. He got out of the Pajero, dropped the Colt's mag and racked the slide: a bullet popped out of the chamber and fell to the ground. He emptied the mag, slipped it back into place, and looked up at the remnants of the dust trail, tipping over the horizon. 'Lastly, you bastard,' he said quietly.

Moshe looked to Cain from under the tailgate. 'Did you say something?'

'Just thinking out loud. Tell you in a sec.'

Cain took the walkie-talkie off the Pajero's roof and tossed it onto the dash. *Clunk.*

The sound, the dead bodies, the location, jogged Cain's memory. 'Tell me Moshe, did you by any chance ever see General Stormin' Norman Schwarzkopf doing one of his press conferences?'

Moshe stared out at the skyline. He appeared to be deep in thought, contemplating what to say… 'We've just had our own Operation Desert Storm,' he said. 'I once met General Schwarzkopf.'

'Really?' said Cain with a look of amazement. 'If you don't mind me asking. How?'

'Our old friend in Florida introduced me.'

Cain remembered Joseph's tattooed arm and silently mouthed 'MOSSAD.'

Moshe read Cain's lips. 'That's the one.'

'Joseph never told me.'

Cain and Moshe looked at each other for a long few seconds and Cain silently acknowledged the sacrosanct confidence Moshe had shared with him.

'I never told you,' said Moshe. 'When I left Israel, it was four weeks before I arrived in New York.'

'Always good to take the scenic route.'

'Indeed it is.'

'Especially when you have time to kill.'

Moshe showed a rarity, he smiled. 'Time to go.'

As the Toyota moved away, the waiting vultures scurried across the desert floor while others on the wing spiralled down to join the feast.

'Meals on wheels,' Cain said.

'Indeed.'

Cain handed Moshe the Colt .45. The strike pad on the slide told Moshe what he needed to know. 'Lastly.'

Arriving back at the blockers' last stand, more winged shadows were already in attendance, in the air and on the sand. Kobus' second lieutenant was waiting in the shade of a bullet-riddled vehicle next to plastic bags and a pile of weapons lying in the sand. Cain stopped the Toyota beside him, opened the driver's door and stepped out. 'All done?'

'Yes boss, I got everything.'

'Let's load up.'

An hour later, Cain glanced down again at the time on the clock on the dash. 'Kobus should be there by now.'

Moshe said, 'He will get Hennie to the doctor in time.'

The lieutenant, sitting on the back seat, unscrewed more bottles of water, passed them round, and checked Moshe's arm again. 'Hennie will be OK, yes boss?'

'Hennie will be OK,' Moshe answered with a reassuring look.

In the rear-view mirror, Cain could see the look of desperation on the face of the lone lieutenant. The two lieutenants had grown up with Hennie and his younger brother, they were all life-long friends. 'You know better than anyone,' said Cain, 'Hennie is like his father, like you, strong as an elephant.'

The lieutenant immediately felt reassured. 'Yes, boss.'

'Have a swig of my Lucozade in the esky. It'll make you feel better.'

'Thank you, boss.'

On the outskirts of Sandorp, Cain drove the Toyota into a warehouse to be greeted by a hive of activity. An inspection team soon lifted the tailgate and started checking through everything taken from the blockers and their accomplices, bodies, and vehicles. All the guns used by Kobus, his son, his lieutenants, Cain, and Moshe were collected – along with Lastly's Colt .45 – and thrown into a burning furnace.

Kobus came out of a side room, rolling down his sleeve to cover the plaster on his arm. Silence descended on the warehouse as all eyes turned to Kobus. He took a long, deep breath and sighed, 'Hennie has lost a lot of blood. The doctor has removed the shrapnel from his legs and stitched the nick in his artery. His chest wound is not serious. Thank God, he will be OK.'

The warehouse erupted into a chorus of cheering, applause, and whistling. Everyone could see the palpable look of relief on Kobus' face as he raised an arm and waited for the cheering to die down. '*Dankie* (Thank you), *dankie, dankie*,' he said, with a deep sense of gratitude. Catching sight of Cain and Moshe with his arm in a sling, Kobus gave them a special look of appreciation and they wandered over.

'Good to hear Hennie is on the road to recovery,' Moshe said with a sigh of relief.

'Glad you are safe,' said Kobus. 'Let's get the doctor to have a look at your arm.'

While Moshe was having his wound stitched, Cain told Kobus what had happened to the Pajero. Kobus eventually laughed, easing the tension of the past few hours. 'Wankers! I won't forget that one.'

Thirty minutes later, one of the Afrikaners, having inspected the Toyota and Land Cruiser, called Kobus over. After a short conversation Kobus beckoned Cain and Moshe to join them. Kobus held out his hand and placed a now broken tracking device into Moshe's palm. 'It was found under your Toyota.'

Moshe and Cain stared in disbelief – and down the barrel of

a pistol.

Cain instinctively flexed his fingers as Kobus touched the forearm of the Afrikaner aiming the pistol and shook his head.

'Thank you for being so cautious, but not today.'

The Afrikaner reluctantly relaxed his finger on the trigger. Killing Moshe would have been a simple case of payback for treachery, while terminating the Englishman would have been a welcome reprisal for the death of his ancestors, killed by the English more than a hundred years ago in the Boer Wars. The Afrikaner lowered his pistol.

The look on the Afrikaner's face, reminded Cain of what he had often said: 'Will they ever let bygones be bygones?'

'Let's have a talk,' Kobus said, leading the way. In the warehouse office, accompanied by a bottle of the Afrikaner's favourite Richelieu brandy, a bucket of ice, and cans of coke, the three men sat at a table and went through the day's events. It took quite a while. They all eventually came to the same conclusion, regardless of the tracking device under the Toyota, there had to be an informant at Kobus' mine to make sure the diamonds and cash were on board the vehicles. All three men looked at the bags and cases on the table next to them, containing cash and rough to the value of US$2m plus.

Kobus surmised, 'The informant could only have made a call to confirm it.' However, for the time being at least, Kobus had enough on his plate. Finding the mole would have to wait for another day. 'I'll leave you to find out who and why the tracking device was placed under your Toyota.'

Outside in the light of the late afternoon, Kobus pointed to a 4x4. 'This is a rental,' he said, handing the keys to Cain.

'Much appreciated.'

'Thank you my friend,' Moshe added.

'Once your Toyota is repaired,' said Kobus, 'I will have it delivered to you in Jo'burg.'

'Send me the bill when—'

Kobus raised his hands and Moshe fell silent. 'I will pay the bill.'

Kobus gave his two lieutenants a wave and they walked over to join them. The lieutenants said their farewells, shook hands, South African black man-style – double grip, two position hold, three-time crunch – and with a nod from Kobus they headed off to be with Hennie.

Moshe, Cain and Kobus all embraced. '*Dankie, dankie* (Thank you, thank you),' said Kobus. '*Gaan goed* (Go well).'

On their way back to Jo'burg, Cain speculated, 'I wonder how long it will take Kobus to find the mole?'

'There is an old Sicilian proverb: 'revenge is a season in hell'.'

Cain glanced sideways. 'Talking of revenge, there's something I want to tell you.'

Moshe took a somewhat theatrical look at his watch. 'Since we only have a nearly two-hour drive ahead, you don't have much time.'

'Are you sitting comfortably?'

'Indeed I am.'

'Once upon a time, back in London, I used to occasionally take pictures for a Government intelligence agency. It resulted in me killing a man who was . . .' Cain sighed, 'You're going to love this one – Lastly's twin brother.'

Thursday – Summary

Talking on the phone to Marius Cain rounded off his synopsis of the attack in bandit country.

'At least,' said Marius, 'you and everyone else are all in one piece, well, just about.'

'Thankfully.'

'Moshe staying in the Sempre Aqui Hotel for the next week is a good idea.'

'Just until his arm is out of the sling. Better to be safe than sorry.'

'Give him my regards when he wakes up.'

'Will do.'

'By the way, I had one of my people take their dog for a walk, in the park across the drive from your 'fortress' on Tuesday morning and yesterday afternoon. On both occasions, there was no sign of Smokey or anyone loitering.'

'Thank you for checking.'

'Pleasure. However, the supposed cigarette butts Smokey left behind are actually spliffs.'

'Bergies don't have the money to buy spliffs.'

'So Smokey, whoever he is–'

'Is not a bergie.'

'We obviously have quite a lot to talk about when you get back. Let's meet up on Monday.'

'OK.'

'Take care.'

Cain drove Moshe, in the rental 4x4, to have lunch with Neilson and Catarina.

Moshe's arm in a sling inspired a number of humorous comments and, when he mentioned he'd fallen down a flight of stairs, no one pried further.

Moshe said, 'I'm afraid your delivery will be delayed by a few days. Please accept my sincere apologies, lunch is on me.'

'You definitely took a *step* in the wrong direction,' said Neilson. 'No rush.'

Catarina placed a hand on Neilson's arm. 'So you will not have to take an extra *trip* yourself?'

And with smiles all round, the waiter arrived at the table. Lunch is served.

They all enjoyed their usual relaxing time together, talking business and pleasure, before Neilson and Catarina's taxi arrived to take them to the airport.

Back in the Sempre Aqui, Moshe and Cain made a conference-style cell phone call to Kobus… Hennie was well on the road to recovery. Kobus' people had circulated rumours about how the shootings were just another gang-on-gang killing spree which had happened, either on Tuesday evening or Wednesday morning. A guard Kobus had employed just a couple of months ago had gone missing. And the supposed new client he was delivering the diamonds to was now, not so unexpectedly, unavailable – more than just coincidence they all surmised. Rounding off their call, Kobus said, 'I'll be keeping the cash deposit the supposed new client left with me to help pay for everything that's happened. Talk to you later.'

Cain and Moshe sat at a table in a quiet corner of the Sempre

Aqui gardens, having a drink, having a chat – out of sight, out of mind.

'Because you have not heard from the minister,' said Moshe, 'let's not waste our time speculating about if or how he could have been involved in the planning of the attack.'

'Or why Lastly's Colt .45 was in the Pajero.'

'Indeed. Let's allow the minister another 24-hrs to respond.'

'Why not. Cheers.'

Friday

In the Sempre Aqui, Cain and Moshe finished reading the stories about the shoot-out in bandit country in the evening newspapers.

'Same as the daily papers,' said Cain. 'Just another gang-on-gang killing spree.'

'Looks as if the rumours put out by Kobus' people had the desired effect.'

'I doubt police will waste too much time on it. The *Docket* will soon be closed.'

'I'll give Kobus a call over the weekend to congratulate him and have a chat.'

Cain asked, 'You sure you don't want to come down to Cape Town with me?'

'I'll be fully occupied.'

'What are you up to?'

Moshe smiled. 'The laptop Célia ordered for me will be delivered tomorrow morning.'

Cain showed a look of absolute amazement. 'Really?'

'I will be having daily classes with a young lady. Célia has arranged it all for me.'

'Congratulations.'

'I did it all,' said Moshe, 'when you went out to fill the rental 4x4 with petrol and checked it over for me in case I needed to drive it next week.'

'I look forward to receiving my first email from you.' Cain checked the time on his Breitling. 'Time to go.'

Moshe stood up. 'We should have heard from the minister.'

'He has now had more than enough time to respond.'

'Don't hold your breath.'

'Any respect I may have had for him has gone. From now on I'm just going to refer to him as Zokwana.'

'Don't forget to give your Jeep the once-over for any bugs – and of course, let me know if you hear from, err, what's his name, oh yes, Zokwana.'

Cain grinned. 'Will do,' he said, shaking hands with Moshe, injured-man-style. 'Talk to you tomorrow. See you a week on Sunday.'

'Take care.'

Cain walked down to the unmarked 4x4-shuttle – with his suitcase in the back – waiting to take him to the airport.

Part Six

Returning to Cape Town

Actions speak louder than words.

Abraham Lincoln

22

Blade – A Cut Above The Rest

Early on Saturday morning, Cain found a tracking device under his Jeep.

He drove out to an industrial parking lot, where he placed the bug onto the back of a truck about to leave for Windhoek, the capital of Namibia, 1500km away.

Follow that one.

After getting back to the 'fortress', Cain phoned Moshe to enquire about his arm – all was well – and tell him about the tracking device.

'To save you asking, I have not heard from Zokwana. Let's wait to see if Marius can shed any light on the situation when we meet on Monday.'

They went on to discuss their business agenda for the days ahead.

Rounding off their conversation, Cain asked, 'Have you received your new laptop?'

'Yes – and the young lady will be here in ten minutes to give me my first lesson.'

'I'll leave you to it. Have a good time.'

'Indeed.'

Cain idled away the rest of the day with Tarah. They went sunbathing on one of the mostly deserted northern beaches to savour the peace and quiet. And after having a picnic lunch to keep them away from the crowds, they enjoyed an hour of stone-skimming and shark tooth hunting before they went back to the 'fortress' for a shower and a shag.

When Cain dropped Tarah off at her flat, he waved to Sharlise up on the balcony. They would soon be leaving for a night at Carlton's.

It had been a welcome, wonderfully relaxing time for Cain.

In the early hours of Sunday morning, Cain walked out onto the sundeck to feel the coolness of the early morning breeze soughing through the dark and quiet. The 'Cape Doctor' had come to visit. Looking down, on the deserted drive, he noticed another streetlamp was no longer working, leaving the small quadrangle of park in almost total darkness. A speck of light appeared under the small copse of trees. Cain realised: Smokey was once again lighting a spliff, keeping an eye on the 'fortress'.

Why am I not surprised.

Cain contemplated how the attempted payback for the punch-up in the Land Rover and the carnage in the dojo would pale into insignificance compared to what they – whomever they may be – might now be planning in the wake of the cluster-fuck in bandit country. Cain felt Smokey was putting the 'fortress' under siege.

At the end of a siege, comes invasion.

Cain looked out to the horizon, where a 'rolling pin' of candyfloss cloud was trundling its way across the ocean towards the coast. He counted the number of seconds between the streaks of lightning as they struck water and the sound of thunder rolling in. The lapses in time told him the storm would make landfall in an hour, perhaps ninety minutes. He gave the crescent moon above a last look.

Perfect timing.

He walked back through the bedroom into the dressing room and pressed a button. The wall of mirrors glided to one side to reveal shelves filled with knives, various types of weaponry, ammunition, and firearms – most of them legal. It was time to send a message.

A few minutes later, a balaclava-clad figure camouflaged in dark clothes, left the 'fortress', crept across the drive, effortlessly jumped over the wall, and landed down on the grass in the small park without making a sound. Cain cautiously moved towards the speck of light amid the trees and made his presence known:

'Morning. You're back again. Didn't you fancy a run up to Namibia?'

Smokey looked up at Cain. 'Mind your own fuckin business, white shit.'

'Who sent you?'

Smokey got to his feet, took a last drag of his spliff, flicked the butt into the air, and moved a few feet closer towards his unexpected visitor.

Cain remained motionless, with his arms folded. With his finger on the trigger of his concealed, throwaway Beretta, hooked to a lanyard around his neck, 'I'll ask you again, who sent you?'

In one fluid motion, Smokey produced a sixteen-inch panga machete in his hand and scythed it through – because Cain instinctively stepped back – the vacant air between them.

> When death and danger are upon you the slow-motion
> movie in the mind distorts time.
> What might seem like an eternity will, in the event, only
> be the beginning.

Cain immediately moved to one side as the panga machete sliced sideways through the air once more, missing him by a whisker. Backing towards the cover of the branches, Cain led Smokey towards him. When Cain positioned his back against a tree. Smokey lurched forward – and everything happened at once.

The panga slashed down through the air. Cain darted to one side, let go of his throwaway Beretta and, grabbing hold of the swordstick-style blade in his sleeve, he launched himself matador-like, into the air. As the panga hit the trunk of the tree, Cain plunged the blade into Smokey's back. Smokey gasped, slowly fell forward, the blade went through his heart, and he crumpled to the ground.

Cain withdrew the blood-soaked blade.

Quickly went through Smokey's pockets to find his cell phone.

A bolt of lightning carved its way through the sky.

Thunder filled the air.

And the first drops of rain began to fall.

The message had been sent.

Along one of the many miles of curving coastal roads – carved out of cliffs – Cain stood on *suicide ledge*: where only the jumpers were predisposed to make a last stand.

Some sixty feet below, the sight and sounds of the waves beating against the rocks, seemed to be playing-out in perfect harmony with a pair of Southern Right Whales, breaching half a mile out. Cain tossed the now snapped-in-half swordstick-style blade down into the ocean. He'd managed to save the Beretta for another day. He looked up to see *Moby & Dick,* breach one last time, before he climbed back up the rock face, to his waiting Jeep.

Cain floored his right foot, turned the wheel, and turned up the volume.

Steve Harley & Cockney Rebel were singing: *Make me Smile.*

> *You've done it all*
> *You've broken every code*
> *And pulled the rebel to the floor . . .*

'Not yet,' Cain said.

On the veranda of Melissa's restaurant, 'Good to see you,' Peter said, shaking hands with Cain.

'Perfect timing,' Cain remarked seeing the waitress arrive with the coffees and carrot cake.

'I saw you parking.'

Cain poured the coffees, allowing Peter – as always – to update him on the latest news. 'A bergie got himself killed in the park outside your place last night.'

Cain feigned a look of surprise. 'Are you joking?'

'Not this time, I was wondering if it was Smokey.'

'I only got back from Jo'burg on Friday night. I'd forgotten all about Smokey.'

'You didn't see or hear anything?'

'Nothing,' said Cain. 'When I saw the storm approaching, I was feeling tired. I closed everything up and went to bed. I slept like a log, woke up in the fireplace.'

'Not again,' Peter groaned.

And with smiles all round they had a bite of their carrot cake and a sip of their coffee.

Cain commented, 'When I went out onto the sundeck this morning, I wondered what the police tape was doing there in the park. How did the bergie die?'

'Stabbed, apparently, but not with the sixteen-inch panga they found embedded in the trunk of one of the trees.'

'A panga? Jesus Christ,' said Cain, showing apprehension. 'It must have been one of those bergie bashes; when they drink too much they start fighting over nothing and end up killing each other.'

'Probably. The police found a load of smoked spliff-ends on the grass.'

'Did they find any empty bottles of moonshine?'

'No,' said Peter. 'The killer, or killers, must have taken them with them.'

'Sounds about right: waste not, want not.'

'If the police thought it was anything more than a bergie bash, they would have been knocking on doors, looking for any possible witnesses. It wouldn't surprise me if they've already closed the case, especially since the thunderstorm would have more than likely washed away any incriminating evidence.'

Remembering what Peter had said about Smokey some two weeks earlier, Cain decided to end the subject of conversation. He grinned, 'You were right, the bergie became the corpse in the copse.'

Peter smiled. 'Such is life. I have to tell you, Shaffie the micromanager who never delegates, had his new pair of sandals nicked from outside his mosque on Friday. It's the second time in a month.'

'The cost of religion.'

'Sure is, you should have heard him ranting. He now keeps an old pair of slip-ons in the footwell of his SUV.'

'He can now truly, in every sense of the word, put his foot in it.'

Peter and Cain looked at each other and burst out laughing… Another coffee later, rounding off their opinions about the

Sunday's front pages and putting the world to rights, Peter checked his watch. 'The Arsenal kicks off in half an hour.'

'Time to go?' Cain suggested.

'My goal in life.'

And with smiles all round. Cain said, 'Bearing in mind what happened in the park, could you come over to my place one day for a beer and help me decide on a couple of places for security cameras? I was thinking I could have one overlooking the park.'

'Good idea. Will do.'

23

Monday – Week Four – Recap

Kimberley started to open up and over, triggering the alarm system's thirty-second warning. Cain felt for the Walther P99 in his waist, but the incessant beeping soon ceased and the security door opened.

On reaching the top of the stairs, Marius called out, '*Namiddag* (Afternoon).'

'Glad you could make it.'

'*Ag perfekte* (Ahh perfect),' Marius said, as he eyed the steaks marinating on the kitchen island.

'Road kill.'

Marius laughed; they shook hands and embraced like great friends do. 'Good to see you are still alive,' Marius said quietly.

'We live to fight another day.'

However, when the two men drew back from each other, one particular unanswered question still lingered in the space between them. 'Unlike Smokey,' Marius said.

Cain nodded. 'It was time to send a message.'

Sitting at the kitchen island, Cain poured the wine, and explained what had happened.

Marius said, 'Smokey was another rogue freelancer – an ex-member of the 33s – brought down from the north.'

'And now he's been brought down in every sense of the word. Good riddance. Cain reached into a drawer under the kitchen island and pulled out two cell phones. One had a piece of sticky tape on the screen with the password 1234 written on it. 'This is the one I took off Windows; the one I received the call on from Smokey. And this is the one I took off a dead Smokey. Sorry I wasn't able to get the password for you.'

'My people will open it. Windows has, in effect, always been Zokwana's gofer, so the numbers you faxed to me, from what is a burner cell phone, have turned out to be very useful. I'm sorry I cannot go into more detail.' Mac placed the two cell phones in his jacket pocket.

Mention of the 33s reminded Cain of what had been said during his telephone conversation with Marius, ten days earlier, about the tattooed guard he'd seen at Zokwana's residence.

Marius asked, 'What are you thinking?'

'Are those ex-33s rogue freelancers, the *Suits,* still watching Zokwana?'

'Yes.'

'Are you telling me officially or unofficially?'

'Touché,' said Marius. 'I'll keep you informed as things progress. Tell me about Jo'burg!'

Over a glass or two of red wine they delved a little deeper into Cain's past few days with Moshe, the attack in bandit country, and all it entailed.

'I can confirm,' said Marius, 'the blockers' bodies have been identified – they were also ex-33s rogue freelancers. And with no evidence to suggest otherwise, the police have marked the *Docket* as nothing more than another gang-on-gang killing spree. The police won't be opening a major investigation any time soon.'

Out on the patio, both men stood by one of the most respected of altars in Afrikaners folklore – the braai – taking in the aroma of steaks grilling over burning hickory.

Cain enquired, 'Any ideas on where Windows and Lastly are?'

Marius shook his head. 'We have to assume they were initially both going to take part in the attack in bandit country, but when Windows unexpectedly got himself laid up after being shot in the dojo, Lastly led the attack.'

Cain turned the steaks over. 'So the brawn, not the brains, led the charge. Sounds about right. Could they both be dead or is that just wishful thinking?'

'If they were. I'm sure the police would have found out by now from their various township informants.'

'So they must be waiting for the dust to settle and their wounds to heal.'

'Undoubtedly. We need to take a step back in time to the night we first met.'

'The attempt on your life – really?'

'Bear with me.'

'I'll go get the Tardis.'

Marius smiled. 'Good idea.'

Cain placed the steaks on the plates. 'Lunch is served.'

'*Lekka*,' said Marius, placing their glasses on the pub-style garden bench.

Over steaks and salad, the conversation continued. Marius said, 'After you left me that night, I went off with my people to search for the gunman, the running man who had doubled back and shot dead the wounded gunman.'

'I must confess,' said Cain, 'from up on the hillside I did see you being helped into the 4x4.'

'Why am I not surprised. We checked the perimeter roads, but we found nothing. Let me tell you a story.'

'Fire away,' Cain grinned, topping up their wine glasses.

'We certainly did,' said Marius. 'I now believe the original plan for the gunmen, after the assassination, was to meet Windows at a pre-arranged rendezvous point to change vehicles. He would then drive them to a place they had been told would be safe, where they could hide out and be paid. But in reality they would have been driven to a location where Lastly was waiting to kill them. To cut a long story short, when the running man told Windows I was still alive, I believe an argument erupted. I'll leave the rest to your imagination. On the following day, a member of the public found the body of a man by Kirstenbosch Botanical Gardens, near the minister's residence. He had been beaten, shot in the stomach, and left to die. That was two years ago. And almost two weeks ago, Windows dumped Gospel's body in almost the same place. Gospel had also been beaten, shot in the stomach, and left to die.'

'Zokwana must know it was Windows who killed Gospel.'

'Undoubtedly,' Marius agreed. 'Two years ago, the local police believed the death was just another gang-on-gang killing, so they didn't investigate.'

'Talking about the attempt on your life,' said Cain. 'I've never asked you – why has there never been another attempt?'

'In a nutshell, within a month of the attempt, there was a very short, very deadly gang war. Several leading members of the 33s were killed and a number of reprisal killings followed. It was a period of great instability. I knew of several police officers who were on the take, so in return for wiping their slates clean, so to speak, they changed their allegiance. Unfortunately, the gang member who had been instructed to issue the contract to have me assassinated was one of those killed in the reprisal killings, so I never found out who issued the contract. Sorry, you were saying?'

Realising Marius would not divulge anything more, Cain said, 'I was just wondering who Zokwana is answering to.'

'Aren't we all?'

Cain had always attributed his tendency for nicknaming things and people – like the Galt Mile Gang and Mischief to his affable character, his sense of humour. Whereas others, especially those he had used in his past life in London, were always for a more serious purpose: to help maintain a degree of clarity and perspective in his own mind.

'May I suggest,' said Cain, 'we give a nickname to the man who is telling Zokwana what to do. How about *Defunct.*'

Marius smiled. 'He soon will be.'

'Allow me to thank you again,' said Cain, 'for the story you put out to the media about the supposed black man who stole my Jeep and wrote it off, to protect my identity.'

'It was the least I could do.'

'Since the black man did not exist, he has never been found. Therefore the police *Docket* on finding him must still be open, yes?'

'Indefinitely.'

'For the past two years I have been driving both a Mercedes and a Jeep. When I first met Windows, he enriched his own ego by telling me he had many talents. Assuming he is still alive, he will be hell-bent on getting back at me for the punch-up in the Land Rover, the carnage in the dojo, and now – we have to assume Lastly is alive and has told him – the failure of the attack in bandit country.'

'But for now, he'll be constrained by his convalescence, and possibly his fear of Zokwana.'

'What if,' said Cain, 'while waiting for his wound to heal, he does a bit more *lying around* of a slightly different kind. He could weave together faked and circumstantial evidence connecting me to the night they tried to kill you. To prove I was the person driving my Jeep. Remember what you said earlier about police officers on the take?'

Marius nodded.

'Windows would tell Zokwana I had bribed the police to make them proclaim the driver of my Jeep was a black man.'

'An interesting scenario,' Marius responded. 'Such a story would undoubtedly get Windows back into Zokwana's good books and *Defunct's* good favour.'

'What if *Defunct* is the same man who ordered your assassination?'

'If that were the case,' said Marius, 'if he believes you foiled the assassination attempt on my life, he might get a degree of satisfaction by having you killed.'

'Having me killed would, as far as Zokwana is concerned, still leave Moshe alive to cut those rough diamonds for him.'

'Assuming Moshe is not killed with you.'

Cain cast his mind back to what Windows had said in the Land Rover: "Unfortunately, Lastly's twin brother was killed in London… our business will be a tribute to him."

Cain speculated, 'Can we be sure Windows did not just go directly to *Defunct*, circumventing Zokwana for financial gain? To pay for his dream of moving to London with Lastly?'

'If Windows and Lastly did know *Defunct's* identity, it could explain why your Jeep and Moshe's Toyota had tracking devices placed under them. We have assumed Smokey was working for Zokwana. What if he was, in fact, working for *Defunct* via Windows and Lastly?'

'So has Windows been reporting different things directly to *Defunct* and Zokwana?'

'We just don't know for sure. But all being well, we soon will.'

'Meantime,' said Cain, 'Windows could literally be lying in a bed, in every sense of the word, watching it all going on around him.'

'Watching it all being done for him.'

Cain frowned in frustration. 'Let's have another drink.'

'Good idea! And before I forget, thank you for faxing me the details of the supposed new client who phoned Kobus, demanding an immediate delivery of his rough to Jo'burg. I'll find out if he knows Zokwana. What are your plans for the rest of the month?'

'I will be here in Cape Town for perhaps a week, getting things organised. Then I'll be going back up to Jo'burg to be with Moshe for a few days before I fly out to Guangzhou or Hong Kong.'

'Your annual visit.'

'It's always good to meet up with Bill and Greg.'

'Since you're only going to be here in South Africa for no more than a week or two, I must ask you to stay away from Zokwana. I don't want you to rattle his cage.'

'As you wish. I'll maintain a low profile.'

'Watch your back.'

'Understood.'

Tuesday – Update

Cain was standing on the sundeck of the 'fortress' under a clear blue sky, taking in the 22°C heat of the day. He admired the panoramic view from Table Mountain, across the gap to Lions Head, along the ridge to Signal Hill and of course, over the ocean. He gave the park below a careful scan, but it was completely deserted.

A double-toot of a car horn interrupted Cain's train of thought. He watched the BMW turn onto the forecourt and come to a stop. Peter stepped out with his briefcase in one hand and a Melissa's restaurant carrier bag in the other.

'Afternoon,' Peter called out. 'Good to see you.'

'Hi Peter,' said Cain, waving down at him.

As Peter approached the front gate it opened.

'I'll get Mr. Ed to let you in,' Cain announced with a grin.

Peter glanced up. 'Stop horsing around.'

'Nice bag you're carrying there. I'll put the kettle on.'

The two men sat at the kitchen island enjoying a coffee and the carrot cake Peter had picked up on his way back from Constantia.

During a tour of the 'fortress' they agreed the upgrades, Peter was handed a set of keys, along with a list of secondary-alarm codes. The work would be carried out under his personal supervision while Cain was away.

Peter was under the impression Cain's annual visits to Hong Kong and Guangzhou were to meet up with old friends. While his trips up to Jo'burg were to – like he did in Cape Town – negotiate property deals and take care of those he had purchased and rented out.

'Don't forget,' said Cain, 'the codes are written back to front.'

'Got it.'

'Let's go have a drink.'

In Carlton's, Sharlise and Tarah greeted Cain and Peter. 'Great to see you!' they chimed, before all four hugged and kissed Spanish-style.

In the background, *Moby* was singing *Extreme Ways*.

Whilst having a chat with Cain, Tarah glanced to their side. 'Look,' she whispered. Exhibited on two walls, framed, colour – painting-sized – photographs of a beautiful, scantily clad female were on display. Only her facial features were completely hidden. They were all for sale.

'Is it you?' Cain asked, eyeing Tarah's breasts. She breathed in deeply, pressed herself against him and stuck her tongue out.

In the background *Feargal Sharkey* started singing *A Good Heart*, causing Tarah to carousel away. Cain sighed – along with many others – as he watched her crossing the floor to the rhythm of the music before disappearing down the steps into the restaurant. It would turn out to be an evening when bets on the female's identity were not the only thing wanting to be laid. Only Tarah's best friend Sharlise knew it was Cain who had taken the photographs some two months earlier. Purchases would be paid to Carlton's. Jason and Tom would then take their commission and secretly pay the balance to Tarah.

Having climbed the four steps up to the old oak bar, Sharlise arrived at Cain's side, holding two pints of beer.

'You always 'come' with a beer,' he said quietly.

'Let me know when you can 'come' in pints,' she whispered.

'Only when I see you two pole dancing.'

'You will,' Sharlise said, as she placed the beers on the table in front of Peter – and went off to attend to other customers' requests.

'What did you say to her?' Peter enquired.

'Just a joke,' said Cain with a bit of a grin, 'about the pictures on the wall.'

'Quite a *pair*,' said Peter, raising his glass. 'Cheers.'

'Chugalug. For my first taste of sin.'

'With Tarah or Sharlise?'

'I wish,' said Cain, giving his standard reply to such a question. Leo appeared behind the bar, immediately providing Cain with a perfect distraction. 'Evening Leo.'

'How's the pizza?' Peter called out.

Leo smiled and raised a glass. 'Bog off,' he mouthed, and they all laughed.

The Carlton brothers, Jason and Tom, were in attendance. They all shook hands and enjoyed a drink with Cain and Peter, before excusing themselves to greet other customers and get ready for the night ahead. Cain and Peter at their usual corner table, went on to enjoy a bite to eat, the company of others, a few games of backgammon, and a Jägermeister shooter or three. Carlton's relaxed 'sundowners' eventually gave way to the evening's gathering of diners and drinkers. Cain checked the crowd and the time on his Breitling.

'Time to go?' Peter asked.

'One more game,' said Cain with a grin 'So you can buy the loser's shooters.

Peter laughed. 'Piss off.'

Back at the 'fortress' Cain sat comfortably in the lounge, watching TV, having a drink, waiting for Tarah to call.

Wednesday

Cain's phone rang: no caller ID appeared. He pressed the button. 'Morning.'

'Mr. Edwards,' said a familiar voice.

'Detective Inspector Davis.'

'How are you, Cain?'

'I'm good Jerry. I've just got back from a run.'

'I'm aching.'

'Why are you aching?' said Cain. 'Are you still lifting *you know* who into the boot of your car to get her into Prince Charles' (Highgrove) home?'

'No comment,' said Jerry, maintaining his usual composure. 'I've just finished a refresher course with the SAS, you know who and where.'

'Know it well.'

'A reminder of the good old days.'

'Such is life.'

'And death,' Jerry jibed. 'What are you doing?'

'I'm on the sundeck.'

'I'm freezing.'

'Some people have all the fun.'

'Sod off.'

After a minute of good-humoured comments, Jerry said, 'I've just been informed I will be in your area very soon. I'll send you a date one evening.'

Jerry had just used a code, telling Cain he would be landing in Cape Town in twenty-four hours' time.

'Is the visit official or unofficial? Shall I get the flags out?'

'No, just the beers and ciders . . . seriously, it's a bit of both really, but mostly low-key. Not too much fanfare.'

'You'll be with your Principal?'

'Don't be Naïve.'

Jerry had once again used an anagram of a nickname – known within certain circles – for the member of the Royal Family he now personally protected.

'I'll be here,' said Cain. 'I'll get a few packs of your favourite springbok biltong for you.'

'Thank you. We'll be able to meet up at some point, I'll let you know where and when.'

The chat with Jerry had put Cain on a charge: it had to be done. With his Beretta, keys, cash, and mobile in hands, he headed down the stairs – and seeing his maid, he called out, 'See you later Marigold.'

Sitting at the kitchen island having a cup of coffee and a sandwich, Marigold took little notice of Cain, who was dressed only in a T-shirt, underwear, and socks. She'd seen it all – well almost all – before. She checked the Gaudi clock on the wall: 11:58am.

'Mad dogs and Englishmen go out in the midday sun,' she said quietly with a smile.

Moments later a crash-helmeted figure, clad in black leather, riding a BMW 1150GS motorbike, filtered through the city traffic.

Years earlier, when Cain had purchased his first Jeep Grand Cherokee in South Africa, he had considered buying a Harley Davidson as well. But the law stated he had to wear a crash helmet. Therefore, knowing he would be losing the thrill – both mentally and physically – of the wind being in his hair, he had decided to buy a BMW 1150GS instead.

On Camps Bay Beach road Cain came to a stop at the 'robots'. He eyed the distant bikini babes bathing on the beach, while other scantily clad lovelies were parading along the prom.

How great it would be to tarry for a while.

But instead, he coiled his fingers for another reason, he dropped a gear, rather than his trousers and as smooth as silk – no *jerking...!* off he went.

He again checked his rear-view mirrors to make sure no one was following him. The 1150GS breezed the peninsular coastal roads to the Cape of Good Hope at an easy pace. He then headed north, passing Boulders Beach and its colony of penguins, before he stopped around the corner in Fish Hoek, by the side of a favourite fish and chip shop. Minutes later, he was sitting on a wall eating his cod and chips with a can of coke, looking out over False Bay.

False. False people, false activities: where will it all end?

Walking back to his 1150GS a great name came to mind:

Coffin Cheaters.

It all placed a different attitude towards his more-of-a-free-spirit attitude to life – and now (after what had been happening) his more a free spirit attitude to death.

In the late of the afternoon, Cain was sitting at his desk

talking on the phone with Moshe.

'How's your arm?'

'Getting better.'

'How's your laptop?'

'I just pressed the button. I've sent you my first email.'

Cain heard the ping from his own laptop and opened his emails. 'Got it. Congratulations. I'll reply when we finish our call.'

After a brief roundup of what was going on, Moshe moved the subject of conversation on to business. He confirmed the man from Lesotho – with a delivery of rough – would meet Cain in the beach town of Hermanus, a two-hour drive from Cape Town, on Friday at noon.

Rounding off their conversation, Cain said, 'I'll give you a call after the meeting.'

'Of course.'

'Take care.'

'Shalom.'

Friday – A Stone's Throw

Cain drove into Hermanus, famous the world over for its whale-watching trips. He quickly scanned the ocean for any sign of Moby and Dick having a splash, but the late morning waves were calm. He drove around for a while, checking his mirrors to make sure he was not being followed.

At noon he met a Lesotho diamond merchant who was visiting friends in the area and had decided to combine business with pleasure. Finishing off their coffees Cain said, 'If you decide to come down to Cape Town let me know, lunch or dinner will be on me.'

'If I do, I'll give you a call,' said the merchant, handing Cain a small plastic shopping bag. 'Take care.'

After driving over the Hottentot Mountains and safely through Sir Lowry's Pass, Cain turned off the freeway to take the beach road… He checked his mirrors again, but no one was tailing him and pressed the button on his mobile, Peter answered.

'Hi,' said Cain, 'I will be passing by High Constantia, fancy joining me for lunch?'

'Very affluent, very posh. But sorry not today, I have a pressing engagement?'

'In the biblical sense or in the gym?'

'Piss off.'

'If she changes her mind, you know where I am.'

'High Constantia, got it, I'll press on then,' Peter joked. 'Enjoy your lunch.'

Some time later, in a quiet corner of the car park under the shade of a line of oak trees, Cain removed a leather wallet from the plastic shopping bag. He made a call to Moshe on his mobile to confirm everything had gone to plan, and he was now in High Constantia, just for a change, to have lunch.

Payment for the rough would be made once Moshe had made his final evaluation. Such trust – although now mostly consigned to a bygone era – still existed among a handful of traditional and trustworthy merchants in South Africa and Lesotho; merchants who still lived and abided by the old, established system of honour and integrity.

Cain strapped the leather wallet to his waist under his summer shirt, removed his Beretta from under his thigh, placed it in his backpack and exited the Jeep. As he approached the upmarket arcade of shops, boutiques and *al 'fresco* restaurants he zapped the Jeep's central locking and dropped the keys into the side pocket of his backpack. Looking up, he saw Jerry with another man, the Principal, walking towards him. Professional protocol instantly came to the fore. Despite the surprise, Cain and Jerry subtly acknowledged each other's presence while acting like perfect strangers. But old habits die hard, Cain instinctively checked the people around them, just in case. A black man wearing a grey long-coat and sunglasses stepped out from behind an old oak tree some twenty feet behind Jerry. The man's hands were in the pockets of his open coat and he had an exaggerated swagger in his gait.

Cain, sensing something wasn't quite right, eased his hand down into his backpack and, taking hold of his Beretta, he realised what was wrong: Long-coat had his hands in his pockets, but he had no fucking arms.

When death and danger are upon you – the slow-motion

movie in the mind, distorts time.
What would seem like an eternity for many:
Would for Cain and Jerry in reality, only be: Tick-Tok,
a second – or two.

'Gun, gun,' Jerry shouted, drawing his Glock from his hip holster, and stepping in front of the man he was assigned to protect, the Principal – just the one thought came to mind.

Why is Cain not turning? Dear God no.

And Jerry opened fire.

As Cain aimed his Beretta, a short-framed automatic machine pistol appeared in the hands of Long-coat, who was now walking towards him. Cain opened fire.

Long-coat took the hits to his chest. His strength evaporated and, falling to the bloodied ground, he pulled the trigger. In the blink of an eye the short-framed automatic machine pistol discharged a sweep of some thirty 9mm rounds across the ground. People started screaming, running, and diving for cover.

Jerry's target stumbled, falling to his knees; Jerry's final shot finished the job. Cain and Jerry glanced at each other. 'Got your back. Go!' Cain shouted.

Jerry immediately escorted the Principal away, talking on his radio. Seconds later, a Mercedes saloon skidded to a halt beside them. The Principal opened the back door and dived in with Jerry following, and it sped off. Cain was well aware the safety of the Royal Family was the absolute priority: nobody would be racing back any time soon to save him.

As the shouts of security guards and the crackle of police radios grew louder, Cain grabbed his backpack off the ground, quickly hunched himself over and scuttled away in the manner of a terrified civilian, using parked cars for cover.

Amid the noise and chaos, Cain heard a burst of gunfire. A vehicle instantly accelerated away, but a second salvo shattered the windscreen, and the vehicle crashed into a scouting security van. A gun fight was now in full swing. Cain scanned the area around him, trying to figure out what the hell was going on. A Mercedes immediately came sideways – rally car-like – around the end of a row of cars towards him. He aimed his Beretta, he heard Jerry's voice call out, 'Take a ride.'

Cain turned to see a dead man lying between parked cars and, a few feet away, Jerry changing the mag on an MP5 machine gun. The Mercedes skidded to a stop between them, and the rear door opened. 'Taxi!' the Principal – hunkering down on the back seat – called out. Cain leapt into the back of the already moving Mercedes and Jerry jumped into the front.

Minutes later, the speeding Mercedes passed through the main gates of a private estate, protected by armed guards.

As the Principal exited the vehicle, he was surrounded by armed men who moved like shadows, escorting him into the mansion. Lockdown had been initiated. The Mercedes immediately moved away into a warehouse-style garage where for all the obvious reasons: security, its number plates would be changed, never to be seen again.

After an obligatory strip search to ensure Cain had not been bugged, he was directed into a drawing room where quite unexpectedly, Jerry introduced him to the Principal.

Sometime later, 'It is good to have met you at last,' said the Principal, bringing their meeting to an end. 'You owe me a drink.'

'Of course sir, anytime.'

And with smiles all round, Cain and the Principal shook hands. 'Thank you again sir, for coming back to save me.'

The Principal, in the manner of a Royal Family custom said nothing but his look said it all. Cain stepped back, bowed, and left the room. A minute later, waiting – as instructed – by the door. Jerry appeared. 'Time for a debrief.'

Cain updated Jerry on what had been going on in his life over the past five weeks. 'The safety of the Royal Family and the Palace Pups is the absolute priority.'

Jerry verbally time-dated the tape, and turned the recorder off. 'Thank you for telling me. The rough diamonds you are carrying certainly look impressive. Nice to see you have the necessary documentation to go with them.'

'Always.'

As they stepped into the light of the afternoon, Cain saw his Jeep parked out front. 'What a pleasant surprise! Thank you.'

'We've checked it over. There was no tracking device.'

'Not like last week.'

'Talking of Jeeps . . .'

'What?'

Jerry put on his best police-officer-in-court voice. 'It has been brought to my attention M'lud, the number plates on the Jeep are false.'

Cain nudged Jerry's arm with his elbow. 'I wonder who could have done such a thing.'

'Sod off.'

They both laughed, but not too loudly.

'Guilty as charged,' Cain said, holding up his hands.

'The original plates,' said Jerry, 'were in a bag in the boot.'

'Did you say *were* in the bag?'

'I've already had them changed, just in case someone spotted the number in the Constantia, car park.'

'Bit like the Mercedes...' Cain grinned knowingly.

Jerry smiled. 'I've taken the packets of my favourite springbok biltong out of the back.'

'I purchased them this morning in case you gave me really short notice to meet you.'

'Thank you. Who do you think was the target today?'

'Not sure.'

'Nor am I. By the way, I've already contacted Marius in Cape Town. He is now fully aware of what has happened.'

'Of course.'

'It will allow him to advise those investigating the case and help keep a lid on it. A courtesy he greatly appreciated. As soon as the dead gunmen are identified we may get a better idea of who their target was.'

'So,' said Cain, 'you have carried out your first kill today. Or was it two?'

'Jerry smiled. 'Two.'

'Congratulations. You feeling OK?'

'Like you, I now know how it truly feels to be at death's door.'

'Join the club.'

'Inspector Davis!' one of the Palace Pups called from the main entrance.

'Time for me to go,' said Jerry. 'We'll be heading back to

London before the end of the day.'

'I thought you would,' said Cain, with a feeling of regret. 'Thank you for saving me.'

Jerry shrugged and smiled. 'We saved each other. 'Never forget the Royal Family's love and respect for their faithful two and four-legged pets. That's why the Principal broke protocol and ordered me to return to the car park to rescue you.'

'He shouldn't have – and you were not obligated to obey such a command.'

'We both broke the rules.'

Cain and Jerry embraced like best friends do.

'Thank you again,' Cain whispered.

'The Royal Family owed you one,' Jerry replied.

'Perhaps they did.'

Two hours later.

Having completed his *pressing engagement*, Peter sat on the side of the bed and turned on his cell phone: a plethora of messages and missed calls flashed onto the screen. Anxiously, he pressed the speed dial. He was relieved to hear it being answered.

'Cain, you all in one piece?'

'I'm fine. Why shouldn't I be?'

'There was a shooting at High Constantia at lunchtime.'

'Seriously?'

'People were killed. Didn't you see it?'

'Thank God I wasn't there. I decided instead of eating alone without you, I'd rather make myself a salad, have a can of beer, and sit out on the sundeck.'

'You missed all the action?'

'Fortunately.'

Peter went on to speculate about what might have happened and Cain played along until he found out what he wanted to know. Peter had turned off his phone for the duration of his *pressing engagement*. He had not spoken to anyone, so no one else had known of Cain's whereabouts.

'See you on the morrow,' Cain said.

'Will do. Don't go shooting off anywhere.'

'Only in the biblical sense.'

Cain and Peter both laughed and ended the call.

Peter walked back into the bedroom. 'There's been another shooting.'

'Why are we not surprised,' said the beautiful young black woman lying naked on her bed.

'Come again!'

Friday Evening.

Cain was alone in the 'fortress'. His phone rang but no caller ID was displayed.

'Mr. Edwards.'

'Detective Inspector Davis.'

'We are you-know-where, waiting to leave, so just a quick call. The initial indicators point more to you being the target than my Principal, but there's one problem with such a scenario.'

'I'm still alive?'

'Aren't we all. We know you were not followed. We know you only decided to go to High Constantia at the last minute. We know neither you nor your vehicle were bugged.'

'True.'

'So how come the gunmen were already there, waiting for you?'

Saturday – Manipulation

Cain was sitting at the kitchen island having a coffee, reading the front page of the morning paper. Under the headline 'Heroes', the story, next to a photograph of two security guards, read:

> 'Security officials have confirmed two gunmen were shot
> dead during a shoot-out, and two others were killed after
> the vehicle they were trying to escape in crashed into a
> security van, and the occupants opened fire'.

Cain's phone rang, he answered it.

'I'll have to be brief,' said Marius. 'The call from Jerry yesterday certainly put everything into perspective. I'm not directly involved, of course, but I was able to make a few calls to save the police and others from expending a lot of unnecessary time and energy. The authorities managed to keep a lid on what really happened and, because no innocent bystanders were killed or injured, the police declared the security guards the heroes of the day.'

'Smart move.'

'The media instantly jumped on the bandwagon and dedicated their front pages to them.'

'I'm just reading the story. Any leads?'

'Not yet, wait one . . .' Marius went offline for a few seconds then came back on. 'I have to go.'

'OK.'

The line went dead.

Cain could imagine all the *games* Marius and many others would have to contend with – behind closed doors – in the coming days:

Complicat-ions, explanat-ions, implicat-ions, justificat-ions, ramificat-ions.

The politicians would now have all the proverbial *ions in the fire* they needed to designate blame and take the credit for themselves.

Part Seven

Johannesburg, South Africa

The Sting

True friends are like diamonds – bright, beautiful, valuable, and always in style.

Nicole Richie

24

Update – Betrayal

On Sunday, Cain arrived in Jo'burg on the morning flight. He collected his suitcase, picked up his Glock 27 from the security kiosk, and headed for the exit where an unmarked 4x4-shuttle was waiting to take him to the Sempre Aqui Hotel. Célia, as always, greeted Cain at reception to sign him in.

'Breakfast for two at 10am,' said Célia with a smile, handing Cain the key to his room. 'Moshe will be joining you. Your favourite corner table in the restaurant has been reserved.'

'Thank you.'

At 10am, Cain and Moshe greeted each other and embraced like great friends do.

Cain said, 'Good to see there is no sling on your arm. All OK?'

'Getting better,' said Moshe. 'But no lifting.'

As they drew back from each other, Cain grinned. 'Will you be rejoining the Pajero Club?'

'I'll *hand* such a task over to a female friend,' Moshe responded, as they took their seats at the table.

Over breakfast, the two men talked about Moshe's laptop-learning skills before they turned to business.

'How was Cape Town?'

Cain brought Moshe fully up to date on the death of Smokey and the shootout in High Constantia involving Jerry and the Principal. It was a long conversation.

'Jerry made a valid point,' said Moshe. 'So how come the gunmen were there before you?'

'There doesn't seem to be an answer.'

'Indeed there doesn't.'

'Perhaps they were just there to shoot each other?' Cain said sarcastically.

'Perhaps,' said Moshe. 'Let's go to Jewel City.'

'Good idea. It's Sunday, so no traffic.'

220

Out in the parking area of the Sempre Aqui, Cain walked around Moshe's now unmarked Toyota 4Runner. 'They did a perfect job.'

Moshe opened the passenger door. 'They certainly did.'

Out on the road, Moshe said, 'I have spoken with Kobus and Hennie.'

'How are they?'

'Very well. Hennie is well on his way to being fully recovered. The guard who went missing – they found him,' Moshe said, frowning.

'I bet that hurt.'

'Probably. They found out what happened.'

'Do tell.'

'Apparently, a stranger started chatting to the guard one evening when he was in a *shebeen* and bought him a drink. A few innocent questions led to a few more drinks. By the end of the evening, they'd had quite a chat. Under the pretence of lending the guard some money, the stranger gave him some cash. Apparently, the stranger said, *Just to keep things between the two of us. No harm done.* A few days later they met up again in the *shebeen* – and more cash was passed to the guard, under the table with a burner cell phone. We know what eventually happened.'

'Where is the guard now?'

'Suffice to say, he will never be seen again.'

'And the stranger?'

'He has disappeared. He does not answer his cell phone – the only number the guard ever called – it is permanently turned off. Kobus' people cannot find any trace of him.'

'Perhaps, having served his purpose, he has also been laid to rest?'

'I believe what I am about to tell you will confirm he has been. While you were flying up to Jo'burg this morning, Kobus rang me. The supposed new client who demanded an immediate delivery of his rough to Jo'burg was found shot dead in an underground car park last night.'

Cain smirked. 'So all three have been taken out – what a surprise.'

'Indeed.'

In their office in Jewel City, Moshe and Cain placed their laptops on their desks, powered them up, and checked their emails. Cain removed a strapped, leather wallet from his waist. 'These are the rough from Lesotho.'

'I'll send them a message to let them know their delivery is now with me.'

'I'll make the coffee.'

Minutes later, Moshe moved the subject of conversation on to all things China.

'Bill and Greg will be glad to see you again.'

'Always a good time.'

The Guangzhou showroom had exceeded all expectations. The Dutchman who had invested the US$450,000 had been fully repaid – and remained one of Bill and Greg's elite 1% clients.

Kay had proven herself to be extremely efficient. She was now overseeing the day-to-day running of the showroom on an almost full-time basis, while tending to the requirements of her own wealthy clientele. Her weekly reports were beyond reproach, while her analysis and occasional suggestions were always greatly appreciated and often acted upon.

Susie Su, a director in a financial consultancy business, continued to introduce her privileged and influential clients to the world of 'all that glitters is not gold', so they could buy investment diamonds. Both ladies continued to maintain their impeccable reputations for honesty and integrity, for which they were well respected.

Moshe rounded off their conversation. 'Zhang has turned out to be an excellent salesman.'

'And Hadley,' said Cain, 'tends to lord it over the showroom, like it's his own little fiefdom, but he certainly does look after things. They're both very good at what they do.'

'Indeed. But neither of them are businessmen.'

'True.'

'Everyone has again done exceptionally well. Bill and Greg will be paying their Christmas bonuses into their accounts two weeks before the Chinese new year in January.'

Cain was getting out of a taxi by the entrance to Jewel City when the rumblings of 4x4 vehicles and a screech of tyres gained his immediate attention. One hundred officers of the anti-crime force – the Scorpions – jumped from their trucks and entered the diamond centre.

Cain pressed the button on his mobile.

'Morning,' Moshe said.

'Hi,' said Cain. 'I'm down at the entrance to Jewel City watching dozens of Scorpions entering the main gate.'

'Must be a raid.'

'It's going to be a bad day for the dishonest dealers.'

'Indeed. Don't come in. Go have a relaxing day. I'll call you when it's over.'

Cain got back in the taxi contemplating what to do – and it drove off.

Moshe soon heard the thunder of marching boots and the barking of military orders in the hallway outside his office, followed by shouts of protest and arguments. All of which synced perfectly with what Moshe was watching on the screen by his desk. Eventually, one of the Scorpions looked up at the CCTV and gave a wave. Moshe pressed a button and the door opened.

***

From the back of the taxi en route to the Sempre Aqui, Cain could see the rush-hour traffic was coming to a stop – and so was the taxi heading in the opposite direction.

'Must be an accident,' said the taxi driver. 'Not a lot I can do.'

Cain noticed a shopping mall he had never been to on the other side of the junction.

I'll go have a look to idle the time away.

Some fifteen minutes later, he was sitting in a café reading a newspaper, when he heard a female's voice, 'Morning Cain.'

He looked up to see Hadley's wife Bekha, more a Victoria Principal than a Claudia Cardinale. 'Morning, what a pleasant surprise. I thought you were in Prague.'

'I'm just passing through. I stopped off to see a couple of old girlfriends. Are you waiting for Moshe? I haven't seen either of you since we first met some two years ago.'

'Sounds about right. Moshe won't be joining me.' Cain gestured. 'Would you care too instead?'

And the waiter arrived to take their order.

After the customary pleasantries, Bekha told Cain, because she was fluent in English and had an American passport, allowing her to travel freely around the world, she had been employed by an import/export company, based in Prague. It was the beginning of a leisurely morning: chatting amiably over coffees and doughnuts with fresh orange juice, before wandering around the shops.

'Time to head back to my hotel,' said Bekha. ' I have a few calls I have to make.'

'OK. I'll get a t–'

'Since you have nothing to do,' said Bekha, looking at Cain seductively, 'why don't you come with me?'

Getting the inference, Cain grinned. 'Love to 'come' with you.'

An hour later, Cain and Bekha were lying in bed, wrapped around each other and chatting. Eventually, Bekha looked at her wristwatch. 'I have a meeting; I'm going to have to throw you out.'

'OK,' Cain said, fondling her breasts… kissing her neck.

'I could always be a few minutes late.'

Monday Evening

Cain stepped out of a taxi, onto the forecourt of the only pole-dancing club in the upmarket suburb of Rivonia. 'Good guess,' he said to the smiling driver as he paid the fare.

'I knew it was where you wanted to be.'

'You wouldn't believe me if I told you,' Cain grinned, and he walked away.

Some fifty metres down the street of the village-sized, outdoor shopping precinct Moshe was waiting at a table, in a quiet corner of the Slug & Lettuce with a bottle of red wine and filled glasses already on the table.

Moshe said, 'The raid on Jewel City by the Scorpions was carried out to ensure the diamond merchants had the necessary documentation to verify the origin and legality of all the rough we have in our possession. Any rough not verified has been confiscated.'

Cain asked, 'Did the Scorpions arrest anyone?'

'Not yet, but several merchants who obviously did not have documentation tried to use the excuse they'd left their keys at home so they couldn't open their safes. They were thinking schoolboy tactics would give them time to offer a backhander, but their safes were sealed. They have clearly forgotten the Scorpions can never be bribed.'

'Those merchants are only delaying the inevitable.'

'Indeed they are.'

Cain told Moshe how he had bumped into Hadley's wife – and what had happened.

'You were seduced,' said Moshe, 'makes a change. Under normal circumstances you never tell anyone who you have slept with. Let's not tell Hadley.'

Cain grinned. 'Let's not. She told me he phones her on occasions, he still hasn't signed the divorce papers. He believes he can get her back; he offers to pay for her to visit him in Guangzhou.'

'How does she respond?'

'She says "I'll think about it." She also says, "Tell me how well the Investment Diamond Showroom is doing and perhaps I will." She certainly has a way about her.'

'Sounds as if she's just playing him along, looking for money.'

'What a surprise.'

'Indeed.'

And the waiter arrived at the table. Dinner is served.

Cain and Moshe spent the next couple of days in Jewel City conducting business, going out occasionally for a Reuben sandwich lunch, and communicating with Bill and Greg.

On Wednesday evening, Cain went to martial arts training with Eddie, the Master, always a privilege and later, he went to town on Bekha – a pleasure.

On Thursday morning, Cain was saying farewell to Bekha in her hotel room. She was leaving for the airport to catch her flight to Prague. 'I'll pay for your taxi,' said Cain, taking a US$100 note from the US$1000 he always kept hidden in his backpack and handed it to Bekha. 'Have a meal on me.'

'Oh thank you,' said Bekha. 'You always carry a pile of cash down there?'

'Might do.'

Bekha checked the time on her wrist. 'The taxi will be here in ten minutes.'

Cain grinned and Bekha got down on her knees.

On Thursday afternoon, Cain received a phone call from Marius: he would be in Jo'burg on the following day. Cain and Moshe offered to buy him dinner.

Friday Evening

In the private dining room of the Sempre Aqui Hotel, Cain, Moshe, and Marius greeted each other like great friends do. Over a relaxing dinner the three men reviewed everything that had happened during the past five weeks.

'You heard,' said Marius, 'about the shooting of Kobus' supposed new client in an underground car park?'

Moshe responded. 'Kobus rang me the morning after to tell me.'

'For various reasons I cannot go into detail. Suffice to say the new client was being watched by plain clothed police officers. In the underground car park a man, casually walking past him carrying a shopping bag with car keys in hand, unexpectedly pulled a revolver and fired three bullets into his heart and chest.'

Cain said, 'Carrying a shopping bag with keys in hand, a clever deception.'

Marius agreed. 'When the plain-clothes police officers made their presence known the gunman immediately opened fire on them. He was shot and, unfortunately, killed.'

Cain asked, 'Do you know who he was?'

'The police have not yet identified him, but his tattoos tell us what we already suspected – he was an ex-33s rogue freelancer.'

A waiter arrived to clear the table and returned with the coffees, a J&B, a Richelieu brandy, and Vera Lynn and supersonic. They toasted each other before Moshe went on to tell his story about the Scorpions' raid on Jewel City. Cain mentioned his unexpected encounter with Bekha.

'Interesting,' said Marius. 'I'll run a check on Bekha.'

'Good idea – just in case, thank you,' said Cain. 'I have to ask you the obvious question – any news on Windows or Lastly?'

Marius showed a rare momentary look of irritation. 'Despite the police offering a reward for any information leading to their arrest, they really have disappeared without trace.'

'Hopefully someone will come forward.'

'You never heard from Zokwana?'

Cain shook his head with a look of contempt. 'Nothing.'

'He will not last much longer in government. The media are gathering momentum on reporting his corruption and the South African president has just announced his complete faith in him.'

Cain grinned. 'Once the president of a country announces his complete faith in a minister, we know they usually end up resigning, good riddance.'

Marius smiled. 'The clock is ticking. When Zokwana leaves government, regardless of the reason, he will continue to act as a go-between for one of Africa's most powerful crime kingpins. Probably, the one we have nicknamed *Defunct,* facilitating all his trafficking enterprises.'

'Why are we not surprised?' Cain sighed.

'It explains why Zokwana has already purchased a property in Jo'burg. It is rumoured he already has a country estate, registered to an off-the-shelf company.'

'Where is it?'

'I don't know – I only heard about it yesterday afternoon.'

'Try asking the landscape artist Gina Du Toit about a farmhouse estate she painted somewhere in the Limpopo province in the last year or so.'

'There is a connection?'

'When I went to Zokwana's residence there was a painting of a Victorian farmhouse on the drawing room wall, above the fireplace. It was dated 1989, but if I'd got any closer, I swear I would have smelt the paint drying.'

Moshe asked, 'How do you know it was Limpopo?'

'All the baobab trees.'

'Well spotted,' Marius said.

'Her studio is a block down from Carlton's,' Cain added.

'I'll send someone over to see her.'

'Talking of days gone by, there's something I need to tell you about me, Jerry, and those *schwarzes* Lastly and Zokwana.'

'No need,' said Marius. 'While you have been up here in Jo'burg I received the file from the British on the killing of Lastly's brother in London. It must have been flagged because I received a phone call from a man called Mac. He filled me in on some of the redacted lines. He knows we are meeting this evening; he sends his regards.'

'I guess, deep down,' said Cain, 'all three of us have always known about each other. But of course, we never asked.'

'Indeed,' Moshe agreed.

'Now we are all on the same page,' said Marius, 'well almost, I have to tell you. If either of you had been fluent in Afrikaans, I would have wanted to recruit you. But not speaking my language: *Sou net die dood van jou gewees het* (Would only have been the death of you).'

'Talking of the death of me,' said Cain, 'do you have anything more on who the target was at the shooting in High Constantia?'

'It was you – Jerry and the Principal being there was purely coincidence. They have been informed you were the target.'

'How do you kn–'

Marius raised a hand, politely interrupting Cain. 'You will be leaving for Guangzhou on Sunday, yes?'

'For about two weeks.'

'When you get back I will fully update you and Moshe. We will then be in a position to coordinate a response.'

'For now,' Moshe politely suggested, 'let sleeping dogs lie.'

All three men raised their glasses. 'Have a good trip,' Marius said.

'Indeed,' Moshe agreed.'

'Stay safe,' Cain replied.

***

Early next morning, Cain and Moshe were sitting at their desks in Jewel City, chatting amiably about the day's agenda, turning on their laptops.

While having coffee and doughnuts, Cain received an email from Jerry:

Hi Cain,
Trust all well.
Before I start – just to let you know, I am all in one piece, everything is OK.
I was diagnosed with a brain tumour, I'm in hospital; I was operated on two days ago. I didn't tell you because I didn't want to worry you. I am scheduled to leave hospital in forty-eight hours. When you phone me on my cell phone, if I don't answer it will be because I am asleep. Will buzz you back when I wake up.
Cheers – although I now have a period of being on the proverbial wagon.
Jerry

After getting over the shock, talking with Moshe, Cain phoned Marius, booked a seat on the next available flight to the UK and gave Jerry a call. There was no answer, so he left a good-humoured message. He also phoned Mac in London as a courtesy and, following protocol, he mentioned what Marius had told him over dinner in the Sempre Aqui the previous evening.

'Thank you for telling me,' said Mac. 'I knew you would.'

'Pleasure.'

'It's been good talking to you,' said Mac, rounding off their conversation. 'Once Jerry is settled back on the *Disponible,* give me a call. It will be good to meet up again.'

'Of course.'

Cain spent the next few minutes looking at his diary with a very sympathetic, supportive Moshe before having a conference call with Bill and Greg in Hong Kong.

As the Boeing 747 lifted off, Cain looked down at Johannesburg's city lights.

He couldn't help but contemplate the events of the past few weeks: The punch-up with Windows and Lastly in the Land Rover. His fight with Gospel and Windows being shot in the dojo. Finding Lastly's Colt .45 after the attack in bandit country. Killing Smokey in the small park in front of the 'fortress'. The shoot-out with Jerry and his Principal in High Constantia. And last of all, meeting Bekha in Jo'burg.

He analysed all the conversations he'd had during the past few days.

He felt a slight niggle in his subconscious.

Why do I have the feeling I've missed something?

Part Eight

London, England

Best friends are always there for you,
no matter what

25

December 2003 – Post-Op

Arriving at Heathrow Airport, Cain switched on his mobile to check for any messages. There was just the one from Jerry:

> *Hi Cain,*
> *Your first visit to the UK for quite some time – now sod off.*
> *You have your keys to the Disponible. Let yourself in.*
> *You know where I am. See you when you get here.*

In the private room of the hospital Jerry said, 'Thank you for the J&B, Jameson, Lucozade, and Red Bull. The doctors were not amused. Oh yes and thank you for the packet of three – the nurses were amused.'

'Well, since you're not allowed to drive, I thought you might like a ride.'

'Sod off,' Jerry said – and they both laughed like best friends do.

'After the surgeon has examined me again tomorrow afternoon, I'll be free to leave.'

'OK. I'll come to collect you.'

'Great.'

For the next week they stayed on the *Disponible*, allowing Jerry to recuperate at a leisurely pace, talking all things past and future.

For the following fortnight they had a relaxing time. They visited the properties they owned to check them out, went to Jerry's local gym to have a carefully orchestrated exercising session. And in what had always been, in days gone by, one of their favourite restaurants, located on the Thornton Heath Pond Roundabout, South London, they had a steak.

'Our first steak without a bottle of Saint-Émilion,' said Jerry, raising his glass of Red Bull. 'Cheers.'

'Not for long,' said Cain, lifting his pint of London Pride. 'Chugalug.'

During several telephone conversations between Cain, Moshe, Bill and Greg, the following was agreed and confirmed by email: Cain would delay his next visit to Guangzhou until after Christmas and the New Year. The new schedule convinced Moshe the time had come: he would visit Israel for the first time in many years. Bill and Greg – between visits to Guangzhou – would be in their office in Hong Kong.

Cain would then fly to Guangzhou in early January to meet with Bill and Greg – and along with H&Z, Kay, and Susie Su, prepare for the Chinese new year on January 22nd.

The days leading up to Christmas were, as always, very busy. Therefore, depending on how Jerry was feeling, they would either stay in or go early to a restaurant to enjoy the festive spirit before the celebrating masses arrived. On returning to the *Disponible*, they would settle down to watch episodes of their favourite TV series – *The Prisoner, The Sweeney, Tour of Duty* – and one of the latest movies.

When Jerry went alone to his office party, his boss sent a car to collect him and deliver him home in the early hours of the morning. Cain was still awake watching a movie when Jerry returned.

'How'd it go?'

'Great. It's the first time I've ever been given a lift home because I didn't have a drink.'

When they went to the hospital for Jerry's penultimate check-up, his surgeon gave him the all-clear to return to work in the New Year, but with conditions. 'For the first few weeks you will be desk-bound. No active duty.'

'Understood,' Jerry responded.

'I'll see you in a few weeks,' said the surgeon, 'And don't forget, no alcohol allowed.'

On Christmas Day, on board the *Disponible,* Jerry was feeling a bit tired again. Cain cancelled lunch at the Dorchester and put a turkey in the oven. Afterwards, they sat and unwrapped their presents together. Cain placed the various gun magazines Jerry had arranged to be sent over from America, along with a bottle of J&B, and cans of London Pride on the table. Jerry tried on the assortment of hats to keep his head warm during the winter until his hair grew back. He opened a mah-jong board game, a porcelain teapot, a tin of Gunpowder green tea, and a bottle of Lee Kum Kee soy sauce. There were also several packs of his favourite: springbok biltong.

'I was going to give them all to you when you next came to Cape Town,' said Cain, 'but here we are.'

'Great, thank you.'

Cain got up, lifted cases of Red Bull into the saloon, and gave Jerry a box. He opened it and lifted out a deactivated Glock 19 pistol.

'Something for you to practise with here on the 'yacht' until you start carrying again.'

'Perfect,' said Jerry, dropping the mag and racking the slide with perhaps the greatest look of appreciation Cain had ever seen.

'Where's your holster?'

'In the wardrobe.'

'Shall we?' Cain said.

Jerry went to the wardrobe and came back with his holster on his waist.

Cain said, 'He was so quick he was fast asleep.'

'Fastest gun in the west,' Jerry quipped, placing the Glock in his holster.

Cain grinned. 'Like when you saved my life in High Constantia a few weeks ago.'

Jerry smiled. 'And you saved the Principal and me.'

Cain opened a tube of Smarties and placed one on the back of Jerry's hand, positioned horizontally next to the Glock.

Jerry had to draw the Glock, aim it, and pull the trigger before the sweet hit the floor.

Practice makes perfect.

On New Year's Eve they stayed on the *Disponible.* Out on the deck they listened to the Big Ben bongs counting down to midnight.

'Happy New Year,' they said as they embraced like best

friends do and enjoyed a Red Bull and pint of London Pride, watching the fireworks.

'2004. Here we are.'

'Cheers!'

26

Monday – January 5th, 2004

Jerry got a taxi to the Royal protection office where, for the next few weeks, he would be working a four-day week on the administrative side of things, leaving Cain on the *Disponible* to start preparing for his trip to Guangzhou.

First off, Cain powered up his laptop to check his emails. Moshe confirmed again he was having a wonderful time in Israel. He would book his flight back to Jo'burg after talking to Cain to coordinate their schedules and commitments for the weeks ahead. But there was no rush, January was always a very quiet month for them.

Cain then read what Bill and Greg had written, six hours ahead, from Hong Kong:

A few hours ago we were with a client in her car when we saw our investor, Teun the Dutchman, standing outside a restaurant talking to Zhang. A taxi then pulled up, they both got in. We have not seen them since. Nor have we heard from them.

If we had not been with the client, we would have stopped to confront them. However, having been given time to consider the situation, we thought it best to let you know and have a chat first.

Cain was well aware Teun the Dutchman – who he had never met – was one of the elite 1% clients Bill, Greg, and Riley had done business with in Perth, Western Australia. And years later, Teun had been the one who had invested the US$450,000 into Bill and Greg's investment diamond showroom in Guangzhou.

Cain closed his eyes. In his mind's eye he saw his beautiful Riley smiling at him – and for the first time in a very long time he watched the magic movie in his mind as they revisited all the islands, parks, the Outback, beaches, and restaurants they had been to together.

'But only diamonds are forever,' he whispered, as a tear ran down his cheek. Seconds later, having wiped his eyes, he typed a reply:

I'm up and running. If you are alone and able to talk,
give me a call. If not, give me a time.

Cain's phone immediately rang, he pressed the button. Bill and Greg confirmed they had no idea why Teun the Dutchman was in Hong Kong, meeting with Zhang. It was a completely unexpected scenario. They weren't sure what to do.

Cain's earlier thoughts about Riley gave his memory a nudge. He suggested: 'Email Teun's PA to tell her you have unexpectedly been given two pink diamonds to sell, from the Argyle mine in the Kimberley district.'

'Good idea,' Bill said.

'Tell her they are known to be beyond rare. And if Teun would like to see them, you will – because you have to visit another client in Switzerland – be happy to fly via Amsterdam to present them to him.'

'Nice one,' said Bill.

'We'll pad it out a bit,' Greg added.

After sending the email to Teun's PA, Bill and Greg received a reply an hour later:

Dear Bill and Greg.
Good to hear from you. Happy New Year.
I'm sorry to tell you Teun is with relatives and friends
in warmer climes.
He will not be back in Europe for another ten days.
He will have to miss out on the pink diamonds.

Bill and Greg then had a conference call with Cain and Moshe. They all faced a simple reality: Teun did not want to admit he was in Hong Kong. Therefore, they had to conclude his meeting with Zhang had been orchestrated – not accidental.

As a precaution, Bill and Greg would immediately ask Kay to examine the company's finances, stock lists, and financial transactions, especially cash, to see if there was anything suspicious – and ask Susie Su to keep her ear to the ground.

Bill and Greg would inform H&Z that Cain would not be arriving in Guangzhou for at least another ten days. It would allow the rest of the week to pan out. But in reality, Cain would arrive in Guangzhou on the following Sunday and secretly meet up with Bill, Greg, Kay and Susie Su on Monday morning.

Meantime, a hold would be put on all diamonds going to the showroom. And H&Z's Christmas bonuses would, for the time being, be withheld.

Wednesday – January 7th

Cain – for the first time in many years – entered Mac's office.

'Morning,' said Mac, getting to his feet with a most welcoming smile.

Cain grinned, 'Good to see you.'

Stepping towards each other, exchanging pleasantries they shook hands and embraced like a father and son.

Mac said, 'It's certainly been a while.'

'Too long.'

After they both made a number of good-humoured comments about looking fit and being healthy, Mac did as expected; he examined Cain's right hand... 'You're still a young man,' said Mac, 'a lot has happened during the years you've been away. Tell me what you've been up to.'

Over coffee, Cain went on to tell Mac about Guangzhou, Zhang's secret meeting with Teun the Dutchman in Hong Kong, Bill and Greg's subsequent email to his PA, and the not-so-truthful reply they had received.

There were several things Mac had planned to tell Cain, but after hearing Cain's story he concluded: he needed to make a number of enquiries first. 'Keep me updated.'

'Will do.'

Changing the subject of conversation, Mac said, 'Marius and I have crossed paths on an investigation into an organisation involved in the illegal trafficking of cash, drugs, guns and girls across Africa, into Europe and the UK, involving Zokwana.'

'You know Zokwana was the man in the taxi in 1992?'

'Yes,' said Mac. 'Marius and I have exchanged a great deal of information. How long will you be in China?'

'Now I know Jerry is well on the road to recovery, I will be there for my usual two weeks.'

'You will, of course, come straight back to London to meet up with Jerry.'

'Yes, so I can spend some time with him, however long he needs.'

'Having spoken with Marius I realise you have many unanswered questions about what has been going on in South Africa.'

'Especially if what is now your joint investigation is linked to the attempts on my life.'

'When you get back from Guangzhou I will fully update you. We will then be in a position to coordinate a response.'

'Those are the exact same words Marius said to me in the Sempre Aqui.'

Mac smiled, checked the time on the clock on the wall and said, 'Let's have lunch together.'

Friday – Old Times

Late in the morning – after the rush hour traffic – Cain drove Jerry out to Berkshire to see the countryside, breathe in the fresh air, and have a bite to eat. They stopped outside the Windsor flat they had once lived in to take a look, reminisce, and have a laugh.

'If it comes up for sale again,' said Cain, 'we'll buy it for old times' sake and rent it out.' Cain put Jerry's Land Rover into first gear.

'Not quite the 351 V8, Windsor *flat* used in Starsky's Gran Torino. You OK, Hutch?'

'Sod off.'

Along the A4 on the outskirts of Slough, Cain stopped at the red lights where their great friend Adam, a gay fellow photographer, had been killed in a car accident many years before.

'Hi Adam,' Jerry said.

'We just stopped by to say hello again.'

Cain and Jerry looked at each other, remembering the famous one-liner from the classic TV series *The Prisoner* all three of them had always used when parting company: *'Be seeing you,'* they both said – and the lights turned green.

They had a couple of drinks in Bray, in The Crown and in the Hind's Head, two pubs at either end of the main street where they would often say hello to the great Michael Parkinson having a drink with the hilarious Jimmy Tarbuck. It turned out to be a great session of reminiscing before they drove to what had always been their favourite Chinese restaurant, the Chef Peking on the outskirts of Maidenhead.

Saturday Afternoon – Time To Go

Cain and Jerry meandered along their well-trodden path of jests and gibes, and they embraced like best friends do.

'Have a relaxing weekend,' Cain whispered. 'Take care.'

'Will do.'

However, as they drew back from each other, a feeling of concern still lingered in the space between them. 'Be careful,' Jerry said quietly.

'I will.'

Jerry was going to drop into his office to while away the first few hours without Cain before he took a taxi back to the *Disponible*, where a female friend would be spending the rest of the day, perhaps weekend, with him.

'Enjoy your 'ride' in every sense of the word,' Cain quipped.

'Sod off.'

'Put it on,' said Cain. 'I've got to see it.'

Jerry, already smart in his work suit, stepped back and placed the 007 hat – a Christmas present from Cain – on his almost completely bald head.

'Licence To Kill.'

Part Nine

Shamian Island, Guangzhou, China

The value of actions lies in their timing.

Laozi

27

Moshe had never had any desire to go to China. However, towards the end of his trip to Israel, he'd suggested on the phone to Cain, 'Since I am already halfway there, I could fly on to Guangzhou.'

'Why not?' said Cain, somewhat surprised. 'You have clearly developed a travel bug.'

'I'll finally meet Bill, Greg, Kay, and Susie Su.'

'We'll show you around.'

'Hopefully,' said Moshe. 'I will be able to lend a hand so you can get back to see Jerry sooner rather than later.'

'When I leave for the UK, you should come with me – Jerry would be more than pleased to see you again.'

'If there are no demands for an immediately return to Jewel City I will. Thank you. Once you have booked your flight to Guangzhou, email me the flight details. I'll see if I can match your timing.'

Sunday January 11th

Cain and Moshe got out of the taxi and walked across a now pedestrianised bridge onto the historically magnificent Shamian Island, where no cars were allowed. The iconic 19th century colonial architecture, along the now paved, silent tree lined avenues, and beautiful gardens – *far from the madding crowd* – proved to be an absolute sanctuary. It was a perfect setting for wedding photographers taking pictures; for tourists posing next to memorials, in front of historic buildings and hotels – one of which they would be staying in. Located in the Liwan District, a twenty minute drive from the centre of Guangzhou, it was truly the perfect location. Out of sight, out of mind.

In the late of the morning, Bill, Greg, Kay, and Susie Su

arrived at the hotel.

Cain introduced them all to Moshe. It turned out to be a memorable first hour of socialising, having tea and coffee. Moshe studied them all appreciatively: Kay, 40, slim and petite with shoulder-length hair, was attractively turned out in a blouse and trouser suit. Susie Su was equally gorgeous with a chic page-boy haircut, sleek dress, and French designer boots. While Bill and Greg, sharply dressed in stylish suits, looked like top executives.

After the waiter arrived with refreshments, Moshe got down to business.

'On Friday afternoon I received a phone call from a trusted senior official in one of the Jewel City certification offices. I was told when H&Z were employed by their miserly merchant employer, Hadley had been selling diamonds on behalf of a third party – and before he left for Guangzhou, US$10,000 in cash went missing from a transaction he had brokered.'

Everyone looked concerned.

'Was Zhang in on it?' Cain asked.

'Nobody knows.'

'If you have only just found out, it must have all been kept very quiet.'

'Yes, very,' said Moshe. 'Merchants are very reluctant to let it be known they have been conned or turned over. Everyone knew of the problems H&Z were having getting their commissions from their miserly employer. So when they resigned to come to Guangzhou, nobody was surprised or gave it a second thought, especially since Hadley is supposedly an honest and trustworthy devout Scientologist.'

Cain sighed. 'Let's not even talk about the honesty of religion.'

'Months later the powers that be had Hadley blacklisted. He will never again be able to enter or work in Jewel City. The full extent of his dishonesty and stealing may never be known. I'm sorry, I should have known,' said Moshe apologetically. 'It is my fault. I–'

'We are both to blame,' Cain said.

Bill held up a hand. 'Greg and I had background checks done on Hadley and Zhang before we employed them, but we found nothing, so we are all to blame.'

'We are,' Greg agreed.

Moshe turned to Bill and Greg. 'You told us how, over these past few years since leaving Australia, you wondered if Teun the Dutchman's drug habit could ultimately become an addiction.'

'On the rare occasions we have met him in recent years, he always looked slightly higher,' Bill confirmed.

'The Flying Dutchman,' said Moshe. 'Despite his wealth – and being a member of the elite 1% clientele – do you think he could have become a drug dealer?'

The question left everyone momentarily pondering what the answer could be.

Greg looked to Kay. 'Your turn.'

Kay confirmed as requested, she had re-examined the company's finances, stock lists, and financial transactions, especially cash.

'Zhang is selling diamonds without telling us,' said Kay. 'When I was in showroom updating, checking everything, I sat at Zhang's desk.'

Greg politely interrupted 'Your English is certainly getting better every day.'

'Thank you. When Zhang not in office and Hadley talking to client I look in Zhang's desk drawers to see what there. I saw envelope full of cash. I thought it was company cash, so I checked it. There was false invoice for US$9,000 with it. Zhang is buying diamonds in Hong Kong for his, not our clients.'

'How do you know?'

'Early next morning, Zhang was talking to supplier in Hong Kong on his cell phone, down in parking area. I walked past him. I hear what he said. He didn't see me because he was sitting with his back to hedgerow. He looking other way, talking loud, and speaking English to show off.'

'What did he say?' Bill asked.

Kay removed a notebook from her briefcase. 'I write it down so I not forget.'

'Take your time. No rush.'

'Thank you,' said Kay as she perused a few pages. 'Ah yes, here it is. Zhang say to man on phone: You have them? Next he say: When I get to Hong Kong, I must go bank first because it close early, then dealer. Then last he say he will be there at 5pm, before I catch train back to Guangzhou. He then end the call.' As Kay placed her notebook back into her briefcase she said. 'As I move away I saw Hadley sitting next to Zhang.'

'Your English is very good,' said Moshe. 'Did Hadley phone anyone?'

'No. I only ever hear him talking on phone to his mother. He calls her mommy. He speaks to her at least three times a week.'

'Mommy,' said Cain. 'Seriously?'

'Yes.'

Greg looked to Susie Su. 'Your turn.'

'I have found out when you speak to clients who do not speak English, Zhang no longer translates what you say word for word. He decides if what you say not to his liking, he tells them whatever he wants to. He tells them you are all foreigners; you don't understand the Chinese way. When you say no to people, Zhang says maybe. When you ask for something he says consider. When you ask to meet them again, he tell them I let you know. Zhang has told a lot of people he is now the boss, you all work for him.'

Bill asked, 'Any idea how long this has been going on?'

'From what I have heard, not too long.'

For the next hour they all discussed ways of trying to find out why Teun the Dutchman had met Zhang in Hong Kong – and how to conclude the inevitable.

On a more positive note, Bill and Greg produced documents confirming the profits the investment diamond showroom had made during the past year.

'As a thank you,' said Bill, gesturing to Kay and Susie Su. 'We will be paying H&Z's annual bonuses into your accounts.'

'We can never be without you,' Greg said.

'Ladies,' said Cain, 'you are true professionals. *Xièxie* (Thank you).'

'Indeed, well deserved,' Moshe added.

Moshe glanced up at the clock on the wall. 'Time for me to buy you lunch.'

In the private dining room, chopsticks delved into the banquet of chicken asparagus, crispy duck, kung pao pork, shrimp, broccoli, steamed vegetables, and rice laid out on a lazy rotating Susan tray in the centre of the table. The meal quite unexpectedly turned out to be a celebration, so they ordered champagne too.

During the course of the next three days, Bill, Greg, Cain, and Moshe met with H&Z in the showroom. Later, they met Zhang on his own in Bill and Greg's lawyer's office, where Zhang was made a director of the investment diamond showroom business.

Meanwhile Kay, and Susie Su were informing their wealthy clients, they would be taking an extended holiday together, abroad.

Forty-eight hours later, all the directors of the investment diamond showroom business – except for Zhang – resigned. Bill and Greg informed their elite 1% they would be leaving Hong Kong to return on a permanent basis to New York.

On the following evening, Moshe, Bill, Kay, Greg, and Susie Su boarded an aircraft for Johannesburg. They would stay at the Sempre Aqui Hotel and wait for Cain to leave Guangzhou. After Cain had met with Jerry in the UK, he and Moshe were to be best men at two weddings: Bill and Kay, Greg and Susie Su were to be married in the USA.

On Sunday afternoon, Cain left Shamian Island and booked into the Taojin Hotel, located at the end of a dead-end street overlooking the Huanghuagang Commemoration Park in Guangzhou, a fifteen-minute walk to where H&Z were working in what was now Zhang's showroom.

Cain would now put the finishing touches to what had been organised.

28

Monday – Set Up

In the late of a Chinese afternoon Cain was on the phone to Moshe, Bill and Kay, Greg and Susie Su in Jewel City.

Bill confirmed, 'H&Z have employed two Chinese girls to work in the showroom. The girls were interviewed by H&Z several weeks ago, so something was obviously already in the making. Kay and Susie Su initially heard about it on the grapevine.'

Moshe said, 'Hadley now has his own little fiefdom again to lord it over, just like he did when he was here in Jewel City.'

Greg added, 'We know Zhang has learnt how to stroke Hadley's ego and over-inflated sense of self-importance. But of course, the loyalty of the two girls will be to Zhang, a Chinaman, not Hadley, an American. Zhang now has total control and free rein to go about his daily dishonesty.'

Minutes later, having discussed the plans for the night ahead, Cain said, 'Thank you ladies and gentlemen. I'll let you know how it goes.'

Monday Evening

In the Taojin Hotel, Zhang was meeting with a young woman who had visited what was now his showroom earlier in the day. They had a drink, had a chat, and wandered over to the elevator. In her room, Zhang sat on the bed, but the young woman immediately left the room and Cain stepped out of the bathroom.

Zhang showed a look of total incredulity.

Cain said, 'Time to have a chat.'

'I won't–' Zhang stammered, getting to his feet, but Cain stepped forward and slammed him against the wall.

'After everything Bill, Greg, Moshe, and I have done for you – everything you were not able to achieve on your own or with

Hadley – you both turn out to be liars and thieves.'

'But I can ex–'

Before he could say another word, Cain frog-marched Zhang towards the door. Zhang thrust out a hand to grab the handle, but Cain threw him sideways into the bathroom and pinned him against the shower wall with a hand around his throat. Zhang immediately saw the point of a blade hovering in front of his face.

'Lie to me again,' said Cain, 'and I'll take your fucking eye out.'

Cain eased the pressure on Zhang's throat. Gasping for air, spectacles lop-sided on the end of his nose and goggle-eyed with fear, he attempted an apology. 'Sorry,' he gulped.

After a little more 'encouragement', Zhang made his confession. It had all started when Mr. Kwan, the owner of the Major Casino in Macau – who had visited the showroom in Guangzhou – had given Zhang cash to buy diamonds for him in Hong Kong. Once Zhang was on the bandwagon, the amounts of cash soon started to increase substantially.

'I also buy for his business friends,' Zhang said.

'Who are they?'

'I don't know – I never meet them.'

Cain realised Mr. Kwan had been using Zhang to launder money, allowing those behind

the scenes to retain their anonymity. 'You met with Teun the Dutchman in Hong Kong. Why?'

Zhang balked, 'How did you know?'

'I'll ask the questions,' Cain said with a look to kill.

'Teun showed us emails saying Bill and Greg owed him US$445,000. He said they refused to pay it back: their debt, not my debt.'

'You didn't think to ask Bill and Greg if it was true or if the email was genuine?'

'Err, why would Teun lie?'

'Same reason you do.'

Such perfidy.

Zhang closed his eyes, screwed up his face and stayed silent as Cain continued. 'How much are you paying Hadley?'

'I told Hadley Teun phoned me, asking me to buy diamonds

for friends in Hong Kong. I told Hadley it was a cash deal. I gave him few hundred dollars and told him it was half the commission, to keep him happy.'

'No honour among thieves.'

Cain waved the blade again in front of Zhang's face and decided to take a gamble of a slightly different kind 'Tell me about the Dutchman's drug-dealing.'

Zhang's eyes, bulging from the pressure across his throat, took a breath as best he could and nodded: the pressure eased. 'Teun knows people in Hong Kong who sell drugs. I went there to collect cash and buy diamonds for them. They gave me commission, but just for diamonds. I don't deal drugs – no problem.'

'*Caveat emptor* (Let the buyer beware),' Cain said.

'Who is Emptor?'

'The man I have paid to kill you.'

Zhang's fear heightened; his mouth opened but no sounds came out.

'The diamond ring on your finger,' said Cain, 'where did you get it?'

'Teun bought it for me. It sealed our deal.'

'Give it to me.'

'But–' Zhang started to protest.

Cain waved the blade, allowing Zhang to take the ring – instead of what he feared, may be his finger – off.

'What are the names of the people Teun sends to meet you?'

'It's not Teun who sends people,' said Zhang. 'I just have a burner phone with a Hong Kong number. They call me with a code word. They change the code word and number every month.'

'Try again,' Cain said waving the blade.

'Lee. It only name I ever heard.'

'Lee – first name or surname?'

'Ah, I don't know – No one I meet ever says more than one or two words to me.'

'Where are they from?'

'They are all Chinese.'

Cain stepped back and jabbed Zhang in the stomach.

'Argh!' Zhang cried out, believing he'd been stabbed – and

sinking to the floor, he pissed his pants.

Cain pressed the button on his burner cell phone, saw it ring and turned it off. Zhang, realising he had been punched, not stabbed, slowly got to his feet.

Seconds later, the door to the room opened and the young lady Zhang had met – who had been waiting in Cain's room across the hallway – appeared.

Cain said, 'If you go to the police or tell anyone else about what has happened here this evening, this young lady will say you tried to rape her.' Seeing how bad Zhang's urine-stained trousers were, Cain concluded their meeting. 'Now *piss* off.'

With Zhang out of the room, Cain handed the young woman, a high-class hooker hired for the 'sting', a wad of cash. 'Thank you,' he said, 'have a relaxing night.'

'I will.'

Cain spent the rest of the night in his room, writing on his laptop what Zhang had said to him, and putting together what should happen next.

After he emailed his thoughts to Moshe, Bill, and Greg – who were waiting in the late of the afternoon in South Africa to read it – he got a beer and sat on the sofa to have a think.

Tuesday – Paint it Black

In the late of the following evening, Cain was again on the phone in his hotel room talking to Moshe, Bill and Kay, Greg and Susie Su, who were all sitting around the table in a private conference room in the Sempre Aqui Hotel.

'It's been quite a day, getting it all done,' Bill said.

'We've talked to you more times today than we have in a whole year,' Greg added.

'But it's well worth it,' Moshe said.

'I have to thank Kay and Susie Su again,' said Cain, 'for enlisting the beautiful young lady who led Zhang well and truly up the garden path.'

'You're welcome,' Kay and Susie Su responded.

'We are ready,' said Moshe, 'let's hit send.'

On cue, they all emailed a situation analysis of H&Z's diamond smuggling and dishonesty to the relevant Beijing and

Hong Kong authorities, the Shanghai Diamond Exchange, and the Chinese consulates in London, Washington, and Michigan – Hadley's home state. Information outlining Teun the Dutchman's drug dealing activities were sent to the taxation offices in Belastingdienst, various police departments in Amsterdam, and the Chinese embassy in London. Meanwhile, in Barcelona, Sofia – Cain's and Jerry's friend – was posting copies of those same documents to various other authorities.

Cain had first met the beautiful Sofia – more a Salma Hayek than a Penélope Cruz – when he had been living in the UK. They had both hailed the same taxi on Oxford Street in London when he had been with Jerry. They all became good friends, allowing Cain and Jerry to visit her in Barcelona.

Cain considered Sofia to be his secret little treasure: a consultant on international tax law and fluent in Catalan, Spanish, English, and French, she had worked her way through the financial capitals of the world before returning to her home in Spain. Now in her late thirties, she ran her own company based in the tax-free principality of Andorra, shifting money on the periphery of legality, but all perfectly above board: out of sight, out of mind.

Her exceptional clientele were from around the world: it was fair to say Sofia had friends in very high places, the Pyrenees being among them, where she would often be seen in the King of Spain's entourage in Baqueira-Beret during the skiing season. In summer, she would often go to Barcelona, the beaches along the coast, and of course, Mallorca to again join the king's entourage.

Before Cain had travelled to Australia, he had nicknamed Sofia his PTPA – Part-Time Personal Assistant – and Sofia had always referred to him as her PTPS: Part-Time Personal Shag. When Cain went to Florida, his change of career had allowed him to enlist Sofia's professional services for one or two of his elite 1% clientele.

Bill said, 'Well, that lot will certainly put the cat among the pigeons. The way it is written, suggests a disgruntled diamond smuggler in Hong Kong or perhaps a dodgy client in China, who

Zhang has ripped off, is getting his revenge.'

'Thank you,' Cain said.

'As for the information about Teun, I would see it as coming from a drug addict who was conned in some way, deciding to even the score. The untraceable email addresses you arranged were a nice touch,' said Greg.

'Here comes the judge,' Moshe suggested.

'Hopefully,' said Cain. 'Have you heard anything from Teun or his PA?'

'Not a word,' Bill confirmed.

The rest of the call dealt with what Cain would do before leaving China.

Wednesday

Cain walked out of the FedEx office – he had sent Zhang's diamond ring to Sofia in Andorra as a present. He hailed a taxi to take him to Xianlie Middle Road Police Station, where he met with a crime officer to have his grievances against *H&Z* officially recorded. The officer's knowledge of the English language was rather limited, so he phoned the immigration department to ask if he could borrow one of their bilingual officers to help him out.

Thursday

Cain returned to Xianlie Middle Road police station, where Officer Luó read through the documents pertaining to the formation of the diamond investment showroom, Hadley's status in China, and Cain's synopsis. 'If GemGia no longer sponsors Hadley, who is?'

Cain answered, 'I believe they have falsified the necessary documentation to renew his sponsorship. Perhaps Lawyer Shen, who did the registration, is involved.'

'I will look into this,' said Officer Luó. 'Immigration is my field of expertise.'

After Officer Luó had made a phone call, Cain unexpectedly found himself hitching a ride in the back of a police van. 'This is quite an experience,' Cain said.

'Try not to make a habit of it,' Officer Luó responded.

And with smiles all round they arrived at the Luyuan Road police station.

In an interview room with three police officers, Officer Luó took on the role of translator, allowing Cain to tell his story… In a very sympathetic and understanding way, the police officers explained how the diamond and financial side of his dispute could only be investigated by customs and revenue. The officers made a number of calls and provided Cain with the names and contact details of those who spoke English and would be in a position to offer assistance.

'*Xièxie*,' said a grateful Cain, shaking hands with the police officers. And after the customary bows, accompanied by Officer Luó, he left the police station.

'Thank you for all your help,' said Cain, standing by the police van.

'You're welcome. Can we give you a lift?'

'Thank you for the offer, but I'll take a walk,' said Cain. 'I'm staying at the Taojin Hotel.'

'Good choice – lovely views over the park.'

'Yes, very relaxing.'

'I will let you know about Hadley's status. Good luck.'

'*Xièxie.*'

'Pleasure,' said Officer Luó, as they bowed and went their separate ways.

Walking back to the Taojin Hotel, Cain was pleased he had enlightened the authorities to the corruptness of H&Z and possibly Lawyer Shen. On the following day, he would stop by the diamond investment showroom to tell *H&Z* the police were investigating them before catching his flight back to the UK to see Jerry.

Being safely out of China, Cain would email and post all the information about Teun the Dutchman's drug dealing with *H&Z* to the Chinese customs and revenue officers in Guangzhou, whose details had been given to him by the officers in Luyuan Road Police Station.

Back in his hotel room, Cain got a beer out of the fridge and checked his emails. There were already two replies from the information they had all sent out only two days earlier.

The Dutch tax authorities wrote:

I have spoken with a colleague; he will see it is brought to the Director's attention.

The Chinese immigration authorities replied:

We are looking into this; it is already an ongoing investigation.

With beer in hand, Cain scrolled through the rest of his emails. There was one from Sofia. He opened and read it...

'Dear God, no!' he cried out; the beer bottle crashed to the floor and shattered.

My Dearest Cain,

Have been trying to call you, but your mobile is turned off. I phoned Jerry this morning to say hello but a fellow officer, sounding really distressed, answered his phone. There's no easy way to say this: I'm so sorry, but Jerry collapsed and died last night.

I'm so sorry Cain. I didn't want to tell you this way, but I knew I had to let you know.

It is such a tragedy. I'm crying. I have to go now.

Love, Sofia x

Cain stared at the message in total shock and disbelief. He checked his mobile: he'd turned it off when he had arrived at Xianlie Middle Road police station and when he left, forgot to turn it back on. Powering it up, he saw the missed calls from Sofia.

He phoned Jerry's office and spoke to his boss. Jerry had collapsed in his office, among his friends and fellow Palace Pups. He'd been rushed to the hospital, but he never regained consciousness.

Cain quietly asked, 'What was the cause?'

'Unforeseen complications – is all we know for now. We are all absolutely devastated. I'm so sorry Cain. Please accept our condolences.'

Cain ended the call, and a tear ran down his cheek.

Detective Inspector Jerry Davis had always been a copper's copper, the best of the best.

During the first years of his career as a bobby on the beat he was promoted to Sergeant and transferred to West End Central police station. One morning he discovered a flaw in the Prime Minister's security protocol that inadvertently alerted everyone in advance as to which exit the PM's car would take when leaving Downing Street. His subsequent commendation – as reported in the Metropolitan Police newspaper, *The Job* – had been well deserved.

Jerry had come from a time when ex-military personnel were proud to join the Force, when they were welcomed with open arms.

It was all before:

The ex-military were banned from joining the Force.

The university kids with zero experience were fast-tracked into the higher echelons of the Force by their political friends to do what they – not the people – wanted.

The Bobby Blunders had started taking control.

The Party Frocks – the PFs – decided the most essential training a copper could ever have, three years on the beat (always referred to as the Bible of Basics), was too old-fashioned and should be scrapped.

Party Frocks decided it would no longer be a police force – something to be reckoned with – but a *service* that, by 2004, was already becoming ineffectual and a laughingstock.

Cain remembered their 'steak-outs' together with a bottle or two of Saint-Émilion. They would then head home to watch one of their favourite TV series: *The Prisoner*, *Tour of Duty* or *The Sweeney*. And then they would stay awake into the early hours, Cain with a bottle of J&B and Jerry with his Jameson, talking about many things: the promises broken by various lying governments. The identity of those who ruled from behind closed doors: the Bilderberg Group, the Illuminati, and the conspiracy theories surrounding the deaths of Marilyn Monroe, Kennedy, and Princess Diana.

Cain had often said, 'We will have to write that book when

we retire.'

And Jerry had always answered: 'All those secrets: perhaps we will.'

Cain knew Jerry had been with the boys on the day Princess Diana had died.

And when Cain and Jerry finally decided to retire, they would have their bucket list of adventures ready and waiting for them. They were going to load up their cameras and spend their summers on the *Disponible*, sailing Europe's waterways and sampling the delights of booze, 'birds', steaks, and wine.

And when the autumn leaves would start to fall, they had planned to take a flight across the equator to the next summer: driving a 4x4 across Africa to photograph the wildlife. Great times had lain ahead, but now their bucket had been kicked over.

After moving into the newly built 'fortress', Jerry had arrived for another of his annual leaves, climbed the outside steps for the first time and, seeing the stable-style, red, front door, had asked, 'Is Mr. Ed in?' And they had both burst out laughing.

And from somewhere, Cain heard the theme song from one of their favourite TV series, *Tour of Duty*: the Rolling Stones singing *Paint It Black*:

> *I see a red door and I want it painted black . . .*
> *I could not see this thing happening to you . . .*

Cain closed his eyes, watching the magic movie in his mind as they revisited all the places in the UK, Australia, the USA, and South Africa they had been to together.

And from somewhere, real or imagined, *Terry Jacks* sang *Seasons In The Sun*:

> *Goodbye to you my trusted friend*
> *We've known each other since we were nine or ten*
> *Together we've climbed hills and trees*
> *Learned of love and ABCs*
> *Goodbye my friend it's hard to die*
> *When all the birds are singing in the sky*
> *Now that spring is in the air*

'But I wasn't there for you,' Cain whispered. 'Please forgive me.'

He burst into tears.

29

Saturday – Smash & Grab

It had not been a good night for Cain: overwhelmed by confusion, anger, denial, sadness, and frustration he had floundered in his misery. He had not felt such emotions since Riley's death in Western Australia. He had emailed Sofia, to thank her – and Mac, Marius and Moshe to tell them the bad news. And at the end he wrote: *Please don't phone me for now. I'll call you later.* Nor had he slept – he was in a tragic, unimaginable world of his own.

He phoned room service to order coffee before getting himself ready.

On entering the investment diamond showroom Cain did not see Zhang, but no matter – he kept on going.

I'll invade Hadley's little fiefdom. Rattle his cage. Take a look at the female staff.

'Morning,' Cain said politely to the two salesgirls, who showed a welcoming smile – and looking at Hadley he let rip. 'Well if it isn't the ungrateful, lying, thieving little prick. And I do mean *little*,' he chided.

Hadley was rooted to the spot, speechless.

'Have you given Bekha a call?' said Cain. 'I must admit I have *given her one!*'

'What do you want?' Hadley blustered. 'What have you been saying to the authorities?'

Hadley's response told Cain what he needed to know: the situation analysis sent to the Beijing and Hong Kong authorities, the Shanghai Diamond Exchange, and Chinese consulate in London, had been acted upon.

Cain retorted, 'After everything Bill, Greg, Moshe, and I did for you. Everything you could not have achieved on your own or with Zhang, you both turn out to be deceitful liars and thieves. You also, personally owe me US$5,000. You will pay the price.'

As Cain turned to walk away…

'Yes, get out,' Hadley ordered with a dismissive wave of his hand to impress the two salesgirls. 'You have stolen money. It will be the death of you.'

Hadley's mention of the word death instantly slowed the turntable in Cain's mind. He eyed Hadley's mouth moving, but with everything from the previous day, still reeling through his mind, he heard nothing. He sank into the depths of grief stricken rage that had last engulfed him when Riley had been killed – the depths of hell.

> When death and despair are upon you the slow-motion
> movie in the mind distorts time.
> What may seem like an eternity will, in the event, only
> be a second . . . or thirty.

Cain stepped purposefully behind the showcase closest to him and tipped it over. The two salesgirls screamed as he continued to walk around the showroom, pushing over each of the showcases one by one sending a sea of diamonds and shattered broken glass cascading across the floor. Totally shocked, Hadley stared in horror and disbelief at the destruction of his little fiefdom. On reaching the doorway, Cain looked back at the showroom.

Hadley shouted, 'You will go to prison for this.'

As Cain picked up a chair, lifting it high, his mind snapped back to normality – and Hadley instantly cowered. Cain looked at the devastation around him: he'd made a terrible mistake. He took a breath. He would not allow anyone to see how badly he felt. He glared at Hadley. He grinned. 'Happy (Chinese) New Year,' he called out. 'We will meet again when you are back in your hometown of Detroit with mommy.'

Hadley's jaw dropped – watching Cain turn and walk out into the mall.

> Tick-Tock. … Thirty-seconds. Time had moved on …
> and Cain sat down on the chair.

The sight and sounds of the girls screaming and shattered broken glass cascading across the showroom floor had attracted the attention of passing shoppers. Realising the six-foot Englishman was no longer on the rampage, just sitting and waiting, they congregated along the glass front of the showroom to watch Hadley on his hands and knees, crawling his way across a sea of glass and debris.

Cain stood up, took a couple of photographs with his Canon sure-shot for posterity and, retaking his seat, he began to contemplate the possible consequences of his actions. And the TV series, *The Prisoner* came to mind:

"You are Number 6," said the new Number 2.

Cain wondered what his number would be.

Two uniformed police officers appeared at the top of the escalator.

Part Ten

Incarceration

*The inner is foundation of the outer.
The still is master of the restless.*

Lao Tzu

30

Arriving at Luyuan Road police station, several officers recognised Cain from his previous visit. They immediately engaged in conversation with those escorting him.

An hour or so later, the door to the interview room opened, Cain got to his feet. 'Officer Luó,' he said with a look of abject regret.

The two men respectfully bowed and shook hands. 'What have you done, Cain?'

'I'm afraid I have made a terrible mistake.'

'Yes, you have.'

Cain had no intention of using the tragic death of Jerry as an excuse for his actions; he did not want the authorities to start delving into his past. 'I'm afraid an uncharacteristic moment of anger and frustration got the better of me.'

'At least no one has been injured,' Officer Luó sighed.

'I realise,' said Cain, 'bearing in mind all the assistance you and your fellow officers gave me previously, this is not how you expected me to behave. Please accept my sincere apologies.'

'Would you like tea?' Officer Luó asked, by way of accepting Cain's apology.

'Yes, a tea would be wonderful.'

'Please follow me.'

In the main office, Cain took a seat at one of the empty desks. Officer Luó said, 'The damage you have caused exceeds US$1000. It is therefore classified as a criminal offence. For a Chinese citizen an arrest, charge, and detainment would be mandatory, but because you are British, I can bend the rules. If Zhang will agree to you paying repairs and reparation, I can keep you out of prison. If not . . . well it's not a place I would want you to go to.'

'He will not agree to me making a payment.'

'You don't think so?'

'No way.'

'I will speak to him. Do you have a lawyer?'

'Will having a lawyer prevent me from going to prison?'

'I'm sorry, no. Once you are inside the system, it will take many weeks to get you out. The British Consul would be informed, and someone would visit you within the first ten days.'

Cain realised he was about to miss Jerry's funeral. Nothing else mattered anymore.

As predicted, when Zhang met with Officer Luó, he steadfastly refused to agree to anything that would result in Cain's freedom. Even worse, his arrogance prevented him from understanding the finer nuances of being advised how grateful the authorities would be if the Englishman were not incarcerated. Agreeing to compensation would save prison officers having to facilitate an Englishman for many weeks, police officers being committed to hours of paperwork, and courts an unnecessary number of hearings.

Officer Luó informed Cain of the situation. 'Would you be willing to meet Zhang?'

'Of course,' Cain agreed, knowing the meeting would have witnesses.

Some fifteen minutes later, Zhang strutted into the main office with his hands on his hips. He had quite obviously been to a barbers shop. He looked even more like – Kim Jong Un – the son of the leader of North Korea – the *hair* apparent. He sat on a chair in the middle of the floor, facing Officer Luó, spreading his legs and leaning forward to rest his hands on his thighs, thumbs and elbows outwards. Cain was not the only one to notice the peculiarity of Zhang's posture. The three police officers present were bemused.

Straight out of Dumb and Dumber, Cain thought, *the scene with the man on the loo.*

Ignoring Cain, Zhang stared at Officer Luó. He did not seem to comprehend the situation: Cain was sitting at a desk at the side of the room, drinking tea, whereas Zhang was sitting in the middle of the room, where the accused are usually placed.

'I knew Cain would come back to China,' Zhang announced

arrogantly. 'You owe the investor Teun the Dutchman US$450,000. You're trying to make your debt my debt. I am the owner of the showroom. I won't deal with you.'

Cain responded as instructed by Officer Luó. 'You were made a director of the investment diamond showroom only a week ago, when Bill and Greg resigned because of your dishonesty – and Hadley's too. As for your accusation regarding the US$450,000, please show the evidence to the police. Tell me, is your smuggling of diamonds from Hong Kong into China and selling them under the counter making enough money for you and Hadley?'

'I don't know what you talking about. We are not dishonest – you are.'

'Hadley is working here in China illegally.'

'Not true. He not illegal.'

'I used my UK registered company, GemGia, to sponsor him, to get him his work visa, and subsequently renew it each year to allow him to work here in China.'

'Teun the Dutchman arranged his work visa, not you.'

'Please remind Hadley he personally owes me US$5,000.'

'He doesn't owe you any money. The investor provides all the money.'

'Where did you get the diamonds for the showroom?'

'From the investor, Teun the Dutchman, not you.'

'Everything you have said is the truth?'

'Yes.'

'Thank you,' Cain said.

Got him!

'Just so you know,' said Cain, 'I have spent the last two days meeting with the police and immigration.'

Zhang glanced at Cain and back to Officer Luó. 'He cannot–'

Officer Luó raised his hand. 'Be silent,' he said and, looking at Cain, 'Please continue.'

'I have provided the police and an immigration officer with copies of all the documentation relating to the opening of the investment diamond showroom by Bill and Greg and the investments made by Teun the Dutchman and myself. I have provided copies of our visitor visa applications and the letters of invitation you wrote, relating to the business and work visa for

Hadley. I have also provided bank statements. They prove Teun the Dutchman's investment of US$450,000 was paid back to him over a year ago – and I transferred US$5,000 into Hadley's personal bank account in South Africa.'

The penny had finally dropped. Zhang's composure left him, he stared down at the floor.

'You're a liar and a thief,' Cain said.

'You going to jail,' Zhang countered.

Officer Luó gestured to one of the police officers – Zhang was led out of the room – and turned to Cain. 'I see what you mean.'

Alone in the interview room, Cain used his mobile to phone Sofia. Condolences were followed by tears before Cain gently explained his predicament.

Sofia opened Cain's file: he had no living family or relatives, so she pulled out his emergency situations list. She saw Jerry's name at the top and burst into tears again. Cain realised what Sofia had probably done. A few seconds later, Sofia came back on the line. 'I have already opened Jerry's file. You know he left everything to you.'

'We left everything to each other.'

'I'll speak to your lawyer in London. He will take care of the *Disponible*, your properties, everything in your absence. Do you have a lawyer there in China?'

'Not yet, but I'll sort it out.'

Awkward seconds of silence followed. Neither of them quite knew what to say.

Cain quietly asked, 'Please send an e-mail and fax to Moshe in Jo'burg. Let him know what has happened.'

Cain knew the ex-Mossad man – still with Bill, Greg, Kay and Susie Su – would immediately inform Marius down in Cape Town and Mac in London.

'I'll send it immediately after we finish our call,' Sofia said.

'Thank you for helping me. Don't forget, when you inform the British Foreign Office of my predicament, you have to tell them you are my fiancée or they will not communicate with you.'

None of the usual jokes and gibes such a comment would have provoked were exchanged.

Sofia asked, 'How can I contact you?'

'I have no idea,' said Cain, feeling drained. 'I have to go now.'

'Take care.'

Hadley sat opposite Officer Luó, telling him several diamonds were still unaccounted for, inferring Cain had stolen them. 'Where else could they possibly be?'

Officer Luó picked up two sheets of A4 paper and looked at Hadley. 'These are signed witness statements from the two salesgirls employed in your showroom. Let me translate a part of it for you:

"Cain picked up a chair and walked straight out of the showroom. He did not pick up any

diamonds or take anything else from the showroom. He did not re-enter the showroom."

Officer Luó looked up at Hadley, who visibly paled and stayed silent.

'As you said, where else could they possibly be? Now get out. I expect you to be back within the hour.'

Fifty-five minutes later, H&Z were back in front of Officer Luó. He looked up at Hadley.

'You have found the diamonds?'

'Yes sir, they were–'

'What a surprise,' Officer Luó interrupted.

They are both habitual liars.

Officer Luó immediately placed an already prepared statement – confirming all the diamonds were accounted for – in front of H&Z and instructed them both to sign it. When H&Z walked out of the police station, they did not see the looks of contempt on the faces of the police officers watching them.

Back in the main office, Cain read through his statement, initialled the minor alterations and corrections, and signed each page. Next, he pressed his right-hand index fingertip onto a red ink pad and fingerprint-stamped each of his initials and signatures. He had just signed away his freedom, Chinese-style.

In another room he was searched, photographed, and his height and weight documented. Finally, his fingerprints were taken before he was led back to the interview room where he sat alone, waiting. *Tick, tock.*

When Officer Luó entered the interview room, Cain respectfully got to his feet.

'Sorry,' said Officer Luó, 'but you are now out of my hands.'

'Thank you for trying. You have the folder with all the documentation I gave you?'

'Yes,' said Officer Luó. 'I have it safely in my briefcase.'

The two men bowed, shook hands, and Officer Luó walked away.

At 7:30pm, two officers entered the interview room. 'You stay night,' said the senior officer, pointing at the floor and, gesturing with a hand, he put imaginary food in his mouth. 'You want?'

Cain gave the senior officer a look of appreciation with a nod of his head. 'Yes please.'

The junior officer raised his hand and rubbed his thumb along his fingertips. Cain got the gist; he laid cash on the table and the junior officer took RMB 40.

Thirty minutes later, taking his first bite of the chicken and rice, Cain made a gesture of thanks to the officer sitting by the doorway.

During another lonely, sleepless night, full of memories, full of regret, he remembered Jerry's second annual leave in South Africa.

Cain had driven them along the Garden Route at a leisurely pace. They'd stayed in the coastal towns of George, Knysna, and Plettenberg Bay before arriving in Port Elizabeth and heading inland to the Addo Elephant National Park.

There, they spent a couple of days following the elephants, while at night they sat on their balcony enjoying a J&B and Jameson, watching the tusks go by.

On the return cross-country route, Jerry had said, "Stop a sec. I've never seen this many in my life."

On the roof of the Jeep, Jerry stood taking pictures of the

'Plast-a-teak' flora of South Africa: dozens of plastic bags blown in the wind and caught on farmland barbed-wire fencing.

"Elephants' condoms," Cain had quipped, and they had laughed like best friends do.

In the town of Oudtshoorn, the ostrich capital of the world, they did the bird thing, visited the Cango Caves, had a lazy lunch, and drove down the 27km twisting mountain road called the Swartberg Pass. It was a truly memorable journey, on which they had stopped many times to enjoy the panoramic views, stand on the vertiginous precipices, and to take a picture or three.

In the late of the afternoon, they drove through the magnificent vineyards, the fruit and olive orchards – past the apricots and figs – to the small town of Prince Albert, located on the periphery of the Great Karoo, the lamb producing centre of South Africa.

After they had booked into their hotel, they went out for a wander. They soon found an *al 'fresco* restaurant where they had relaxed for the evening, sampling the local wine, the local produce, and a leg of lamb with just a touch of mint sauce.

Their last day had been a drive over the Du Toitskloof Mountains for lunch in Stellenbosch and a shopping spree in the Oom Samie se Winkel store, a national treasure, operating in much the same way as it had when it first opened in 1904.

At the Cheetah Outreach, they had leant on the rail overlooking the main attraction, a cheetah named Hemingway. "A Hemingway of a different kind," Cain had said.

"On a landscape of a different kind."

"How was the good old USA when you were last there?"

"Don't be *Naive*," said Jerry. 'The key to your answer on this one is very different from the Florida key(s).'

Jerry had again used the word *Naive*, an anagram of a nickname – known within certain circles – for a member of the Royal Family.

Cain knew Jerry would eventually get around to telling him what had happened, just as he would, had their roles been reversed and the proverbial shoe was on the other foot. He just had to go with the flow, and, in good time, all would be revealed. Cain had grinned, "We will have to write that book when we retire."

"All those secrets . . . perhaps we will."

The pen is mightier than the sword.

Edward Bulwer-Lytton

<h1 style="text-align:center">31</h1>

Sunday – Transported

On the following afternoon, Cain stood in the open doorway of his hotel room with his wrists cuffed behind his back, watching police officers packing his belongings into his suitcase.

Back down in the hotel reception, the dishevelled, unwashed white man, standing head and shoulders above the three officers who flanked him, proved quite a spectacle to the staff and guests who passed him as he waited at the counter. One of the officers removed cash from Cain's backpack side-pocket and paid his hotel bill.

Sitting in the back of a police van for the second time in as many days, Cain remembered what Officer Luó had said: "Try not to make a habit of it."

An hour out of Guangzhou, the van turned off the freeway to enter the *Guangdong Prison and Detention Centre.* At the barrier, the police van came to a stop for the security check. Moving off again, the van approached Cain's new horizon: a ten-metre-high, solid brick wall that appeared to stretch for miles. At the T-junction, the van turned left, onto the perimeter road. A hundred metres further on they passed through an open gate under a concrete archway into a large, deserted square and came to a stop in front of a guardroom. Once out of the van, one of the police officers – who had watched Zhang being interviewed in Luyuan Road police station – removed Cain's cuffs and said with a sympathetic look, 'Take walk.'

Cain nodded. '*Xièxie.*'

Leaving the police officers with the prison guards, Cain stretched his arms and legs, wandering across an empty staff car park towards a line of unoccupied office buildings. It was a Sunday afternoon, all was quiet.

Thinking again about Jerry, Cain turned back and stared at the enormous solid steel, cantilever gate in the ten-metre-high, solid brick wall – part of the new horizon.

He heard *The Eagles* singing *Hotel California:*

I had to stop for the night . . .
This could be heaven or this could be hell . . .
There were voices down the corridor
I thought I heard them say . . .
Any time of year – any time of year – you can find it here . . .
You can check out any time you like
But you can never leave.

Escorted by all three police officers, Cain stepped through the single Judas gate onto a deserted, inner perimeter road. As they crossed the road he realised the solid concrete wall ahead of them, stretching some fifty metres to his left and a hundred or so to his right, was the back of a single-storey building. And the two twenty-feet-wide cantilever gates built into the concrete wall, were made of vertical steel bars that reached from the ground up to the roof. On reaching the bars Cain could see straight across a seventy-feet-wide expanse – the restricted zone – to a second pair of identical cantilever gates. They were the entry and exit point for everyone and everything on wheels.

As the old saying goes, Cain thought, *one way in (on the right) and one way out (on the left).*

Beside the pairs of cantilevers two much smaller Judas-style gates – only big enough for one individual at a time to step through – were closed.

A chorus of incessant beeps accompanied the partial opening of the cantilever gate. Cain and the three police officers stepped through, the beeps changed to buzzes and the gate closed behind them.

To his right, an unoccupied desk was the checking-in point for a large visitors' waiting area, lined with rows of benches facing a long office-style reception counter. Cain glanced up to see security cameras on all sides, surveying everyone, everything around him. He looked to his left, across the restricted zone: a solid concrete wall ran the width of the building. At one end, a steel door provided the entry point for the visitors' cell block to meet with prisoners. And at the other end, a one-way window of black glass, allowed unseen guards to keep watch.

To the sound of footsteps and a door closing, Cain turned to see a warden marching towards him, talking in Chinese. Seeing Cain's wrists were not cuffed, the warden raised his voice with a tone of anger gesturing with a hand.

The senior police officer stepped forward to have a few words… a minute later their conversation ended seemingly on good terms. One of the police officers turned to Cain. 'You go now.'

Cain shook hands with the police officers. '*Xièxie,*' he said, bowing respectfully, and stepping back he waited for the next command. The warden couldn't believe his eyes.

Ten minutes later, Cain was standing naked on a square of steel grating, in the middle of a large room – the processing facility. Several desks and a door were positioned along one wall. A line of three-tier lockers along another. And a massive cage made of wild west-style prison bars – crammed with thrown-in suitcases and bags – filled a corner.

None of the prison guards spoke more than a word or two of English. Hence, when one of them walked past Cain, spiralling a hand, he once again, got the message. He turned around to follow the lead. They both squatted down and after spreading their legs, they placed an elbow against each knee, leant forward and jumped up and down. The guard gestured with a waving hand for Cain to continue and stood up, leaving the guards at the *rear* – in every sense of the word – to see if there were any illegal secretions, namely drugs, dropping to the floor.

When Cain was eventually told to stand up, a guard pointed at a small bar of soap on a steel table fixed to the floor, next to a steel grating. As Cain picked it up, a spray of icy cold water from a hosepipe hit him, a shiver of shock ran down his spine. After he had quickly washed himself down he – as instructed – returned the soap to the table, did a 360-degree turn to get himself rinsed off and the flow of cold water stopped. Standing dripping wet, realising he would not be given a towel he wiped himself down with his hands. Still slightly damp and feeling cool, he walked naked over to his suitcase, where a guard, removing some of his clothes, held up his jeans and indicated with a pair of scissors: if he wanted to wear them in prison, the zips would have to be cut out. Cain gave the guard a shake of his head.

'Get clothes on.' the guard said.

Wearing his long-sleeved shirt and baggy beach shorts, minus the cord, Cain took his backpack over to the warden sitting at a desk. The warden took out the envelopes, opened them and gasped at the amounts of cash: several thousand US dollars in various currencies. The warden tossed the Chinese 10-cent notes – worth about a penny each – into a drawer and looked up at Cain. 'For Chris-mas.'

Cain grinned with a nod of agreement to say on the warden's good side. 'OK.'

His laptop, mobile, keys, credit cards, IDs, passport, and cash were inventoried and placed in a clear plastic bag. When all was done, a guard sealed the bag and laid it down on the desk. The warden turned the register towards Cain and held out a pen. 'You sign.'

Cain signed both the register and the seal on the plastic bag – and placing his index finger onto a red ink pad he signed everything again Chinese-style. The warden tore out the perforated yellow slip of paper from the register and handed it to Cain. 'You keep. You lose, you no get back,' he said, placing his free hand on the sealed plastic bag.

'*Xièxie*,' said Cain, 'thank you for all your guidance.'

'Go,' said the warden, pointing at Cain's suitcase lying on the floor. Cain stood watching a guard rummaged through his suitcase, bundling up four pairs of his boxer shorts, two pairs of socks, and two blue long-sleeved T-shirts.

With the bundle in hand, Cain was escorted barefoot back through the visitors' waiting area into the restricted zone and through the second cantilever entry gate. The beeps changed again to buzzes, and the gate closed behind them.

Across a ten-metre wide driveway, Cain scanned a tennis court-sized park surrounded on three sides by an elevated walkway and what appeared to be one end of a two-storey H-block. However, the upper floor – enclosed by glass – showed Cain it did not accommodate prisoners. Instead, it was one section of an interconnected observation gallery that allowed the guards to walk around all the H-Blocks, watching the prisoners, indoors or outdoors, below them. Cain was not too surprised to see a guard sitting up on the balustrade of an open window with a cigarette in the corner of his mouth, keeping an eye on the new arrival. The guard taking a drag, revealing a single speck of light in the dullness of the late afternoon, and the puff of smoke drifting in the air, reminded Cain of a certain ex-33s rogue freelancer under a small copse of trees, opposite the 'fortress' in Cape Town.

I can't have another Smokey in my life. I'll nickname him Ciggy-lee.

A short walk along the driveway brought Cain to the door of the medical centre. Inside, a lone doctor took a sample of blood to test for drugs and carried out a rudimentary health check. For most of the time Cain managed to stand or sit with his arms semi-folded across his stomach or by his side, preventing the doctor from noticing the imperceptible small scar on his side or six inch one on his wrist.

'You all OK,' the doctor said, and the guard led the prisoner away.

On reaching the top of a short flight of steps, Cain was guided along the side of the H-Block's elevated walkway, overlooking the park, past two pairs of black metal doors marked 125 and 124 and came to a stop outside the pair marked 123.

The guard – who did not speak English – looked up at his tall prisoner and momentarily hesitated. Cain sensed something wasn't quite right, but he had no idea what, so he simply, already standing to attention, gave a respectful nod... and the guard reached for the keys.

When the main door opened, Cain was expecting to see a corridor, perhaps a row of cells. Instead he went down three steps into a deserted, white-painted concrete-walled room – some seventy feet long and ten feet wide. And to the sound of the main door being slammed shut, a steel bolt sliding, a chain being dragged through iron rings and a key turning, *Click* – he stood alone.

Cain looked up. Fluorescent tubes in the ten-metre-high ceiling lit the room, and a CCTV kept an eye on everything down below. Around the tops of the walls, several small

rectangular steel-barred openings provided the air for the room
– and a few drops of rain, splashing through them fell to the
floor.

Glad I missed the rain. I'm damp enough.

To Cain's left, three steps up, a steel sliding door was
closed. To his right, a row of clear fifty-litre plastic storage
containers were stacked – some two metres high – in the corner
against the walls. Each one appeared to be filled with clothes,
the odd tube of toothpaste, bars of soap, packets of biscuits and
things he did not know, with labels in Chinese he could not
read. As he walked the length of the room he eyed the various
items of men's clothing hanging on most of the rounded-knobs
– on either side of him – stuck in the walls.

I'll nickname this open space: the laundry-room.

Against the back wall, Cain was surprised to see a Wild
West-style rectangular water trough, made of concrete with a
tap next to it, not above it. Against the side wall, a six-foot long
slab of concrete, accommodated a Chinese porcelain, squat-
down toilet at one end with a twelve-litre bucket full of water at
the other. It was a looland with a *flush valve* of a slightly
different kind. And having a half-metre high, concrete, mini-
wall on its open two sides with a gap to step through, Cain
came to terms with a whole new perspective on privacy.

Cain turned around. Up above the main door, Ciggy-lee was
leaning on the inner balustrade of the observation gallery – on
the safe side of Wild West-style steel bars – looking down at the
new arrival. He removed the cigarette from the corner of his
mouth with one hand and pointed down at the steel sliding door.
Cain walked back towards what was the entry point to his new
world – and waited.

The steel sliding door scraped open – and Cain stepped up
into room 123. It was a wider version of the laundry room.
Opposite him, along a one-metre-high, two-metre-wide
platform – stretching the length of the room – a dozen Chinese
and one black prisoner were sitting motionless staring at him.
Above them, the (painted) numbers, 1-29 were evenly spaced
along the length of the wall. At the far end of the platform,
standing under the number 24, a single prisoner wearing an
odd-looking beanie stared at Cain for a long few seconds,

before he returned his attention to the open paperback in his hands.

On the other side of the room, half a dozen prisoners were sitting on a shorter, centred platform with the numbers 30-40 painted along the wall.

Could get crowded in here.

Hi, my name is Cain,' said the only white man in the room. 'Afternoon.'

Nobody moved or spoke as the steel sliding door scraped to a close behind him.

From under the number 1, a prisoner, perhaps in his late twenties, wearing a yellow waistcoat, slid himself to the edge of the platform, dropped himself down into a pair of slip-on sandals and, stepping forward, addressed Cain. '*Nihao* (Hello),' he said. 'You English.'

'Yes.'

'We have English speaking,' said the yellow waistcoat and, shouting, 'Afam! Afam!' he beckoned the new arrival to follow him.

Watched by the silent inmates, Cain walked barefoot along the central aisle between the two platforms, noting the pairs of plastic and rubber slip-on sandals neatly laid out along both sides. When they reached Number 19, a much older-looking prisoner, probably in his late fifties, moved away from the young black man he had been talking to and sat alone, watching Cain.

Hi,' Cain said to the black man. 'You must be Afam.'

'You must be Cain.'

After the yellow waistcoat spoke in Chinese to Afam, he spoke in English, 'You help new prisoner.'

'Leave it to me.' Afam turned to Cain, 'Every room has two Yellow Jackets. They are the ones in charge. I would like to introduce you to Zen. He is the Number One here in room 123.'

'Pleased to meet you,' Cain said holding out his hand.

After the customary pleasantries in both English and Chinese, Zen gave Afam a grateful wave and walked away.

Cain asked Afam, 'You speak Chinese as well as English?'

'Just a little. You are from England?'

'From London. And you?'

'Uganda.'

Afam turned himself around, his shackled ankles had been chained through a solitary, five-inch iron slave ring, embedded in the concrete platform.

'Are you always chained?' Cain asked.

'Just for today.'

'What did you do?'

'Breathing while black.'

'You have little other choice.'

'True. Most Chinese hate black people – they won't even shake hands without wearing gloves. Where do you live in England?'

'I used to live in London, I now live in South Africa.'

And shaking hands, South African black man-style – double grip, two position hold, three-time crunch – Afam realised Cain was more than likely telling the truth. The sound of Chinese voices made everyone look up at the observation gallery, a small TV had been turned on. Several prisoners gathered near the end of platform two, under the number 38 to watch the start of a game show.

'The TV always comes on at this time,' said Afam, 'but not too loudly.'

The analogue clock under the TV, in the centre of the front wall, confirmed the time: 6pm.

When Zen shouted out various commands, Afam gestured for Cain to watch what was going on. As several prisoners pulled out a number of fifty-litre plastic storage containers from under the platforms and started removing various items, Afam started his briefing: 'Every prisoner has to wear his yellow or grey jacket at all times, on top of whatever else he is wearing.'

Cain could clearly see all the prisoners were wearing black or dark-blue tracksuits under fleecy jumpers or army-style jackets with a grey – except for the two wearing yellow – sleeveless jacket on top. But in reality, the 'jackets' were waistcoats.

I can't be bothered to ask why. I'll just go with the flow.

A prisoner walking barefoot along the platform, knelt in front of a very precisely folded, triple-stacked duvet, under the number 20, and moved it along by precisely one number. A second prisoner then placed another, not so new looking stack in its place.

'It's our bedding,' said Afam. 'They are heavy-duty, double sized duvets. In this cooler time of the year, we have to fold them in two to cover ourselves. Only one duvet per prisoner is allowed. If you are lucky, the one they have given you might be quite clean. When you wake up in the morning, you will fold it military-style and place it back against the wall under your number 20.'

Cain glanced around the room; all the stacks were folded under their respective numbers. 'Why is no one sitting on them?'

'We are not allowed to touch them until 9pm.' Afam eyed Cain's damp shirt and beach shorts. 'You will be rather cold here. And if you stay long enough, you will be very hot. There is no heating or air-conditioning in the rooms.' Afam looked up at the small rectangular steel-barred openings around the tops of the walls. 'We only get the not-so-fresh Chinese air.'

As Cain removed his damp shirt to put on his T-shirts, many of the pale Chinese gazed at his deep all-over tan. 'You like the sun,' Afam commented.

'Always. This is the natural colour I go to when I am on the beach.'

'I know the feeling,' Afam chuckled, looking at the backs of his black hands.

Zen appeared on the centre aisle beside them and handed Cain a grey jacket. 'You always wear this,' he said.

'Of course.'

After a few words in Chinese to Afam, Zen spoke in English to Cain, 'You sit. You talk. No move.'

'OK.'

Zen again gave Afam a grateful wave and walked away.

A prisoner handed Cain a red twelve-litre bucket and scurried away.

'Put it on floor,' said Afam. 'It is not allowed on the platform. All items given to you now go in it. You'll get things from prisoners in this room or from others who have been released, moved to other places, or executed. The authorities provide nothing. You must thank each prisoner; it is the custom.'

Thus began a ritual of appreciation, as Cain bowed to each prisoner and thanked them as they presented him with a toothbrush with half the handle cut off, a tube of toothpaste, a pair of plastic mugs in amber and beige, a brown face cloth, a bar of soap, two shampoo sachets, a toilet roll, and a plastic drinking bottle. A one-litre-sized rectangular plastic container was placed on the platform next to Cain. He lifted the lid to see a white Chinese plastic soup spoon inside.

'The bowl is what they put our food in,' said Afam, 'and the spoon is what we eat it with.'

Last of all, a pair of used slip-on sandals were placed on the floor next to Cain's bucket.

'Not the bucket list we dreamed of Jerry,' Cain whispered quietly with a feeling of self-condemnation.

'Sorry,' said Afam. 'I missed what you said.'

'Oh nothing,' Cain sighed shaking his head. 'Just thinking out loud.'

'When you on platform you must be bare foot. Sandals not allowed.'

Seeing Afam was rather round-faced and somewhat overweight, Cain asked, 'How long have you been here?'

'One month.'

'Apart from Zen, does anyone else in this room speak English?'

'Some know a few words,' said Afam. 'You will be pleased to know you are the only white man here.'

Cain surveyed the room. 'So I am.'

Afam chuckled again. 'No, not in this room, I mean in the whole prison.'

'Really?'

'You are the only white man out of eighteen hundred.'

'How many black men?'

'About one hundred, from many different African countries.'

'None of them Americans or Europeans?'

'No. I can see you did not have your head shaved.'

Cain noticed Afam's near-bald head and glanced around the room. No one had any hair.

'New arrivals' heads are always shaved,' said Afam. 'I wonder why they didn't shave yours?'

'They wanted to, but I stood up so they couldn't reach.'

Afam laughed, 'Really?'

'The guards didn't ask or try. Has everyone in here just arrived?'

'No. The guards bring the shaver to the room once a week. The Chinese prisoners always shave their heads and so I do. At the same time, the guards bring in a pair of nail clippers, no scissors allowed.'

Cain watched Zen sit down on an upturned bucket on the floor at the end of platform two, by the steel sliding door. Picking up papers in one hand, with a pen in the other, he commenced writing on the page of a ledger. Several prisoners crowded around him to read what was being written.

'Zen is holding your papers,' said Afam. 'You are being officially logged into room 123.'

When Zen finished writing, he closed the ledger, spoke a few words in Chinese, and the prisoners around him wandered off to watch TV, talk with others, have a read, have a chat and watch the white man.

Afam said, 'The second main door behind Zen, always stays closed. Only the much larger food flap in the centre of it is ever opened, three times a day for our food bowls to be passed through.'

Cain saw one of the prisoners kneel down at the end of platform one and push open the rectangular steel flap of a military-style pillbox. Cain realised he had not noticed the flaps when on the walkway. He expressed a momentary look of self-annoyance, perhaps sadness.

Deep down, his mind was on other things.

Afam guessed what Cain was looking at and asked, 'The pillbox yes?'

'Well spotted.'

'The pillbox is the only way the guards communicate with us. One of them passed your papers and grey jacket through it to Zen before they opened the steel sliding door to let you in. If at any time the Yellow Jackets want something, they leave a note wedged in the flap of the pillbox for the guards to see when passing. At all other times, it must remain closed.'

'Why is the prisoner looking out?'

'Who knows? The guards will soon see the light and without warning, it will be slammed shut. Ouch,' Afam joked, as he held up his hand, fluttering his fingers.

Cain grinned. 'Painful,' he said.

I know the feeling.

'When it comes to deliveries,' said Afam, 'if something is too big to be passed through the pillbox, the guards will try the food-flap before having to open the main door. You have noticed the Number-2 Yellow Jacket sitting on his upturned bucket with his back against the front wall.'

'All he seems to do is sit there with his arm laid out along the platform's edge, tapping his fingers.'

'Beware of the Number-2 Yellow Jacket,' said Afam. 'His name Liu Jin. He is slightly mad. With him we have to be extra careful.'

'I know the type,' said Cain. 'We can nickname him Liu-ny, loony.'

'Very good,' said Afam as he pushed Cain's shoulder like a long-time friend would. He was clearly pleased to have someone to communicate with, especially someone who had lived in Africa. 'Now would be a good time for you to put your things away,' Afam, suggested, stretching himself, moving his feet, rattling the chains. 'I will have to stay here and watch. Make sure you put everything correctly in place on the shelving and you fold your face cloth exactly like all the others. Those are the rules. Never break them.'

'Will do.'

Cain picked up his food bowl, slipped on the sandals… they were a size too small, and picked up the bucket. At the end of platform two, many buckets were lined up: some were empty, others were full of what looked like wet clothing, while two were filled with rubbish – bin buckets. Above the buckets, concrete shelving filled half the wall. Cain placed the items he had been given: His toilet roll on the top shelf; his food bowl and spoon on the next; his plastic drinking bottle on a narrower rack below; his toothbrush and toothpaste in his amber-coloured mug at the end of the next shelf; and his bar of soap and shampoo sachets in his beige-coloured mug on the end of the lowest shelf. Everyone else had stamped their precious belongings with black ink or product stickers to give each one a unique identity, a stamp of ownership. Cain's items, unmarked, gave him a unique identity in their anonymity. He took the last item, the eight-inch square brown face cloth, out of his bucket and turned to face a much larger looland in the back corner, spanning half the width of the room. Being closer he realised the three-feet-high side wall was in reality, another horse-style, concrete trough full of water. Memories of his jokes with Jerry about Mr. Ed came sadly to mind. As he sighed he noticed for the first time a little Chinese man sitting alone at the end of platform one in the corner, half hidden by the triple-stacked duvet under the number 29, reading a magazine. He was wearing a red jacket.

A Red Jacket. I'll have to ask Afam who he is.

Cain stepped through the gap in looland's half-metre high, concrete, mini front wall. Two squat-down toilets shared just one twelve-litre bucket full of water. On the back wall above the single tap at knee height, a row of rounded-knobs numbered one to twenty-nine were positioned at shoulder height. Twelve of the knobs had identically folded eight-inch square face cloths hanging from them. Cain folded his face cloth and hung it on the number twenty. On the side wall, the rest of the rounded-knobs, numbered thirty to forty, had another six cloths hanging from them. Cain did a quick calculation: *13 + 6 = 19*. But with Red Jacket, there were twenty prisoners in the room.

I'll ask Afa–

Cain's empty bucket tumbling across the floor interrupted his line of thought. He turned to see the prisoner wearing the odd-looking beanie glaring at him like a madman, waiting for a reaction.

'No problem,' Cain said as he walked to the side of looland, stepped over the mini front wall and giving the glaring beanie a wide berth, he retrieved his bucket, placed it in line with the others under the shelving and backed away.

As Cain sat down under his number 20. Afam said, 'The beanie man is a mad one.'

'I'll nickname him Mad-Hatter,' Cain quipped.

Afam showed a look of amusement. 'Always keep him at a distance.'

The Mad-Hatter started walking along the centre aisle, singing horrendously out of tune.

'Will do,' said Cain. 'Especially when he's singing. Tell me where do we have a shower?'

Afam gestured towards looland with a nod of his head. Cain turned to see a naked prisoner empty a bucket of water over his head, place it back under the tap, and start washing himself down with a bar of soap.

Cain turned back to Afam. 'Now I know,' he said. 'Don't tell me the eight-inch square face cloths are our towels?'

'Yes.'

'Is there any hot water?'

'No. And to save you asking. To wash our clothes, we put the bucket under the tap, fill it up and wash your clothes in it.'

'Drinking water?'

'The dustbin at the other end of the room under the clock is filled each day with drinking water. Take your drink bottle and it will be filled for you.'

9pm – The stacked duvets were laid out.

Cain and Afam sat with their backs against the wall and their legs between the folded duvets, talking about the daily routine. Cain soon began to feel very tired. He had only slept for a total of some three to four hours during the last two days, since reading Sofia's email. 'You will have to excuse me,' he said to Afam. 'I think I'll lay down now, I'm feeling rather tired, it's been one hell of a day for me.'

'I understand. You have to sleep with your feet against the wall, not your head.'

'OK,' Cain said. He couldn't be bothered to ask why. Staying fully dressed; to stay warm, he got under the folded duvet. 'Night,' he said quietly to Afam. 'See you in the morning.'

'I'll be here.'

As Cain folded a corner of the duvet over to make a semblance of a pillow, he realised the platform was only six feet wide, so he could only just stretch out his legs. He closed his eyes.

In his mind's eye, he saw Jerry and Riley with their arms

around each other, just like they were in the many photographs he had taken. "We're OK," they said.

After several minutes of painful reminiscence, Cain rubbed his eyes, trying to hold back the tears.

Come and get me.

32

Monday – Week One

7am – Wake Up.

The morning alarms had their desired effect on the sleeping prisoners in the H-blocks.

'Afam! Afam! Time to start day,' shouted Zen the Yellow Jacket as he made his way along platform one, stepping over and around prisoners as they awoke. On reaching Number 19, Zen faked a kick to Afam's side, smiled, and sat down on his overweight stomach. 'Good morning.'

'Go away, I'm busy,' Afam politely responded.

'Morning Cain,' Zen said.

'Morning Zen.'

After exchanging a few words with Afam in Chinese, Zen stood up, pretended to kick Afam again and, with his slip-on sandals in hand, he stepped over to the edge of the platform to start his day.

Afam sat up and, seeing the look of curiosity on Cain's face. 'Zen's game is a morning ritual,' he said, with an air of exasperation.

'Every day?'

'Not quite.'

With a bit of guidance from the chained and shackled Afam, Cain performed the first deed of the day. He triple folded their duvets with military-style precision and placed the completed stacks under their respective numbers, 19 and 20, against the wall. He then sat down next to Afam to observe the morning rush hour:

To watch the prisoners entering looland.

Take their face cloths off the knobs on the wall. Soak them under the running water from the solitary tap. Wash and wipe their faces and hands. Rinse their face cloths and hang them, perfectly folded, back onto the knobs on the wall.

Step out to get their mugs off the shelf. Step in to fill their mugs with water. Step out to clean their teeth, gargle and spit over the mini front wall onto looland's floor. And rinse their mugs in the horse-style trough, before putting them back on the shelf.

Re-enter looland to take a piss in the pot. Wash their hands and rinse their sandalled feet under the tap. Step out of looland.

Cain realised, despite the prisoners best efforts, the morning's ablutions were always going to be a somewhat crowded affair. Especially when – in the middle of it all – one prisoner remained squatted down over one of the two porcelain squat toilets with a loo-roll in one hand and a magazine in the other, oblivious to everyone and everything going on around him.

'You would think,' said Cain, ' he could wait until the crowd thinned out a bit.'

'He does it quite often,' Afam said with a look of contempt.

'I'll nickname him Pot Man.'

'Good idea,' said Afam, giving his legs a limited stretch. Seeing the last of the prisoners enter looland and Pot Man stepping out, he said to Cain, 'It your turn. Please bring our food bowls with you when you come back.'

'Will do.'

Red Jacket arrived and handed Afam an empty bucket.

'It's for me to piss in,' Afam said.

Cain refrained from making any 'piss people off' jokes. 'I'll leave you to it.'

Some ten minutes later, Cain and Afam were emptying dry noodles into their plastic food bowls.

'Just follow what they all do,' Afam said.

Cain walked down the centre aisle and placed the food bowls alongside the others on platform two. He put their plastic spoons on the upturned lids next to the bowls and returned to Afam.

'Drop the empty packets into one of the bin buckets,' said Afam, handing them to Cain. 'Everything must be kept perfectly tidy. You'll soon see why.'

'OK.'

'I'll guide you through the rest of the day. You will soon get to know the routine.'

'Thank you, I appreciate your help,' said Cain. 'When will they take the chains off your ankles?'

'At ten o'clock.'

8am – Breakfast Time.

Zen called the prisoners onto the end of platform one where they sat cross-legged and in silence in two rows, facing the sliding door.

When the senior prison officials and guards – occasionally accompanied by government and/or military personnel – appeared up on the observation gallery, Zen, standing to attention on the centre aisle, shouted, in Chinese, 'All present and correct, sir.'

On hearing Zen's declaration, the prisoners were allowed to either continue facing the door or respectfully look up at the passing officials. Cain looked up to see several men in various uniforms and a woman in plain clothes.

And once they were gone, Zen gave the command to disperse.

Minutes later when the food flap in the door banged down noisily, the two food-fetcher prisoners each grabbed two food bowls off the platform, and the rush began. The two empty food bowls were handed to Liu-ny, standing by the open flap. He passed them one by one through to the servers, who filled them to the brim with boiling-hot, slushy rice and passed them back. Liu-ny handed the filled bowls to the food-fetchers, who quickly returned them to their places on the platform and picked up two more.

When all the bowls were full, the food flap slammed shut and Zen gave the command, allowing the prisoners to pick up their very hot food bowls, put their spoons in them and, using the upturned lids as trays, sit and eat wherever they wanted to.

'We will have to nickname those who serve up the food,' said Cain as he stirred the rice, waiting for it to cool down and the noodles to soften. 'How about Steam-pots?'

Afam chuckled, 'The Steam-pots are females from a separate prison around the corner.' Seeing Cain looking across at an older prisoner, sitting on platform two, stirring one of four food bowls, full of rice, he decided to explain, 'We get two or three extra bowls of food every mealtime. Zen must know one of the Steam-pots. Zen tells the older prisoner to hold up the spoon and dish out the extra food to anyone who wants it. I know it's only rice at breakfast time, but you'll soon see many prisoners still want to have it.'

'We'll nickname him Hand-Out,' Cain suggested.

As breakfast came to an end, Cain watched the prisoners walk down to looland, wash out their food bowls and spoons, put them back on the shelves and begin their assigned, daily chores.

'I'll do yours for you,' Cain said to Afam.

'Thank you.'

8:15am – Clean-up.

Since Cain was the last prisoner into room 123, he should have been heir to the throne of the Last Man's Kingdom, the loolands – and assigned to clean them. But the timely arrival a week earlier of a Red Jacket had saved him.

Afam explained how the Chinese prison authorities and prisoners always deemed a Red Jacket to be a contagious individual; an untouchable who would be permanently kept at arm's length by those around him and rarely spoken to. Red Jacket stayed and slept at the end of platform one, under his number 29, with his personal effects and clothing kept in his fifty-litre plastic storage container under him, opposite his kingdom of looland. No other prisoner ever slept under the number 28 next to a Red Jacket who was always the last to eat, the last to drink, the last to wash, the last to do everything, before he set about doing his daily chores. After breakfast, lunch, and dinner, Red Jacket would clean up all things disgusting in and around the two loolands using just a scrubbing brush, a bar of soap, and elbow grease – without any rubber gloves.

'How does a prisoner get to be a Red Jacket?' Cain asked.

'I have no idea,' said Afam. 'When I asked Zen, he told me to never ask again. He will be coming to talk to you in the next minute or two.'

Zen explained to Cain, with help from Afam, what his daily chore would be. He would be partnered with a convicted shoplifter, to perform the second-worst chore of the day: swabbing the platforms and the floors in both rooms.

'Unfortunately,' said Afam with a shake of his head, 'Red Jacket was not here when I arrived in room 123, so you are very lucky.'

Cain showed a look of empathy. 'At least you only had to do it for a couple of weeks. I'll nickname the shoplifter whose helping me: Take-Away.'

Afam smiled, 'You have a great sense of humour.'

Cain and Take-Away dropped two bath towel-sized cloths into a bucket of water, wrung them out, rolled them up, and laid them end to end under the number 30 across the width of platform two. Next, they squatted down, side by side behind the cloths, put their hands on them and pushed them along the length of the platform (avoiding the stacked duvets) and back again. After they had washed and wrung out the cloths again, they commenced their second push along the length of platform one, while the other prisoners stood in the centre aisle watching the performance.

After Cain and Take-Away had again washed and wrung out the cloths, the other prisoners, with sandals in hand, stepped up onto the now dry platform two. They looked down at Cain and Take-Away performing their third push of the morning – along the centre aisle – and back again, before rinsing and wringing out the cloths and leaving them in the empty bucket.

The experience left Cain with just the one thought in mind:

Bath towel-sized cloths can be used to clean and dry the 'floors' but not the people.

8:30am – Work Time.

Cardboard trays of beads and thread were distributed to the prisoners sitting in their own preferred groups of twos, threes and fours, leaving Cain and Afam together and Red Jacket alone, under his number 29. The task involved threading a thin black lace through the centre of a single oval black bead and knotting the ends precisely, making a kind of ponytail band. The work was fiddly, mind numbingly boring and, for those prisoners detained long-term, it caused calluses, cuts, and blisters.

Zen and Liu-ny occasionally walked around the room inspecting the completed hair bands before tipping them into buckets under the clock on the front wall.

9am – Sort Out.

When the steel sliding door opened, Cain and Take-Away took their cloths and bucket full of water into the laundry, watched by Zen standing in the doorway.

And for Cain, as he knelt down, the lyrics of a great song came to mind: *Chubby Checker* sang:

Yeah, let's twist again . . .
And round and round and up and down we go again . . .

Once the floor was almost dry the prisoners collected their dried clothing hanging on the walls. The work buckets containing the completed hair bands and bin buckets were placed in the laundry room by the main door, waiting to be emptied.

Meanwhile, Afam sat watching the prisoners scouring room 123, making sure everything was in place.

10am – Roll Call & Inspection.

Everyone resumed their cross-legged, straight-backed positions on platform one, and waited. The sound of a turning key, a sliding steel bolt and a chain being dragged through iron rings on the main door, broke the silence. Mr. Lài, flanked by two prisoners wearing green jackets – the Trustees – entered the room.

Zen, sitting under his number one, shouted, 'All present and correct, sir.'

The roll call followed. Everyone shouted his number, in sequence:

Cain shouted, '*Bā* (Eight).'

Mr. Lài, wearing his black uniform, black tie, white shirt, and white cotton gloves, looked every inch a product of the Chinese system. He picked up the opened ledger and pen left by Zen on the end of platform two, read the report, signed it, looked at Cain, and nodded. He spoke a few words to the prisoners – but what? Cain had no idea. As Mr. Lài returned the ledger to the end of platform two, he issued orders and, accompanied by one Green Jacket, he left the room.

Zen and two other prisoners immediately jumped down off the platform into their slip-on sandals and, bending over like chimpanzees on the run, they scampered after Mr. Lài, leaving everyone to get on with the rest of the morning's chores. Everything was carried out at a frenetic pace, without delay, without complaint and, most of all – under the watchful eyes of Liu-ny and the Green Jackets – without question. The bin buckets were taken out of the laundry room, emptied, and returned while the work buckets were emptied and refilled with more materials. A Green Jacket eventually went over to Afam and unchained him.

Once everything was done, Zen scrambled out through the main door and onto the walkway, where he squatted down in front of Mr. Lài.

Afam told Cain it was compulsory for all prisoners to squat down and stay still when a guard entered a room. And when a guard escorting a prisoner stopped walking – regardless of the location the same rule applied.

'If you don't,' said Afam. 'The guard(s) will knock you to the ground.'

Cain realised when he had been escorted by a guard to the main door of room 123 on the previous evening. When he had remained standing. When the non-speaking English guard had remained silent, he should have squatted down.

Thank God the guard did not knock me down. Thank you.

Mr. Lài handed Zen a packet of cigarettes – the currency of containment. It was the morning's reward for a job well done. Zen quickly opened the packet, placed a cigarette between his lips and Mr. Lài gave him a light before dismissing him with a wave of his hand.

Zen scurried back into the laundry room with the main door slamming shut behind him.

The smokers all gathered around him to have a fag, a five-minute break, and a chat. The non-smokers, namely Cain and Afam, were left sitting alone on platform one, where they watched a prisoner performing a Tai Chi form on platform two. The prisoner, in his mid-fifties, was only 150cm tall. 'I'll nickname him Shor-tee,' Cain whispered.

'I wonder what he's doing?'

'I know it well,' said Cain. 'It is called a Tai Chi Quan-42 Short Form.'

'A short form for Shor-tee,' Afam said with a bit of a chuckle.

'He performs it perfectly,' Cain said, sadly remembering his own performances with Jerry in the dojos, on the deserted beaches, and on Devil's Peak. But he didn't mention it.

10:45am – Work Stopped.

The cardboard trays of beads, thread, and hair bands were stowed under the clock on the wall while any bits and bobs were dumped in the bin buckets by looland. Once everything was in place, the prisoners again placed their empty food bowls, with spoons on the lids on the end of platform two before they dispersed to sit and chat.

11am – Lunch.

The Steam-pots banged down the food flap noisily, prompting the two food-fetcher prisoners to begin their frantic mealtime chore, passing food bowls to Liu-ny and receiving filled ones from him.

Minutes later, after Zen gave the word, Cain and Afam settled themselves under their numbers, 19 and 20, waiting for their bowls, containing green vegetables and three meatballs, topped to the brim with hot slushy rice, to cool down.

'Instead of the meatballs,' said Afam, 'many of the Chinese prefer the thumb-sized pieces of pork. I tried them once, but there was too much fat.'

'I'll take your word for it.'

'Two days a week, the green vegetables are replaced by cooked tomatoes. And one day a week the meat is replaced by a slimy, soggy sort of pasta.'

'Always in the same boiling hot slushy rice?'

'Yes. Lunch and dinner is always the same meal,' said Afam. 'So no surprises ahead.'

11:15am – Clean-up.

When the prisoners finished eating, they washed their bowls and as instructed, started checking out the room to make sure everything was in place. They then did whatever they had to: like washing their clothes in a bucket before hanging them out in the laundry room.

11:45am – Close.

The steel sliding door to the laundry room closed. The prisoners unfolded their stacked duvets, laid them out under their respective numbers and settled down.

12 Noon to 2pm – Rest Time.

Two prisoners would wear the yellow jackets to keep vigil over those sleeping or reading: no talking or going to looland was allowed.

Cain laid under the duvet fully dressed and folded a corner over to make a semblance of a pillow. 'See you in a couple of hours,' he whispered to Afam.

Afam smiled. 'What a surprise.'

Cain closed his eyes. In his mind's eye, he saw Jerry and Riley again, with their arms around each other. Adam, their great photographer friend who had been killed in a car crash, appeared by their side. "We're all OK," Adam said.

Once more, fighting back tears, Cain had just the one thought in mind:

Wish I was with you.

33

Tuesday – Tiger Chair

In the cold light of the late morning, Cain was still wearing just his grey jacket, his T-shirts, beach shorts, and two pairs of socks, which made his one-size-too small sandals two sizes too small. He squatted on the walkway and held up his hands. A guard, wearing a jacket and gloves, cuffed his wrists. It was Cain's first time out of the room. It was good to breathe in the outdoor air, see the park, and look up at the cloudy, grey sky.

Down on the inner perimeter road, a line of chained and manacled prisoners, like a chain gang from a thirties movie, were being loaded into the back of a police van.

Why are they chained in such a way? Where are they being taken?

In the heated visitors' cellblock, at the start of a long hallway, six Chinese and two black prisoners were already squatting in a line, their backs to the wall, waiting to be summoned. As they watched the white man hunkering down at the end of their line beside them, they showed varying degrees of surprise, but nothing was said: no talking was allowed. An expressionless face peered down at Cain through the bank teller-style security glass of the guard's office. Cain could see the guard was pouring himself a hot cup of tea.

Ten minutes later, Cain was told to stand up and led along the hallway into an interview room. The room was divided in two by floor-to-ceiling bars. On Cain's side, there was a Chinese torturers, steel, tiger chair. Once Cain was seated, a guard swung its hinged front shut. Cain's ankles were now locked into place, while his wrists were manacled to the chair's built-in table. For the first time in his life, Cain was completely helpless and at the mercy of everyone and anything around him. A female police officer sitting on the other side of the bars started the talking, while her male colleague did the typing. Cain recited – as requested – what he had previously said to

Officer Luó on the day of his arrest. In mitigation, Cain explained again how he had tipped the cabinets over in an inexplicable moment of anger and frustration. It was a misdemeanour rather than a crime, and he hoped the matter could be resolved quickly. The female officer did not respond, handing Cain his statement with a pen and red ink pad. 'Please sign it.'

Cain could see it was typed in Chinese. 'Is there an English version?' he asked.

'No.'

'Can I have a copy?'

'Not allowed.'

He realised he had no choice, so he reluctantly, signed, dated and red ink fingerprint-stamped all where required and handed everything back, through the bars, to the female officer.

'Thank you. We go now.'

The officers packed their things, pressed the button to summon the guard, and left the room. Cain was soon released from the chair and taken along the now deserted hallway to the entrance of the visitors' cell block, where he was placed in the deserted return room. He caught sight of the time on the guard's wristwatch: 12:05pm; Rest Time had started. Knowing no prisoners would be moved until after 2pm, Cain sat down on a concrete bench along one side of the room, opposite a red bucket. He kept his distance: he didn't have to guess what was in it, the stench told him.

Shit.

As he sat alone for the following two hours: he closed his eyes to watch the magic movie in his mind, as he and Jerry revisited all the places in the UK, Australia, the USA, and South Africa they had been to together. And with a sense of sadness after he had analysed what had happened in the past few days. He had to ask himself:

Why had the police today interviewed him again? Could what the police had typed in Chinese not be what he had said? And recollecting what Zhang had told him about what was going on in Hong Kong, he was relieved the police had not mentioned anything about drugs. A sigh of relief was his only outward sign of emotion.

When Cain eventually arrived back in room 123, the clock on the wall said 2:25pm.

The prisoners were all sitting in their preferred groups, having a chat, and threading the beads to make the hair bands. Cain spotted Afam sitting with the much older looking Chinese man, whose name was Jiang, who spoke only Chinese. Cain gave Afam a nod: they would talk later.

'Your food on the shelf,' Zen called out.

'*Xièxie*,' Cain responded.

Sitting alone on the end of platform two, Cain opened his food bowl to see it was filled with cold, slushy rice, tomatoes, and a soggy sort of pasta. Taking his first spoonful, he could see Red Jacket sitting alone at the end of platform one, facing the wall, under number 29.

3pm – The steel sliding door opened, and the afternoon schedule began.

Cain was sitting next to Afam threading beads when the pillbox steel flap flipped up, immediately summoning Zen. A minute later, Zen called out Cain's name. Cain got up and moved quickly along platform one to kneel down next to Zen. He could see the face of the female police officer from his earlier interview looking at him. She said, 'You will be detained for another four days.' She walked away and the steel flap closed.

Cain realised she had immediately walked away so he could not ask the obvious: Why four days? Then what happens?

What Officer Luó had said came to mind:

"Once inside the system, it will take many weeks to get you out."

4pm – Work Finished.

Once the prisoners had put away the cardboard trays of beads, thread, and hair bands they went into the laundry room and waited. To the sound of a steel bolt sliding, a chain being dragged through iron rings and a key turning, they squatted down, the main door opened, and Mr. Lài stepped in. After a few words, he handed Zen the customary packet of cigarettes.

While the smokers were in the laundry room enjoying their

afternoon reward, Cain and Afam were alone on platform one, they talked about Cain's interview while watching Shor-tee performing a Tai Chi form.

When the smoking session came to an end, the prisoners dispersed to do several things: their washing, sort their storage boxes, have a chat, take rest.

4:30pm – Clean-up.

Cain and Take-Away grabbed their cloths to begin their cleaning work.

Yeah, let's twist again . . . And round and round and up and down we go again.

The rest of the prisoners stood watching, as usual, sharing an occasional joke, a jibe and a laugh or two, making fun of the white man. Having finished their work, Cain and Take-Away parted company. Cain sat down and shoved his cold hands under his jacket, trying to get them warm.

4:45pm – The steel sliding door closed.

After the food bowls were laid out on the end of platform two, the prisoners made sure everything was tidy, everything was in place.

5:15pm – Observation.

The prisoners were summoned again to sit at the end of platform one, waiting for the senior officials and guards to conduct their second tour of the day, passing by on the observation gallery. Once more, Cain looked up instead of straight ahead. He wanted them to see he was showing the greatest of respect.

5:30pm – The food flap opened.

Minutes later, having completed his good deeds for the day, Hand-Out picked up his food bowl and walked to the end of platform two, where he was welcomed by Zen, Liu-ny and two invited others – the chosen few – to join them for dinner.

The prisoners were left to their own devices for the rest of the evening. Some took their buckets to looland to have a shower, but not Cain and Afam: it was too damn cold.

6pm – The TV sprang into life.

The beginning of documentary hour.

7pm – China News.

Afam watched it and if there was anything of interest, he translated a lot of what was being said. It occasionally provided a subject for conversation.

7:30pm Weather Forecast.

Cain and Afam watched the weather report, waiting for the city of Guangzhou to appear. The symbols, icons, and numbers were self-explanatory to Cain, although the damp and cold of room 123 was enough of a weather forecast for all the prisoners.

7:40pm – International News.

Again Afam's occasional translation of a few words was always greatly appreciated. But aside from the clues offered by photos and film footage, Cain could only guess as to what was going on.

'You do not want to learn to speak Chinese?' Afam asked.

Cain was well aware when prisoners were supposedly helped with translations in a foreign land, they were often being lied to for any number of reasons – maybe just a joke. They did not realise, instead of saying nice to meet you, how are you, can you show me – they were saying go fuck yourself, you're full of shit, can you shag me. It caused many tragic, painful and deadly consequences for the prisoners.

Cain turned to Afam with a perfect excuse. 'I tried to learn French many years ago. My memory just isn't good enough. I can remember how to say hello and thank you but not a lot more. Hopefully, we both will not be here long enough to need to learn.'

8pm – China v Japan War.

The action-packed war series, based on the 1930's war between China and Japan, always gained the prisoners' undivided attention.

9pm – The prisoners unfolded their stacked duvets.

Several prisoners went to sleep, some read, and others, like Cain and Afam, sat talking.

9:30pm – In the middle of a programme, the TV screen went blank.

The prisoners completed their night-time routines.

10pm to 7am – Lights Out – Suicide Watch.

In reality, the lights stayed on 24/7.

The room was silent. No talking or going to looland was allowed.

Cain gave Afam a wave and stepped down onto the centre aisle. Cain and Take-Away – both wearing yellow jackets – began the first Suicide Watch of the night. They walked along the centre aisle to make sure no prisoners faces were covered, to make sure they were all breathing. They took up their positions in the middle of the aisle, level with the numbers 12 and 26 on the wall and stood to attention. The waiting game had begun.

When the senior officials and guards appeared up on the observation gallery, performing their last walk-by of the day, Cain and Take-Away ceremoniously knelt on one knee and bowed to honour the country's president – a man whom many Chinese hated – and honour the country they all loved.

Once the officials had passed by, Cain and Take-Away got to their feet and checked the time on the clock on the wall. They had been standing for thirty four minutes.

Cain sat on his upturned bucket on the centre aisle: it was forbidden to sit on or lean against a platform. When Cain heard footsteps, he got to his feet and looked up at the observation gallery to acknowledge the night guard, passing by on the first of his every twenty minutes walk-by routine.

Cain looked down at Take-Away, sitting on a bucket, sound asleep under the clock on the wall: a blind spot for the guard – out of sight, out of mind.

At the end of their two-and-a-half-hour shift, Cain and Take-Away woke up their relief team and handed over the yellow jackets. All prisoners, depending on how many were in the room, had to perform a Suicide Watch at some point between 10pm and 7am or during Rest Time, from noon to 2pm, every two to three days.

Cain laid himself in his duvet and having spent the past two hours thinking about all that had happened during the past week, he closed his eyes with a sense of regret, a feeling of remorse, trying to come to terms with reality.

34

Thursday Morning – British Consul

Cain was surprised to find himself in the medical staff's administration office, next to the medical centre where he had been examined on the day of his arrival.

At the end of a row of desks, Ms. Carrie Hutt, the Pro-Consul Corporate Services Officer of the Corporate Services and Consular Section of the British Consulate-General in Guangzhou, introduced herself.

The sight of the incredibly overweight blonde woman's white blouse and buttons being stress-tested to infinity and beyond, stretched the very fabric of plausibility itself. Cain pondered the potential 'fallout', should Louisiana's finest threads fail the challenge.

'Good to meet you,' said Cain, holding out his cuffed wrists, 'Please excuse the 'jewellery'.'

Cain was surprised to see Mr. Lài at the back of the room with a group of senior prison officials, guards, other uniformed men of varying seniority, and a woman in civilian clothing. They were the same people he had respectfully observed passing by on the observation gallery earlier that morning. They all showed a look of absolute surprise to see Cain shaking hands with Ms. Hutt.

Quite a crowd, I wonder why they are all here? What's going on?

Ms. Hutt introduced her young Chinese translator, Kim. The sylphlike figure in her twenties, with shoulder-length hair, wearing a black trouser suit over a white blouse, could have been a younger version of the beautiful Kay or Susie Su. The contrast between Ms. Hutt and Kim could not have been greater.

An English bulldog and Chinese cracker.

Cain apologised, 'Unfortunately, I've been wearing these same clothes for the past five days now. I have not shaved and there are no mirrors. Please excuse my appearance.'

'I understand,' came the deadpan reply with a look to match from Ms. Hutt. 'Please take a seat. How are you feeling?'

'I've been better.'

'I have to start by telling you I cannot give you any financial assistance or discuss your case. Is there anything you would like to ask?'

'I have never been in this situation before, so is there anything you would like to tell me?'

'I advise you to get a lawyer.'

'After being interviewed by the police yesterday, they told me I would be held here for another four days. So what happens next?'

'I strongly advise you to get a lawyer,' Ms. Hutt responded, avoiding the question. 'We have heard from Sofia, your fiancée. She was the one who alerted the Foreign Office in London of your arrest.'

'You are in contact with her?'

'Yes.'

'Please let her know we have met and I'm OK. I assume you have already given her the name, address, and phone number of where I am being detained?'

'Anything else?' Ms. Hutt asked, avoiding the question.

'The beach shorts and T-shirts I am wearing, especially at this time of year and in unheated rooms, are not really the best of options. Could you arrange a couple of tracksuits for me? My fiancée will pay you or I will when I get out.'

'You may wish to read these,' Ms. Hutt said, sliding a dossier across the table.

Cain saw a list of lawyers' names, addresses, and telephone numbers – nothing more – on the first page. He flicked through the rest of the dozen pages, each of which contained advice on being a prisoner and information on an organisation called Prisoners Abroad.

Cain looked up at Ms. Hutt. 'Thank you for this – what am I supposed to do with it?'

'Choose a lawyer.'

'I'll choose the first one on the list, Gregory Smythe.'

'Gregory Smythe will be informed.'

'Thank you,' said Cain, placing the dossier back on the table.
'Wh–'

'Our new ambassador, Johnathan Trenchard, who arrived last week, will of course do all he can to help.'

Cain had been taken by surprise, but he didn't show it. In the blink of an eye he relived what had happened back in 1996, when he was in hospital, after being shot at the polo ground. When he had elbowed Trenchard in the throat – and said, "Bye Trash-card, sorry Trenchard."

Trenchard certainly will do all he can but just to settle an old score, not to help me.

'You have several friends,' said Ms. Hutt, 'who are police officers in the UK.'

The comment struck a nerve, Cain took a breath... 'Yes, several good friends.'

'Is there anything else I can help you with?'

'How about getting me the tracksuits?' Cain suggested.

'I'll see what can be done.'

'Talking of the police,' said Cain. 'Hadley is now working illegally in China, while Zhang is smuggling diamonds into China from Hong Kong and selling them for cash. I wait to see what the police and Chinese authorities will do with those two.'

At the mention of the Chinese authorities, Ms. Hutt fidgeted uneasily. 'I cannot discuss your case,' she reminded Cain.

'I have not asked you to.'

'We cannot interfere with the legal process.'

Kim raised her hand to the side of her mouth and whispered to Ms. Hutt, who looked across to Mr. Lài and the others. A conversation in Chinese ensued, at the end of which Ms. Hutt and Kim got to their feet. 'I have to go now,' Ms. Hutt said.

'I look forward to seeing you again.'

'I am only allowed to visit you every thirty days.'

That last comment didn't take Cain by surprise – and once again what Officer Luó had said in the Luyuan Road Police Station came to mind:

"Once inside the system, it will take many weeks to get you out."

For appearance's sake and the benefit of the video cameras, Cain got to his feet, held out his cuffed wrists and, shaking hands with both Ms. Hutt and Kim, he politely said, 'See you in thirty days. Take care.'

Whilst Cain was being escorted back to room 123, on reaching the top of the steps to the walkway he came face to face with Mr. Lài, and instantly squatted down. Mr. Lài held out a hand and Cain, having no choice, handed over the dossier Ms. Hutt had given him.

'Tank yoo,' Mr. Lài said, and walked away.

When Cain entered room 123, he checked the time on the clock on the wall – 11:45am – and the steel, sliding door closed behind him. He took his food bowl off the shelf, laid out his duvet, and sat next to Afam. He did not tell Afam about the unexpected location of the meeting or the number of officials in attendance, but Afam did chuckle at the description of the very large British Consul.

'I'll nickname her Jabba the Hutt,' Cain said.

Afam checked his own waistline. 'I've lost a few pounds; Jabba must have found them. At least you've met someone from your consulate.'

Sensing the frustration in Afam's tone. Cain asked, 'Have you not met anyone from your embassy yet?'

'It's a long story. I'll tell you–'

Zen's voice echoed across the room and silence prevailed: it was noon. Rest time: no talking allowed.

Afam, along with most of the other prisoners, ensconced themselves under their duvets to take a nap. The two designated Yellow Jackets took up their positions, all was quiet.

Whilst eating, Cain came to terms with a simple reality: Trenchard was already using his authority to settle an old score. To administer payback. Making Ms. Hutt say and do exactly what she was told.

The procedure Mac (in London) would adhere to after receiving the email from Moshe, telling him Cain was in a Chinese prison, would be precise. Trenchard would be told if anything was said about Cain's past to arouse the curiosity of the Chinese, intelligence authorities there would be 'dier' consequences of a slightly different kind.

But what Trenchard would surreptitiously do behind closed

doors to disrupt and hinder the legal process to delay Cain's release would be achieved.

Friday

Zen summoned Cain into the laundry room. In front of the main door, Cain squatted down, and a Green Jacket handed him a bundle of clothing.

'*Xièxie*,' Cain said with a look of appreciation. The main door closed.

'Anything you not want,' said Zen. 'Give me for others.'

'OK.'

Sitting under his number 20, Cain sorted through the bundle of clothing. He put on an army-style jacket, it was almost the right size and a pair of dark-blue tracksuit trousers turned out to be three inches too short.

'They look quite clean,' said Afam.

'Better than nothing,' said Cain, putting his grey jacket back on. 'I feel warmer already.'

'You think Jabba the Hutt, or your ambassador arrange this?'

'Possibly.'

Back at the British Consulate, Ms. Hutt was complying with what she had been instructed to do. She faxed Ambassador Trenchard in Beijing a transcript of her conversation with Cain and made a phone call to confirm it had been received.

In Andorra Sofia received an email from a Foreign Office representative in London:

> *Our British consul has met with Cain. He is being*
> *detained in Guangzhou and asks us to pass on the*
> *following message: I am OK. No need to worry.*

Sofia checked her emails again, but there was nothing more. She couldn't believe it.

35

Monday – Day 7 – Whatever Next?

Zen laid his yellow jacket on the edge of platform one, next to the pile of neatly folded clothing he would never wear again.

At the far end of the room, Zen stood in front of the shelving on the wall and to the sounds of cheers and congratulations the ritual began. Theatrically, he picked up his drinking bottle, soap, food bowl, toothbrush and mugs one at a time and dumped them in a bin bucket. And after stepping in and out of looland, he did the same with his face cloth. As he walked the length of room 123 for one last time, he exchanged several words with various prisoners standing on the platforms. In the laundry room, to the sound of a steel bolt sliding, a chain being dragged through iron rings and a key turning, he squatted with his slip of yellow paper – the only item a prisoner was allowed to take from the room – held tightly in one hand. When the main door opened, he scampered onto the walkway and squatted down in front of Mr. Lài. Zen was going home to his wife and child, never to return. It left Cain – and perhaps others too – with just the one thought in mind:

When will I ever be released?

Over lunch, Afam told Cain what Zen had said to him earlier that morning, whilst sitting on his stomach one last time.

'So,' said Cain, 'Liu-ny as we call him, truly hates black and white people. As you mentioned when I first arrived: he is slightly mad.'

'Yes. He's now the new Number One Yellow Jacket, so we no longer have Zen to keep him restrained, and Hand-Out will no longer receive any extra food bowls at mealtimes.'

Later that afternoon, during the customary smoking session in the laundry room, Liu-ny announced his new rulings – and Afam tending to his clothes, hanging on the knobs, did his best to listen in… After the prisoners dispersed Afam informed Cain: 'Liu-ny has issued the order, we will no longer be given

306

toothpaste and soap or noodles to put in our breakfast rice. That's all I heard. When he realised I was listening he started whispering.'

6pm – The TV sprang into life, the steel sliding door opened, and everyone fell silent. Liu-ny scampered through into the laundry room and squatted down facing the main door.

Minutes later, three new prisoners entered the room and Liu-ny, holding the necessary documents, sat on his upturned bucket at the end of platform two. He signed them into the ledger and looked at the daily chores schedule to adjust the assignments. He looked across the room at the black and white prisoners and smiled.

Tuesday

When it came to the chores of the day, it did not go unnoticed by the prisoners in the room that Cain had not – unlike Takeaway – been upgraded. He was still cleaning the platforms and the floors with one of the new arrivals, a young man called Huì fēn.

As for Afam, his two-hour Suicide Watch was now always at the worst time – between 1am and 5am. But on the good side, Hand-Out became the new Number Two Yellow Jacket.

Thursday

For the first time in seven days, Cain left room 123. He squatted by the main door, raised his hands, and the guard, Ciggy-lee, cuffed his wrists. As he was led along the walkway, it felt good to be stretching his legs again, breathing in the outside air, viewing the park and looking up at a cloudy grey sky instead of a ceiling.

In the interview room, Cain waited to be pinioned in the tiger chair, but Ciggy-lee left it open, walked out of the room and closed the door, allowing Cain to sit fairly comfortably.

On the other side of the bars, the female translator introduced herself and the prosecutor sitting next to her. Cain marvelled at the Chinese justice system: he was about to have an interview with the prosecutor before he had even chosen, let alone met, a lawyer to represent him.

Via the translator, the prosecutor questioned the veracity of Cain's statements. When Cain did not rise to the bait, the prosecutor looked Cain straight in the eyes and pointed his pen. 'You not tell truth.'

'Please,' said Cain, 'take a look at the work and visitor's visa applications for Hadley, myself and the accompanying letters of invitation from Zhang. They will confirm I am the only one who is telling the truth.'

For the next thirty minutes Cain answered the questions. The female translator finished Cain's statement and passed it, along with a pen and ink pad, through the bars. Cain was surprised to see it was typed in English. He read, signed, dated, and red ink fingerprint-stamped it before handing everything back. Without a word being said, the prosecutor and translator packed their things, pressed the button to summon the guard, and left the room.

Cain sat alone, waiting for Ciggy-lee.

Saturday

For lunch and dinner Liu-ny occasionally told the Steam-pots not to put any meatballs in Cain's food bowl. It prompted Afam, who was still a few kilos overweight, to surreptitiously share his own with Cain, who was already beginning to look rather thin.

In the early hours of the morning, Cain and Huì fēn – both wearing their yellow jackets – were sitting on their upturned buckets on the centre aisle, halfway through their Suicide Watch. Cain closed the magazine on his lap to hide his 'diary' – a scrap of paper on which he was making the briefest of notes about his day-to-day experiences – and placed it down on the floor behind him. When he heard footsteps, he got to his feet – he was level with the number 26 on the wall – and looked up at the observation gallery to acknowledge the night guard passing by.

See you again in twenty minutes.

Cain looked down at Huì fēn sitting on a bucket, sound asleep under the clock on the wall: the blind spot for the guard – out of sight, out of mind. Cain walked to the end of platform two, where he returned the pen he had been using to where it was always kept, under the ledger. Prisoners were forbidden to keep a diary or notes relating to their incarceration. When being released they would often be searched for any such notes or the telephone numbers of other prisoners they might have written on scraps of paper, on the inside of their clothing or on their bodies. If caught, their release would often be delayed for several hours – or several days.

When Cain got back to his bucket on the centre aisle he picked up the magazine and opened it. He started to read through all he had written in his 'diary' once again. To memorise every word, everything he had experienced, playing his own version of the memory game: *I packed my bag. . .* because sooner or later he would.

At the end of the two-hour shift, Cain and Huì fēn gave the two prisoners assigned for the next shift a wake-up tap on their shoulders and handed them the yellow jackets.

Cain laid on the magazine. In the morning he would conceal it in the folds of his triple stacked duvet against the wall. He closed his eyes, thinking about all he had written… and fell asleep.

36

Mr. Lài sat at his desk in his comfortable, high-backed leather chair, smoking a cigarette.

Opposite him three prisoners, sitting on upturned buckets next to Cain, were also smoking their way through a cheaper packet of twenty on the desk, courtesy of Mr. Lài. Despite the door being open, the office filled with smoke. Cain had no choice but to endure the 'lung-lashing'.

Alex, one of the three prisoners – from other room(s) – turned to Cain, gestured with his free hand at the document on the desk and acting as an interpreter said, 'Mr. Lài say you must choose lawyer. Please make choice.'

Cain remembered what had been said during his meeting with Jabba the Hutt, some ten days earlier:

"I'll choose the first one on the list, Gregory Smythe."

"Gregory Smythe will be informed."

However, Jabba had not said who would inform Gregory Smythe or when. Cain had been about to ask those very same questions, but Jabba had interrupted him. He had instantly been totally distracted by the mention of Trenchard's name, followed by the hurtful comment:

"You have several friends who are police officers in the UK."

Knowing he had no choice, Cain knelt forward onto the floor in front of the desk to look at the document. It was of course the same one he had read before from the dossier Jabba the Hutt had given him, and Mr. Lài had subsequently taken from him. He read again through the list of names, addresses, and telephone numbers. Although they were all English names, in reality they were all Chinese lawyers based in Guangzhou. He again, chose the first name on the list, Gregory Smythe. He signed, dated, and red ink fingerprint-stamped it and handed it to Mr. Lài.

Mr. Lài smiled.

'Wait,' Alex said.

Mr. Lài handed Cain another document, written entirely in Chinese.

'You must sign it,' Alex said.

Cain watched Mr. Lài tip himself back in his chair, raise his foot to the edge of the table and, gently rocking himself, take another drag of his cigarette.

Cain turned to Alex. 'What is this document?'

'It authorisation.'

After Cain completed his signing, dating, and red ink fingerprint-stamping ritual, he reached forward across the desk and placed the document next to the first one. Mr. Lài dropped his foot to the floor and his chair tipped him forward to within an arm's reach of the documents. He studied them both for a few seconds before handing Cain an envelope.

Alex said, 'Please write lawyer name.'

Cain wrote the name Gregory Smythe on the envelope. Mr. Lài removed the cigarette from his lips and, eye to eye, with Cain, he slowly exhaled. Both men saw through the smokescreen. Cain got the unspoken message: Do as you are told.

Mr. Lài stood up and the prisoners immediately scurried around, piling the buckets in a corner, before squatting in attendance. As Mr. Lài walked out of his office the prisoners – seemingly on an invisible leash – got to their feet and followed him.

When Cain returned to room 123, Afam asked, 'All OK?'

'Yes,' said Cain, 'Mr. Lài needed me to sign a document. The first step in appointing a lawyer to represent me.'

During Rest Time, whilst sitting on his duvet with his back against the wall, Cain came to terms with a simple reality:

Mr. Lài was getting a – customary – back hander. And by using Alex with the other two prisoners as witnesses: if push came to shove, they would say whatever they were told to – for their own safety – to exonerate Mr. Lài.

It left him with just the one thought in mind:

Are the Chinese in cahoots with Trenchard?

And because Alex and the other two prisoners were in different rooms Cain would probably never see them again. But if he did he knew the rules: When prisoners were out of their room, no talking was allowed.

He took a look around the room: under number 34 there was no stacked duvet, just an empty space. Jiang, the older man who often spoke to Afam in Chinese, was gone.

37

Monday – Week Four Begins.

Officer Luó sat listening to Lawyer Shen Tang Liáng: 'Hadley's work visa renewal was applied for and accepted by Teun the Dutchman. Zhang brought me the necessary documents signed by himself, Cain, and Hadley.'

'You did not speak to Cain?' Officer Luó enquired.

'There was no reason to, I had everything I needed from him in writing.'

'May I see the documents?'

Lawyer Shen pulled out a folder from a filing cabinet and handed it to Officer Luó.

After browsing through the pages, Officer Luó said, 'All in order, thank you. Would you be kind enough to make a copy for me.'

I'll double check this.

'Of course.'

Officer Luó appreciated Bill, Greg and Cain had employed Lawyer Shen, a man of the highest integrity for all the obvious reasons.

Thursday

In the Luyuan Road police station, Cain's arresting officer was sitting at his desk, smoking a cigarette, feeling very annoyed. He had tried to help Officer Luó keep Cain out of prison, but Hadley and especially Zhang's obstinacy had foiled them. During the following weeks he had spent many arduous hours explaining to senior officials – and filling out paperwork – why there was now an Englishman in the system. His phone rang, he answered it.

'*Nihao*, Officer Luó here. I have good news; I have checked it out – we can kill three birds with one stone.'

Mad-Hatter's odd-looking beanie wasn't a hat at all. It was a rolled up, cut off sleeve from a fleece – knotted at one end – and plonked on his head.

Mad-Hatter was a hardened drug dealer who had spent many years behind bars. He had a reputation for being unbalanced, unpredictable, and prone to violence: a reputation that allowed him, unchallenged, to irritate other prisoners in a number of ways. Usually by walking aimlessly up and down the centre aisle of room 123, singing horrendously out of tune or loitering a little too close for comfort.

Having been to the loo, Cain stepped up onto the edge of platform one, under his number 20, and realising he had forgotten to take his bottle of water off the shelf he stepped to his right to turn around. His feet were swept out from under him. He crashed sideways, down onto the edge of the platform and onto the floor. Mad-Hatter jumped up onto platform two and smirked down at Cain before joining the other prisoners watching TV. Cain cautiously got himself up to a kneeling position, and with his elbows and palms on the edge of the platform he heard Afam's voice: 'You have to stay down for it to be finished. If not,' he said, glancing up at the clock on the wall, 'you have five minutes.'

Cain slowly got to his feet and, feigning injury, he staggered across the centre aisle into the open space at the end of platform two, in front of the buckets under the shelving on the wall and fell to his knees with his head in a hand.

Meanwhile, at the opposite end of the centre aisle, Liu-ny had been sitting on his upturned bucket with his back against the wall, watching Cain being taken down. He grinned contemptuously with his arm outstretched, tapping his fingers on the platform – and seeing Cain staggering towards the back of the room he gave Mad-Hatter a nod.

Knowing a great deal of money was on offer, Mad-Hatter seized the opportunity to give Cain a final beating. He strode the length of platform two, singing as tunelessly as usual.

'Stop.' Hand-Out shouted, but Mad-Hatter kept on going.

Cain remained motionless, looking sideways from the far corner of his eye, through the tiny gap between his fingers. When Mad-Hatter jumped off the end of platform two, Cain threw himself sideways, into the shins of the flying legs, causing a twisting body with flailing arms to hit the floor. Several prisoners were astounded to have seen what had happened. To see Cain quickly dragging Mad-Hatter to the end of platform two, where a fist to his stomach curled him up.

Cain checked the time on the clock on the wall and sat on the end of the platform with a foot on Mad-Hatter. *Out of sight, out of mind*, he thought. *Any second now.*

As the guard passed along the observation balcony – doing his normal twenty minute assignment – he glanced down, saw nothing unusual and continued on his way.

Hand-out immediately instructed prisoners to attend to Mad-hatter, to check if any bones were broken. Cain walked towards a shocked Liu-ny to scare him, thinking how great it would be, if they were not in prison, to break his tapping fingers.

I Know how it feels.

Hand-Out jumped down from platform two in front of Cain and shook his head. Cain reluctantly gave Hand-Out a nod of acceptance, turned and walked away.

Sitting with Afam, Cain gave his shoulder and side a rub.

'How are you feeling?' Afam asked.

'OK, just a couple of bruises.'

'I'll get you your bottle of water,' Afam said sliding to the edge of the platform.

Cain looked to the end of the room to see Liu-ny being confronted by Hand-Out and two of his followers.

Afam arrived back with the bottle of water – and with a look of relief, he stated, 'Mad- Hatter has no broken bones. Well done.'

Sunday Evening

Hand-Out finished talking to Afam and strolled off to join the others watching TV. Liu-ny, however, remained sitting alone on the obligatory bucket, at the end of platform one, browsing through a magazine. And Mad-Hatter was resting where he had been moved to. Under the number 32 – across the centre aisle – on platform two, reading a paperback. He was no longer out of sight, out of mind.

Afam sat next to Cain to translate what Hand-Out had said.

'Liu-ny told Hand-Out you accidentally tripped and fell off platform one onto the floor. It made you very angry with yourself. When Mad-Hatter tried to go past you to get his bottle of water off the shelf, you attacked him out of frustration.'

'So Liu-ny is definitely in cahoots with Mad-Hatter.'

'Yes. If Mad-Hatter had beaten you up, it would have been a perfect story. No prisoner would have dared to call the Number One Yellow Jacket a liar.'

'Do we have any idea why they did this?'

'Liu-ny refuses to say anything more and Mad-Hatter isn't saying anything at all. Nobody has been seriously hurt. Therefore everyone wants to forget it.'

'Nobody,' said Cain, 'wants to jeopardise how long they are kept behind bars.' Cain

looked at Afam with a sigh of relief, with just the one thought in mind:

Did Trenchard have anything to do with this?

'There is some good news,' said Afam. 'From tomorrow, your food bowls will be full again. We will be given toothpaste, soap, and a daily packet of noodles to go with breakfast.'

Cain asked, 'Will I still be cleaning the floor?'

'No. And my Suicide Watch hours will be rotated again, like everyone else.'

'Great.'

'It didn't go unnoticed how well you–'

A blast of machine gunfire, the sound of prisoners shouting and artillery shells exploding interrupted what Afam was about to say; the war TV series, *China v Japan* had started.

'Let's watch some proper action,' Cain said.

During the TV adverts, the sight of several attractive young females prompted a few more shouts from the prisoners in the room, and probably a few memories as well.

'There may be a few wankers in the room before the end of the night,' Cain joked.

Afam showed a look of absolute surprise and told Cain a story about how the consequence of masturbation is death.

'With a stroke of luck,' Cain joked, 'you will tell me who told you.'

'My church,' said Afam with a very serious look. 'God is always right.'

'I wouldn't know,' said Cain. 'I've never spoken to him.'

Afam went on to explain how he knew his belief to be true.

'Just for the record,' Cain whispered, 'are you telling me you've never had a wank?'

Afam was mortified by Cain's use of a forbidden word, referring to an act of debauchery. 'Never,' he declared. 'I don't want to die.'

Cain sensed he had already overstepped the mark so he made a complimentary comment, 'I certainly prefer you to be alive.'

I'll ask Afam why I'm not dead another day.

'It is time to pray,' said Afam. 'Would you like to join me?'

'Thank you for the offer, but it's not something I do.'

'God is always right,' Afam insisted, as he knelt and crawled towards his triple stacked duvet against the wall. He closed his eyes and, with his hands clenched tightly together against his forehead in what looked like an act of desperation, he prayed. Cain heard him recite the same words over and over: *The power of our Lord Jesus Christ . . .*

Slowly the sound of prayer became more muffled as Afam's face and hands sank into his altar – his stacked duvet against the wall.

Cain had found out a little more about Afam. But not quite what he had expected.

38

Tuesday – Week five

Standing on the end of platform one Liu-ny finished his announcement, causing several prisoners to burst into frenzied activity – and Afam translated what had been said for Cain, 'I will be leaving in thirty minutes. It is time for me to go to a room with other black men.'

Cain put his hand on Afam's shoulder. 'The time has come, the walrus said . . .'

Afam placed his hand on Cain's arm. '. . . to talk of many things.'

'Of shoes and ships and sealing wax.'

'Of cabbages and kings.'

'Where did you learn the poem?' Cain asked.

Afam chuckled, pushing Cain's shoulder again like old buddies do. 'When I was very young, a missionary and his wife stayed in our village for a year. Lewis Carroll was their favourite poet.'

'How wonderful.'

'It was. I have to pack my things.'

'Of course.'

Five minutes later, Afam placed his full bucket on the centre aisle and for the last time, sat on the edge of platform two, in front of his number 19, next to Cain.

'It is time to talk about what I have never told you, what you never asked me. I came to Guangzhou to stay at a friend's house. In the middle of my first night, a loud engine noise, breaking glass, and men shouting, woke me up. The Drug Enforcement Squad had broken in.'

'What was the engine noise?'

'A helicopter – the SWAT team came in, from the balcony on the roof.'

'There must have been a lot of drugs?'

Afam showed a look of guilt, of regret. 'Yes there were. I'm a drug dealer.'

'I have to ask,' said Cain. 'Was Jiang, the old man you were often talking to, also a drug dealer?'

'Yes.'

'You'll be transferred to the same place he was?'

'I hope not.'

'Why's that?'

'He was executed.'

'I had no idea. I–'

'I also have a slight problem, I am actually from Nigeria, but I have a Ugandan passport. It is the easiest way to obtain travel visas. When the Ugandan Consul visited me here, she soon realised I was not fluent in their language, I was not a Ugandan. I told her I have a Ugandan wife. I thought it would make a difference, but it didn't. She suspected the worst, she just walked out. I was soon informed they had discovered I was travelling on a false passport.'

'Will the Nigerian Embassy help you.'

'I now do not have a passport – real or false – from any country. No one will help me. Just out of interest, do you have a wife?'

'I've had several!'

Afam chuckled. 'When you are released, I have to ask, will you please contact my wife for me.'

'Assuming I get out first, of course I will. Tell me her name?'

'Davika. She doesn't even know if I am alive, let alone where I am. We have two children.'

'I'm sure you will see them all again soon,' said Cain, trying to be positive.

'I also have a cousin here in Guangzhou.'

'He is also a drug dealer?'

Afam hesitated momentarily. 'Yes. Will you also contact him to let him know what has happened to me?'

'Of course.'

'His name is Cheks. We grew up together.'

'So he knew the missionary and his wife who stayed in your village for a year?'

Afam chuckled again, 'Yes, Lewis Carroll also became his

favourite poet.'

Cain glanced up at the clock on the wall. 'Time is running out. Give me the phone numbers, quickly now. I'll memorise them for now and write them down tonight.'

Seconds later. 'Davika is in Bangkok,' said Afam, 'so it will be very easy to contact her.'

Cain realised the country code for Davika's phone number was Thailand. 'I thought you said your wife is in Uganda?'

'My other wife.'

Cain grinned. 'Tell me another time.'

'When we meet again.'

'I look forward to it.'

'You will not forget to phone Davika and Cheks for me?' Afam asked, looking for reassurance.

'I give you my word.'

And they shook hands, Nigerian-style: it started with a two-time crunch – and as their hands slipped back from each other, they stroked each other's palms with their fingertips before they finally snapped their finger and thumb.

As Cain walked with Afam carrying his bucket to the steel sliding open doorway, Afam said, 'Cheks has a friend, who has been to South Africa, you would like him. Perhaps you should meet up with them.'

'Hopefully you will be with us.'

Looking down into the laundry room, Cain and Afam could see Shor-tee, Red Jacket and two other prisoners squatting down with their storage containers in front of them.

Cain asked, 'Just so I know, what is the name of Cheks' friend here in Guangzhou?'

To the sound of a steel bolt sliding, a chain being dragged through iron rings and a key turning, Afam said, 'It's a strange name, Lastly,' and quickly stepping down into the laundry room, he squatted on the floor with his bucket in front of him and looked up at Cain, now also squatting by the open sliding door.

Although Cain was horrified his face gave nothing away, he grinned, they gave each other a wave, their time together had come to an end.

Cain spent many hours thinking about the possible implications of what Afam had told him – and what Kay had overheard when Zhang had been talking on a burner phone, sitting next to Hadley, making arrangements for another of their illegal diamond deals in Hong Kong.

You have them? When I get to Hong Kong, I must go bank first because it close early, then dealer. Then last he say he will be there at 5pm, before I catch train back to Guangzhou.

Cain thought about what Zhang had revealed when pinned against the shower wall in the Taojin Hotel.

Lee. It only name I ever heard.

Cain contemplated: knowing, both Kay and Zhang's spoken English was not 100%, could she have misheard. Or had it been another, simple mispronunciation?

Cain quietly whispered:

'Then Last he say or Then Last, Lee say or Then Lastly say.'

39

Thursday – Week Six – Jabba the Hutt

After many days of coldness and having no one to talk to, Cain was pleased to be in the warmth of an interview room, in the comfort of an unlocked tiger chair, meeting with Jabba the Hutt and Kim.

Cain enquired, 'Why is there a Chinese man sitting in the chair behind you?'

'He is listening in,' said Jabba. 'To make sure we do not discuss your case.'

'Makes a change from the group of people who were behind you when we first met in the medical centre.'

Jabba did her usual: she ignored Cain's remark – and seeing he had not shaved or cut his hair since being imprisoned. 'How are you?' she enquired.

Despite the sight of Jabba's blouse and buttons, being stress-tested to infinity and beyond, Cain decided to say it anyway. 'I'm losing weight.'

'I have all the lawyer's papers here for you to sign. Unfortunately Gregory Smythe does not represent criminal cases but recommends Lawyer Nigel, who is very good.'

'May I suggest you add the lawyer's areas of expertise to the list, it might help.'

'It is not our list,' Jabba said dismissively handing Cain the papers. 'We have marked where you need to sign.'

'I appear not to have any choice,' said Cain, taking and signing the papers. 'Will you make sure Sofia, my fiancée, receives Lawyer Nigel's contact details?'

'Of course.'

Handing back the papers and pen, Cain asked, 'Have you heard from Sofia?'

'Yes, she sends her love.'

Cain knew Jabba was lying. Sofia would never send her love. 'Did Sofia say anything more?'

Jabba looked down at her notes. 'I have brought you two books, *Brideshead Revisited* and *Chronicles* by Bob Dylan.'

'Thank you, *Brideshead Revisited* is a classic TV series starring Anthony Andrews and Jeremy Irons. I've watched it more than once.' What Cain had said, momentarily left him with just the one thought in mind:

Always watched it with Jerry.

'I believe so,' said Jabba. 'I have left them with reception, they will be inspected and, all being well, given to you. Is there anything else?'

'I would like to know what is stopping Sofia from opening a shopping account for me so I can, like the other prisoners, purchase pre-packed foods and clothing.'

'We will look into it. Are they treating you well?'

'The British or the Chinese?'

Jabba did her usual: she ignored the remark. 'Lawyer Nigel will be here soon.'

'I won't hold my breath.'

'He will guide you through the legal process. Jabba looked at her watch, gave Kim a nod, and said, 'We have to go now.'

For the benefit of the CCTV Cain's cuffed hand reached through the bars and they all shook hands. The Stooge in the background showed a look of amazement as he pressed the button to summon the guard before following Jabba and Kim out of the room.

Back in room 123, Cain checked the time on the clock on the wall: noon – Rest time.

Sitting alone in the silent room under his number 20 he opened his now cooler food bowl to see it was another meatballs day, in the usual slushy rice.

When Rest time ended, Cain was unexpectedly summoned back to the interview room, where Lawyer Nigel and his female colleague, Melly, introduced themselves.

For almost six weeks, the British Consul had done nothing, but now, only two hours after signing the authorisation, Cain was sitting in front of Lawyer Nigel. Cain realised it had all been prearranged. It left him with just the one thought in mind:

Who chose Lawyer Nigel? Trenchard or Officer Luó? Or was

Cain apologised for his unshaven, dishevelled appearance and they got down to business. Lawyer Nigel did most of the talking, leaving Melly to record the minutes of the meeting. He confirmed: once he had obtained the case papers from the police and prosecution service he would be in a position to take a view on the charges.

Cain described his meeting with the female police officer who had said he would be held for another four days and the prosecutor who had accused him of not telling the truth.

'My supposed statement I had to sign for the police was typed in Chinese. But the ones for the prosecutor were in English. Both before I had even met my own lawyer.'

'You recall the dates?' Lawyer Nigel asked.

'I'm trying to,' said Cain as for the benefit of the CCTV – looking down at him and listening – he raised his hand to theatrically count his fingers before giving what he believed to be the correct days. 'Sorry,' he said, 'I have no idea what the actual dates are.'

Cain's deception would prevent the prison authorities from suspecting he may have a near photographic memory or was secretly keeping a diary of some sort. He really did not want the Green jackets to conduct a search in room 123.

'It must seem very strange, going through all this for such a minor misdemeanour,' said Lawyer Nigel with a look of understanding. 'But this is China. This is how the system works.'

'What will you be wanting to charge me?'

'RMB10,000.'

'I take it the British consul has already given you the details of Sofia, my fiancée yes?'

'Ms. Hutt has already sent them to me.'

'Sofia will make the payment. Please keep her up to date about what is happening.'

'I will email her later today.'

'Please ask her why she has not yet opened a shopping account for me so I can buy what I need.'

'I will look into it.' After confirming how long the first part of the legal process would take, Lawyer Nigel brought the meeting to a close. 'We will be back in two weeks.'

Cain signed and red ink fingerprint-stamped the necessary agreement and authorisations. 'Look forward to seeing you.'

And for the second time in a day Cain reached through the bars, and they all shook hands.

After dinner, with nothing to do or anyone to talk to, Cain sat alone under his number 20, keeping an eye on Mad-Hatter. The steel flap unexpectedly opened and Hand-Out – because Liu-ny was having a piss – squatted down to see what was wanted. Seconds later Hand-Out wandered along platform one... and handing Cain the two paperbacks: *Brideshead Revisited* and *Chronicles*, he whispered, 'I no tell you, tomorrow you leave. You be searched.'

'*Xièxie,*' Cain said, surprised but very grateful for the tip-off.

In the early hours of the morning, during Cain's Suicide Watch session, he repeatedly read through his 'diary' – the scrap of paper he had hidden – making sure he had memorised everything to date, especially, the names and phone numbers Afam had given him.

Friday – Day 39

At 7am, Cain meticulously folded his bedding, placed it against the wall, and sat waiting for looland to be a little less crowded. During his morning's ablutions, he surreptitiously dropped his now torn up 'diary' into one of the toilets, picked up the bucket and flushed them all away.

At 10am Mr. Lài arrived for roll call and inspection. After he had read and signed the register, he turned to Cain. 'Half-hour you leave.'

Cain filled his bucket with his two mugs, toothbrush, tube of toothpaste, plastic food bowl, bar of soap, drinking bottle, a sachet of shampoo, and face cloth. From the drawer under his number 20 he topped up his bucket with his boxer shorts, socks, two paperbacks, and what was left of his toilet roll. Last of all, he carried his stacked duvet the length of platform one and placed it against the front wall under the closed steel flap next to all the others waiting for a new arrival.

At 10.20am Cain walked up to Hand-Out. 'Thank you for helping me,' he said, holding out his hand.

'Welcome.'

Both men had wanted to say more but lacked the language to do so.

When Cain reached the sliding door he turned to give the prisoners, especially Hand-Out, Take-Away and Huì fēn a wave followed by a respectful bow of appreciation. When he spotted Liu-ny and Mad-Hatter sitting together looking at him, he gave them the finger and stepped down into the laundry room.

At 10.30am Cain was strip-searched in the laundry room by two Green Jackets. After he had put his clothes back on he squatted down next to his bucket, waiting for Ciggy-lee, now standing by the main door to give the command.

***

On the day of Cain's transfer, when Europe eventually woke up for breakfast, Sofia arrived at her office in the Principality of Andorra. Her PA told her the news: an email from a Lawyer Nigel in Guangzhou had been received.

Also, the London Foreign and Commonwealth Office had emailed Sofia the name and address of the prison in which Cain was being detained, along with details of how to open a prisoner's shopping account. Sofia was more than angry: for the past six weeks she had been repeatedly phoning and emailing the FCO asking for that information.

Within twenty-four hours, Sofia had discovered the shopping account details emailed to her by the FCO were incorrect. She immediately phoned and emailed the FCO to point out their error and requested an immediate response.

40

Seven Days Later

Fists were flying down on the centre aisle: two prisoners were fighting.

One of the fighters was a getaway driver who loved American cars, while his twenty-year-old adversary had produced counterfeit scratchcards and sold them. Cain had nicknamed them Maybach and Scratch.

Other prisoners were keeping their distance by staying up on the platforms. When the Number One Yellow Jacket tried to separate the two fighters, he was shoved aside. Cain stepped in to help, only to receive a punch to his stomach and an elbow to his chest for his efforts. Since no weapons were involved, Cain decided to let it be, he didn't want anyone – after what had happened against Mad-Hatter in room 123 – to witness or be on the receiving end of his fighting prowess.

When the Number Two Yellow Jacket, standing on the end of platform two, got the OK from his Number One, he turned, reached up to the emergency intercom alarm by the top of the steel sliding door, slammed his hand against it and called for help.

The sound of a guard shouting up on the observation gallery, followed by the pounding of boots along the walkway, alerted the prisoners to an imminent invasion… The steel sliding door opened and Mr. Fán, flanked by four baton-wielding Green Jackets, shouted his commands.

Welcome to room 309.

All the bystanders squatted down immediately with their open hands above their heads to show they were not holding anything. The Green Jackets then waded in to separate Maybach and Scratch. Maybach offered no resistance; he yielded to instructions without hesitation and squatted down with his hands in the air. Whereas Scratch, took a swing at one of the

Green Jackets before being struck with a baton, and having his legs kicked out from under him, he crashed down onto the floor. Order had been restored and silence prevailed.

Mr. Fán summoned the Number One Yellow Jacket; he scampered across to his master's feet, like an obedient dog being brought to heel.

While the Number One Yellow Jacket was explaining what had happened, an irate Scratch, still down on the floor, swore loudly and kicked out at one of the two Green Jackets standing by his side. A nod from Mr. Fán told the Green Jackets what to do. Scratch was soon curled up in a ball gasping for breath – the result of a kick to his stomach.

When Mr. Fán summoned Maybach, he scampered along the centre aisle and squatted down. A verbal tirade from Mr. Fán was followed by Maybach apologising profusely, begging forgiveness. It was all he needed to do; he was no fool. Maybach and the Number One Yellow Jacket were then dismissed, and they backed away.

The Green Jackets dragged Scratch along the centre aisle and placed him at Mr. Fán's feet. During an exchange of words Scratch raised his voice and raised his hand. Mr. Fán's kick hit Scratch across the side of his head, knocking him to the floor. As Mr. Fán issued various commands, one of the Green Jackets left the room while two others frog marched Scratch back along the centre aisle, dragged him up onto platform one, and held him under the number 19.

When the other Green Jacket returned to the room, Scratch was cuffed, and his ankles shackled and chained to a solitary, five-inch iron slave ring, embedded in the concrete platform. It reminded Cain of when he had first met Afam in room 123.

Mr. Fán and the Green Jackets then left the room, the steel sliding door closed, and the prisoners got to their feet.

That evening Cain – under his number 30 at the end of platform two – completed his nightly English lesson for Kuo, the Number One Yellow Jacket: a charming young man in his late twenties. He had been a director of a computer robotics company before being arrested, for alleged patent infringement.

'Your English is excellent,' said Cain. 'You are easily ninety per cent fluent.'

'Thank you.'

Mr. Fán and the guards believed Kuo had been framed – by the corrupt directors of a company he had been associated with – and should not be in prison. But of course they never admitted to having such an opinion. Kuo should have been a Green Jacket but, having not been convicted and sentenced, the rules would not allow it. However, none of that mattered anymore. Ten days earlier, having been detained for twenty-three months, he finally had his last day in court. He was found guilty. He would be released in eight weeks.

The Number Two Yellow Jacket, who spoke only Chinese, chatted only with Kuo and rarely communicated with any other prisoner in room 309. Instead, he spent most of the day sitting on his upturned bucked at the end of platform two, posed like a famous *Auguste Rodin* sculpture, pondering life, or reading magazines. Hence, Cain had nicknamed him Thinker.

Across on platform one, Scratch had discovered the handcuff on one of his wrists had inexplicably not been tightened sufficiently enough to prevent him – with a spit of saliva – from pulling his hand through the open cuff. He waved the free hand victoriously.

Anyone else would have looked on the upside of the Green Jacket's error, kept quiet, and used the situation to the best of his advantage, but not Scratch. He proceeded to ratchet the cuff's mechanism to show everyone his cuffed hands before performing the hand-release trick over and over again. Scratch then got to his feet and added to his repertoire by imitating what could be best described as Leonardo da Vinci's *Vitruvian Man,* stretching out his arms and legs in triumph.

Kuo looked at the clock on the wall. 'Sit down!' he shouted at Scratch in a panic.

But Scratch, glancing at Kuo had lost track of time as well as his sensibility, and following Kuo's line of sight he came face to face with the guard doing the twenty-minute walk-by up on the observation gallery. The guard stopped, observed Scratch's outstretched arms, saw the open cuff hanging from one of his wrists, and shouted a command at Kuo. Seconds later, Scratch was sitting with his hands well and truly securely cuffed.

Saturday

The daily routine in all the rooms was basically the same with a few variations. In room 309, after the wake-up call and the morning's ablutions, the prisoners would carry their duvets – all casually folded anyway they wanted – to the far end of platform one where they were stacked in rows to a height of five feet against the back wall, under the numbers 28 and 29, opposite looland. Cain was then left to carefully place cardboard sheeting around and on top of the piled up duvets to give them the appearance of being in a perfect cardboard box.

After the 10am Roll Call & Inspection, the prisoners in room 309 watched two Green-jackets dragging a shouting, struggling Scratch into the laundry room, where he received punches to his stomach and silence prevailed. He was then hauled out onto the walkway.

As for the daily work, it wasn't beads, it was Christmas decorations of various types for the world markets. Cain had been given the task of quality control man: he checked every item for any flaws.

'Any problem,' said Kuo starting the day. 'You report directly to me.'

'Of course,' said Cain. 'Thank you.'

7pm – Unpack.

The Chinese news starting on TV was the signal for Cain to unpack the cardboard from around the piled up duvets. Hence two hours earlier than in room 123, the prisoners were allowed to lay out their duvets to make themselves comfortable. To get off the coolness of the platforms.

Kuo and Thinker laid their duvets out lengthwise, at the end of platform two and, lying down, warmly wrapped with their heads on pillows made of bundled-up clothing, they were very comfortably looking up at the TV, with other prisoners sitting behind them.

At 2am, in the silence of the night, Cain and Maybach were woken up – and handed the yellow jackets. It was the start of their two-hour Suicide Watch shift.

Sitting on his upturned bucket on the centre aisle, Cain removed his 'diary' – an A4-sized sheet of proper paper given to him by Kuo – from inside a magazine. He had already rewritten everything that had happened to him while he'd been in room 123 and with pen in hand he had brought his notes on his day-to-day activities in room 309 up to date. He then went back to day one to read it again, to play the memory game:

I packed my bag... Hopefully sooner rather than later.

Sunday

Outside the main door, Mr. Fán had a quiet word with Kuo, initiating a frenzied race around the rooms. Kuo finally took a fifty-litre plastic storage container – with a bucket and clothes on it – out onto the walkway and squatted down. All traces of Scratch had been removed: he would never be seen again.

Mr. Fán stepped into the laundry room to personally hand out the cigarettes. It was his way of telling the prisoners: *You have seen nothing. You say nothing.*

And with the warning in place, Mr. Fán handed Kuo his lighter to do the honours.

41

Monday – Week Eight – Brat-fetch

It was a more monotonous day than usual for the prisoners. The steel sliding door was closed: it was a national holiday. Cain was sitting under his number 30. Seeing the guard walking along the observation gallery Cain heard his own version of the great *Herman's Hermits* song:

> *No work today, it's not a common sight*
> *But people passing by, all know the reason why*

Minutes later, Cain and Kuo were quite unexpectedly walking along the sidewalk – without handcuffs – escorted by a guard. And feeling a touch of warmth, Cain looked up at a glimmer of sunshine.

Spring is in the air.

They soon found themselves in Mr. Fán's office, sitting on upturned buckets in front of his desk. It was Mr. Fán's second English lesson with Cain who was able to clarify and talk about many things in the UK and Kuo, being pretty fluent in English, more than just helped with the translations. Kuo helped himself to a cigarette from one of the packets on the desk in front of him, but not from the superior brand, always kept out of reach. The informal lesson proved again to be a welcome respite from the confinement of room 309.

Kuo translated for Cain, 'What did you think of the scuffle between Mr. Fán and Scratch?'

Cain realised the question was referring to when Mr. Fán had kicked Scratch in the side of the head. Looking at Mr. Fán, Cain chose his words carefully, but spoke convincingly. 'When it happened, I was squatting in the centre aisle. My hands were on the back of my head. I was looking down at the floor, trying to keep my balance, so I didn't see anything. Sorry.'

When translating, Kuo reinforced Cain's statement with

additional words of his own. Suitably satisfied, Mr. Fán smiled.
'Would you like tea?'

'Yes, please sir.'

A hot drink for the first time in two months.

Some twenty minutes later, Ciggy-lee appeared at the door
and exchanged a few words with Mr. Fán who looked at Cain.
'You have a visitor.'

Outside, Ciggy-lee unexpectedly handed Cain the cuffs, so
he could put them on himself. In the empty visitors' cell block,
Cain was able to look out through the pane of the one way black
glass, across the deserted restricted zone to a totally unoccupied
visitors waiting area. And in the deserted hallway,
glancing through the bank teller-style security glass of the
guard's office, the emptiness told him he was the only prisoner,
out of eighteen hundred, receiving a visitor.

Whatever is going to happen will be a surprise.

Ciggy-lee left Cain in a tiger chair unrestrained. A man in
his forties, in civilian clothes, accompanied by a police officer
in uniform carrying a typewriter, entered the room. Cain was
astonished to see a young girl, perhaps aged eight, with them.
When the young girl started screaming, the man let her out of
the room to run freely in the visitors' empty corridor. A prison
guard soon appeared, and politely instructed the man to go and
get her.

For the rest of the supposed interview, the man left the room
on several occasions to *brat-fetch*. He also received a number of
calls on his cell phone. Seeing the man hand the phone to the
young girl for a third time, Cain assumed the calls were
personal, probably putting together the final touches for their
bank holiday lunch and afternoon's activities. Between
checking the time on his watch and playing *brat-fetch,* the man
managed to ask Cain a few questions about what had happened
in the showroom. At the end of the charade, Cain was assured
everything had been documented and would be looked into. The
man handed Cain his supposed typed statement – in Chinese –
of what had been said, along with a pen and red ink pad. The
fact that the police officer had stopped typing long ago and
taken the statement out of a folder had not escaped Cain's

notice. The man told Cain to date the statement seven days earlier and sign it.

'Seven days? Why would I do that?'

'Because you want to get out of here,' said the man. 'If you prefer, I can come back in six weeks' time so we can start again.'

Cain realised he had no choice, so he signed, backdated and red ink fingerprint-stamped the document before handing everything back.

When the man with his briefcase in hand and the police officer carrying the typewriter were led out of the room by the *brat*, they didn't press the button to summon the guard. Cain looked up at the CCTV. 'I wonder who that man was?'

Back in room 309, Kuo sat contemplating what Cain had told him about the *brat-fetch* saga. But of course, Kuo's twenty-three months in prison, along with his three appearances in court – and the four lawyers he had sacked – made him realise nothing really surprised him anymore.

Tuesday

After Rest time, Cain received his very own fifty-litre, plastic storage container. He opened it, but there was no food inside. The paltry number of items inside confirmed what he believed would happen: Sofia's attempts to open a shopping account for him were being blocked. He looked down at his thinner wrists, hands, ankles, and feet.

How much weight have I really lost?

42

Wednesday – Week Nine

It had been nearly four weeks since Lawyer Nigel and Melly's first visit.

Cain apologised for his unshaven appearance and politely stated, 'I received a plastic container containing two tracksuits, a tube of toothpaste, a few bars of soap, and packets of shampoo, but there was no food, no correctly sized clothes, no underwear. Why has Sofia not opened a shopping account for me?'

'I thought she had.'

'Who sent me the plastic container?'

'Allow me to check what's going on. I'll get back to you.'

'With all the weight I've lost, I could certainly do with something extra to eat.'

'How much weight have you lost?'

'I'd guess eight kilos.'

'Rather a lot.'

'Perhaps more than Ms. Carrie Hutt from the British Embassy has lost,' said Cain sarcastically. 'Or should I say *found*?'

Lawyer Nigel smiled without comment.

Cain went on to describe the meeting he'd had on Bank Holiday Monday with the anonymous man accompanied by the *brat-fetch* child and a police officer. 'I had to backdate the statement by seven days and sign it.'

Lawyer Nigel expressed a look of surprise. 'Really? I'll find out what that was all about. Anything else?'

Cain silently shook his head.

'I have now reviewed your case files,' said Lawyer Nigel. 'You face a maximum of three years in prison. It must seem very harsh for such a minor misdemeanour, but this is China.'

Cain got the distinct impression Lawyer Nigel was giving him the worst numbers first, playing the psyche game. 'It is very harsh,' he said, playing along. 'Is there any good news?'

Lawyer Nigel told Cain how there were several facts in his favour: he had not inflicted any physical injuries on Hadley, Zhang or the two girls; he had not stolen any diamonds from the showroom; he had not absconded from the crime scene; and he did not have a criminal record. 'These facts will all be testimony to your good character,' said Lawyer Nigel. 'They will be looked upon favourably by the judge.'

Cain showed a look of appreciation.

Lawyer Nigel added, 'I need to obtain what is called a 'letter of forgiveness' from Zhang to present in court. It will be a major influence on the judge and will automatically reduce your sentence by one third. Unfortunately, a payment has to be made to Zhang for the letter.'

'How much?'

'I estimate RMB80,000 for the damage you caused and reparation.'

'You did not mention this before,' said Cain in his very affable way. 'Is there anything else I will have to pay?'

'If all goes to plan, no.'

'Payment for the 'letter of forgiveness' far exceeds the cost of replacing the showroom cabinets. It is nothing more than bribery.'

The look on Lawyer Nigel's face confirmed Cain's suspicions.

'I will have to meet with Zhang as soon as possible.'

'Make sure you emphasise I will serve the maximum sentence of three years. Do not mention the possibility of a reduction in sentence. The longer Zhang believes I will be in prison, the happier he will be – and easier to deal with.'

'You believe Zhang wants you to be imprisoned for a long time?'

'Yes, that's all he wants. Let's not give him any reason to believe I will be out any sooner.'

'That will not be difficult. Once I have the 'letter of forgiveness' I will approach the prosecution to find out how hard they intend to push – and arrange the earliest possible court date.'

'How long will it all take?'

'Several weeks.'

Cain signed, dated, and red ink fingerprint-stamped the minutes of their meeting, along with a separate authorisation for Sofia to transfer more money to Lawyer Nigel's company account.

The meeting left Cain with just the one thought in mind:

Will Trenchard bribe Zhang not to sign a 'letter of forgiveness'?

43

Monday – Week Fifteen

For the previous few weeks, the daily routine had remained predictably the same. Mr. Fán continued to have his English lessons once, sometimes twice, a week in his office. It allowed Cain and Kuo an opportunity to stretch their legs, have an occasional plastic cup of hot tea and for Kuo, have a smoke from the help-yourself packet of cigarettes on the desk.

In the evenings, after an English lesson with Kuo, Cain would relax alone under his number 30, slowly reading *Brideshead Revisited* and *Chronicles.*

However, there had been one 'surprise': the daily work had changed from making Christmas decorations to folding and glueing various coloured pieces of cardboard together to make matchbox-sized cases for jewellery and rings.

Having finished their evening English lesson, Cain and Kuo were having a few sweets and the Chinese people's favourite, pistachio nuts, while talking about the future.

Cain said, 'Thank you again for sharing some of the snacks you buy with me.'

'My pleasure . . . when you eat, you make no noise – you keep your mouth shut.'

Cain grinned. 'Eating quietly with our mouths' closed is a tradition in the west.'

Kuo unexpectedly raised a hand. Cain stopped talking and followed Kuo's line of sight up to the TV to see a portrait of Ambassador Johnathan Trenchard staring down at him.

Kuo turned to Cain. 'The British Ambassador has been killed. He crashed the car he was driving on a freeway on the outskirts of Barcelona in Spain.'

'How tragic,' Cain said, keeping a lid on his true feelings, feigning a look of shock.

The news left Cain contemplating:

Could the crash have been more than just an accident?

Tuesday – Surprises

Sitting in the tiger chair, Cain once again faced the prosecutor's accusations, via the female translator, challenging the veracity of his statements and suggesting he had not been an investor or director. 'You not tell truth,' the prosecutor said again. 'You just friend.'

'If, as I suggested when we last met,' said Cain, 'you had looked at the work and visitor's visa applications for myself and Hadley, and the accompanying letters of invitation from Zhang, you would clearly see I am not the one who is a liar.'

The female translator did her thing, but there was no response from the prosecutor.

At the end of what turned out to be a session of disagreement, the female translator finished typing Cain's statement and passed it through the bars with a pen and red-ink pad. Cain was surprised to see it was again typed in English. After reading through it, he said, 'It says, I deliberately wanted to push over the showroom cabinets. You infer my actions were planned and premeditated, which is not true. This is my sixth interview, and six times I have stated, I acted in an inexplicable moment of anger and frustration. You must correct the wording.'

Cain tried to hand it back, but the female translator and prosecutor conferring in Chinese did not take it. They then all sat silently staring at each other. Cain let the statement fall down onto their table, prompting the prosecutor to say a few words. Eventually, the translator picked it up, changed the wording, and handed it back.

Cain read it, signed, dated, and red ink fingerprint-stamped all where he had to, especially the corrections, and handed everything back through the bars.

The prosecutor and female translator packed their things and, without saying another word, they left the room.

Ciggy-lee appeared in the doorway, summoned Cain, and led him into one of the interview rooms on the opposite side of the hallway. Cain was surprised to see Jabba and Kim waiting for him. He immediately noticed there was no stooge sitting in the third chair behind them. Cain realised it was all over, the sentence had been decided, and from now on it would just be a charade.

Ciggy-lee said, 'Take seat,' before he walked out of the room, closing the door behind him.

As Cain sat down in the tiger chair he apologised for his unshaven, dishevelled appearance and noticed a number of paperbacks: *Titus Groan, The Van, Artemis Fowl* and *Sometimes A Great Notion,* next to a newspaper and an *Economist* on the table.

'A present for you,' said Jabba. 'Once they have been inspected you will get them.'

'What a wonderful surprise seeing both you and the novels. Thank you again for *Brideshead Revisited* and *Chronicles.*'

'Lawyer Nigel has asked me to tell you Zhang has written the 'letter of forgiveness' and accepted the payment. He will now press for the earliest court date. As soon as he has more news, he will come to see you. I'm sure you can appreciate there was little point in him coming all the way out here today and charging you for his time when I could do it for him.'

Cain grinned, 'Free of charge. Please thank him for me.'

'I have to tell you the authorities were considering bringing further charges against you, but they have decided not to, so you have nothing to fear.'

Cain got the distinct impression Jabba had made the comment to make him feel – after he was sentenced – he had got off lightly. Or perhaps now, without Trenchard telling her what to do and say, the paperbacks, newspaper and *Economist* on the table were helping her to make amends.

'Thank you for telling me,' said Cain, 'such is the Chinese system.'

'I will be leaving in two days; this will be our last meeting.'

Cain's professionalism immediately came to the fore. He decided not to tell Jabba he knew Trenchard was dead. He did not want their last meeting to end – for Jabba at least – on any sort of bad, perhaps tragic terms or with a sense of reckoning.

Cain grinned, 'Why are you leaving, you have been promoted?'

'I have—'

The visitors' door swung open – interrupting what Jabba was about to say – and the prosecutor and female translator walked into the room. Jabba and Kim turned to see who it was and stood up to have a quiet few words. Jabba then turned to Cain. 'I have to go now.'

'It's been good meeting both you and Kim. Thank you for all your help.'

The prosecutor was visibly shocked to see the great courtesy and cordiality between Cain, Jabba, and Kim. He was horrified to see Cain shake hands with Jabba and astonished to see Kim actually put her hand through the bars to do the same. It was more than he could take: his eyes looked as if they were going to pop.

As they all left the room, Jabba led the way. She added a whole new dimension to the saying: Line Abreast.

Back in room 309, Cain discovered Kuo had been released. Thinker led Cain down the centre aisle to a pile of hardback books under the number 30. 'From Kuo,' said Thinker, saying what Kuo had taught him. 'I am new Number One Yellow Jacket.'

'Thank you,' said Cain with the biggest of grins, holding out his hand. 'Congratulations.'

'*Xièxie.*'

As Thinker wandered off, Cain got up onto platform two, sat down, picked up the first volume, and read the front cover of *The Three Kingdoms*. It was a five-volume chronicle of Chinese history between 220-880 AD: a tale of corruption, lies, deceit, deception, and murder. Sadly, it was the Bible for business in China. All young men were advised to read it before starting out in life; it's message was what they aspired to.

That evening, the metal flap opened. Thinker immediately jumped up onto platform one to see what was wanted. A guard passed through the paperbacks *Titus Groan, The Van, Artemis Fowl,* and *Sometimes A Great Notion.* But not the newspaper or the *Economist.* Thinker called Cain to the front of the room and handed him the paperbacks.

Cain sat under his number 30 next to the piles of books and

closed his eyes, wondering, for how many days, weeks or perhaps months he would – to pass the time – be reading them.

44

Tuesday Morning – Week Seventeen – Day 113.

After Kuo had been released, Mr. Fán never again invited Cain to his office for English lessons.

It was another month before he was taken out of room 309 again. As he was escorted along the driveway it felt good to be stretching his legs again, to see the sun shining, to breathe in the warmer summer air, and to look across at the small park.

In an interview room he sat unchained once again in a tiger chair to be briefed by Lawyer Nigel.

'So you will appear in court in seven days.'

'Just out of interest,' said Cain, remembering what Jabba had told him during their final meeting, 'have the authorities at any time considered bringing further charges against me?'

Lawyer Nigel looked at Cain curiously. 'Not that I know of. Why do you ask?'

'Just wanted to know.'

'Anything else I can help you with?'

'My visitor's visa for China has now expired. Would you check on what the procedure is for me getting out of the country?'

'OK.'

'Will Zhang or Hadley be in court?'

Lawyer Nigel smiled. 'Zhang will not be there.'

'What about Hadley?'

Lawyer Nigel puffed himself up. He had been waiting until the end to deliver his news. 'Hadley was deported from China to the USA last week.'

Cain grinned, 'Good riddance.'

It's all part of the charade – everything has already been decided.

Cain arrived back in room 309 in time for the daily delivery of the air conditioning: it was summer and sweltering. Cain helped to push two one-metre-square blocks of ice through the steel sliding door and along the centre aisle, where they were placed twenty feet apart. The prisoners broke off bits of ice and wrapped them in items of clothing to make a cooling ice pack. They also placed their bottles of drinking water against the ice blocks to cool them down. No ice was ever put in the prisoners bottles or into the dustbin full of drinking water at the front of the room.

Cain had been surprised by how much the ice blocks reduced the temperature in room 309. That evening, he sat under his number 30. He slipped in his earplugs, made from toilet paper, to lessen the monotony of the Chinese language from around the room and the TV. He picked up a book and opened the pages before he closed his eyes for a few seconds of deliberation.

Jabba had left China, Hadley was probably now in Detroit with mommy, and Trenchard had been killed.

Why?

Thursday – The Men In Black

Cain squatted down on the walkway and held up his hands, but a guard he had never seen before told him to stand up. As he got to his feet he was turned around – and for the first time since being arrested, his wrists were cuffed behind his back. He was marched quickly along the walkway, turned into an area he had never been to before, pushed into a room – and the main food flap door closed behind him.

The steel sliding door to the laundry room was closed. Both platforms were stacked with boxes from end to end; some were overflowing with the various materials needed for the prisoners' daily work. There were dozens of one-gallon tubs of glue and flat transport packs piled high, waiting to be assembled and filled.

Halfway down the room, two men wearing black suits, shoes, ties, and white shirts were standing on either side of the centre aisle with an upturned bucket between them.

As Cain got closer, he could clearly see one of the men was the spitting image of the actor Kien Shih, who had played the part of Han in the movie *Enter The Dragon*, starring Bruce Lee. The other man looked a bit like Roger Willie, who had played the Navajo Private Charlie Whitehorse in the WW2 movie *Windtalkers*.

'Good morning sir,' Cain said, with a respectful bow of his head.

The men in black: I'll nickname them Han and Navajo.

Navajo gestured to the bucket. 'Take a seat.'

As Cain sat down, the men in black removed their jackets – revealing empty shoulder holsters – before sitting on the edge of the platforms on either side of their target.

'You will be pleased to know,' said Navajo, 'Zen and Kuo, your past Number One Yellow Jackets are both happily at home with their families. I'm sure you are looking forward to being released as soon as possible, assuming of course there are no problems.'

'I cannot see any problems sir.'

'Tell us about how the investment diamond showroom came into being?'

As Cain started to explain, Han removed a notebook from the briefcase by his side and put pen to paper. When Cain had finished, and after a number of questions, Navajo said, 'Tell me what Zhang is doing in Hong Kong.'

Navajo's use of *is,* not *was,* alerted Cain's sense of awareness. 'All I know,' said Cain, 'is what I said to Zhang in the Luyuan Road police station, in front of Officer Luó and several other police officers: Zhang is smuggling diamonds into China from Hong Kong and selling them under the counter, we have faked invoices produced by Zhang to prove it.'

Navajo asked, 'You have been to Hong Kong?'

'On several occasions, to meet with Bill and Greg before we went to Guangzhou.'

'Have you ever met Mr. Kwan the owner of the Major Casino in Macau?'

Cain was taken by surprise, but he didn't show it. Despite what Zhang had told him when pinned against the wall in the Taojin Hotel, he had never mentioned Mr. Kwan to Officer Luó, Jabba the Hutt, or Lawyer Nigel because without any proof, it was just hearsay.

'No sir,' Cain answered. 'Nor have I ever been to the Major Casino in Macau. I never gamble.'

'You are aware Ambassador Trenchard is dead?' Navajo asked.

'Yes sir. I saw it on the TV news. Kuo translated the story for me. He apparently crashed the car he was driving on a freeway on the outskirts of Barcelona.'

'You are aware Ambassador Trenchard was a homosexual?'

Cain showed a look of surprise. 'No sir, I had no idea.'

'Why do you think he went to Spain?'

'It is common knowledge the coastal resort of Sitges, about an hour's drive from Barcelona, is the gay capital of Spain. Perhaps Ambassador Trenchard was going there.'

'You have been to Spain and Sitges?'

'I have been to Spain on holiday several times, but I have never been to Sitges.'

Han and Navajo looked at each other and communicated without saying a word. Han turned to Cain. 'Tell us what you know about Teun the Dutchman?'

'He used to be one of Bill and Greg's clients. I have never met him. The documentation I gave to Officer Luó proves Zhang was lying about the supposed $450,000 I owe him.'

'Why would Teun the Dutchman tell Zhang and Hadley such a story?'

'I have no idea. I only found out about it when Zhang said it to me in front of Officer Luó after I had been arrested, so I have not been able to ask anyone to find out.'

'Do you know where Teun the Dutchman lives?'

'I have been told he is based in his home city of Amsterdam, nothing more.'

'You do know of course the Dutchman is a drug dealer.'

Cain showed a look of absolute surprise. He frowned for a moment, as if trying to comprehend what had been said. Seconds later, he looked up at Navajo. 'The D–'

'The drug dealer in Spain or South Africa?' Navajo interrupted.

'Sorry,' said Cain. 'I don't understand. I was about to ask you to clarify: The Dutchman is actually dealing in drugs? But you said Spain or South Africa. Sorry, I'm at a loss.'

Navajo looked at Han, who gave him a nod, turned a page, and made a note.

'Officer Luó from the immigration department is looking into your case,' Navajo said.

'I am honoured,' Cain said, and he bowed his head as a sign of respectful thanks.

'This is a confidential meeting, you understand, between just the three of us,' said Han, somewhat threateningly. 'Even if you are on the steps of the aircraft, we can bring you back. If we meet again, you are going to be staying here for a very long time.'

Cain got the inference. 'I understand sir. My lips are sealed. We will not be meeting again.'

The men in black communicated again without saying a word. As Han stood up, Cain took a kick to the stomach, he folded over – and a smack across the back of his head knocked him to the floor.

'Just a reminder,' Navajo said.

Cain stayed still, silent, listening to the sound of receding footsteps. A minute later, the unknown guard uncuffed Cain's wrists and gave him a bottle of water. Cain sat up, took a gulp, and looked up at the clock on the wall. It was 1:50pm, almost the end of Rest time.

Back in room 309, Cain gave a nod to the waiting prisoners and shrugged, indicating nothing new had happened. The prisoners took this as a positive sign, mistakenly believing Cain had been with his lawyer in one of the interview rooms. They proceeded to talk among themselves, speculating as to what the Englishman's fate might be. Cain got his food bowl off the shelf and sat under his number 30 to eat his still warm meatballs and rice, thinking about his meeting with Navajo and Han. As he rinsed out his food bowl and spoon in looland he had one particular thought in mind:

The drug dealer in Spain or South Africa?

What on earth had the men in black been trying to find out?

45

Tuesday – Week Eighteen – Chain Gang & Court

Cain stood with his ankles shackled and chained and wrists cuffed behind his back.

Wearing the prisoner's sleeveless, grey jacket over his creased, long-sleeved white shirt, tracksuit pants – always too short – and the slip-on sandals, now far too big, he waited for the command.

All eyes turned to look at the source of the sound: the chains scraping along the floor into the courtroom. Cain felt like he was in one of those 1930's chain-gang movies.

In the public gallery, Cain recognised the two Chinese salesgirls from the showroom. One let out a gasp, horrified by the sight of the bearded, longhaired, bedraggled, skeletal figure in chains. They turned to each other and held hands, almost cowering: they were the ones who had informed Officer Luó Cain had not stolen any diamonds.

'*Xièxie*,' Cain said quietly to himself, unable to convey his thanks.

A calm and disciplined atmosphere prevailed in the courtroom. Cain was led to a single chair. 'Sit,' the guard said.

On either side of Cain, some two metres distant, the opposing counsels sat at their respective tables: Lawyer Nigel and Melly on his right nodded and smiled, while the prosecutor on his left, ignored him and the translator looked up just briefly from the papers she was looking through.

One of the officials made an announcement, everyone stood up, three judges arrived through a side door, and the courtroom came to order. Retaking his seat, Cain looked up at the judges, waiting for the charade to begin. In his mind he heard *Steelers Wheel* singing their great 1972 song:

> *Clowns to the left of me,*
> *Jokers to the right:*

As directed, Cain stated his name, and apologised to the court for his appearance.

The proceedings were conducted in Chinese, with the only questions in English coming from the prosecutor's translator. Cain was again accused of not telling the truth. When the prosecution finished their cross-examination, the female translator surprised Cain by asking him, 'Before we bring the proceedings to a close is there anything you would like to say?'

Cain was astonished to discover Lawyer Nigel was not going to question him. He quickly glanced at Lawyer Nigel, who looked back at him blankly. It confirmed what Cain had long suspected: Lawyer Nigel was a part of the charade.

Cain stood up. 'I would be most grateful to be able to say a few words.'

'Please look and speak directly to the judges.'

Cain began by apologising for the damage he had caused in the showroom, before repeating everything he had said to Officer Luó in Luyan Road police station, written statements and subsequent interviews:

'I have provided the police and Officer Luó, an immigration, officer with copies of all the documentation relating to the opening of the Investment Diamond Showroom by Bill and Greg and the investments made by Teun the Dutchman and myself. I have provided copies of our visitor's visa applications and the letters of invitation written relating to the business.' Cain looked to the female translator. 'Please,' he said.

The female translator stood up, repeated word for word – in Chinese – what Cain had said, and sat down again, allowing Cain to continue.

'I have also provided bank statements. They prove Teun the Dutchman's investment of US$450,000 was paid back to him over a year ago, and I did transfer US$5,000 into Hadley's personal bank account in South Africa. Hadley had been working in China illegally for many months. His deportation by the Chinese authorities proves my case, yet I am the one who is in prison and now before this court. Thank you for listening to me.'

Cain turned to the female translator and bowed respectfully. With pen in hand, she picked up one of the documents in front of her, stood up and repeated again, word for word – in Chinese what Cain had disclosed.

The judges conferred before peering down at the English defendant. The senior judge in the centre looked sternly over the tops of her spectacles at Cain. 'You have told the court the documentation Officer Luó has in his possession will verify everything you have said is true.'

'Yes, your honour.'

You know that already.

The senior judge stared down at Lawyer Nigel, with a look that said it all: Why have you not presented the evidence given to Officer Luó?

Lawyer Nigel, on the verge of respiratory failure, stared down at his notes. The senior judge looked at the English defendant again. 'You will be sentenced in seven days.'

'*Xièxie,*' Cain said as he respectfully bowed before sitting down.

A week later

Cain was back in the courtroom and, once again, all eyes turned as he shuffled in, chained and cuffed. The guard led Cain to the single chair. 'Sit.'

The opposing counsels were back at their tables. This time, however, there was just a lone judge, already seated on the bench.

It left Cain again with just the one thought in mind:

Clowns to the left of me,
Jokers to the right:
Here I am.
Stuck in the middle with you.

'Stand up,' the guard ordered.

Cain got to his feet and respectfully stood to attention.

'You will be released in twenty-one days,' the lone judge

announced.

The gavel hit the block.

Cain bowed.

The charade was over.

46

Repercussions

Zhang was still trying to deal with the repercussions of Hadley being deported when he heard about Cain's impending release. He was on the phone to Mr. Kwan, the casino owner in Macau.

'You sure you never said anything to Cain about what you are doing for me? You sure he knows nothing about us?'

'No, I told him nothing,' said Zhang. 'He doesn't know – I told you this before, it all OK.'

'For your sake, it had better be. You have forty-eight hours to get to Hong Kong.'

'But there is no one to take care of showroom.'

The line went dead.

Zhang's phone was soon ringing again. He listened to Teun the Dutchman's ranting. 'You told me Cain would get two to three years in jail.'

'I tell you what Lawyer Nigel told me when he gave me money for my 'letter of forgiveness'.'

'This is your mistake.'

And again, the line went dead.

Teun turned to another line of a slightly different kind. A line of white powder on his table. He took a snort and his drug-addled brain gradually traded fact for fiction, until it was clear in his own mind it was not his fault. Because he was never, ever, wrong.

Zhang sat alone in the showroom, knowing he had lied to Mr. Kwan. He put his cell phone back in his pocket, took off his glasses, and placed his elbows on his desk. Rubbing his eyes he tried to come to terms with what was happening. The long-term consequences of his, Hadley and Teun's conspiracy were proving to be more devastating than he could ever have imagined.

All these problems, he thought, *and Cain not even out of prison yet.*

352

47

Tuesday – Day 148 – Week Twenty-Two – Release

Cain sat watching the clock on the wall as the seconds passed by, *tick, tock*: it was nearly midnight. The second-hand finally hit the mark.

My 'cell-bye' date has finally arrived. Today I walk free.

He curled up in the duvet and went to sleep.

At 7am, as was the custom in room 309, Cain, along with Maybach, finished his last Suicide Watch. Minutes later, to a round of applause, Cain was the first to place his duvet in the corner. He then sat under his number 30: he would be the last man to enter looland.

During his morning's ablutions, he surreptitiously took the shreds of paper out of his pocket – his 'diary' – and, bending down to pick up his bucket, he dropped them into the toilet and flushed them all away.

Minutes later, wearing his long-sleeved white shirt and tracksuit bottoms, he completed the ceremonial removal of his items from the shelves, the knob on the wall and dropped them into the bin bucket. And, as instructed by Thinker, he placed his grey sleeveless jacket, his T-shirts, and his books on the end of platform two: nothing could be taken from the room except what he stood up in.

At 10am there was the usual roll call and inspection. After Mr. Fán had signed the ledger and placed it back on the end of platform two he smiled at Cain and spoke to Thinker before the usual procedures began.

At 10:45am, after saying his farewells to fellow prisoners, shaking hands, and bowing respectfully, Cain heard for the last time the sound of a steel bolt sliding, a chain being dragged through iron rings, and a key turning. The main door opened.

Mr. Fán looked down at Cain. 'Time to go,' he said in English.

'Yes sir.'

Mr. Fán and Cain, with his hands uncuffed, made their way along the walkway, leaving a guard to close the door behind them.

In the medical centre, Cain stood on the scales: sixty-six kilos. The doctor stared at the Englishman's skeletal figure and checked his file. Since the day he had arrived he had lost a total of sixteen kilos in weight. Back at the doctor's desk Cain signed, dated, and red ink fingerprint-stamped his records, confirming he was alive and well.

Outside, across the driveway, Mr. Lài was standing by the steps leading up to the walkway to room 123, overlooking the park – and above him, Ciggy-lee was sitting on the balustrade of the open window, smoking a cigarette. They both gave the uncuffed prisoner a nod – and Cain, respectfully did the same.

In a different room off the arrivals corridor, Cain's suitcase and backpack were already by the counter. He handed over his yellow slip, sat on the floor, discarded the far-too-big slip-on sandals and put on his now far-too-big Timberland boots. He took the clear plastic bag, broke the seal, and opened his backpack. He saw what was wrong: it had been ransacked, it was a mess, but he ignored it.

'OK, OK?' said the guard, holding out a pen and tapping the ledger. 'You sign.'

'All OK.'

As Cain signed, dated, and red ink fingerprint-stamped the ledger, the guard gave Mr. Fán a quick look of relief. Cain then placed the contents of the plastic bag into his backpack.

Seconds later, for the last time, Cain stepped through a partially opened cantilever gate, the beeps changed to buzzes and the gate closed behind them. With Cain doing all the carrying and Mr. Fán doing all the talking, they crossed the inner perimeter road, and passed through the partially opened solid steel, cantilever gate in the ten-metre-high, solid brick wall.

From the pathway Cain looked out over the now completely full staff car park and the occupied prison office buildings. On reaching the open gate under a concrete archway, Cain took a last look back. 'Bye,' he said quietly.

As they walked along the outer perimeter road Cain could

see Lawyer Nigel and Melly waiting at the barrier.

Lawyer Nigel and Mr. Fán had a brief conversation before saying their goodbyes.

Shaking hands with Mr. Fán, Cain sensed his smile was nothing more than a veneer.

Cain stepped back and bowed as a sign of respect: he wanted to leave on the best of terms.

And the only white man, no longer in a prison of 1800, turned and walked away.

Part Eleven

Guangzhou, China

If you leave prison with hatred, anger, and bitterness, you are still in prison.

Nelson Mandela

48

Time

Cain relaxed on the back seat of Melly's Mercedes four-door saloon, enjoying his first hour of freedom and chatting amiably with Lawyer Nigel.

By the time Melly had parked on the forecourt of the Taojin Hotel, Cain had just one question remaining: 'How do I book into the hotel without a visa?'

'I have to go to a meeting,' Melly said, extricating herself from the situation.

'That's OK, I have all the help I need.' Cain got out of the Mercedes, opened the front passenger door and looked down at Lawyer Nigel. 'After you.'

Lawyer Nigel had deliberately avoided mentioning the visa situation, hoping it would have allowed him to leave with Melly and disappear. He looked up at Cain and got out of the car.

In the hotel's reception, for the first time ever, Cain was confronted in a full-length mirror by his bearded, long-haired, bedraggled, skeletal appearance. He took a breath; his unshaven beard hid the look of horror on his face. At the same time, the hotel manageress gave him a look of disdain. However, when she saw his passport photograph the penny dropped. She realised he was the handsome, suntanned guest who had been led out of the hotel in handcuffs many months before. She gave Cain a look of sympathy. 'Your visa is out of date. I cannot book you in.'

Using the hotel's landline, Lawyer Nigel made a few phone calls and, after finding out the way to renew the visa, Cain left his bags with reception and the two men set off. As they walked the length of the bustling Taojin Road, the people gave Cain more than just a passing look. And standing next to his smartly dressed lawyer, wearing a suit and carrying a briefcase, at one of the many bus stops on the main road, other people waiting, kept the pale, skeletal figure at a distance. Stepping onto the bus, Lawyer Nigel appeared to exhibit a look of excruciating pain when he paid the equivalent of fifty US cents for the fares before they took their seats.

'Well I certainly didn't expect to be on a bus today,' Cain commented.

'We could do nothing until you were free,' said Lawyer Nigel. 'You have to appear in person at the immigration department to get your visa renewed. We will be there in twenty minutes.'

'OK.'

Despite the visa hiccup, and not being in a taxi, Cain was at ease. He was now a free man, watching the world go by. It was good to once again see the crowded streets, the people – not the prisoners – having a chat, having a cigarette, beneath cloudy summer skies.

When Cain and Lawyer Nigel stepped down off the bus, some of the passengers showed a look of relief. On the sidewalk, passers-by stepped away, preferring to keep the bearded, long-haired, bedraggled, skeletal figure at a distance.

Arriving through the doors of the Immigration Department, a few words from Lawyer-Nigel with the security guard were needed before Cain was allowed to proceed.

On the third floor of the super-modern building, Lawyer Nigel pulled a number from the ticket dispenser, and they took a seat. They soon had the row to themselves as others shuffled away – and no one sat in the row in front of them. They were soon called to one of the counters, where Lawyer Nigel's professionalism and explanation appeared to garner a degree of sympathy from the immigration officers. The whole process – including having a photo taken – took less than thirty minutes. 'Come back in ten days,' an officer informed them, handing Lawyer-Nigel a receipt for Cain's passport.

'*Xièxie*,' Cain said as he got to his feet and bowed.

Outside on the kerb. 'I'll pay,' Cain said, raising his hand to hail a taxi. The wary driver slowed to take a closer look at the skeletal white man and decided to pass him, *Bye* – in every sense of the word. But on seeing the smartly dressed Chinaman – Lawyer-Nigel – also flag him down, he came to a stop.

As the taxi moved through sparse midday traffic, Cain

spotted two Nigerian men, wearing *bubas*, *sokotos* and *Abeti Aja fila*-style damask hats, walking on the sidewalk. He had never seen Nigerian men wearing such traditional clothing on the streets before: they really did stand out. Cain then caught a fleeting glimpse of another Nigerian, also dressed traditionally, walking towards the two other men. He twisted himself in his seat and stared out of the back window. But the taxi, moving with the flow of traffic and the bustling people walking on the sidewalk, limited and obstructed his view.

Lastly! Could it really have been him?

Seeing Cain twist and turn, Lawyer Nigel asked, 'What is it?'

Cain relaxed back into his seat. 'I saw a man I know rather well. Perhaps I'll meet up with him before I leave China.'

Back on the bustling Taojin Road, Cain tapped the driver's shoulder to pull over and turned to Lawyer Nigel. 'Let's take a walk.'

Seeing Cain pay the driver, Lawyer Nigel asked, 'Can I have the taxi's receipt for my expenses?'

'Of course.'

Cain handed Scrooge Lawyer Nigel the receipt: a trifling sum of RMD24, the equivalent of US$4.

As they walked along the street, Cain bought a few beers, crisps, fruit, and a bar of chocolate from one of the kiosks. Lawyer Nigel translated for Cain at the barber's: 'He will come in tomorrow at 11am. Shave off his beard and cut his hair.'

As requested, Lawyer Nigel took photographs of Cain standing in front of the Taojin Hotel – and in reception, the immigration department's visitor's visa renewal receipt did the trick, Cain finally checked in.

'Time for a beer,' said Cain. 'Care to join me for a farewell drink?'

'OK,' Lawyer Nigel said – knowing he would be getting the drink for free.

Up in his room, Cain looked for a bottle opener.

'Give the bottles to me,' Lawyer Nigel said, holding out his hands and, placing the top of a bottle in his mouth, he removed its top using his teeth.

Cain was amazed. 'Jaws,' he said with a grin.

Lawyer Nigel removed the second top from his mouth. 'All

Chinese people can do this. Cheers.'

They talked about Cain's prison life and how it felt to be back on the outside. Lawyer Nigel took a last swig of his beer, placed the empty bottle on the table, and checked the time on his watch. 'I have to go.' He rounded off their conversation by reminding Cain not to go near the showroom. 'If you do, Zhang will immediately go to the police and tell them you have threatened him or even worse, anything to have you re-arrested.'

Lawyer Nigel got to his feet, opened the last two bottles of beer using his teeth, placed one back on the table, and handed the other to Cain along with the receipt for his passport. Cain realised he would not be seeing Lawyer Nigel again. They shook hands and respectfully bowed, but not as friends. Cain watched Lawyer Nigel take a few steps along the hallway before closing the door. He sat on the sofa, placed a piece of chocolate on his tongue and savoured the taste. His passport would be ready in ten days. He would have just enough time to do what had to be done.

He emptied his ransacked backpack onto the bed: his reserve of US$1000, kept at the base of a pocket liner, had been stolen. He remembered the quick look of relief the guard had given Mr. Fán when he had signed the ledger; signed away any chance of making a complaint. He realised it was partly his fault, for on the day of his arrival at the prison – with Jerry's death still reeling through his mind – he had forgotten all about it. Hence, he was left with just the one thought in mind:

How did they find out the cash was there?

He put his phones on charge, plugged in his laptop, and got his backpack in order. After a very long hot shower his pale, bearded, longhaired, skeletal reflection in the mirror looked back at his diminished self:

I definitely need a few steaks and days in the sun.

And picking up his Canon sure-shot he set about taking a few pictures of himself.

Getting dressed, he made a hole in his belt to prevent his jeans from falling to the floor and put on a now over-sized shirt. He phoned room service, ordered coffee and a mix of Chinese dishes without the rice. He sat down, gazed at his laptop screen, opened a Word document and played another version of *I packed my bag*. He typed: *Day One – Room 123*, and from memory, for better and for a lot worse, he relived the last five months of his life.

When he had eventually finished his diary of detainment, along with his meal and coffee, he checked his emails: Sofia, as expected, had sent him a number of updates regarding various personal and business matters, accompanied by a number of suggestions and things she was taking care of. He read her summary of the correspondence she'd had with the British Consul and Lawyer Nigel:

1. For the first six weeks you were in prison, I repeatedly phoned – leaving messages – and emailed the FCO to ask where you were being detained.

2. Six weeks after you were arrested, I received an email from Lawyer Nigel telling me he would be representing you – along with your signed authorisation to send monies to his account.

3. On that same day, the London FCO emailed me the name and address of the prison in which you were being detained and details of how to open a shopping account for you.

4. I tried to open an account for you, but the account numbers were incorrect. I phoned and emailed the FCO, pointing out their error and politely requested an immediate response.

5. Despite several days of repeated requests by phone and email, the FCO did not respond.

6. I informed Lawyer Nigel. He said he would open the prisoner shopping account for you. He said he needed another €1000 over and above his agreed fees. I sent it.

Cain realised Lawyer-Nigel had kept all but a fraction of the €1000 for himself. He had been the one who had sent the couple of tracksuits and bare essentials in the fifty-litre plastic storage container to room 309. The cost of which would have been nothing more than US$75. The miserly Lawyer-Nigel had lied and left Cain to starve.

When released from prison, Cain had wanted to ask Lawyer Nigel many things: Why Jabba had chosen him? Why hadn't a shopping account been opened? Why had he not presented in court the documents – given to Officer Luó – proving H&Z were liars?

But of course, Cain already knew the answers: miserly Lawyer Nigel was just doing whatever would make him the most amount of money – and doing what he was told.

Cain checked the time on his Breitling on the table; it was too big now to be on his wrist. The time in Andorra would be 10am. He was well aware if Sofia found out he had lost sixteen kilos in weight she would be absolutely devastated, so he decided not to tell her. He removed the burner cell phone SIM cards from the lining of his suitcase, placed one in his Chinese cell phone and dialled a number. 'Morning. *Que pasa?* (What's happening?)'

'You're out!' Sofia almost screamed. 'How are you? Where are you?'

'I'm OK – I'm in the Taojin Hotel in Guangzhou.'

'Having a beer?'

'Having my second one. Cheers.'

I'll mention it now to start on a low note, end on a high.

'I've read your emails, thank you for sending the two wreaths from me and you to Jerry for his funeral. Please, for now, let's leave it there. Bless you.'

'I'm looking at a fabulous diamond ring on my finger,' Sofia said to raise Cain's spirits.

'Glad you like it.'

It will definitely look better on you than it did on Zhang.

An exchange of jokes about Cain being Sofia's fiancée were followed by a brief resumé of his time behind bars – but he talked only of the good times, the funny times, to make Sofia feel happy. 'By the way,' said Cain, 'were you in direct contact with Jabba the Hutt?'

'No, she never made contact with me.'

By midnight – China time – Cain had also spoken briefly to

Moshe in Jo'burg and Marius in Cape Town. But of course they had all stayed with the protocol of days gone by: they would wait until they were face to face to discuss more serious issues. Cain had also sent emails to Bill and Kay, Greg and Susie Su, congratulating them on getting married in the USA. Cain soon received a great response from them all. But Cain had not spoken to everyone he had wanted to: he would not be having a friendly chat with Jerry. He remembered, when they were with Adam in the UK, their old saying: *"Be seeing you."* But he wouldn't be seeing Jerry ever again. He closed his eyes and watched the magic movie in his mind as they revisited all the places they had been to together in the UK, Australia, Florida, South Africa, and Spain. Also, one of the books he had read in room 309 was a reminder of the great 1981 TV series they had watched more than once.

Lord Sebastian Flyte in *Brideshead Revisited*:

You're to come away at once, out of danger. I've
got a motorcar and a basket of strawberries and
a bottle of Château Peyraguey – which isn't a
wine you've ever tasted, so don't pretend.
It's heaven with strawberries.

A tear ran down Cain's cheek.

49

Wednesday – Point Blank

Cain sat in the barber's chair taking photographs of his hair being cut and his beard being shaved off.

The suitably refreshed, skeletal figure attracted a little less attention as he took a stroll through the Huanghuagang Commemoration Park, next to the Taojin Hotel. It was a wonderful experience to be able to walk for more than twenty-three steps in a straight line – the length of the prison rooms – without coming up against a brick wall and having to do a U-turn. He eventually took a breather and sat on some steps overlooking a fountain.

By a hedgerow a young girl, no more than five or six, watched an old lady performing Tai Chi. The young girl stepped forward and began to mirror the old lady's every move – becoming a reflection-in-time, some seventy years apart. He wondered if they were related, perhaps a grandmother and granddaughter.

In his mind's eye, he took a step back in time. He watched Jerry mirror his every move when they were young, learning karate in the dojo, practising in the garden shed and, when they were older, on the beaches in Perth, Florida, and South Africa. He then saw Jerry, Riley, and Adam with their arms around each other. "We're all OK," they said. "Take care."

Sorry Jerry, I wasn't with you to say farewell. My fault.

Once again, Cain's eyes welled with tears.

Thursday

Cain had always despised drug dealers, so he didn't care if Afam ended up being executed, like Jiang had. As for meeting up with Afam again, he would only do it if Mac or Marius deemed it necessary. But because Afam had looked after him in room 123, Cain was a man of his word, he did what Afam had requested. He took one of his hidden burner cell phone SIM cards out of his suitcase, put it in a cell phone he had just purchased in a local store, and sent an SMS to Afam's wife Davika in Thailand, explaining he had a friend who had been in prison with Afam and signed it 'Freddy'. He soon received a reply. He sent a few good-hearted comments, explained how Afam had not yet been sentenced, and gave the address and phone numbers of the prison.

He then sent the same message to Afam's cousin Cheks, with an extra couple of lines:

Afam suggested we could do business together.
If that's OK with you, give me a call.
I look forward to hearing from you. I'll buy you dinner.

Friday

Posing as Freddy, Cain received a very guarded call from Cheks.

'Freddy' explained – with a strong American accent – how his friend, who had been in prison with Afam, had been deported. The following conversation remained somewhat tense, especially when discussing if they should meet up.

'So,' 'Freddy' commented: 'The time has come, the walrus said.'

'To talk of many things,' Cheks responded.

'Of shoes and ships and sealing wax.'

'Of cabbages and kings.'

'You and Afam were with the missionary and his wife in your village,' 'Freddy' said.

'Afam told your friend about us.'

'On the day he was released.'

'Lewis Carroll was our favourite poet.'

'Mine too.'

'Freddy' went on to talk about South Africa and casually mentioned Lastly.

'Lastly is away for a few days,' said Cheks. 'He'll be back at the end of next week.'

'Let's have dinner one evening, as I suggested. You will both of course be my guests. Dinner is on me.'

'I'll convince Lastly,' Cheks said appreciatively.

'I know a great restaurant – the Luming restaurant, overlooking Lu lake. Give me a call when Lastly is back. I'll book us a table.'

Hearing the name Luming, Cheks said, 'Wouldn't miss it for the world.'

Using another burner SIM card, Cain phoned an American number to speak to Mac who was really in London. It was a very precise, military stye discussion. Mac ended it with three simple words: '*Silence is Golden.*'

Cain removed the SIM card from the phone, crushed it under foot and flushed it down the toilet.

Saturday To Wednesday

Cain spent the next few days eating well, having a beer or two, walking in Huanghuagang Commemoration Park, carefully exercising his pale, skeletal body, and buying the few things he needed. He made two burner cell phone calls to Mac regarding the days ahead and exchanged coded emails with Marius and Moshe, regarding the weeks ahead.

One afternoon, he was walking back to his hotel when a Chinese man he had never seen before standing on a corner said, 'Silence is soon to be golden.'

Without answering, Cain followed the stranger into a side street where – without any of the country's CCTV's looking down on them – he was handed a small bag and the stranger walked away.

In his hotel room, Cain opened the bag, removed the Chinese Tokarev .7.62mm semi-automatic pistol, loaded it and screwed on the silencer.

Thank you Mac.

Next, he phoned Marigold, his maid in Cape Town, had a chat, and gave her a list of the clothes, trainers, and toiletries he wanted packed into suitcases.

'The suitcases will obviously be rather heavy,' said Cain. 'Just leave them in the bedroom. A friend of mine will collect them and carry them down the stairs rather than the pole.'

Marigold laughed. 'Look forward to seeing you.'

'In a few weeks' time. Take care.'

Cain then sent Marius an SMS on a burner cell phone, removed the SIM card, crushed it under foot and flushed it down the toilet.

Thursday

Cain finally received a call from Cheks.

'Hi,' said 'Freddy'.

'Lastly is back.'

'Let's meet up tomorrow evening – a great way to start the weekend.'

'Good idea.'

A minute later, they had agreed a time and place to meet near to the Luming restaurant. 'I look forward to meeting you,' 'Freddy' said, before he rounded off their conversation with a further incentive. 'We can put together a letter to send to Afam to cheer him up.'

Friday

In the immigration department, Cain collected his passport stamped with a new visitor's visa.

Back in his hotel room at 8am, European time Cain phoned Sofia.

'Morning. I have my passport.'

'Wonderful.'

'Please book a seat for me on a last flight tonight to Jo'burg. If there is not a seat available, book me on a last flight to anywhere in Europe where I will not require a visa?'

'Anything for this ring on my finger,' Sofia seductively whispered. 'Anything for my PTPS (Part-Time Personal Shag).'

'My wonderful PTPA (Part-Time Personal Assistant),' Cain replied.

'I'll have an answer for you within the hour.'

In the darkness of the night, Cain stood under the cover of trees, behind a hedgerow, watching the entrance to the Luming restaurant some fifty metres distant. It was the same restaurant where he, Bill, Greg, Kay, and Susie Su had enjoyed a wonderful dinner on several occasions. It was the perfect secluded setting, away from the city, next to a park, overlooking Lu lake.

Cain watched through a monocular: the taxi dropped Cheks and the one and only Lastly off at their rendezvous point. They sought cover from the drizzling rain under the shelter of the now deserted visitors' viewing stage. They would not venture nearer to the five-star Luming without 'Freddy'. It was out of their league: they were gofers, bagmen, not kingpins.

Lastly looked as fit as ever. Cain opened his umbrella, walked along the pathway, and crossed the road. Having lost sixteen kilos in weight, he was in no position to get physical: he had no strength, he had to keep his distance.

'Glad you could make it,' Cain called out with a truly strong 'Freddy' American accent. Pleased to be acknowledged, the two men stepped forward and Lastly taking bullets to his legs, fell to the ground. 'On your knees,' 'Freddy' said to Cheks, 'give me your phones.' And looking down at Lastly, 'Freddy' said, 'Hands on your head *NOW*.'

Absolutely horrified, trying to come to terms with reality, Cheks did what he was told. As he divulged the unlock codes, 'Freddy' tapped them in to make sure the numbers were correct. Cheks then received a kick to the side of his head, knocking him unconscious, to the ground.

'Freddy' raised the umbrella. 'Good to see you again, Lastly,' Cain said with his own English voice. 'Hand me your phones and I will allow you to tend your wounds.'

Lastly handed them over, divulged the unlock codes and Cain tapped them in to make sure the numbers were correct.

Trying to stop the bleeding, Lastly hatefully said, 'Minister Zokwana told me you killed my brother.'

'Only because he was trying to kill me.'

'Pity he didn't.'

'Talking of killing people, you tried to kill Moshe and I in bandit country. Windows would have been with you if Gospel had not shot him in the stomach.'

'How do you know?'

'You left your Colt .45, with a strike pad from a box of matches stuck on the slide, in the Pajero. Wanker!'

'Fuck off white shit.'

'Tell me what I want to know, and I will let you live. Who sent you to China?'

'Minister Zokwana.'

'When did you start meeting Teun the Dutchman in Hong Kong?'

'About a year ago.'

'What is the name of the man who tells Zokwana what to do?'

The sound of one beep from a vehicle's horn made Cain glance to his side, Lastly started pulling a gun, Cain looked back and staring straight into the haunted eyes of a dead man staring straight back at him he fired the Tokarev .7.62mm semi-automatic pistol: a single bullet entered Lastly's forehead and the dead man lying, stayed on the ground. Seeing the road was clear, Cain ran to the slow moving vehicle, got in the back and ducked down, out of sight, out of mind.

In a warehouse, everything was carried out military-style: Cain handed the Tokarev pistol to the man who had given it to him, the man who had been driving the vehicle. At a table he wrote the cell phone unlock codes on sticky notes and stuck them on each one. He took off every item of clothing he had been wearing, especially his shoes, latex gloves and put them in a bag. From the boot of another vehicle, he took the clothes he wanted to wear from his suitcase and got dressed.

Minutes later after throwing the bag into a furnace, Cain was sitting in the back of a taxi on his way to the airport.

Thank you Mac.

While on the flight, Cain couldn't stop thinking about how he should have flown back to England six months earlier to meet with Jerry, and years before how he should have flown with Riley to save her – and her parents' lives.

In his mind's eye Cain could see Jerry, Riley and Adam

standing together, waving to him.
If only I was with you.

Part Twelve

The Land of the Baobab Tree, South Africa

The dead cannot cry out for justice.
It is a duty of the living to do so for them.

Lois McMaster Bujold

50

Reunited – Updates

On landing at Johannesburg airport, Cain received an SMS:

Ready and waiting, room 13 – lucky for some.
Take Care. Talk to you later.

It was the first SMS Moshe had ever sent him.

Cain saw the Jeep parked in the allotted space in a corner of the airport car park and checked the registration number – just to be sure.

Thank you Marius.

The driver's door of the Jeep unexpectedly opened, and a black man stepped out. Cain froze, dropped his suitcase, and checked the space around him.

'Morning,' the black man said.

In the quiet of the pause, Cain was totally astounded. 'I don't believe it,' he said a little louder than intended.

'Long time no see.'

Cain grinned as he removed the cheap Chinese baseball hat and sunglasses he'd put on before leaving the plane and held out his arms to embrace the man in front of him.

'Good to see you whitey,' Agent Omara whispered. 'You've lost your tan. You OK?'

'Yeah, all OK, Harry. I just wanted to pale into insignificance.' And with smiles all round. Cain added, 'I've also lost some weight.'

'Just a bit. Mac told me, you owe me a beer, I've come to collect.'

'Make that two.'

Maintaining the humour, Agent Omara carried Cain's suitcase for him and placed it in the back of the Jeep. Cain immediately noticed his other two suitcases in the back.

Thank you, Marigold, my wonderful maid.

Agent Omara handed Cain the keys to the Jeep. 'You remember how to drive?'

Appreciating the mirth, 'Might do,' Cain answered.

As they opened the doors, Agent Omara said, 'There are a few things I need to tell you before you go, because I will not be travelling with you.'

In 1972, a teenage Agent Omara had arrived in the UK with his Ugandan parents. They were among the many thousands who had fled the murderous dictatorship of Idi Amin Dada. Agent Omara's father, a doctor, and his mother, a nurse, found employment in a hospital in Essex, and their teenage son went off to school. At the age of eighteen, the young Agent Omara joined the Army. He served in Europe and parts of Africa where he was highly commended for acts of bravery.

In 1992, when Cain and Agent Omara had been on the London stakeout, when Cain had knifed Lastly's twin brother to death, Agent Omara had been in the early days of a one-man undercover investigation. His task was to meet and work with members of a particular criminal drug world – one being Zokwana who he ended up spending quite a lot of time with.

Zokwana had sought refuge from apartheid South Africa by moving to the United Kingdom. He was nothing more than a minion on the periphery of the undercover investigation into drug gangs. As for the twin brothers, Agent Omara had no idea they even existed, let alone knew Zokwana.

Days after Lastly's twin brother had been knifed to death, Zokwana had watched Nelson Mandela giving a speech on TV. He realised the impending election in South Africa would be the downfall of the president, F.W. de Klerk and the end of apartheid. It was a green light for him to return to his home country and get a foot on the ladder while putting his enemies in their graves.

When Zokwana had met Lastly in the café in Brixton, all he had wanted to do was cajole Lastly into going back to South Africa with him. A feat he achieved by promising a fitting funeral for Lastly's twin brother, back on African soil.

Within days, Zokwana had caught a flight back to Jo'burg and Lastly, who was illegally in the UK, hitched a ride on a container ship heading for Durban. Meantime, Zokwana's file was shelved by Agent Omara and time moved on.

'Because Zokwana and I had become reasonably good friends in London,' said Agent Omara, 'when he returned to South Africa and eventually entered parliament I sent him a card of congratulations with one of my burner cell phone numbers. I did it on the off chance he might reply, and at some point in the future our friendship might come in handy.'

'Good idea,' Cain agreed.

'I must admit, I was surprised when he called me one day. To cut a long story short, here I am working for him in South Africa. Only Mac, Moshe, Marius and his people, plus you now know who I really am.'

'Congratulations.'

'Sorry to have lumbered you with all this as soon as you've got off the aircraft, but I wanted to see you again and tell you face to face, hence I volunteered to deliver the 4x4 with your suitcases.'

'Thank you, at least I can begin to get things into perspective.'

'I know you have many questions,' said Agent Omara. 'Marius can't meet you until Thursday or Friday. He will fly up to Jo'burg, Moshe will pick him up. It is best you all talk together to ensure you are all on the same page.'

'I understand,' said Cain. 'Will you be joining us?'

'Unfortunately, no, but Marius will keep me informed.' Agent Omara smiled. 'It will be a great long weekend for you all.'

'It will be,' said Cain, grinning. 'I'm looking forward to it already.'

Agent Omara opened the glove compartment. 'I thought you would appreciate a pocket-sized Walther PPK for the time being.'

'Good idea – thank you.'

'The keys and alarm code to the lodge you are staying in are in the envelope. I understand you've been there before.'

'Friends of Moshe and I, Neilson and Catarina from Mozambique took us there once. We've stayed there since on a couple of occasions when driving to and back from Maputo.'

'Moshe arranged for a local supermarket to stock up the lodge with all the necessities for the weeks ahead, so everyone believes tourists are staying there.'

'Great. I'll take an occasional visit to the local store to replenish anything I need.'

Agent Omara removed a burner cell phone from his pocket and handed it to Cain. 'You will be receiving a few calls,' he said as he checked the time on his watch. 'That's about it for now. I have to go.'

A few amusing comments about diets, rice, steaks, and beer later, the two men shook hands, but they did it South African black man-style – double grip, two position hold, three-time crunch – allowing Agent Omara to maintain his undercover identity. 'Take care of yourself white-shit.'

'You too, you black bastard.'

They burst out laughing and embraced like such men do.

A step in the right direction

Driving a Jeep again and watching the world go by once more made Cain feel pretty good. He turned off the freeway into a well-known tourist spot and parked on the forecourt of a small motel, in a quiet corner away from the crowd.

Outside room 13, he raised his hand to knock, but the door opened. He found himself looking down at a gorgeous, slim, black female in her early thirties, wearing a T-shirt and short skirt.

The female smiled welcomingly. 'Hello. I can see you need my services. Please come in.'

'That obvious, huh?' Cain said with a grin.

In the bathroom, Cain started to undress. He was about to have more than one shower, his body scrubbed, his face shaved, and his hair trimmed, before being manicured and pedicured.

Afterwards, Cain looked at his doppelgänger, now wearing a perfectly pressed long-sleeved shirt and jeans. Although they were somewhat loose-fitting, he felt perfectly groomed, invigorated, and his resolve was strengthened.

'All OK?' the female asked.

'I feel a hundred times better. You're fantastic. How much do you owe me?' he joked.

'Nothing. It's all been taken care of.'

But Cain put cash on the table anyway. 'Don't forget, this never happened.'

'Of course.'

They kissed, cheek to cheek, by the open door. 'Thank you,' said Cain. 'Take care.'

'You too.'

Watching the man with no name walk away, the female was overjoyed by the cash he had left on the table but saddened by his appearance. Although she had worked for Marius on a number of occasions, no questions were ever allowed. She was left wondering what could have happened to have left the polite, pale, skeletal, English-sounding man in such a state. Seeing the man disappear around a corner of the motel, she said quietly, 'Bye . . . look after yourself.'

Back in the Jeep, Cain slipped on his Serengeti shades and switched on the radio. The great Cape-Talk Radio presenter John Maytham was starting his afternoon drive show.

Time to truly get the wheels into motion.

Some four hundred kilometres east of Jo'burg, Cain turned off the N4 highway – known as the Maputo Corridor – and drove up to the main gates of the Marloth Park Wildlife Sanctuary. The guard checked Cain's pass, gave the security booth a wave, and a single gate opened. Cain entered a world of freedom, where there were no fences. A world where the zebras, giraffes, kudus, blue wildebeest, nyalas, impalas, and many other species roamed freely; a world where, on or off the trails and tracks, around the various country-style homes and rental properties, the wildlife always had the right of way.

The isolated old country lodge Cain (and Moshe) had visited several times before came into view, as did those blocking his way.

'A welcoming committee,' Cain said with a sigh of appreciation. 'Just what I needed.'

The Jeep coasted slowly to a stop... Cain switched off the engine, stepped out onto the dirt track, stretched his arms and climbed up onto the roof rack. He breathed in clean, fresh air, looked up at the fading light of the early evening sky – and back down at those blocking his way. A baby giraffe with its mother, were standing in the driveway, observing the antics of the skeletal figure now sitting on the roof of the Jeep. A few metres away, several ever-skittish zebras, kicked out their back legs, raising up dust, and let out their high-pitched calls before returning to their less frenetic, quieter grazing.

Cain would let the dust settle: he was content to sit and relax, free of any concrete walls, steel bars, city buildings, and other people around him. He was surrounded by nature – a sight for sore eyes – in one of the most beautiful, most fertile areas of South Africa, where the Afrikaans people had a saying:

"As jy 'n besemstok plant, dit sal groei. (If you plant a broom handle, it will grow)."

Cain eventually eased himself down onto the dirt track, removed the suitcases from the back of his Jeep, slung his backpack over his shoulder, and slowly dragging the three suitcases along, one at a time, he made his way around the skittish zebras and past the giraffes on the drive to the front door of the lodge.

In the entrance hall, a grandfather clock's hourly chimes broke the silence. Cain checked the time, closed the door and, with the Walther PPK in hand, he went for a wander – just to be sure. Leather sofas, cushions, a coffee table, and bookcases filled the lounge. Through the glass patio doors he could see an old wooden railway sleeper dining table, chairs, and a braai overlooking the fountain in the garden. At the top of the curved staircase, Cain wandered around the open three-sided gallery. In a quiet corner, an obligatory vase and two dolls, sitting on intricately patterned doilies on a table, fulfilled the tribute to Afrikaans folklore. Once he'd checked all of the en suite bedrooms, he decided – as always – to sleep in the one with the king-size bed. After he had lugged the suitcases up the stairs and unpacked, he checked the drive: the giraffes and the zebras were gone, so he re-parked the Jeep.

Feeling somewhat exhausted, he helped himself to a can of beer from the fridge, plus a takeaway chicken salad and sat on a stool at the kitchen island. As he finished eating he received his – welcome back – conference call from Mac, Marius, and Moshe.

Some time later, he quietly opened the patio doors, stepped out, sat in an old rocking chair and watched the wild boar drinking at the fountain. He relaxed under the night sky; an empty can in one hand, and nothing in the other. He breathed out, long and slow, contemplating what the future may bring. He heard the grandfather clock chime 10pm:

Time for a nightcap.

As he dropped an ice cube into a highball tumbler and poured his J&B, deep down he knew where he should have been: on the *Disponible.*

In his mind's eye, he saw Jerry, Riley, and Adam with their arms around each other.

"Just keep us in your thoughts," they all called out. "Be seeing you."

And once again he heard *Sarah Brightman & Andrea Bocelli* sing their beautiful song:

Time to say goodbye.

A tear ran down his cheek.

51

Untraceable

For the next forty-eight hours, Cain had a relaxing time. He was beginning to feel quite good, though he didn't look it. He started each day by cooking himself a full English breakfast, or having fruit, watching the news on TV, checking emails, and making phone calls.

For lunch he would grill himself a *filet mignon* steak, ostrich, or lamb chops on the braai out on the patio, with steamed vegetables or salad and a glass or two of red wine.

During the afternoon, he went for a walk to stretch his legs, enjoy the countryside, say hello to the wildlife, and back at the lodge have a snack of whatever he felt like.

For dinner, he would eat whatever he fancied, and depending on the evening's temperature – it was winter in South Africa, not summer – he would go for a walk or exercise, watch the TV. He drank water copiously – it was all part of his health regime, to get himself back in the real world.

Wednesday

Cain re-opened one of the two suitcases in which Marius had placed a few items after Marigold had packed them.

Cain pulled on his now not-so-tight-fitting leather shooting gloves, slipped his Galco Miami shoulder holster into place and threaded his gun belt through the loop in the strap, the loop in the hip holster, and the loops in his jeans. He looked at his gaunt reflection in the mirror: everything was all rather loose. But on the more positive side, the thinner the target, the harder it is to hit. He raised his arms and gave his hips a shake: if he hadn't put an extra hole in his gun belt and put on two pairs of boxer shorts, his jeans would have fallen to the floor. He lowered his arms – for the time being it was something he would have to contend with.

From among his various untraceable weapons and ammunition, he extracted a throwaway Beretta 96. He fed the 40cal Critical Defence Hydra-Shok rounds into the mag and slipped it back into the well. The sound of the slide – sending the first round into the chamber – was the first step in preparation for the road ahead. He aimed the 96.

Marius and Moshe arrived at the old lodge in Marloth Park on Thursday afternoon. Cain was standing in the drive, waiting for them. The three men immediately embraced, like great friends do, exchanging the usual humorous comments, tinged perhaps with a touch of concern.

'Dear boy, you have certainly lost some weight,' said Moshe. 'I didn't realise–'

'Compared to some,' said Cain, 'I got off *lightly*. Excuse the pun.'

'Good job we brought the Eskies full of lamb with us,' said Marius. 'It's a special delivery from this year's Hantam Vleisfees Calvinia Lamb Festival in the Great Karoo. We brought a few steaks too.'

Suddenly, the rear passenger door of the Toyota opened. 'I don't believe it,' Cain said, completely surprised.

'How are you?' Mac said, and they embraced like father and son.

'I'm OK,' Cain quietly answered.

Some time later, after unpacking and settling into the lodge, the four men pulled the tabs on their cans.

'Welcome back,' Marius said.

'Good to see you,' Moshe said.

'Glad you got here sooner, rather than later,' Mac added.

'I reached my '*cell-bye*' date.'

And with smiles all round, they toasted each other.

As they relaxed on the sofas in the lounge, Cain told his story.

Many questions later, Moshe said, 'We can only be betrayed by the people we trust. I'm sure the men in black will be paying Zhang a visit sometime soon. As for Hadley, it's good he was deported – a degree of justice was served. Bill and Greg have told me he is back home in Detroit with mommy, trying to re-enter the diamond business.'

'I spoke to the newly married couples very early this morning,' said Cain. 'Bill and Greg are keeping an eye on him. They have been informing all and sundry – especially his Church of Scientology – about his dishonesty.'

'Serves him right,' Moshe said.

'I'll pay him a visit when we go to the Big Apple to see them,' said Cain. 'Kay and Susie Su told me Afam has been convicted of drug dealing and sentenced to fifteen years in jail.'

'Compared to many,' said Mac, 'he got off lightly. You came back from China after six months instead of two weeks. A lot has been going on. You have quite a lot to catch up on. And just so you know, Marius, Moshe and I, with you included are now aware of everything there is to know about each other – well almost.'

'So, we are all on the same page,' Cain said.

'We have to be,' said Marius, 'in preparation for the road ahead.'

'Let's have another beer.'

As they all sat around the kitchen island, they would start to talk about all the things protocol had not allowed them to discuss on the phone. They would now all talk freely, about anything and everything, the past, the present and the future.

'I'll start,' said Mac. 'On the day you were arrested, seconds after Moshe received the email from Sofia explaining what had happened, he forwarded a copy to both Marus and I.'

'She is perfect.'

'Indeed,' Moshe said.

'You all are,' Cain responded.

And Mac continued, 'We know, as far as anyone is concerned the Bureau does not exist. We are just an ordinary *Trailing Arrest Team*. The people I have to answer and report to, immediately reminded Trenchard how you were nothing more than – as reported at the time – a servant to the Royal Family who was accidentally shot. He was told, if any rumours started circulating, he would be held to blame, Her Majesty The Queen would have him immediately recalled back to the UK and he would be dismissed. Let's not forget, Buckingham Palace refused to name you. Your identity would forever, especially since you were wearing a false beard, remain anonymous.'

'Pity I wasn't wearing it in the hospital.'

'When a copy of your passport was brought to the attention of Ambassador Trenchard – as protocol dictates – it confirmed you were definitely the 'Agent Smith' he had confronted.'

'Point taken,' said Cain. 'Such is life.'

'He was, as you suspected responsible for delaying your legal process, keeping you behind bars, having you starved. Payback, When I eventually found out, I had to put a stop to it.'

Cain looked at Mac expectantly. 'Looks as if you did.'

Mac smiled. 'When Trenchard was told to stop interfering with your legal process, he flew to Barcelona without informing London. I did not have anything to do with his death. His autopsy proved he was high on drugs and alcohol.'

'Do you believe his car crash was an accident?'

'The Spanish authorities' investigation is still ongoing. I'll let you know.'

'Of course.'

'When Jabba the Hutt as you call her, returned to London, I had her interviewed. She had, as expected, simply followed Trenchard's orders. She revealed a lot about what she had heard was happening behind the scenes. But in all fairness, being in Guangzhou, two thousand kilometres from Trenchard in Beijing, she was unaware of what was really going on. However, to cut a long story short, Marius and I did manage to piece a few things together to help with our joint investigation.'

'Where is she now?' Cain asked.

'She is at the British Embassy in Moscow.'

'Working for you?' Cain speculated.

Mac smiled. 'Let's just say she has her own best interests at heart.'

Cain sensed Mac had subtly divulged a little more than he normally would. 'Nice one.'

'In your absence, I ran a check on Teun the Dutchman – as a favour to you – to find out where he is and what he's up to. However, in light of what you have told us about the men in black asking about a drug dealer in Spain or South Africa, plus of course our ongoing investigation into all the phone numbers

from Lastly and Chek's burner cell phones Marius and I are –
just to be sure – having the Dutchman fully investigated. We'll
let you know what transpires.'

'I owe you one,' Cain said.

'We'll add it to the list.'

'For the moment,' said Marius, 'let's just deal with what we
have to.'

Moshe, in his inimitable way, moved the subject of
conversation on to other things to ease the pressure. He handed
Cain a gift-wrapped box. 'A present for you.'

Cain unwrapped the box: inside was a brand-new Beretta
.9mm semi-automatic pistol. He picked it up, dropped the mag
and – as protocol dictated – racked the slide to show everyone it
was not loaded. As he turned his hand to slip the mag back into
place, he noticed a diamond had been studded into the side of
the grip. He looked up at Moshe.

'A present from a friend,' said Moshe. 'A man who likes to
mine his own business.'

Cain grinned, 'I'll have to phone Kobus to thank him.'

'I had it registered on your firearms certificate, so it is legal.'

Marius said, 'A pleasant change for you.'

And everyone laughed, though not too loudly.

'It will be my preferred daily carry,' said Cain. 'But not until
we get our lives back to normal.'

'I've cut the 3-carat rough given to you by Windows and
Zokwana,' Moshe said, handing Cain a *brifka.*

Cain read the numbers Moshe had written on each of the
brifka's four corners. 'Top quality,' Cain said appreciatively.

'It's amazing what I can do with a nail file.'

Cain laughed at their long-standing joke. 'Another reason for
you truly being the master – you never cease to amaze me.'

Moshe acknowledged the compliment with a rarely seen
smile. 'I have also cut all of the ten rough Zokwana personally
gave you.'

'What are they like?'

'Grade D, all top quality.'

'We won't be giving them back.'

'Compensation,' Marius suggested.

'Indeed,' Moshe said.

Cain grinned. 'We have only one thing for Zokwana.'

'Don't we all,' Mac said.

Moshe checked the time on his wrist. 'Time to eat,' he suggested. 'Something with rice?' he teased.

'Ric White, next clue,' Cain grinned.

The men all juggled the anagram in their minds. 'Very clever,' said Moshe, 'is that your new name, now you are almost without a suntan?'

'I'll try not to *pale* into insignificance.'

Everyone laughed. Marius walked out to the braai to fire it up. Cain started to make the salads, Mac decanted a first bottle of red wine, and Moshe fetched the steaks from the esky.

Over a relaxed early dinner, whilst talking about various times and places, Cain eventually told his story about why Afam was not a wanker and had two wives, provoking a great deal of laughter. And Cain's account of how 'Freddy' had lured Cheks and Lastly to their meeting gained a round of applause.

'So,' said Cain, rounding off his story, 'nobody will ever know 'Freddy' was really me.'

As early evening darkened into a starlit night, the four men sat – under the pyramid-flamed patio heaters – watching the wildlife at the fountain, talking about what the future may bring, about how one number on Lastly's burner cell phone had allowed Marius and Moshe to trace where and what Windows is now doing.

'The old-style, Costa Beach Hotel on the outskirts of Maputo,' said Cain, 'overlooking the Indian Ocean has a great seafood restaurant. Moshe and I have eaten there several times. If Windows is there, it will be the perfect location.'

Mac asked, 'Why do you say that?'

'I'll let you know.'

Mac smiled. 'Maputo, the capital of Mozambique – we need eyes-on. Any suggestions?'

'Surprisingly,' said Cain, 'we know just the man.'

'Indeed,' Moshe agreed, giving Cain an appreciative smile.

'Time for you to say hello.'

52

Friday Morning – The Man In Mozambique

'Hey Cain, good to hear from you. How you doo-in?' Neilson said in his usual way.

'Good to be back in South Africa,' said Cain, 'Moshe is here with me, he's listening. You two can have a chat when we're finished.'

'It will be good to see the two of you together again,' said Neilson. 'We were all getting fed up with the empty chair at the table.'

'Looking forward to it.'

Cain gave Neilson a brief synopsis of the activities of the man they were looking for…

'So,' said Neilson, 'to summarise, the man is involved in the trafficking of cash, drugs, guns, and girls across the borders.'

'Yes. Guess where he is staying, fancy an oyster?'

Neilson laughed. 'How convenient. The Costa Beach Hotel just happens to have our favourite seafood restaurant.' Neilson had always suspected there was more to both Moshe and Cain than meets the eye, but of course, any questions would have to wait until they were once again face to face. 'The man you are looking for, what's his name?'

'Windows: a fit-looking black man in his early thirties, about 5ft 9ins tall with a short, vertical scar under the left of a pair of very wild eyes.'

'Drugs?' Neilson queried.

'Probably the crystal-meth kind they call *Tik*, here in South Africa. Windows was shot some eight months ago, so he has two bullet hole scars at waist level, entry and exit, left side.'

'I have seen him at the hotel on several occasions.'

'You sure?'

'Yes. A couple of months ago I was standing by the front of the hotel with Catarina waiting for a client to arrive in a taxi. The man you call Windows was walking along the promenade towards us. As he put his T-shirt on before going into the hotel, I saw the scars on his side, and when he said afternoon, I saw the scar under his eye.'

'That has to be him,' said Cain, as he looked around at Moshe, Mac and Marius, all silently listening, silently nodding. 'For the time being, we just need to know if he is there.'

'I'll check it out when I get back.'

'You are not in Maputo?'

'Catarina and I are away for a long weekend. We will be back on Sunday night. I will book a table; we will have dinner at the hotel on Monday evening. I will find out what is going on.'

'Moshe and I will of course pay you for your time, your meals, taxis, everything.'

'Thank you, much appreciated.'

'Have fun. Enjoy the oysters – hope they work!'

'Oh, yes always,' said Neilson. 'I'll phone you on Monday evening when we are back home, after dinner.'

'Take care,' said Cain. 'I'll hand you over to Moshe for a chat.'

For the rest of the day Cain, Mac, Marius, and Moshe relaxed, playing catch-up. There were many questions Cain wanted to ask Mac and Marius, but experience told him, some things were best left on a need-to-know basis. Or a don't need to know basis. Or perhaps on this occasion: All in good time, all would be revealed.

The six o'clock chimes of the grandfather clock reminded Cain to take a leg of lamb and chops – from the Festival in the *Great Karoo* – out of the fridge. As the men began the preparations for dinner, Marius walked out to the most respected of altars in Afrikaners folklore – the braai – to fire it up. It was the beginning of another great festive evening.

Saturday

Cain made a call to Kobus to thank him for the diamond-studded Beretta. Rounding off their conversation he said, 'Please pass on my best regards to your family, especially

Hennie and your two lieutenants. See you soon. I'll pass you over to Moshe to have a chat.'

It was the beginning of another great day.

Cain drove everyone around Marloth Park to see the freely roaming wildlife, which included stopping for a 'zebra crossing' on the road – of a slightly different kind.

As the sun moved towards the horizon, the four men sat with a couple of Eskies on the Crocodile river bank, having a drink, enjoying a picnic. They watched the elephants on the other side of the river warily coming down from the Kruger National Park to the water's edge for their evening drink and session of bathing.

'Mesmerising,' Mac said.

Out on the patio of the old lodge, Cain was again being updated.

'We know Minister Zokwana,' said Marius, 'resigned several months ago. If not he would have been sacked. And now the Mr. Zokwana, having moved to Jo'burg, is enjoying a life of leisure, non-executive directorships, cocktails, and dinner parties.'

'Is he becoming an alcoholic?'

'Not just yet. I have to thank you for mentioning the painting you looked at above the fireplace in the then Minister Zokwana's residence.'

'The Victorian farmhouse surrounded by baobab trees.'

'Yes, you were right; the landscape artist had painted it only months earlier. It was Zokwana who had the false date 1989 painted on it. It is the property Zokwana had purchased, the one I was looking for. And of course it is located in the Limpopo province.'

'Quite a distance from here.'

'It is,' said Marius. 'Zokwana often spends long weekends there.'

'Must be quite an isolated location.'

Marius smiled. 'Agent Omara is keeping us up to speed.'

The four men were having an English breakfast at the kitchen island. They knew it was now a waiting game until Neilson in Maputo, confirmed Windows was in the hotel.

'To save you asking,' said Mac, 'I am travelling under a pseudonym.'

'A private jet back to London?' Cain asked.

'Of course. We will stop at a motel on the outskirts of Jo'burg where a young female will put my false wig and beard back on.'

Taken totally by surprise, Cain grinned. 'An outstanding charade – she is very good.'

'She certainly is,' Marius agreed. 'I will be flying separately back down to Cape Town. Mac and I, regardless of how he may look, really do have to keep our distance.'

Hearing the hourly chimes of the grandfather clock in the hallway, Moshe said, 'Time to load up the suitcases.'

'Time for you to all leave,' Cain said with a sad look of inevitability.

Outside on the drive, all four men, watched by several skittish zebras, embraced like great friends do – and a father would his son.

As Cain gave the Toyota a last wave, the baby giraffe, still no taller than its mother's legs, wandered past. Cain sat down on the front doorstep of the lodge, watching the wildlife. His great time with Mac, Marius and Moshe, reminded him of three other people who were missing in his life.

I need a drink.

53

Waiting Game

Late on Monday evening, Cain's mobile rang; he checked the caller ID and pressed the button. 'Hi Neilson.'

'Hey Cain, how you doo-in?' Neilson said in his usual way.

'Good. How were the oysters?'

'Excellent as always. Windows is now calling himself Ray. He is expected back at the hotel next Sunday and his room is booked for the rest of next week. I will fax you a copy of his fake passport.'

'Thank you,' said Cain. 'I won't ask how you got a copy of the passport.'

'Definitely not,' Neilson interrupted, amiably. 'Catarina and I have booked a table for next Sunday to see if Windows is back. If he returns earlier, I will be informed. I have to go now; I have a busy day ahead of me.'

'We really appreciate you helping us.'

'You're welcome. Talk to you later.'

Cain immediately phoned Marius and faxed him a copy of the fake passport.

'I will phone Mac to let him know,' said Marius. 'Keep me informed.'

'Of course, and I'll phone Moshe.'

For the rest of the week, Cain started taking a daily run as well as a walk, exercising for a longer time – and eating well, putting on a few more pounds.

On Thursday morning he placed a throwaway Beretta 96 in his shoulder holster – and one in his waist holster – with two spare mags on the strap. Standing in front of a full length mirror, 'Looking better,' said his doppelgänger. 'But not by much.'

He sent a few more emails and made a number of necessary phone calls. He spoke to Peter to thank him for, as always, taking care of the 'fortress' in his absence – and as agreed during their last meeting – updating the security: installing the CCTV's and taking care of Marigold the maid.

'Looking forward to having a beer with you,' Cain said, rounding off their conversation.

'Over a few games of backgammon,' Peter suggested.

'Good idea. Especially when you are buying (as the loser of each game) the Jägermeister shooters.'

'Piss off.'

'Cheers.'

One afternoon after taking a run and practicing the karate *katas* and Tai Chi *forms,* Cain opened a can of beer and phoned Moshe to have a chat.

Moshe eventually said, 'To cut a long story short–'

'I'll go get the scissors,' Cain joked.

'Please do.'

During Cain's penultimate visit to Guangzhou – over a year ago – he had unexpectedly been asked by Bill and Greg to travel down to Hong Kong to meet with one of the elite 1% billionaire clients they had all first met in Australia.

On the following day, when H&Z had asked Kay about Cain, she had told them he was spending time with some old friends from Australia who wanted to do business in China.

"In Guangzhou?" Zhang had asked.

Surprised by the question, Kay had responded appropriately. "Of course."

Moshe continued, 'One of Kay's contacts told her Officer Luó discovered the date on the documents you supposedly signed, coincided with a stamp on your passport, proving you were in Hong Kong at the time, not in China. Further investigation discovered your fingerprints were not on the documents you supposedly signed regarding the transfer of sponsorship for Hadley's work visa.'

'Kay and Susie Su certainly have their fingers on the pulse in Guangzhou, despite being in New York.'

'They do. Although Lawyer Shen, claimed he was unaware your signature had been forged, your case prompted further enquiries. He has been taken into custody by the immigration department. There are now several ongoing investigations, but they are not related to you. Kay also told me Zhang's passport has been revoked.'

'So Zhang will no longer be able to go to Hong Kong, serves him right.'

'Susie Su has also been informed Mr. Kwan, the casino owner in Macau, is now too scared to go back to China. He is staying in Hong Kong.'

'Time will tell.'

'Apparently, what you said at your trial has spread throughout the industry. It is the death knell for Zhang.'

'Good riddance.'

'Indeed.'

'I'll send Kay and Susie Su an email to thank them for being so wonderful.'

'I already have,' said Moshe. 'But one from you as well, will be appreciated.'

'I think it's time to have something to eat,' said Cain. 'I'm feeling rather peckish.'

'What are you having?'

'Ostrich.'

'Can you run fast enough to catch one?'

'If I did, would that be a feather in my cap?'

'Very good.'

'Talk to you later.'

'Shalom.'

Late on Sunday evening, Cain took a call from Neilson. 'Hey, how you doo-in?'

'Hi Neilson! All the better for hearing from you. How are the oysters working?'

'Ahh, Cain, I wish it would take another month before I call you. But I am sure my heart would not last. Catarina will be the death of me.'

'Way to go Neilson.'

'Windows is here,' Neilson announced, getting back to business.

'Alone?'

'Yes. When I saw him this evening at the bar, Catarina and I got close and started talking about the views from the top of Table Mountain.'

'A clever ploy.'

'It worked. Having seen us several times in the past, he introduced himself. I will not bore you with the details.'

'OK.'

'He was more than pleased to join us for dinner. He said he had just returned from the north, but he did not say where or why. I did not ask. He told me he would be here for the rest of the week. He will be leaving next Sunday. But again he did not go into detail. We have

arranged to have lunch with him on Tuesday, just to keep an eye on him.'

'Excellent.'

'I will give you a call when I get back home.'

'Talking of home, will you by any chance be in Maputo for the rest of the week?'

'Yes, I am not going anywhere. Why do you ask?'

'I'll tell you on Tuesday afternoon when you call me.'

'As you wish.'

'Just out of interest, has that old hotel on the beachfront been demolished?'

'No, not yet, still standing. It's been deserted for thirty years now and still no running water,' Neilson joked. 'I will let you know when your room is ready.'

'Thank you,' said Cain, suitably amused.

'Sleep well.'

And with laughs all round they ended their call.

Cain phoned Marius. 'Windows has arrived. He will be there for at best, seven days.'

'At last,' said Marius, 'it's time for Plan and Shoot.'

'What is Plan and Shoot?'

'Tell you later.'

'OK.'

Now Marius had a timeframe, he arranged for one of his people to type out a faked letter from 'Ray' (Windows), put a future date on it and, using the signature in 'Ray's' fake passport, had it signed. Having checked the letter, Marius folded it around US$500 in cash and put it in an addressed envelope. He placed the envelope in a plastic bag and took off his plastic gloves with a sigh of satisfaction.

Tuesday – Plan and Shoot

Marius arrived at the old lodge in Marloth Park in a 4x4. Cain walked across the drive to greet him. 'Afternoon.'

Marius greeted Cain, in his own language – the Afrikaans language – like they so often do. '*Goed om the sien jy sit gewog aan* (Good to see you are putting on weight).'

And they embraced like great friends do. As they unloaded the suitcases and sports bags out of the back of the 4x4 and carried them into the lodge… Cain said, 'Neilson called an hour ago, after having lunch with Windows. We are on the same timetable; Windows will be leaving on Sunday. Neilson is now on our payroll for the rest of the week. I offered him, an amount he could not refuse. Moshe and I will pay him. I said I would talk to him again this evening.'

'Perfect. Thank you,' said Marius. 'We just need the next forty-eight hours.' Marius' cell phone rang. He answered it. Seconds later, 'Yes,' he said.

Marius and Cain walked out onto the patio to see two armed black men appear from nowhere. Apart from entering Marloth Park undetected, Cain could see they had not disturbed the wild boar drinking at the fountain.

True professionals.

'Good evening sir,' they both said to Marius.

Cain was absolutely astonished to see who they were. He glanced at Marius.

Marius smiled. 'Allow me to introduce you to Plan and Shoot.'

'Seriously?'

And with handshakes all round, 'It is a code,' said Marius. 'For my most trusted (Agents). In their Xhosa language, in the pages of etymology, their names Cebo and Dubula mean Plan & Shoot.'

'That's what we do,' Dubula said.

'Especially now,' Cebo added.

Marius said, 'We cannot risk Cebo and Dubula being seen here. As far as anyone is concerned they are with their parents on the outskirts of Cape Town having a few days off. I'll explain why later.'

And for Cain, past events came to mind:

Some three years earlier, when Marius had visited Cain
at the 'fortress' for the very first time, there had been a
parked car along the drive.
"Friends of yours?" Cain had asked.
Marius had said, "The two men inside are my most trusted."

Around one year later, Peter had introduced Cain to Cebo,
a supposed guard, who had shot dead one of several
armed burglars at a country residence in Constantia.
Neither Cain nor Peter had known or ever found out:
Cebo's night shifts had allowed him – for Marius –
from up on the top floor to find out who was
surreptitiously visiting the people who lived in the
property across the road, associated with Minister Zokwana.

And eight days later, when Cain had visited the
then Minister Zokwana at his residence Dubula had been
the supposed guard at the gate. But in reality, Dubula
was the man who was unofficially informing Marius of
what was going on.

Cebo smiled. 'Thank you again for the US$400 you and Peter gave me.'

'You're a hero,' said Dubula. 'My friend here gave me half.'

And with smiles all round Cebo and Dubula were shown around the lodge.

All four men spent the afternoon discussing strategies and tactics and afterwards Cain phoned Neilson to coordinate their plans for the days ahead.

As the sun drifted below the tops of the trees Cain, Cebo, and Dubula were talking with Marius around the braai, taking in the aroma of grilled steaks and lamb chops over burning hickory.

'*Ag 'n perfekte einde tot 'n dag* (Ah, a perfect end to another day),' Marius said quietly.

They sat around the railway sleeper dining table in comfortable wicker chairs to enjoy their meal with just the one glass of wine. They would need clear heads for what was coming.

After dinner, under the warmth of pyramid-flamed patio heaters, they drank coffee and went over the plans one last time. They spoke in English, occasionally in Afrikaans, and more than once, Cebo and Dubula exchanged words in Xhosa to better understand the finer nuances of what they were going to do.

'Where we will be taking Windows is a very clever idea,' said Cebo.

'I'm pleased I came up with it,' said Cain. 'It's what you'd call a concrete solution.'

And with smiles all round, Cebo and Dubula knew they would easily blend in with the people in Neilson's country and remain, out of sight, out of mind.

54

Wednesday

In the darkness of the early morning, Marius drove the 4x4 slowly along a length of the Marloth Park perimeter road, nearest to the Maputo Corridor.

'There sir,' Cebo said, pointing at a tree.

The 4x4 stopped and seeing all was clear, Cebo and Dubula immediately jumped out into the woodland, to retrace their steps, to again climb over the perimeter fencing.

As Marius drove off Cain asked, 'When they came in last night, how did they know which route to take?'

'I had a special set of pictures taken by a drone.'

Minutes later, with a last wave, Cain watched Marius drive off. 'Take care.'

After Marius picked up his two most trusted, the 4x4 headed east, along the Maputo Corridor, towards the Lebombo/Ressano Garcia border post with Mozambique. At the R571, the 4x4 turned south towards Swaziland, and on reaching the rendezvous point it pulled over. Cebo and Dubula jumped out to cross the border into Mozambique, where Neilson was waiting amongst trees by a hillside to drive them the 100km to their destination.

Marius would now stay in prearranged accommodation nearby, waiting for the call.

By the end of the day, on the outskirts of Maputo, Cebo and Dubula had reconnoitred the solitary, cul-de-sac-style, beach road:

They'd checked out the area around the incomplete, concrete shell of the Four Seasons Hotel, set back from the beachfront. In 1975, when the Marxist Mozambican government gained independence and took control of the country, the last of the colonial Portuguese workers had poured concrete down the elevator shafts to prevent the hotel's construction from being

396

completed. It had all the hallmarks of a building long-since abandoned and being 25-floors high with 340-bedrooms it had become a towering eyesore.

Cebo and Dubula had then walked to the end of the beach road – getting the lay of the land – to survey the Costa Beach Hotel where Windows was staying and have a walk along the pedestrian pathways leading to another road.

And last of all they caught a taxi to a warehouse-style building, owned by Neilson, where they had a shower, and changed into their pre-delivered clothes for the evening ahead.

At sunset, Neilson drove Cebo and Dubula into the centre of Maputo and dropped them off. They walked along a main street before they hailed a taxi. Anyone who saw them would conclude they were guests in one of the nearby hotels.

Near the Costa Beach Hotel, Cebo and Dubula looked at each other for a few long seconds. They both knew the word Xhosa meant *angry men.*

The time had finally come to settle a long overdue family score.

'*Ekugqibeleni* (At last),' they both said – and Dubula walked away.

In the Costa Beach Hotel, Cebo was sitting on a stool at a table in the bar having a beer. Minutes later 'Ray' walked in, ordered a drink and sat on a stool at a nearby table, sadly thinking again about how Lastly had been murdered, and all it entailed. When 'Ray' heard the young man, talking on a cell phone, mention Cape Town and Khayelitsha, he couldn't resist the temptation. When the call ended, 'Excuse me,' he said, giving the man a wave, 'I heard you mention Khayelitsha, you are from the Western Cape?'

'Yes, I am.'

'So am I.'

'Please join me,' said the young man with an inviting gesture towards a vacant stool.

'Ray' joined the young man and, feeling revitalised, he held up his glass to gain the barman's attention. 'Same again for both of us please.'

'Yes 'Ray',' the barman answered.

After the customary pleasantries, having a good time and finishing their drinks, Cebo suggested they should go to a very private upmarket bar-restaurant full of free drinks and wonderful, sexy females.

'Sounds great,' 'Ray' said, and a short vertical scar creased with a smile, under the left of a pair of very wild eyes.

Cebo removed his passport from of his pocket and held it up. 'Like me 'Ray', you are a foreigner here in Mozambique, we have to present our passports to gain entry.'

'I'll go get it.'

'I'll wait for you by the entrance.'

When 'Ray' returned, Cebo was talking on his cell phone, he held up his hand and 'Ray', staying silent, listening in, realised the friend Cebo had mentioned, who would be coming to the hotel was on his way.

'OK,' said Cebo, rounding off their conversation, 'we'll take a walk along the road to meet you.'

Looking at 'Ray', Cebo said, 'My friend will be our taxi.'

A hundred yards along the road, when Cebo hit 'Ray' across the side of the head knocking him unconscious, he fell into the arms of a man standing by a hedge.

Thursday

In the early light of the morning, Windows woke up to find he was stretched out on his back on a very large thick plastic sheet on a concrete floor, looking up at a concrete ceiling. He tried to move, but his arms had been splayed apart and his wrists tied to the ends of a long steel pole. He craned his neck to see his legs were similarly pinioned. He tried to call out for help, but he had been gagged. Looking around as best he could across a deserted floor at balconies, vacant stairwells, and open lift shafts, he immediately realised he was in the derelict Four Seasons Hotel. His head fell back, hit the floor and the short vertical scar contorted with the pain under his left of a pair of very closed eyes. He momentarily wished he was dreaming. However, a kick to his side brought him back to the real world. He looked up.

'Morning,' said Cebo, removing the strip of duct tape from

across his mouth. 'You have met Dubula.'

Windows recognised Dubula, now standing by his side with a very large hunting-style knife in hand, as a guard from the main gate of what had been Minister Zokwana's residence in Cape Town.

'This must be a mistake,' said Windows, his tone anxious. 'What do you want?'

'Not a mistake,' said Cebo, placing a portable tape recorder on Windows' stomach. 'We are rival gang members, if you answer our questions truthfully you will live. If you do not, things will become slow and very painful before you die.'

'Whatever you want to know, I tell you,' Windows pleaded.

'Good,' said Cebo. 'Who are you working for?'

'Mr. Zokwana.'

As Cebo and Dubula's questioning progressed, they soon came to terms with a simple reality, Windows was lying – in every sense of the word – as he always did. Cebo flicked open a switchblade and waved it in front of Windows' wide eyes.

During the rest the interrogation, Windows became saturated in his own blood, sweat, tears, and vomit. Cebo poured more water from a bottle into Windows' mouth to wash it out, and over his head to cool him down. His chest heaved; his pulse ricocheted off the hype of his heartbeat, he choked, he turned his head to one side, and wretched again. The stench of vomit permeated the air.

Windows' ultimate confessions confirmed what Marius, Cain, and Moshe had always suspected – and during Cain's time in prison in China, what they had uncovered:

The failure of the attack in bandit country had caused Lastly to go into hiding in the Soweto township on the outskirts of Jo'burg. To be with Windows, recovering from the bullet wound Gospel had inflicted on him. After weeks of convalescing, Windows had plucked up the courage to call Minister Zokwana, who responded in full fire and brimstone mode, berating Windows for his lies, for Gospel's murder, and for the failure of the raid in bandit county before slamming down the phone.

But as time had moved on, Minister Zokwana became Mr. Zokwana, and Windows' persistence eventually paid off. Past hostilities and animosities were left to rest. Mr. Zokwana's priorities had changed. Before long, Windows was taking orders from Zokwana again. He was sent to Maputo to open up a new route for the trafficking of cash, drugs, guns, and girls across the borders into the neighbouring countries. Windows bribed officials at the border posts, ensuring he would get his cargo across unhindered. Meantime, Lastly was sent to Hong Kong. His task was to keep an eye on the laundering of drug money – earned through the extensive black community from West and Central Africa, residing in Guangzhou – into legitimate diamonds.

When Cebo and Dubula asked Windows about the assassination attempt on Commander Marius van Rensburg, Windows vowed he had never heard the name, but had been told the two targets were police officers who had ripped off the man who always told Minister Zokwana what to do.

'Your last chance,' Cebo threatened. 'Who tells Zokwana what to do?'

'I don't know.'

'So the white police officer lived, and the black police officer died.'

'Who cares if black cops live or die?'

'We do,' said Cebo, kicking Windows. 'The black cop was my brother.'

'The black cop was my brother-in-law,' Dubula said.

Windows' face wore an expression of pure fear. His bowels and bladder emptied. He was left writhing in a pool of piss and pile of shit. Cebo and Dubula pointed their knives at him.

'No, no, please!' Windows whined. 'You promised I would–'

The knives entered his throat. The *coup de grâce* had been administered.

They cut the duct tape from around the dead man's wrists and ankles, laid the poles on top of him and wrapped the plastic sheet around him. No trace of what had happened was on the floor. They carried the body across to one of the open lift shafts and threw the dead man down into his grave.

RIA – Retribution Is Africa.

55

Thursday Afternoon – Analysis

Cain stood with Moshe and Marius on the patio of the lodge…
waiting.

Moshe had arrived at the lodge, hours earlier – and Marius,
only a few minutes ago.

When Cebo and Dubula appeared by the deserted fountain, it
was the beginning of a welcoming session of congratulations
and shaking hands from Cain and Moshe, with more
compliments from Marius.

Whilst having refreshments – teas, coffees, water and fruit
juices – all five men were seated at the dining room table,
listening to the portable tape recorder Cebo had placed on
Windows' stomach. They stopped it many times to discuss
various points, make notes and put everything into perspective.
When the tape finally came to the death of Windows, Cebo
pressed the button. Respectful salutations for a successful
assignment and grateful comments for personal reasons –
payback – moved all five men to the kitchen island for the
opening of a bottle of champagne.

'Cheers,' they all said.

'It's about time the Four Seasons Hotel had a guest,' Cain
announced.

'A permanent guest,' Cebo remarked.

'*Welcome to Hotel California,*' Cain jested with a tone of
musical rhythm. '*You can check out any time you like. But you
can never leave.*'

Laughter followed, accompanied by several one-liners…
When things had quietened down, Marius said, 'I will have a
copy of the tape sent to Mac in London. One of my people
under the guise of a delivery driver will collect it later and
deliver it to Agent Omara in Jo'burg. He will have a listen
before putting it on a flight. The information Windows gave us,
although limited, about Lastly's drug and diamond dealing in

Hong Kong, will be a great help to Mac's side of our joint investigation. The detailed information about the trafficking of cash, drugs, guns, and girls will assist in putting a number of plans into action. My 'delivery driver' will also take Windows burner and registered cell phones. My people will start to trace all the numbers.'

Cain's mobile rang. He checked the screen, 'It's Neilson,' he said – and silence prevailed.

'Yes they are here, safe and sound,' said Cain, and Neilson continued… 'Perfect,' said Cain. 'Thank you again for everything you arranged, everything you did, and taking care of the two young men we sent over to you. We owe you three.'

'Anytime,' said Neilson. 'Look forward to seeing you soon.'

'When we do, I'll be buying lunch and dinner. Talk to you next week.'

Neilson's contact in the Costa Beach Hotel had confirmed 'Ray' had left a letter for the manager saying he was unexpectedly going to be away for a couple of days. There was US$500 in cash with the letter to add to his account, confirming his return. Cain looked at Marius. 'Your idea, like everything else, is working perfectly.'

'Thank you,' Marius replied, modestly acknowledging the clapping and compliments from everyone standing around him. When things had quietened down, Marius confirmed, 'We will leave Windows' phones turned off. It will make Zokwana and anyone else wanting to speak to him phone the hotel. When told about Windows' letter. It will make them think he is away with a hooker or perhaps high on *Tik* for a couple of days – nothing unusual – and leave a message.'

Everyone nodded with looks of agreement.

'Gentlemen,' said Marius. 'The time has come to have a chat with Zokwana. However because we now know he has ordered Windows to visit him on Saturday afternoon, we will have to pay him a visit him on Saturday morning, as soon as he arrives from Jo'burg.

Friday – Preparation

Cain and Marius were looking again at the photographs of

402

Zokwana's farmhouse on the dining room table, a knock on the front door of the lodge interrupted them.

Marius said, 'I know who it is. I'll go.'

Cain was totally surprised to find himself being introduced to the waitress from Vasco's in Cape Town. The one who had served them their very best peri-peri chicken with rice. Cebo and Dubula then appeared, and they all embraced like great friends do.

'Take care of Lara,' Marius said, and they all went off to have a walk around the lodge, have a drink and have a chat, bringing her up to date.

'Agent Lara,' said Marius hated it when I made her work in Vasco's as a waitress to find out who a certain customer was meeting there. That's why she was a little, shall we say, *irritating*.'

Cain remembered Lara unexpectedly inscribing a heart shape in the froth of Marius' Guinness. 'I thought you were having an affair.'

Marius smiled. 'I never mix business with pleasure.'

'Why is she here?'

'Let's put the kettle on,' said Marius. 'Time for a Rooibos tea.'

'Good idea.'

At the dining room table, Lara was shown the aerial photographs and ground-level views of Zokwana's farmhouse taken by Agent Omara as the team went through their plan once again.

An hour later, Lara took the lead. 'Since Minister Zokwana became Mr. Zokwana he has been spending more time than he should, enjoying a life of leisure, attending many cocktail and dinner parties. Also, his visits to his farmhouse have become more frequent, rather than occasional, and longer. Agent Omara has confirmed when Zokwana is there – a number of hookers always arrive on the same day.

'During Zokwana's absence, the day-to-day security of the farmhouse is left to the cleaning lady and her husband the gardener, who live in a small bungalow in the grounds of the estate. There are no guards on the gate, so they use a simple intercom system for deliveries and the like. But of course, when

Zokwana is on the move he always has his bodyguards with him, the *Suits,* the same ex-33s rogue freelancers who were with him at his ministerial residence in Constantia.'

The bodyguards were a reminder to everyone that the man nicknamed *Defunct,* who was still telling Zokwana what to do, was still protecting him and, of course, keeping an eye on him.

Lara continued, 'Agent Omara has informed me, since Lastly was killed in China, Zokwana has been drinking a lot more and spending a great deal of time on his burner cell phones, going over various financial documents and other records. Unfortunately Agent Omara has never been able to be close enough for long enough to hear exactly what was being discussed. However he can confirm one important factor. The financial documents and other records Zokwana has been going over are photocopies. The originals are kept at his farmhouse. This is an opportunity we have all been waiting for.'

'Indeed,' Moshe said.

'Is Zokwana taking any extra security with him? Any *Suits,* any ex-33s?' Dubula enquired.

'No,' said Lara. 'Zokwana believes Lastly's killing in Guangzhou was either by a rival drug gang or the authorities. Therefore, nothing has been said or happened in South Africa to

necessitate elevated security.' Lara looked to Marius. 'Over to you sir.'

By late afternoon, everyone's suitcases and gun bags had been loaded and their vehicles thoroughly checked over, ready to go. As the chimes of the old grandfather clock brought the proceedings to a close, Marius said, 'I think an early dinner would be in order.'

During the evening meal, everyone again went through the plan of action.

Taking a deep breath, Lara said, 'Boobs or bust.'

'Tit for tat,' Cain jibed.

Everyone burst out laughing.

'When we leave here,' said Marius, 'we will not be coming back. Let's make sure we leave nothing behind.'

'I'll arrange the necessary,' Cain suggested.

'Please do.'

Cain picked up his cell phone and dialled a number:

'How can I help you?' said a familiar voice – the Cleaning Crew.

Improvise, adapt and overcome.

Clint Eastwood

56

Saturday – Clockwork

The chauffeur-driven Mercedes S-class saloon – hotly pursued by an M-class 4x4 – sped through baobab tree country, with Agent Omara at the wheel of a Land Cruiser following closely behind.

Lara's cell phone rang, she pressed the button.

'Situation normal,' said Agent Omara. 'See you soon.'

Lara closed the passenger door of the Jeep and Cain started the engine to follow the convoy of three vehicles from a safe distance. Some five miles further on, Zokwana's convoy swept through the main gate of his isolated country estate and Cain's Jeep entered a nearby farmer's deserted, uninhabited, storage facility to rendezvous with Marius, Moshe, and Cebo.

Everything would now be carried out military style.

Twenty minutes later, Dubula – who had been watching the farmhouse since before dawn – spoke with Marius on their burner cell phones. 'Zokwana's cook, two maids, and his Rhodesian ridgeback arrived in a 4x4 earlier this morning. And four hookers arrived fifteen minutes ago in a saloon. Both vehicles are parked at the side of the farmhouse by the kitchen door. There are two *Suits* outside, sticking to their usual routine. They walk around, keeping a wide berth, but always in sight of each other. And, as expected, the Mercedes and M-class 4x4 have been driven into one of the barns at the back of the estate to be refilled with petrol and given the once over.'

'All is going to plan,' said Marius.

'Don't forget,' said Dubula, 'Zokwana's ridgeback is a pet not a guard dog.'

'So if there is any, trouble, it will only run and hide.'

'It will, if I get close enough. I'll give it a biscuit, like I always did when I was a guard on the gate of the then Minister Zokwana's residence.'

'We are good to go?'

'Yes sir.'

'Cain will pick you up in thirty minutes.'

Fifteen minutes later, Marius jumped out of the back of Moshe's Toyota 4Runner and with a sports bag over one shoulder, he disappeared through a perimeter hedgerow into the depths of Zokwana's farmhouse estate.

And Thirty minutes later, Cain stopped the Jeep on a prearranged part of a country lane, jumped out and got into the back. Dubula, appearing from nowhere, got into the driver's seat. Cain checked the time on his throwaway watch and, catching Dubula's eye in the rear-view mirror, said, 'All set. Let's go.' As Dubula put the wheels into motion, Cain touched Lara's shoulder and whispered, 'Let's see if your 34s can outdo the 33s.'

Lara breathed in deeply. 'Will do.'

Cain slipped a balaclava over his head, drew his silenced Beretta from his hip holster and got down low.

Lara pressed the remote Agent Omara had given her. The main gate to Zokwana's estate opened and the Jeep drove in. The *Suits* showed a look of surprise because they were expecting Windows but not so early in the day. When the nearest suit saw it was Dubula, the ex-guard from Constantia driving the approaching Jeep, he wrongly guessed the white female in the passenger seat was a whore being delivered. The suit gave Dubula a wave and Dubula flashed the Jeep's lights and slowed down. In his peripheral vision Dubula could see the second suit, standing some fifty metres distant, raising the barrel of an AK-47 as he watched the new arrivals.

'Here we go,' Dubula whispered, slowly coasting the Jeep to a stop in the perfect position.

Lara opened the passenger door and, with the most wonderful of smiles, showed off the alluring curves of her beautiful breasts bulging out of a very low-cut neckline. She turned to the suit; her ultra-short skirt had the desired effect: he was hypnotised. From the side of the head restraint, the silenced Beretta double-tapped the suit's heart and the dead man standing, fell to the ground. Lara closed the door. The second suit, blindsided by the Jeep because his colleague had gone to the passenger side, did not see his colleague fall to the ground;

he just saw the driver's window buzz down and the man behind the wheel give him a wave.

From among the baobab trees – out of sight, out of mind – the eighties Israeli Galil Arms R4 Sniper Variant Rifle, produced under licence in South Africa, was as accurate as ever, especially in the hands of Marius, a master sniper. No one heard the bullet leave the barrel at 3000 fps and, in less than three tenths of a second, enter the suit's heart. And a second dead man standing, fell to the ground. Marius immediately got to his feet and set off towards the dead body. Dubula drove towards the front door of the farmhouse. Moshe, with Cebo pressing a remote, drove the Toyota through the reopened main gate and down the drive to park near to the Jeep. As everyone exited their vehicles, Lara loosened her bra, releasing the pressure on her breasts, slipped on her leggings, put on her Kevlar body armour and, along with Cebo, Dubula and Moshe, slipped on a balaclava and gloves.

Cebo skirted around the side of the farmhouse and opened the kitchen door. On seeing the gun-toting balaclava-clad figure in the doorway, the cook, the cleaning lady, and a maid immediately froze – and an unseen hand silently closed a door several feet away to one side of them. Cebo locked the kitchen door. 'Stay together,' he told the three females. Looking at the cleaning lady he asked, 'Where is your husband?'

'Er, outside somewhere.'

Meanwhile – leaving Dubula to move the dead *Suits* – Cain, Moshe, and Lara went through the front door where the second maid, overwhelmed by the sight of the intruders, simply raised her arms in surrender. Cebo then appeared at the far end of the hallway behind her, escorting the kitchen staff.

In the lounge, two girls were drinking wine and watching TV. They stared in total disbelief at the armed intruders. Lara raised a finger to her lips and the two girls, fearing for their lives, stayed silent.

'We are not here to hurt you,' Lara whispered as reassuringly as she could. 'Where is Zokwana?'

One of the girls pointed to the ceiling. 'He is in the bedroom with another two of us.'

'Anyone else up there?'

'Don't think so.'

Leaving Moshe to stand guard, Cain and Lara took the stairs and Cebo headed back outside to give Dubula a helping hand and meet with Marius.

Cain with Lara burst into the master bedroom. On the king-size bed Zokwana was laying naked on his back with one girl sitting on top of him, bobbing up and down while the other kneeling beside him smiled invitingly. Zokwana's hands stopped groping both girls' breasts. The girl doing the bobbing looked over her shoulder at the unexpected visitors, wondering if this was a new sex game. 'Hello,' she said.

'Stay still, hands up,' said Cain, pointing his Beretta. 'And you, stop bobbing.'

The girls giggled, but no one spoke. After the threesome had disentangled, the girls hastily put on underwear before being escorted down the stairs. Lara took the two girls into the lounge, where Moshe had started searching the rest of the staff to confiscate any cell phones.

Cain pushed Zokwana into his office – the library room – and sat him down on a leather chair. An armed Agent Omara immediately appeared from behind a leather sofa, wearing a balaclava.

Meanwhile, the chauffeur of the Mercedes S-class saloon and the driver of the M-class 4x4, having refilled their vehicles with petrol and given them the once over, were driving back to the front of the farmhouse. On arrival, they were surprised to see the Toyota and Jeep parked outside. Getting out of their vehicles, and realising the *Suits* were nowhere to be seen, the M-class 4x4 driver went for his gun, but too late: the bullets from two silenced semi-automatic pistols pierced the skulls of both drivers.

As Marius went inside to join Cain, Moshe stepped out to watch over Cebo and Dubula as they moved the dead drivers' bodies out of sight, next to the dead *Suits*, before re-parking the Jeep and Toyota – facing the main gate – ready to go.

In the library, the balaclava-clad Agent Omara – pointing his pistol – looked down at Zokwana. 'Tell me the combination of your safe in the wall.'

Zokwana showed a look of contempt. 'Do you know who I

am?'

Agent Omara fired a bullet into Zokwana's foot and the man screamed in pain.

'Ouch,' Cain said.

In fear of another bullet, Zokwana gave the combination. Agent Omara immediately went to a picture on the wall, ripped it down, opened the safe, took an empty carry-on case from behind the leather sofa, and started filling it with cash, files, and folders.

Cain took off his balaclava and Zokwana stared at him in shock. 'It's you!' he gasped. 'What do you want?'

'The name of the man who tells you what to do.'

'If I tell you, he will kill me, just like you killed Lastly's twin brother in London.'

'I also killed Lastly in China,' said Cain. 'Oh yes, I almost forgot to tell you – Windows is now with them, friends of mine cut him up.'

Zokwana looked horrified. 'You ba–'

'I will ask you one last time,' said Cain, waving a cutting knife in front of Zokwana's eyes. 'Who tells you what to do?'

As Marius entered the library, he removed his balaclava. Zokwana gasped.

'Give us the name,' Cain demanded aiming the carving knife at Zokwana's balls.

'Tell us now,' said Marius, 'and I will make sure you are taken to another country to live out the rest of your life in sheer luxury.'

Suddenly, the sound of suppressed automatic gunfire rang out. Bullets shattered the library's side window and ripped through Zokwana's back, tipping him onto the floor. Cain, Marius, and Agent Omara instantly dived for cover and sightlessly returned fire.

> When death and danger are upon you, the slow-motion
> movie in the mind distorts time.
> What might seem like an eternity may well be:
> Till death do us part.

Seeing Zokwana go down, the hitman skirted around the

side of the farmhouse towards the front door. He hadn't, however, spotted Moshe behind the Jeep. Two rounds entered the hitman's chest and he fell to the ground.

'Dammit,' Cain cursed, getting to his feet. 'We still don't have the answer.'

'We have company,' Marius said.

The mayhem of the shooting had distracted Lara from the female staff cowering on the floor and the cleaning lady had slipped out of the lounge and disappeared down the hallway into the kitchen. Lara caught a glimpse of her, alerted Marius, and gave chase. On entering the kitchen, Lara had to dive for cover as gunfire smashed into the pots and pans around her.

Seconds later, Cain put his balaclava back on and headed down the hallway in pursuit of Lara, while Cebo went around the side and along the back of the farmhouse to check it out. Dubula stood in the lounge to keep an eye on the females and Moshe stood by the front door to keep watch for any more movement on the outside.

In the kitchen, Cain got down beside Lara who, with a pistol in one hand and a Mossberg in the other, was keeping the hitmen pinned down.

'How many?' Cain asked.

'Two,' said Lara. 'When the cleaning lady slipped out of the library, she must have unlocked the kitchen door to let them in. Cebo told me he'd locked it.'

'Where is she?'

'Don't know, haven't caught sight of her again.'

Seconds later, Cebo's shadow fell through the kitchen's open doorway onto a kneeling hitman's face. The man turned to look, the silhouette fired, and the hitman fell across the floor. Cain looked over the counter to see Cebo standing over the body. 'He's dead,' Cebo called out.

'Just one?' Cain asked cautiously, walking towards Cebo.

'Yes.'

'There's another one somewhere,' Cain warned.

'I came round from the back; I didn't see anyone. There's blood in the doorway, he must be wounded. He could be behind the 4x4 or the saloon parked at the side, or perhaps he has headed round to the front of the farmhouse.'

'Let's go find him.'

Lara said, 'I must have shot him without realising it'

'Well done.'

'I'll double check the rooms around the kitchen.'

'OK.'

Cain and Cebo soon spotted the wounded hitman – with gun in hand – lying by the side of the 4x4's, open driver's door. From behind a baobab tree Cebo sent a couple of bullets into the side of the 4x4 – and as expected the hitman returned fire. Meanwhile Cain was hiding by the front of the 4x4, waiting for the hitman to run out of bullets. But when the hitman fired a last shot it was into his own head. Cebo and Cain approached the dead body, lying in a massive pool of blood.

Cebo said, 'Looks as if Lara's Mossberg blasted an artery. A dead end situation.'

Cain showed a look of frustration, shaking his head. 'Pity our plan to question him didn't work.'

When Lara got back to the library, Marius was pointing his sniper rifle through the glass.

Agent Omara shouted, 'A 4x4 has come through the main gate.'

Marius eventually fired a shot. 'Shit,' he said.

The driver of the 4x4 with a bullet to his head was now dead, but the passenger had grabbed the wheel. Marius found his next target and fired again before making a run for it. The 4x4 crashed into the wall of the library and the dying passenger hurtled through the windscreen, through the shattered window, onto the library floor.

In the silence that followed, maintaining their military precision – time was of the essence – Lara soon found the person she was looking for, hiding in the utility room. She immediately placed the muzzle of her pistol against the cleaning lady's head: 'Tell me.'

A week earlier, a cash incentive had persuaded the gardener and his wife, the cleaning lady to help the hitmen by hiding them for twenty-four hours in their bungalow just a hundred yards from the farmhouse. The promise of being able to loot the property after Zokwana, Windows, and everyone else was dead, had been a convincing bonus. Their role was to distract and divert the attention of those around them to allow the hitmen to accomplish their mission, but the unexpected arrival of the strangers – namely Marius, Cain, Moshe, Lara, Cebo and Dubula – had destroyed their plan.

Lara looked down at the cleaning lady. 'You shouldn't have done it.'

'We're so sorry,' she cried out.

'Where were they from?'

'I'm not sure, but they sounded as if they were all talking Russian.'

'When it was all over, did you really believe the hitmen would let you live?'

In tears, the cleaning lady looked up. 'Will you let us live?' she begged.

Lara pulled the trigger and left the utility room to join Agent Omara in the dining room, interrogating the dead cleaning lady's husband – the gardener – curled up, down on the floor.

'Anything?' she asked.

'The hitmen never told him anything. He believes the language he heard them talking in was Russian.'

Seconds later, they ended their conversation. Lara gave Agent Omara a nod. He pointed the gun at the back of the gardener's head and pulled the trigger. 'Go join your wife.'

Meanwhile, Cebo and Dubula – after photographing and fingerprinting the dead hitmen – carried the bodies of those shot and killed on the outside into the farmhouse.

Marius called everyone to join him for a quick debrief. Lara informed everyone of what the cleaning lady and her husband had confessed to. 'They are now both dead.'

A minute later, a plan of action was agreed. Cebo and Dubula headed into the lounge and lined up the four hookers, the cook, and two maids to tell them a made-up story.

Cebo explained, 'We are undercover agents working for Mr. Zokwana. That is why we are all wearing balaclavas – to conceal our identities. We are sorry if it has scared you.'

'You have saved our lives,' said the cook, with looks of agreement from those around her. 'Thank you.'

'Pleasure. We have also saved the life of Mr. Zokwana. But sadly, others have been killed.' Cebo raised a hand to stop any questions being asked. 'Bear with me,' he said. 'There is still one gunman on the loose. You will now be moved into the cleaning lady's bungalow, away from immediate danger. My armed men will be outside to guard you until the police arrive.'

Dubula handed out some of the cash Agent Omara had taken from the library's wall-safe to the seven females. 'I'm sure this will help you contend with what has happened, with the compliments of Mr. Zokwana. Now, let's take a brisk walk down to the bungalow.'

Meanwhile, Agent Omara – who had not been seen by any of Zokwana's surviving staff – was driving back to Jo'burg. The Land Cruiser had false plates and he was wearing a hat and dark glasses to conceal his identity. He would eventually arrive at a supposed friend's home where he had been for the whole day. Out of site. Out of mind – the perfect alibi.

It was now time to leave. Marius, Lara, Cebo and Dubula, leading the ridgeback all got in the Jeep Cain had been using and drove off. They soon arrived at a deserted private airfield to fly back to Cape Town. Meanwhile, a cleaning crew belonging to Marius' Institute – who had arrived on the private jet – would drive the Jeep to the farmer's deserted, uninhabited, storage facility to do the necessary: no trace of anyone who had been there would ever be found.

In the farmhouse, the smell of gasoline pervaded the air. Cain removed the rubber gloves from his hands and the shoe covers from his Timberland boots and threw them through the front entrance of the farmhouse. He lit a Zippo lighter, tossed it into the hallway, turned his back on the rising flames and walked away.

Watching Cain, Moshe sat at the wheel of his Toyota 4Runner, ready to go.

Later that evening, Cain and Moshe arrived at the Sempre Aqui Hotel.

JIA – Justice In Africa.

Part Thirteen

Unlucky for Some
Cape Town

If you want anything said, ask a man.
If you want anything done, ask a woman.

Margaret Thatcher

57

For the next few days the media speculated about the identity of the dead bodies, burnt to a crisp, found in Zokwana's fire-gutted farmhouse: who might have been killed and why?

Many rumours began to circulate – courtesy of Marius and The Institute – about how Zokwana's corrupt lifestyle had finally caught up with him. Hence, he had fled the country, and depending on which newspaper you read, he had been seen in Nigeria or Saudi Arabia. The whole situation, however, left Marius asking one simple question: who had the hitmen been working for?

Meanwhile, Marius had sketches made from the photographs Cebo and Dubula had taken of the dead hitmen. He put the sources of the information he had gathered down to informants, snitches, and the exemplary work of the police investigation: he would never have to explain how he had managed to obtain photographs of the dead hitmen before they had been burnt beyond recognition. Ashes to ashes, dust to dust.

It was in the main just a 'good news' week, without anyone dropping a bomb somewhere.

It was a time to start putting the last pieces of the jigsaw together.

The beginning of the end.

Friday

As instructed by Marius, Cain landed at an airfield on the outskirts of Cape Town at dusk. He taxied the luggage-loaded Cessna 207 to a quiet parking spot where Marius was waiting in a 4x4 to give him a lift. Everything would now be done quickly and efficiently.

'*Goed om jou te sien* (Good to see you),' Marius said, and they loaded up the 4x4.

"

Back in Cape Town, Marius turned off the 4x4's lights, drove past the 'fortress' and did a circuit of the small quadrangle park – just in case. Cain looked up at Egg, glowing through the bulletproof tinted glass on the first-floor balcony.

Good to see you again. Thank you for telling me.

As Marius drove the 4x4 onto the forecourt and made a U-turn, Cain pressed the button, Ladysmith opened... and a car with its lights turned off came to a stop on the drive.

'Cebo and Dubula?' Cain enquired.

'My most trusted.'

'I didn't notice them following us.'

'Nobody ever does,' Marius said with a smile, reversing the 4x4 into the garage.

Once Ladysmith had closed, the 4x4's doors opened, spreading light into the darkness. Cain headed over to the alarm panel and tapped in the code. As the incessant beeping ceased, he flicked a new switch and the lights came on. As the two men heaved the suitcases up to the dressing room next to the master bedroom, Cain realised various lights in the 'fortress' were already on and the new Spanish-style steel blinds installed on the inside of the first-floor balcony, the top floor sundeck, and all the doors and windows were closed. From the outside, the 'fortress' had looked dark and deserted, preventing any prying eyes from seeing in and any interior lights – except for Egg – from shining out.

Cain remembered how Sofia had suggested in one of her emails, months before he'd killed Smokey in the park, he should have the blinds installed.

'*Viva España* (Long live Spain),' Cain quietly whispered.

'Peter did a good job,' said Marius, looking at the screen for the CCTV's.

'He is the best.'

Once the luggage was unloaded, the two men sat at the kitchen island to have a drink and a French stick with cheese, ham, nuts and olives, talking about all that had happened. As Cain poured a J&B and a Richelieu brandy, Marius said, 'Time to bring you up to date.'

In the dining room, Marius opened his briefcase and laid out on the table copies of the various documents Agent Omara had taken from Zokwana's farmhouse library wall safe. 'Before we have a read,' said Marius, placing a mugshot-style photograph on the table in front of Cain, 'Have you ever seen or met this man?'

Taking a look, Cain said, 'No, never seen or met him. Who is he?'

'Teun the Dutchman,' Marius answered placing a second photograph on the table.

'I don't believe it,' said Cain with a look of incredulity. 'Who took the photo?'

'One of Mac's people.'

Trying to come to terms with what he was looking at, Cain asked, 'When was it taken?'

'When I informed Mac of the date we were going to pay a visit to Zokwana's farmhouse, he decided to have one of Teun the Dutchman's holiday homes, the one in Sitges, watched.'

Cain remained motionless staring down at the photo and stated the obvious: 'So the Dutchman is gay. Is he the reason Trenchard went to Spai–'

Marius raised a hand. 'There is still quite a lot I have to update you on,' he politely interrupted. 'Please bear with me.'

58

Monday

Cain eyed the diamond in the side of the grip of his new Beretta 92: the present from Kobus. He racked the slide – sending the first round into the chamber – and placed it in his shoulder holster. He looked at himself in the mirror.

Need to like to, or prefer to? Or perhaps I just have to – just in case.

The conundrum caused him to survey his reflection, still lacking several kilos in weight, for a few seconds longer than was needed.

Or perhaps, in reality, I just want to.

As he put on his jacket, his burner cell phone rang.

'I'll pick you up in fifteen minutes,' Marius said.

'OK.'

Thirteen minutes later, Cain looked at the CCTV screens one last time: the drive and the park were deserted. He put on a pair of sunglasses and a rugby hat, passed through the stable-style front door, descended the short flight of steps – and waited.

As Marius pulled up in an inconspicuous-looking saloon on the forecourt, Cain stepped through the front gate in the perimeter wall and as the gate closed behind him, one of the saloon's back passenger doors opened. On route, Cain looked again at several vehicles behind them, wondering which one Cebo and Dubula were in.

Meanwhile, at Cape Town's airport, Agent Lara, posing as a customs official at passport control, politely informed a young woman how her suitcase had been accidentally damaged. Discreetly, she led the unsuspecting passenger through a door and along a corridor to a room where she was asked to take a seat.

When Marius and Cain entered the room, the young woman flinched with shock and disbelief – especially when she saw two young black men behind them.

'Hello Bekha,' Cain said.

Mortified, Bekha stayed silent.

'You know why you are here. You will tell us everything,' Cain said softly.

Marius added, 'By doing this the easy way, you will be in time to catch your flight.'

'Or we can do it the hard way,' Cebo said.

'You can't hurt me,' said Bekha. 'If you try, I'll report you to the authorit–'

Dubula shoved a sock in Bekha's mouth before her eyes, full of terror, watched Marius, Lara, and Cain leave the room.

It was not long before Bekha was gasping, begging, and crying. But she had no bruises or blood stains. Cebo and Dubula's professional skills had come to the fore. 'I'll tell you everything you want to know,' she pleaded.

Marius, Lara, and Cain re-entered the room and Bekha told her story. Vitaly the Russian, a crime kingpin now living in Cape Town, was a distant relative. During his early days of climbing the criminal ladder, he had been in Moscow and Bekha had been in Prague, hence they never met. Realising the restrictions imposed by her nationality, Bekha learnt to speak English with just the one aim in life: to obtain British or American citizenship by marrying a national. A year after Bekha had married Hadley, he had suggested they take a break from their life in the USA to visit the diamond centre of the world: Jewel City in South Africa. Knowing Vitaly was in Cape Town, Bekha agreed. Hadley had no idea what she was planning, and weeks later they moved to Johannesburg.

When Bekha first contacted Vitaly, he told her he would soon be visiting Jo'burg, on business, providing the perfect opportunity for her to finally meet up with her long-lost, handsome relative. It was the beginning of a relationship in and out of bed...!

'Good fuck?' Cain asked.

'You or the Russian?' Bekha enquired, raising her eyebrows.

'Very good,' Cain responded.

'Yes, very good, but not as good as you.'

'The Russians are always looking for an opening.'

'Well he found one between my legs.'

'Touché,' said Cain. 'Was Vitaly the reason you and Hadley started living separate lives?'

'Yes. I told him I had a medical condition, so we stopped having sex.'

When Hadley had eventually left for Guangzhou, Bekha had filed for divorce and flown down to Cape Town to be with Vitaly. During the following days and nights, the interconnection between them allowed Vitaly to find out everything he wanted to know – and their intercourse allowed Bekha to get everything she wanted to have.

Vitaly – who trafficked cash, drugs, guns, and girls – soon came to the realisation. Bekha possessed many talents, both in and out of bed. She could be put to good use, especially with an American passport, which allowed her to travel freely. Under the guise of being employed as an executive by an ordinary import/export shelf company based in Prague, Bekha became Vitaly's personal courier, a go between – and anything else he wanted. . . !

In Hong Kong – without Hadley knowing – Bekha arranged for Zhang to meet with one of Vitaly's people. It took no more than the mention of cash to convince Zhang to join Vitaly's latest venture. The plan worked well: Vitaly's drug and diamond dealing charades in Hong Kong were running separately and in parallel with Bill and Greg's investment diamond showroom in Guangzhou. Nobody was any the wiser as Zhang worked both sides of the fence, without any paths being crossed: everything was going to plan.

Bekha looked at Cain. 'Zhang is fluent in Chinese, Mandarin, and English. He was exactly what Vitaly was looking for.'

'And for the right price, totally dishonest.'

'I want you to know,' said Bekha, 'I knew nothing about what happened next until it was too late. I didn't want you to get hurt.'

'Of course,' said Cain. 'I understand.'

Bekha mistakenly believed she had convinced Cain of her innocence. 'Zokwana told Vitaly about your Jeep when it had crashed during a shooting in Cape Town several years earlier. Vitaly was furious, shouting down the phone at me about how the newspapers had reported your Jeep had been stolen, and the police were still looking for a black man who had been driving it. But you who had been driving it. I was travelling at the time; I didn't know what Vitaly was talking about. When he's in such a mood you just listen. I had to wait until we met up again before I could ask what had happened.'

'When did you meet up again?'

'When I was back in Cape Town a few weeks later.'

'Who told Zokwana I was driving the Jeep?'

'It was someone called Windows . . . strange name.'

Cain nodded to Marius. They both realised Windows, when he had been recovering from the bullet wound to his stomach – after being shot by Gospel – had invented the story. He had been as Cain had suggested: lying in every sense of the word.

Cain asked, 'Then what happened?'

'Vitaly tried to have you killed, but you survived the attempt on your life in High Constantia.' Bekha looked at Marius. 'It was payback for foiling the assassination attempt on your life.'

Cain asked, 'How did Vitaly know I was in High Constantia?'

'I have no idea. When you left South Africa you didn't as expected, go to China. He lost track of where you were.'

'Music,' Marius said. Cebo placed a set of headphones on Bekha's head so she could not hear what was about to be discussed. Looking at Cain, Marius said, 'With everything else we now know, it's clear Vitaly is the man you nicknamed *Defunct.*'

'The man who ordered your assassination.'

'Yes.' Marius glanced at Cebo and Dubula, who wanted to avenge the man who had ordered the assassination attempt, causing the murder of their respective brother and brother-in-law. 'We'll take him down.'

'I wonder,' said Cain, 'if Windows, lying in every sense of the word, realised he was telling the truth.'

'We will never know for sure, Zokwana probably told Vitaly things when it best worked in his favour.' Marius gave Cebo a nod to remove the headphones from Bekha's head.

Cain looked down at Bekha. 'Tell me about Teun the Dutchman.'

'Before leaving for China, Hadley told me Teun was the major investor. I obviously mentioned it to Vitaly when talking about Zhang and the showroom in Guangzhou. Vitaly did a check on Teun, and I was sent to Sitges – under the pretence of buying drugs – to meet with him. In reality, I was there to find out what he was up to. It was only after our meeting, when we were having a drink in a restaurant-bar on the waterfront he told me what he was financing in Guangzhou. He was a bit high at the time, trying to impress me, or rather the young boy sitting with him.'

'A young boy?' said Cain. 'How old was he?'

'Fifteen, perhaps – I have no idea who he was. I didn't ask any questions. After I informed Vitaly of what Teun was doing he manipulated Teun to achieve what he wanted.' Bekha took a sip of water from the plastic cup on the table.

Cain asked, 'How?'

'Vitaly told Teun to do as he was told or his parents would be killed.'

'Please continue,' Marius said.

'Vitaly was not too concerned about what might happen to Bill and Greg's investment diamond showroom. If it closed, he could always finance Zhang to open another. He didn't care because, whatever happened, it would not affect what Zhang was doing for him: secretly buying diamonds in Hong Kong, laundering cash.' Bekha looked at Cain. 'However, when you returned to Guangzhou, wrecked the showroom, and got arrested, it put everyone on the radar. Hadley and Zhang had a lot of questions to answer, and not just from the police and immigration. After Zhang met with Lawyer Nigel to sign the 'letter of forgiveness' and receive the payment, he told everyone you would be in prison for at least three years. It allowed everyone to forget about you.'

Cain asked, 'You ever hear about the men in black?'

Bekha looked surprised. 'Why are you asking about a movie?'

'Forget it. What were you doing when we met in Jo'burg?'

'I told you I was just passing through, stopping off to see a couple of old girlfriends. I was telling you the truth.'

'Of course,' said Cain, stroking Bekha's ego.

Makes a change.

'Talking of telling the truth, when we said goodbye to each other in Jo'burg, I took a US$100 note out of my backpack and gave it to you to pay for your taxi and have a meal.

You asked me: You always carry a pile of cash down there? I answered: Might do.'

Bekha showed a momentary look of regret.

Cain asked, 'Who did you tell?'

'I told Vitaly Zhang had told me. How do you know?'

'You were the only person who ever asked, who knew it was there.'

'Vitaly's people told one of the Chinese people on his payroll. He in turn told a senior Chinese guard at the prison you were in, ensuring the cash would be stolen.'

'Thank you Mr. Lài, Mr. Fán,' said Cain. 'Thieving liars.'

'Who?' said Bekha.

'Forget it, just thinking out loud. You obviously never told Vitaly about when we met in Jo'burg?'

'I decided it would be best not to mention it.'

Cain realised Bekha was a player, not a pawn. He looked down at the photograph of Bekha and Teun the Dutchman – taken by Mac's people – sitting in a restaurant-bar in Sitges. 'Tell me why you were in Spain last Friday?'

'He–'

'I'll take it from here,' Marius interrupted raising a hand.

Cain looked at Bekha. 'By continuing to answer the questions truthfully, you will save your life. You will be on the next flight to wherever you want to go.'

As Cain left the room he sadly remembered: being on the flight from Jo'burg to London to see Jerry in hospital, contemplating the events of the preceding weeks, and the slight niggle in his subconscious.

Why do I have the feeling I've missed something?

Closing the door behind them and seeing Cain deep in thought, Marius asked, 'What are you thinking?'

'When I flew to the UK to see Jerry in hospital, I can't believe I didn't realise Bekha was working for the very man whose identity we were trying to discover.'

Marius showed a look of sympathy. 'You had other things on your mind. You were worried about Jerry and keeping yourself and Moshe alive.'

Cain stayed silent and Marius continued. 'When I met you and Moshe at the Sempre Aqui Hotel, you told me about meeting Bekha. I said I would run a check on her, but nothing came up. It was only in recent days, after she met with Teun the Dutchman in Sitges – I won't bore you with the details – it was discovered she has two identities – one blonde, one brunette – and two passports.'

'That must have opened a whole new can of worms for you.'

'Finding her has put many pieces of the jigsaw into place. I'll take care of Vitaly.'

'Of course.'

'Sorry I cut you off back there talking to Bekha, but Teun is now involved in circumstances you will not want to know about and certainly not want to become involved in. Mac will be taking care of him.'

'I feel I'm partly to blame, I'll offer to do it for him.'

Marius smiled. 'I'll give you a call in the morning.'

Minutes later, Cain boarded a private jet to Jo'burg to be with Moshe and stay at the Sempre Aqui Hotel – out of sight, out of mind.

While thinking about what Bekha had confessed to, he momentarily contemplated if Vitaly had arranged for both his US$1000 to be stolen out of his backpack and for Mad- Hatter to attack him in room 123.

I'll never know.

Fearing for her life when Marius revealed he knew she had two passports, Bekha answered all his questions about the drugs, the guns, the girls, and other things related to the joint investigation he and Mac were conducting. Bekha eventually had nothing more to divulge.

'You are free to go,' Marius said.

Bekha showed a look of absolute relief. On the following morning, a drowsy Bekha woke up in a window seat of a Boeing 747. She remembered the customs official (Agent Lara) politely taking her to a ladies' room before buying her a drink while she waited to board the aircraft – nothing more. She lifted the window blind: on the horizon, above a layer of cloud, the rising sun was in full bloom. Seeing a passing stewardess she asked, 'Where are we?'

'Still at thirty thousand feet – we'll be landing in thirty minutes.' Glancing down at Bekha's wrist the stewardess suggested, 'Don't forget to put the time on your watch back an hour.'

'Why?'

'London time.'

'It can't be–' Bekha began, but she dozed off again.

She was supposed to have been on an aircraft landing in Hong Kong.

***

Mac was sitting in his office, having his morning coffee. He had just finished reading the fax Marius had sent him – a word-for-word copy of the interview with Bekha. His phone rang.

'The aircraft has just landed at Heathrow Airport sir,' said a familiar voice – a member of the Bureau. 'We have a wheelchair and vehicle waiting on the tarmac.'

'After the drugs have worn off and she has been thrown in the shower, let me know.'

'Yes sir.'

Bekha would soon be interviewed for a second time regarding her involvement in the trafficking of cash, drugs, and girls into Europe and the UK.

She would never be seen or heard from again.

426

59

PAGAD

During the following few days, documents arrived anonymously on the desks of some of the good men – and some of the bad criminals – around the world. It was signed 'PAGAD'.

Seven days later, the newspapers reported:

'Vitaly The Russian shot dead.

One of Cape Town's most feared underworld figures, Vitaly 'The Russian' Apalkov, is dead, riddled with 10 bullets in a late-night ambush. An armed man with him, believed to be a bodyguard was also killed.

Apalkov, 49, owned Czarina's pole-dancing and strip club in Cape Town. He was known to have had a long history of scrapes with the law.

Police said he was attacked by the occupants of a white Toyota Tazz in the northern suburb of Table View'.

There was a great deal of speculation as to who could have been responsible for Vitaly's death. The usual suspects – enemies and rivals – topped the list, with associates and supposed friends taking second place. However, there were rumours circulating about two Chinese men, dressed in black, who had been seen in a lone Tazz car in the vicinity at the time of the shooting.

PAGAD – People Against Gangs And Drugs – was a notorious coloured vigilante group formed in the mid-nineties in the Cape Flats area of Cape Town. Their methodology was to protect the public by setting fire to drug dealers' properties and killing gangsters in a number of rather barbaric ways.

However, as time moved on, the pendulum began to swing. It

was rumoured PAGAD was connected to various bombings in the Western Cape and responsible for the deaths of ordinary people. The public started to look upon PAGAD as a gang rather than a law-enforcing organisation.

No better than the 33s.

60

Snitch

Cain and Marius were out on the patio at the back of the 'fortress', sitting under the lemon tree on the two rocking chairs with a bottle of red wine on the coffee table between them. Marius looked at his watch. 'It will be happening in ten minutes.'

Cain remembered again the day of the shooting in High Constantia, when he had phoned Peter:

"Sorry, not today, I have a pressing engagement."

"In the biblical sense or in the gym?"

"Piss off."

"If she changes her mind, you know where I am."

"High Constantia, got it. I'll press on then," Peter joked. "Enjoy your lunch."

And when Jerry had arrived at the airport that evening – to fly back to England – what had been said on the phone.

"We know you were not followed. We know you only decided to go to High Constantia at the last minute. We know neither you, nor your vehicle were bugged."

"True."

"So how come the gunmen were already there, waiting for you?"

On the outskirts of Cape Town, in the darkness of the night, a cheap, inconspicuous, fifteen-year-old saloon car made its way into the Gugulethu township and parked on a quiet street. The driver and the passenger, two black men wearing casual gear, sunglasses, and baseball hats, exited the saloon, walked some fifty yards, and knocked on the front door of a small terrace bungalow. A black man opened the door: two bullets from a silenced Beretta immediately entered his heart and he soundlessly fell to the floor. The two assailants stepped into the property and quietly closed the door behind them. A scantily clad woman in the bedroom called out, 'Who is it?'

When the two assailants entered the bedroom the horrified woman, looking down the barrel of a semi-automatic pistol, was convinced to tell her story.

A week before the shooting in High Constantia, she had been paid to deliberately bump into Peter in a shopping mall, initiating a relationship that would involve sleeping with him every day. Hence, when Cain had phoned Peter, inviting him to lunch, she had listened in on the call. She had heard Cain would be in High Constantia for lunch, so she went into the bathroom and secretly made a call to the man who had been paying her; the man who had also, for the right price, been sleeping with her; the man who was now lying dead in the hallway of her home.

'I didn't want to do it,' she said. 'I was forced too. I'm so glad you have rescued me.'

'Who was the man paying you working for?' one of the assailants asked.

'I don't know. I only had to answer to him.'

'You have also been involved in the despicable trafficking of young girls and boys.'

The woman looked irritated. 'But I–'

A double tap to the heart of the lying woman – in every sense of the word – on the bed killed her.

Minutes later, the old saloon car was driving on a main road safely miles away from the Gugulethu township. The passenger pressed the button on a burner cell phone.

Marius answered. 'Yes?'

'Plan and Shoot,' said a trusted voice. 'Mission completed sir. We are all clear.'

'Excellent. Stay safe. See you tomorrow.'

Another clean-up operation had been completed.

Some twenty minutes later, Cain and Marius finished their drinks and strolled down to the garage. As Kimberley opened, Marius rounded off their conversation. 'Give Moshe my regards when you next speak to him.'

'He sent me an email just before you got here. He's having a great time with Joseph, the old master and the Galt Mile Gang in Florida. He asked me when I will be joining them – and suggested you should come too.'

Marius grinned. 'Perhaps I will. I'll be here at two-thirty tomorrow for our conference call with Mac.'

Part Fourteen

Barcelona, Sitges, Spain

Only those who will risk going too far can possibly find out how far one can go.

T. S. Eliot

61

The City of Dreams – Friday Evening

Sofia was sitting on the bed in her hotel room, talking with Cain unpacking his suitcase. He placed two gift-wrapped cardboard boxes in front of her. 'Present for you,' he said.

'What a surprise,' she responded, holding out her hand with a look of expectancy. Cain lifted the switchblade out of the watch pocket of his jeans – the one Sofia had given him years before – placed it in the palm of her hand and settled himself down on the bed beside her. The blade flicked out and Sofia sliced open the tops of the boxes.

'Pretty big chickens in South Africa,' she giggled, holding the two carved ostrich eggshell lamps in her hands. She plugged them in and turned them on. 'Wonderful,' she said, giving Cain a kiss on the cheek. 'I now have ten different *huevos* (eggs), thank you!'

'You sure you haven't got enough now?'

'Oh no,' said Sofia with a very slow, exaggerated sway of her head. 'They are truly wonderful; I can never have too many.'

'Thank you again for the Gaudi clock you sent me.'

'I knew you would love it,' she said, snuggling up to Cain.

It would be an hour or two before they went out to dinner: the beginning of a long weekend together, talking about many things, the good times, and the bad time, coming to terms with reality.

Saturday

Sofia and Cain were strolling along the tree-lined avenue of La Rambla. Entering the fabulous Boqueria food market, Cain was reminded of Maputo's central market in Mozambique.

Neilson and Catarina would love it here.

From the Christopher Columbus monument they continued

walking along the length of the harbour, admiring the luxury yachts and ships moored on the quayside. They checked in on one particular private jetty: the pendant flying above a 96-ft white Ferretti, berthed next to a14-ft parked red Ferrari, confirmed the arrival of one of Cain and Moshe's elite 1% clients.

'I'm having lunch with them at the Ares overlooking the harbour on Tuesday,' Cain said.

'And I'm having lunch with them at the Arenal overlooking the beach on Monday.'

'Touché.'

Sofia smiled. 'Thank you for introducing me.'

'Pleasure.'

'They never mention your name.'

Cain grinned. 'As the old saying goes; discretion is the better part of valour.'

Monday Evening

Cain drove Sofia to the Barcelona airport, from where she was flying to Madrid to meet with clients. Once Cain had unloaded Sofia's suitcase from the back of his hired 4x4 they embraced and kissed cheek to cheek, Spanish-style.

'My PTPS (Part-Time Personal Shag),' Sofia whispered, 'see you on Friday.'

'My PTPA (Part-Time Personal Assistant),' Cain replied quietly.

As they drew back from each other, they sealed their friendship with a kiss on the lips, English style.

Sofia said, 'Hope you have as good a lunch tomorrow with our clients as I did today.'

'Will do. Take care.'

Tuesday

After having lunch with his elite 1% client in Barcelona, curiosity took Cain for a drive along the C32, through the tunnel where – he had been informed – Trenchard had crashed his car. At the end of the tunnel, Cain arrived on the outskirts of

Sitges to start his reconnaissance.

Sitges was a beautiful old coastal town that came to fame in 1893 when the Spanish painter, poet, journalist, and playwright Santiago Rusiñol i Prats took up residence there. The four kilometres of sandy beaches, including one for those who liked an all-over, naked tan, the hotels, restaurants and annual festivals, made Sitges, only 35km's from Barcelona and 20km's from the city's international airport, a major attraction for visitors, tourists – and the like. Sitges was also considered to be the *Gay Capital* of Spain, a coastal resort of *Village People.* Hence, it was easy to understand why the Dutchman had taken up residency there.

At 8pm, Cain parked the hired 4x4 in the garage of Teun the Dutchman's holiday home. Inside the property, Cain met with Agents he had never seen before, who had drugged the Dutchman and Tech people who had copied everything from the Dutchman's computer, laptop, and cell phones.

Cain looked down at the drug-addicted, semi-conscious Teun – wearing a light coral T-shirt, a scraggy scarlet scarf wrapped loosely around his neck, blue jeans, and deck shoes – in an armchair. Although Bill and Greg knew Teun had been taking more and more drugs over the years, they'd had no idea of how bad his addiction had become.

'Every day on the white powder,' said Cain. 'More trips a day than the local bus.

Everything would now be implemented military-style.

They carried the Dutchman down to Cain's hired 4x4 in the garage, opened the tailgate – did the necessary, dumped him in the back and left the property.

Nothing would look out of place when the police eventually arrived.

Minutes later, Cain was driving along the twisty coastal road between Sitges and Castelldefels, carved out of the steep sided rocky mountains. It was very similar to one of the many miles of curving coastal roads – carved out cliffs – Cain had often driven along in South Africa's Western Cape.

In his rear-view mirror Cain could see an Agent following

him, keeping an eye on his back. He drove the 4x4 into a deserted parking area, made a U-turn, and reversed back towards the cliff's edge. He wandered over to the rocks and stood on what was a Spanish version of the Western Cape, coastal roads, *suicide ledge*. He looked down at the waves beating against the rocks some ninety feet below him. He looked out over the *Mediterranean* towards the horizon, but there were no Southern Right Whales – no *Moby & Dick* – having a *splash*.

Cain knew the Dutchman, having been informed of the deaths of Lastly and Vitaly – had just flown back from Prague, where he had tried to find the missing Bekha.

The Flying Dutchman, Cain thought, remembering the nautical tale:

Her sails are full, though the wind is still
The sight of this phantom ship, The Flying Dutchman
Is a portent of doom.

Standing by the back of the 4x4, Cain checked the deserted road, and receiving a flash of light from the Agent, stationary on the curve, he raised the tailgate. He quickly lifted out the still semi-conscious Teun the Dutchman – now shackled in chains and weights – and carried him back over to *suicide ledge*. Cain stood Teun in front of him so they were face to face. 'You are a murdering paedophile,' said Cain. 'The bodies of two young boys have been found buried on the edge of wasteland behind your property. Your DNA was found inside them. As a drug addict this will be a last trip for you. Good riddance.'

Cain turned Teun around to face the dark depths of the Mediterranean below.

When push comes to shove . . . Splash.

It is the set of the sails, not the direction of
the wind, that determines which way we go.

Jim Rohn

Part Fifteen

London, England

If you prick us do we not bleed?
If you tickle us do we not laugh?
If you poison us do we not die?
And if you wrong us shall we not revenge?

William Shakespeare

The Final Chapter

Last Shot

As the private jet turned onto the final approach to Biggin Hill airfield, Cain sat back to enjoy the view. He had taken off and landed there many times. It was where he and a famous TV actor had learnt to fly and – before he had left the UK – become friends.

In the back of a chauffeur driven SUV – for the seventeen-mile drive into central London – Cain sat watching the world go by, contemplating his schedule. He would spend the next two days doing what he had to do alone. He would visit the apartments he and Jerry had jointly owned. The apartments Jerry's life insurance had paid-off the mortgages on. The apartments he now solely owned. He would pack away what he had to. He would go to see the *Disponible* to arrange for it to be shipped to warmer climes. And last of all, he would meet with his lawyer – no longer their lawyer – to tie up a few loose ends, sign his new *Will* – and have a copy of everything sent to Sofia.

He closed his eyes for a moment's respite – he felt for the tissues in his pocket.

A tear ran down his cheek.

Three days later

When Cain met with Mac in his office, the two men immediately embraced like father and son.

Mac respectfully enquired, 'All OK regarding Jerry?'

'Yes, all done,' Cain sighed.

Whilst having morning coffees, Mac updated Cain about how the organisation involved in the illegal trafficking of cash, drugs, guns, and girls across Africa into Europe and the UK had been taken apart. Various members, leaders, and kingpins had been arrested while others, along with Vitaly, had been killed.

'Splash,' Cain said, rounding off their subject of conversation.

Mac picked up several folders lying on his desk and gestured to the sofas. 'Let's take a seat.'

'OK,' Cain said, refreshing their cups and placing them on the coffee table.

Sitting opposite each other, Mac opened one of the folders. 'Please bear with me.'

'Of course.'

'In August 1996, after you were shot at the polo ground, you were the supposed Agent Smith whom Trenchard visited in a hospital. You refused to sign the statement handed to you.'

Cain remembered, the statement, couched in ambiguous terms, represented a total distortion of the facts. Whereas, at the very worst, it could have been construed to be an admission of an unauthorised killing: guilt.

'A month later,' said Mac, 'in August 1996, Trenchard was informed, any aspirations he might have had of becoming a top Whitehall mandarin had been blocked. So he had to re-route his career path. It took him several months before he realised the outgoing prime minister was surreptitiously stifling any chances he might have had of becoming an MP, and perhaps one day a member of the Cabinet. Therefore, any hopes he may have had of entering Downing Street had been closed. He subsequently slithered his way along the corridors of power to where, with a little help from his friends, he got a foot on the rung of the ambassadorial ladder. He soon found himself on the doorstep of the British Consulate in Barcelona. Meanwhile, his wife quietly divorced him. Months later, one of my people had a discreet word with her. She explained how she had returned home earlier than expected one evening, to discover her husband in their kitchen, pouring himself a glass of wine, wearing one of her dresses, standing in a pair of her high heels.'

Cain laughed. 'He had been *skirting* around the truth again.'

Mac smiled. 'He paid off his wife to make sure she kept her mouth shut. She agreed because they had no children.'

Mac leant forward and opened a bottle of J&B and brandy. Cain was somewhat surprised to see Mac pouring alcohol so early in the day. His subliminal alarm bells began to chime.

'Help yourself,' said Mac, placing Cain's glass next to the icebox.

They both raised their glasses. 'To absent friends,' Mac said. 'To absent friends.'

As Mac placed his glass on the table, he said, 'What I now have to tell you is going to be very painful.' He looked Cain in the eye. 'I know how Riley was killed – and why.'

Cain showed a look of absolute surprise. He stared down at the floor, closed his eyes, breathed in and out, long and slow. Seconds later he said quietly, 'Tell me.'

'There is no easy way to do this.'

'I understand. Please do it military-style, precise and to the point.'

'In 1997, Teun the Dutchman paid a visit to his holiday home in Sitges. In a bar of *village people* he introduced himself to an Englishman named Trenchard. During the course of the next few days they got to know one another and stayed together. One evening, the Dutchman was talking about one of his legitimate investments – his trip to Perth to buy diamonds – to impress Trenchard. He mentioned how, late one afternoon, when he had been sitting in the back of a taxi, moving slowly in rush hour traffic, he had watched Riley and a man who he assumed was her fiancé being greeted by Bill and Greg on the patio of a restaurant.'

'We did that many times,' Cain said quietly, seeing them all together in his mind's eye.

'When you were all shaking hands,' said Mac, 'the Dutchman noticed how Riley's fiancé was doing it injured-man-style, because his right hand and fingers were in a splint. To amuse Trenchard, the Dutchman went on to make a few jokes about Riley's fiancé being unable to have a wank, how it was a 'stroke' of luck to have seen them and so on. It worked, Trenchard was laughing – and they fell in love. A couple of days later Trenchard casually got Teun to describe Riley's fiancé.'

'He guessed the fiancé was Agent Smith,' Cain politely interrupted. 'Namely, me.'

'Yes,' said Mac. 'Weeks later, when Trenchard had to visit the Foreign Office in London, he met with the Whitehall superior he always had to answer to. He told the story about how you, the supposed Agent Smith – Riley's fiancé – was now living in Perth, Western Australia. Trenchard only did it in an effort to help rebuild – because he didn't make it into Downing Street – his reputation. His Whitehall superior gave him the impression it was of no importance to anyone. However, I can confirm, around that same time, surreptitious checks were made to confirm the man in Perth was indeed you.'

Cain couldn't believe what he was hearing. He remained silent and Mac continued.

'Trenchard's Whitehall superior, while spying for Russia – a country always in cahoots with Iraq – had played a major part in the administration of the attack on the Royal Family at the polo ground in August 1996.'

Cain remembered what Mac had said to him after he had left hospital about the attack being carried out by al Qaeda in retaliation for Operation Desert Storm. Cain shook his head. 'I can't believe it. Jesus Christ. I met Zokwana in Cape Town years after we were both at the stake-out in the garden square in (1992) London. Then I cross paths – when in a Chinese prison – with Trenchard who I met in the hospital after the shootout (in 1996) at the polo ground. And now Dann the Dutchman who visited Australia (in 1997) before Riley and her parents–' Cain sighed, staring down at; well nothing really – just the floor. 'Coincidence,' he murmured. 'Or has my past life always been truly catching up with me.'

'I now have to tell you why *Jumbo* crashed,' said Mac, before continuing in a precise, military manner. 'On that day at the Margaret River airfield, Riley's girlfriends drove off with their parents, to park in a lay-by near the end of the runway. It was something they always did to give Riley and her parents a wave as they flew past them. As you are well aware, Riley then phoned you.'

Cain closed his eyes, remembering his last-ever conversation with Riley:

'Boo. It's me.'
'What a surprise. All OK?'
'We'll tell you all about where we went for brekkies, lunch and dinner when we get back.'
'I thought you might.'

'We'll be taking off in twenty minutes.'

'In Jumbo,*' said Cain. 'Or are you doing a Harry Potter on a broomstick?'*

'I'll fly Jumbo. *It will be easier to bring the wine.'*

'The corkscrew is ready and waiting.'

Riley giggled. 'Love you.'

'Love you too.'

'Byyyyyyeeeeee.'

Cain looked across at Mac as a tear ran down his cheek. Mac had no option but to continue; he could not drag it out. 'When Riley finished her call, she turned and accidentally bumped into a passer-by. The end of the man's umbrella, lying on top of his pilot's bag, jabbed into her thigh and through the loose-fitting, long-legged chinos she always wore when piloting *Jumbo*. It made her do nothing more than give it a rub. The man apologised and said the umbrella, on such a sunny day, was for his granddaughter in a tripper around the corner, to help keep the sun off her. In fact, Riley had been injected with *ricin*. Riley would lose consciousness within the hour. Killing Riley was payback for you saving the lives of members of the Royal Family at the polo ground and playing a part in the killing of the Jihadist terrorists. The assassin had been told you would be with Riley. He had been ordered to shoot you but when he realised you were not with her he did what he did, we do not know why. Riley's parents were collateral damage, an unexpected bonus, and how he got away, we have no idea.'

Cain sat motionless, speechless, trying his best to restrain the tears.

Mac lifted a box of tissues from under the table and placed them next to Cain. 'I'll go get us more coffee,' he said quietly, allowing the tearful Cain a moment's respite alone. 'I'll be back in ten minutes to answer your questions.'

My PA cannot be allowed to see Cain like this.

When Mac returned, after having a sip of their coffees and a swig or two of their J&B and brandy, Cain asked, 'Who was the assassin?'

'I know who and where he is,' said Mac. 'Please allow me to fill you in on a few more details before I tell you.'

Cain wiped his eyes again with a tissue, blew his nose – and looked up at Mac. 'OK.'

'Going back in history, we all know the Cambridge Five, were students recruited by the Soviet Union. They went on to become spies who passed on information about the UK and our allies to the Soviet Union during War II and the Cold War.'

'They were responsible for the deaths of many people,' Cain said with a sense of regret.

'We have discovered, during the late seventies two more students were recruited, but not from Cambridge. They are known as the Oxford Two.'

'Probably members of the Bullingdon Club,' said Cain. 'The self-centred, narcissistic, Bullshit Club.'

'Through an undercover joint operation carried out by trusted individuals in various departments, which has taken several years, all the parts of a jigsaw puzzle have finally been put together. If I were to go into detail we would be sitting here for hours.'

'All those secrets,' said Cain. 'Perhaps one day you will.'

Cryptology.

'Trenchard's Whitehall superior was recently interviewed by MI5. They were about to arrest and charge him when Downing Street ordered them to drop the charges and release him.'

'Why?'

'For political and personal gain: a day after he was released he disappeared.'

Cain looked up. 'You abducted him?'

'I interviewed him – our way – over a four-day period. I found out everything. After Trenchard told him about you being in Perth, he informed the Russians. As I said, Russia is a country always in cahoots with Iraq.'

'Typical,' Cain said forlornly.

'As a return favour for having been given such information, the Russians found out everything they could about the Dutchman and handed it over. Two weeks later the Whitehall superior met with the Dutchman in Amsterdam to provide him with a number of contacts to enhance his illegal drug dealing along with names of potential clients to buy his investment diamonds. He was told Trenchard, his lover, would be looked after. In return, he paid a rather large amount of money – a percentage of what he was making – into the Whitehall superior's, secret Swiss bank account every three months.'

'Why did Al Qaeda not try to kill me again?'

'We can only assume the Russians, for whatever reason, did not tell them.'

Cain asked, 'Did Trenchard know about his lover's drug dealing connections with Vitaly or – as you informed Marius and I during our conference call last week – the Dutchman was also a murdering paedophile?'

'Unfortunately, as I mentioned to you, he was killed when driving through the tunnel on the C32 to Sitges. He was shot and his car crashed into a wall, so we have not been able to establish exactly what he may have found out or what he was intending to do.'

Cain showed a look of absolute surprise. 'He was shot?'

'Yes. The media were not told and the CCTVs in the tunnel at the time of the shooting were, coincidentally, not working. When the British Consulate in Barcelona was informed they did not even know he was in the country. Rumours are still circulating about a white, motor car occupied by two Chinese men, dressed in black, seen in the vicinity at the time. Although it was recorded on the freeway's other CCTVs, it has never been traced.'

Cain immediately recollected, after the shooting of Vitaly on the outskirts of Cape Town, rumours had been circulating about two Chinese men, dressed in black, who had been seen in a lone Tazz car in the vicinity at the time of the shooting.

'When I was in prison,' said Cain, 'the men in black told me Teun was a drug dealer.'

'Undoubtedly,' Mac agreed. 'There is, to coin a phrase, a long road ahead.'

Cain looked at Mac. 'What happened to Trenchard's Whitehall superior?'

'Rumour has it he has fled the country. A modern-day version of John Stonehouse, the corrupt Labour MP who faked his death in Florida and fled to Australia; a man who allegedly was a spy.'

'What really happened?'

'I did what I believed you would have done. I threw him out of an aircraft from twelve thousand feet above the middle of the Atlantic. He was strapped to a fifty-kilo iron slab. He begged me not to.'

Cain sighed. 'Another *splash*. Thank you. What happened to the money in his Swiss bank account?'

Mac smiled. 'Before he disappeared, he donated it to various veterans' charities around the UK. The account was then closed.'

Cain looked at Mac admiringly.

'I now know who Trenchard's Whitehall superior was spying with, the second member of the Oxford Two,' Mac said.

'So you will be dealing with him.'

'All in good time. The name of the assassin who killed Riley and her parents is Soyen Kotsev, an ex-Russian SVR Agent.' Mac handed Cain a file.

'Where is he?'

'He is now living in Dorset, near to the man who had diplomatic immunity when he shot dead the Metropolitan police officer in London in 1984.'

'How the hell did they both manage to get back into the UK?'

'The prime minister has been in power now for eight years; we know what he's up to. I'll explain another day.' Mac handed Cain a second file, stamped *Termination*.

Cain looked Mac in the eye. 'Both of them?'

'Yes. You will get yourself kitted out with a supply of false hair and beards. You will be issued with false passports, driver's licences, and credit cards. A female agent will then drive you to an isolated country cottage, five miles from where Kotsev and the other murdering bastard are living. She will drive you around for a few days so you can get your bearings, the lay of the land, before she comes back to London. In the garage of the cottage, there will be two cars, two motorbikes, and half a dozen sets of false number plates waiting for you.'

'Perfect.'

And once again Cain would be where perhaps, he always had been:

When the transgressions of a target of primary interest

ascended to a hearing.
When there was only one judge – Mac – in session
and no jury,
Cain would carry out the sentence with characteristic ease.

*I guess sometimes the past just catches up with you,
whether you want it to or not.*

Dabbs Greer

*Life becomes liveable only to the extent that death
is treated as a friend, never as an enemy.*

Mahatma Gandhi